The Sandalwood Tree

www.rbooks.co.uk

Also by Elle Newmark

The Book of Unholy Mischief

The Sandalwood Tree

Elle Newmark

Doubleday

LONDON · TORONTO · SYDNEY · AUCKLAND · JOHANNESBURG

TRANSWORLD PUBLISHERS
61–63 Uxbridge Road, London W5 5SA
A Random House Group Company
www.rbooks.co.uk

First published in Great Britain
in 2011 by Doubleday
an imprint of Transworld Publishers

A CIP catalogue record for this book
is available from the British Library.

ISBN 9780385615426

Addresses for Random House Group Ltd companies outside the UK
can be found at: www.randomhouse.co.uk
The Random House Group Ltd Reg. No. 954009

Typeset in 12/16pt Giovanni Book by
Falcon Oast Graphic Art Ltd.
Printed and bound in Australia by
Griffin Press

2 4 6 8 10 9 7 5 3 1

www.randomhouse.com.au
www.randomhouse.co.nz

For my daughter, Tess

'Death steals everything but our stories.'
Adela Winfield

Elle Newmark lives in the hills north of San Diego, California. Her sensational debut was *The Book of Unholy Mischief*. This is her second novel. Visit her website at www.ellenewmark.com

Chapter One

1947

OUR TRAIN HURTLED PAST a gold-spangled woman in a mango sari, regal even as she sat in the dirt, patting cow dung into disks for cooking fuel. A sweep of black hair obscured her face and she did not look up as the passing train shook the ground under her bare feet.

We barrelled past one crumbling, sun-blasted village after another, and the further we got from Delhi the more animals we saw trudging alongside the endless swarm of people – arrogant camels, hump-backed cows, bullock-drawn carts, goats and monkeys and suicidal dogs. The people walked slowly, balancing vessels on their heads and bundles on their backs, and I stared like a rude tourist, vaguely ashamed of my rubbernecking – they were just ordinary people going about their lives, and I sure as hell wouldn't like someone staring at me, at home in Chicago, as if I were some bizarre creature on exhibit – but I couldn't look away.

The train stopped for a cow on the track, and a suppurating leper hobbled up to our window, holding out a fingerless hand. My husband, Martin, passed a coin out of the window while I distracted Billy with an impromptu rib tickle. I blocked his view of the leper with my back to the window and smiled gamely as he pulled up his little knees and folded in on himself, giggling. 'Not fair,' he gasped. 'You didn't warn me.'

'Warn you?' I wiggled two fingers in his soft armpit and he squealed. 'Warn you? Where's the fun in that?' We wrestled merrily until, minutes later, the train ground to life and we pulled away, leaving the leper behind, salaaming in his grey rags.

Last year, early in 1946, Senator Fulbright had announced an award programme for promising graduate students to study abroad, and Martin, an historian writing his Ph.D. thesis on the politics of modern India, had won a scholarship to document the end of the British Raj. We arrived in Delhi at the end of March 1947, about a year before the British were scheduled to depart from India for ever. After more than two hundred years of the Raj, the Empire had been faced down by a skinny little man in a loincloth named Gandhi and the Brits were finally packing it in. However, before they left they would draw new borders, arbitrary lines to partition the country between Hindus and Muslims, and a new nation called Pakistan would be born. Heady stuff for an historian.

Of course, I appreciated the noble purpose behind the Fulbright – fostering a global community – and I understood the seriousness of Partition, but I had secretly dreamed about six months of moonlit scenes from *The Arabian Nights*. I was intoxicated by the prospect of romance and adventure and a new beginning for Martin and me, which is why I was not prepared for the grim reality of poverty, dung fires and lepers – in the twentieth century?

Still, I didn't regret coming along; I wanted to see the pageant that is Hindustan and also to ferret out the mystery of her resilience. I wanted to know how India had managed to hang on to her identity despite a continuous stream of foreign conquerors slogging through her jungles and over her mountains, bringing their new gods and new rules, often setting up shop for centuries at a time. Martin and I hadn't been able to hold on to the 'us' in our marriage after one stint in one war.

I stared out of the open window, studying everything from behind my new sunglasses, tortoiseshell plastic frames with bottle-green lenses. Martin wore his regular glasses, which left him squinting in the savage Indian sun, but he said he didn't mind; he didn't even wear a hat, which I thought foolish, but he was stubborn about it. My dark-green lenses and my wide-brimmed straw topi gave me a sense of protection, and I wore them everywhere.

We passed pink Hindu temples and white marble mosques, and I raised my new Kodak Brownie camera to the window often, but I didn't see any hints of the ancient tension simmering between Hindus and Muslims – not yet – only the impression that everyone was struggling to survive. We passed mud-hut villages, inexplicable piles of abandoned bricks, shelters made from tarps draped haphazardly over bamboo poles, and fields of millet stretching away into mist.

The air smelled like smoke tinged with sweat and spices, and when gritty dust invaded our compartment, I closed the window, brought out the hairbrush, wash cloth and diluted rubbing alcohol that I carried in my hand baggage, and went to work on Billy. He sat patiently as I whisked his clothes, wiped his face and brushed his blond hair till it shone. By then the poor child had got used to my neurotic need for cleanliness. If you understand the lunatic nuances involved in keeping up appearances you'll understand why I spent an insane amount of time fighting dust and dirt in India.

I caught the madness from Martin. He had come home from the war in Germany obsessed with a need for calm and order, and by the time we had dragged ourselves halfway round the world to that untidy subcontinent I was cleaning compulsively, drowning confusion in soapy water, purging discontent with bleach and abrasive cleansers. When we arrived in Delhi, I shook out the bed linen on the tiny balcony of our hotel room before I let my weary husband and child go to sleep. In the narrow lanes of Old Delhi, crammed with people and rickshaws and wandering cows, I pinched my nose against the smell of garbage and urine and insisted Martin take us back to the hotel, where I checked under the bed and in the corners for spiders. Found a couple and smashed them flat – so much for karma.

When we boarded the train to go north, I wiped down the seats in our compartment with my ever-ready washcloth before I let Martin or Billy sit. Martin gave me a look that said, 'Now you're being ridiculous,' but the tyranny of obsession is absolute and will not be reasoned with. At every stop, chai wallahs, water bearers and food vendors leaped on to the train and sped through the carriages hawking biscuits, tea, palm juice, dhal, pakoras and chapattis, and I recoiled from them, keeping a protective arm around Billy and shooting a warning look at Martin.

At the first few stops, mingled smells of grease and sweat saturated the sweltering air and made the food unappealing. But after several hours without eating, Martin suggested trying a few snacks. I quickly produced the hotel sandwiches I'd packed in Delhi and handed him one, agreeing only to buy three cups of masala chai – gorgeous, creamy tea infused with cloves and cardamom – because I knew it had been boiled. I ate my bacon sandwich and drank my tea, feeling safe and insulated – I would observe and understand India without India actually touching me. But as I munched away and looked out of the window, my heart beat faster at the sight of an elephant lumbering on the horizon. A mahout, straddling the massive neck, urged the animal along with his bare heels, and I watched, strangely exhilarated, until they disappeared in a trail of red dust.

Billy watched women walking along the side of the road with brass pots balanced on their heads, and men bent double under enormous loads of grain. Often, ragged children straggled behind, looking thin and exhausted. Quietly, he asked, 'Are those poor people, Mom?'

'Well, they're not rich.'

'Shouldn't we help them?'

'There are too many of them, sweetie.'

He nodded and stared out of the window.

On our first day in Masoorla I threw open the blue shutters of our rented bungalow, beat the hell out of the dhurrie rugs, and polished all the scarred old furniture. I went over every inch of the old two-bedroom house with carbolic soap and used a quart of Jeyes cleaning fluid in the bathroom. Martin said I should get a sweeper to do it, but how could I trust a woman to clean my house who spent half her time up to her elbows in cow dung? Anyway, I wanted to do it. I didn't know how to fix my marriage, but I knew how to clean. Denial is the first refuge of the frightened, and it *is* possible to distract oneself by scrubbing, organizing and covering smells of curry and dung with disinfectant. It works for a while.

When I found the hidden letters, I had just finished an assault on the kitchen window. I squeezed out the sponge and stood back, squinting with a critical eye. A yellow sari converted to curtains framed the blue sky and distant

Himalayan peaks, now clearly visible through the spotless window, but the late afternoon sun spotlit a dirty brick wall behind the old English cooker. The red brick had been blackened by a century of oily cooking smoke and, just like that, I decided to roll up my sleeves and give it a good scrub. Rashmi, our ayah, deigned to wipe a table or sweep the floor with a bunch of acacia branches, but I would never ask her to tackle a soot-encrusted wall. A job like that fell well beneath her caste, and she would have quit on the spot.

The university chose that bungalow for us because it had an attached kitchen instead of the usual cookhouse out back. I liked the place as soon as I walked into the little compound full of tangled grass and pipal trees with creepers twisting around their trunks. A low mud-brick wall, overgrown with Himalayan mimosa, circled our little compound with its hundred-year-old bungalow and vine-clad verandah, and an old sandalwood tree, with long oval leaves and pregnant red pods, presided over the front of the house. Everything had a weathered, well-used look, and I wondered how many lives had been lived there.

Off to one side of the house, a path bordered by scrappy boxwood led to the godowns for the servants – a dilapidated row of huts, far more than we would ever need for our few staff. At the far end of the godowns a derelict stable nestled in a grove of deodars, and Martin talked about using it to park our car in during the monsoon. Martin had bought a battered and faded red Packard convertible, which had been new and snazzy in 1935, but it had seen twelve monsoons and too many seasons of neglect. Still, the jalopy ran, I had a bicycle, and Billy had his Red Flyer wagon, and that's all we needed.

The remains of the old cookhouse still stood around the back, listing under a neem tree – a bare little shack with a dirt floor, one sagging shelf and a square of mud bricks with a hole in the centre for wood or coal. Indians didn't cook inside colonial houses – a fire precaution and some complicated rules regarding religion and caste – and it must have been some very unconventional colonials who decided to attach a kitchen and install a cooker, bless their hearts.

I hired our servants myself, choosing from a virtual army that lined up for interview. They presented their chits – references – and since most of them couldn't read English, they didn't realize that the bogus chits they had bought in the bazaar were supposedly signed by Queen Victoria, Winston Churchill or Punch and Judy. The only chit I could be absolutely sure was authentic said, 'This is the laziest cook in all India. He strains the milk through his dhoti and he will rob you blind.'

In the end we had a scandalously small staff – a cook, an ayah, and a dhobi who collected our laundry once a week in silent anonymity. At first, we'd also had a gardener, a sweeper and a bearer – a more typical arrangement – but that many servants made me feel superfluous.

I particularly disliked having a bearer, a sort of major-domo who trailed around after me, doing my bidding or passing my orders on to the other servants. I felt as helpless as a caricature of a nineteenth-century memsahib swooning on a daybed. Our bearer had been trained in British house-holds and would wake Martin and me in the morning with a tradition called 'bed tea'. The first time I opened my eyes to see a dark, turbanned man standing over me with a tray it scared me out of my wits. He also served our meals and stood behind us while we ate; it felt like sitting in a restaurant with an eavesdropping waiter, and I was painfully conscious of our conversation and my table manners. I found myself delicately dabbing the corners of my mouth and keeping my spine straight. I could see that Martin felt it too, and meals became an uncomfortable chore.

I didn't want 'bed tea', I didn't want a bearer – always there, always hovering – and I enjoyed feeling useful. So I kept our little house clean and watered the plants on the verandah myself. I liked the natural, jungly look around the bungalow, and the notion of having a gardener struck me as absurd. Martin told me the expatriate community was appalled by our lack of servants. I said, 'So?'

I kept the cook, Habib, because I didn't recognize half the things in the market stalls, and since I didn't speak Hindi the price of everything would have tripled. I kept Rashmi, our ayah, because I liked her and she spoke English.

When I first met Rashmi, she greeted me with a formal bow, her hands in an attitude of prayer. She said, 'Namaste,' then she began giggling and clapping, making her chubby arms jiggle and her bangles jangle. She asked, 'From what country are you coming?'

'I said, "America," wondering if it was a trick question.

'Oooh, Amerrrica! Verry nice!' The ruby in her right nostril twinkled.

Rashmi deeply disapproved of a household with so few servants. Whenever she saw me beating a rug or cleaning the bathroom she would hold her cheeks and shake her head, her eyes round and alarmed. 'Arey Ram! What Madam is doooiiing?' I tried to explain that I liked to keep busy, but Rashmi would stomp around the house mumbling and shaking her head. Once I heard her say, 'Amerrrican,' as if it were a diagnosis. She started sweeping up with neatly tied acacia branches and taking out the garbage. I had no idea where she took it, but it seemed to make her happy to do it. Whenever I thanked Rashmi for something, she would waggle her head pleasantly and say, 'My duty it is, Madam.' I wished Martin and I could accept our lot so easily.

My beautiful Martin had come home from the war in Germany with a shrouded, chaotic underside, wanting everything as neat as an army cot. It's about control, I know that, but he drove me nuts, picking at imaginary lint on my clothing and lining up our shoes side by side on the closet floor, like a row of soldiers snapped to attention. At first I complied and kept everything ship-shape, simply because we didn't need yet another thing to argue about. But I soon discovered that ordering furniture and annihilating dust gave me a fragile sense of control – Martin was on to something there – and I enjoyed imposing my antiseptic standards on India, keeping my little corner of the universe as predictable as gravity.

When an altered Martin came home from Germany, straightening books on the shelf and buffing his shoes until they screamed, he often complained of a metallic taste in his mouth, rushing off to brush his teeth five times a day. I didn't know what he tasted, but I did know he had nightmares. He twitched in his sleep, muttering disjointedly about 'skeletons' and calling out names of people I didn't know. Some nights he'd shout in his sleep and I'd spring up, shocked and scared. I'd dry the sweat from his face with the sheet and kiss the palms of his hands, while his breathing calmed and my heart slowed.

His skin would be clammy and he'd be trembling, and I'd rock him and croon in his ear, 'It's all right. I'm here.' After a while, when it seemed safe, I'd say, 'Sweetheart, talk to me. Please.' Sometimes he'd talk a little, but only about the language or the landscape or the guys in his platoon. He said it bothered him that German sounded so much like the Yiddish of his grandparents; then he shook his head as if he was trying to understand something.

He told me that Germany was littered with castles and fairy-tale villages, all blasted to hell. He said the soldiers in his platoon were an unlikely bunch thrown together by war, men who would not otherwise have met. Martin, a budding historian, bunked with a fast-talking mechanic from Detroit named Casino. Also in his barracks were an American Indian named William Who Respects Nothing, and a Samoan named Naikelekele, whom the men called Ukulele. Martin said they were OK guys, but a CPA from Queens named Polanski – Ski to the guys – had the wide slab face and flat blue eyes that had been behind too many of the pogroms mounted against the Jews, and Martin had to keep reminding himself that they were on the same side.

But Ski cheated at cards and had a nascent anti-Semitic streak. Martin said, 'Of all the decent guys in that platoon, I had to haul Ski back to a field hospital while better men lay dead around us.' His ambivalence about saving Ski haunted him, but it wasn't *the* thing eating at him like acid.

One night, in bed, after having had an extra glass of wine with dinner, Martin knit his fingers behind his head and told me about a mess sergeant from the hills of Appalachia, Pete McCoy, who made a crude liquor with pilfered sugar and yeast and canned peaches. Pete had served an informal apprenticeship at his father's still, deep in the woods of West Virginia, and in a rare, light-hearted moment, Martin did a skilful imitation. He drawled, 'Ah know it ain't legal. But mah daddy's gonna quit soon as he gits a chance.'

I said, 'The nightmares aren't about Pete McCoy's moonshine.'

'Hey, you didn't taste that stuff. Burned like a son-of-a-bitch going down.' His voice became abstract. 'But sometimes the moonshine was necessary, like when Tommie . . . Well, anyway, McCoy was like the medic who brought the morphine.'

I said, 'Who was Tommie?'

Martin looked away. 'Ah, you don't want to hear that stuff.'

'But I do. Talk to me. Please.'

He hesitated, then, 'Nah. Go to sleep.' He patted my hand and rolled away.

World War Two veterans were icons of heroism, brave liberators, and most of them were glad to leave the ugliness buried under the war rubble and get back to a normal life, or try to. But Martin had come home with invisible wounds, and our normal life was as ruined as the German landscape. I wanted to understand. I'd been begging him to talk for two solid years, but he wouldn't budge. He wouldn't let me help him, and I felt worn to a stump from trying.

That business of rolling away from me in bed hurt, but by the time we got to India, I was doing it too. I was becoming as frustrated as he was tormented, and we took our pain out on each other. We hid in our respective corners until something brought us out with fists raised. I couldn't fix our insides, so I fixed our outside. I prowled around the bungalow searching for dust mites to exterminate, mould to slaughter and smudges to wipe out. I vanquished dirt and disorder wherever I found it, and it helped, a little.

The morning I found the letters, I'd filled a pail with hot soapy water and pounced on the sooty bricks behind the old cooker with demented determination. I described foamy circles on the wall with my brush and . . . what? One brick moved. That was odd. Nothing in that house ever rattled or came loose; the British colonials who built the place had expected to rule India for ever. I put the brush down and forced my fingernails into the crumbling mortar around the loose brick, then wiggled it back and forth until it came out far enough for me to grab hold. I teased the brick out of the wall and felt a thrill of discovery when I saw, hidden in the wall, a packet of folded papers tied with a faded and bedraggled blue ribbon.

That packet reeked of long-lost secrets, and I felt a smile lift one corner of my mouth. I set the blackened brick on the floor and reached in to lift my plunder out of the wall. But on second thoughts, I went to the sink first to wash the soot from my hands.

With clean, dry hands, I eased the packet out of its hiding place, blew the dust from its crevices, then laid it on the kitchen table and pulled the ribbon loose. When I opened the first sheet, the folds seemed almost to creak with age. Gently now, I smoothed the fragile paper out on the table and it crackled faintly. It was ancient and brittle, the edges wavy and water-stained. It was a letter written on thin, grainy parchment, and feminine handwriting rose and swooped across the page with sharp peaks and curling flourishes. The writing was in English, and the way it had been concealed in the wall hinted at Victorian intrigue.

I slipped into a chair to read.

Chapter Two

from . . . Adela Winfield . . .
. . . Yorkshire, Engl . . .
September 1854

Dear Felicity,
. . . wrenched my heart to say goodbye . . .
. . . dangerous voyage . . .   . . . storms at sea . . .
. . . Mother persists in . . .   . . . these men . . .   . . . vile
cretins all . . .
. . . miss you terribly . . .

sister . . . joy
Adela

Decades of damp had ruined most of the page. I glanced at the date, thinking, my God, this thing is almost a hundred years old. And those names – Felicity and Adela – how charmingly Victorian. From the sound of it, Felicity lived in India (in this bungalow?) and Adela had written from England.

I shot a quick glance over my shoulder, then smiled at my own silliness. It would make no difference to Martin or anyone else if they found me reading an old letter. It was that hole in the brick wall and the way the letters had been hidden that made me feel like a pirate with illicit booty.

But I was alone. Habib hadn't yet arrived to start dinner and Rashmi was outside, gossiping with an itinerant box wallah in the godowns. I listened, and only Billy's innocent voice broke the house's deep silence. Billy – five years old then, and full of ginger – was carting Spike around the verandah in his Red Flyer wagon.

Spike, a stuffed dog dressed in cowboy gear, had been a gift for Billy's fifth birthday in lieu of the real puppy he'd wanted. Pets had been forbidden in our Chicago apartment and Spike was a compromise. Martin and I splurged on the finest toy dog we could find – a pert Yorkshire terrier with uncanny glass eyes and a black felt cowboy hat. He was snappily clad in a red plaid shirt and blue denim jeans, and he wore four pointy-toed boots of tooled leather. Billy adored him.

But in Masoorla, the rootin' tootin' cowboy had come to represent the easy American life we'd taken Billy away from, and I couldn't look at it without a twinge of guilt. India had turned out to be lonely – believe me, you don't expect that in a country with almost half a billion people – and Spike was Billy's only friend. He talked to the toy as if it was a real dog, and Martin worried whether that was entirely healthy. But I wouldn't have taken Spike away even I'd known the trouble the toy was going to cause later.

I unfolded another page rescued from the wall; it was a water-stained drawing of a woman in a split skirt and pith helmet astride a horse. Martin had told me that English women rode sidesaddle in the 1800s, and I wondered whether this was some sort of cartoon, or was this woman, perhaps, one of those outrageous few who flaunted society? I studied the drawing: she had a young face, thin and plain, and she smiled as if she knew something the rest of us didn't. She held the reins with easy confidence. The brim of her topi shaded her eyes, and only her knowing smile, her lifted chin and that bold costume hinted at her personality. I unfolded a few more pages, all bearing different degrees of damage, but I made out a phrase here and there.

From . . .   Ad . . . Winfield
. . . shire, England
September 1854

Dear Felicity
  . . . last night . . .   . . . a chinless little man . . .
      . . . bored . . .
          . . . a good cry . . .
. . . duty to yourself . . .   but your health . . .
    . . . intrepid Fanny Parks . . . not consumptive . . .
. . . worry about you . . .

The letters were personal, and trying to fill in the blanks felt like peering into these people's lives uninvited. I struggled with a brief pang of guilt before reminding myself that the letters were dated 1855 and the people concerned were long past caring. Still, I glanced at the back door. Gloomy Martin and lighthearted Rashmi would not have cared about the letters, but Habib was a sphinx-like Indian who spoke no English, and I never knew what he was thinking. I always felt a bit off balance around Habib, but he was a reliable cook, who hadn't poisoned us yet with his incendiary curries.

In spite of my reluctance to trust the suspicious snacks on

the train, Martin and I had decided to eat the native food in our own home. Indian cooks had long been preparing English meals – they smirked and called them invalid food – but Martin convinced me that it would be more interesting to eat curries than to teach an Indian how to make meatloaf. 'Either you'll give cooking lessons to a cook who doesn't speak English or we'll eat nothing but shepherd's pie and blancmange.' He grimaced. I knew he was right and he clinched it with the very reasonable observation that 'It will be the same ingredients from the same markets made by the same cook, no matter how they are seasoned or arranged in the pot.'

Unfortunately, Habib's curries were so hot that most distinguishing flavours were lost under the searing spices. Martin, the great promoter of local dishes, said the meals in our house were not consumed but survived. One night, he stared at his goat curry and rubbed his belly. 'OK,' he said, sheepish. 'I know we agreed, but . . .' He sighed. 'Does every meal have to leave blisters?' I nodded, sympathetic. At that point, we both could have done with a little English invalid food.

I tried to get Habib to cut back on the hot chillis with pantomimes of fanning my mouth, panting and gulping cold water. But the silent little man with the skullcap and expressionless eyes only rocked his head from side to side in that ambiguous, all-purpose gesture that no Westerner can completely decipher – the Indian head-waggle. It can mean yes or no or maybe, it can mean I'm delighted or utterly indifferent, or sometimes it seems to be an automatic response that simply means, OK, I heard you. Apparently, it was all about context.

I shuffled the letters, scanning another sheet of writing spoiled by time and weather, and I felt a spurt of irritation with both the letter and the place that had ruined it. I had hoped that cultural isolation would force Martin and me back to each other, but India had not brought us together. India had turned out to be incomprehensibly complex, not a wellspring of ancient wisdom, but a snake pit of riddles entwined in a knot of cultural and religious contradictions.

And speaking of contradictions, India seemed to make Martin simultaneously paranoid and reckless. He still never wore a hat and brushed me off when I offered him a tube of calendula ointment for his red, peeling nose. For his work, he interviewed Indians about their forthcoming independence from Great Britain, which meant walking through the native quarters of Simla and driving the open Packard over steep, rutted roads into the hills to visit remote villages. When I told him to be careful, he laughed, saying, 'I'm a war veteran. I think I can handle myself.' He whistled as he left the house.

But every morning, when I made up our bed, I had to whisk flat the spider cicatrices in the sheet where he had bunched it during angst-ridden dreams. I didn't know whether he was dreaming about India or Germany, but I knew he was not as relaxed as he pretended.

Another mark of his anxiety was his infurating double standard. Even while he roamed the countryside at will, he warned me not to stray too far from home. That chafed. I don't like being told what to do, never have, and I stood up to him. I stuck my chin out and told him we were in India, not wartime Germany, but he stuck his chin out too and told me I didn't know what I was talking about. Any mention of Germany brought a dangerous edge to his voice, so I pulled in my chin and let it go.

I unfolded the last sheets of parchment, and my breath caught. The innermost letter was intact. Several pages had been saved from the worst of the damp, every word preserved by the absorbent layers around it.

from the pen of Felicity Chadwick

Calcutta, India
January 1855

Dearest Adela,
Silly goose! By now you've received my letters from Gibraltar & Alexandria & know I haven't perished on the high seas. I miss you terribly, but it is good to be back in India. How I wish you could join me.

Arriving during the season has been a colossal bore – days spent in stuffy drawing rooms, endless dinners & dances with the same dreary courting rituals between the same desperate women & the same lonely men, all of them becoming silly on Roman punch. I make a point of telling the stodgy gentlemen that I like to smoke & drink, & the bawdy ones that I'm devoted to my Bible studies. Does that shock you? Mother would be appalled, but thus far I have succeeded in avoiding any proposals so my plan is evidently working. Mother & Father are mystified by my lack of proposals & I keep silent, pretending not to understand it either, biding my time until we go to the hills in March. Then I shall escape to the freedom of the mofussil – the wild countryside – all on my own. I've heard about an unspoiled little village called Masoorla & I smell freedom.

I am happy to be back in India, but the multitude of servants who attend us every moment has resurrected an unsettling memory. One day, when I was six, I skipped into the humid cookhouse behind our home in Calcutta & saw Yasmin, my ayah, standing over a pot left to simmer. This was most surprising as Yasmin was a Hindoo & would normally not enter the cookhouse, which she considered unclean, the place where our Mohammedan cook prepared meat, even beef. Yet, there she was.

I had gone into the cookhouse for a snack of guava chaat & caught her in the act of withdrawing her hand from a moonstone urn. She swivelled her head slowly & locked her eyes on to me, her chota mem – little lady – whilst she withdrew a pinch of ash from the urn. Some Hindoos sentimentally save a small amount of a loved one's ashes, & I had last seen that moonstone urn in Yasmin's hands a week earlier when she returned, weeping, from Vikram's cremation. Vikram had been one of our many bearers, & I remembered seeing his body in the godowns covered with masses of marigolds & roses & ready for cremation. I gave Yasmin a questioning look whilst her hand hung poised over the stew pot with Vikram's ashes pinched between thumb & fingertips.

Knowing I would never betray her, my beloved Yasmin released Vikram's ashes into the stew, & I watched them flutter into the pot, into our dinner. She smiled at me & I smiled back. Yasmin was the one who woke me with a kiss in the morning, & sang me to sleep at night. She gave me the patchwork quilt made of sari fabrics that I brought with me to England. It smelled of patchouli & coconut oil, like Yasmin, & do you remember how furious your mother was when I hid it from the laundress? I could not lose those scents to lye soap; it would have been like losing Yasmin again.

I watched Yasmin stir the desecrated stew with a long spoon, & then she gave me an affectionate wink & a handful of guava chaat.

It was our secret & though I did not understand, I was happy to share it with her. After all, I was six & lonely &

accustomed to not understanding. I did not understand why cows controlled the traffic in the street, or why father donned a white kid glove to pinch the servants when he was displeased. Nor did I understand Mother's practice of giving servants a large dose of castor oil as a punishment, or her rule that no servant could come closer to her than an arm's length.

Once, she forgot herself & made to steady herself on Vikram's shoulder as she climbed into the palanquin, then, with a huff of disgust, she withdrew her hand as though from a flame & clambered in on her own. Vikram seemed oblivious, but Yasmin's face had darkened, & a few weeks later, after his sudden death, Yasmin put his ashes into our food. I thought she was playing a joke on Mother.

That evening at dinner, the bearer set down plates mounded with perfumed rice & partridge stew. Mother & Father spooned the defiled stew into their mouths & chewed dutifully. As always, Mother dabbed daintily at the corners of her mouth, & Father blotted his moustache with a stiff damask napkin.

I recall pushing it around in my mouth, probing with my tongue for some gritty texture or aberrant taste, but there was none. I knew Vikram was in my dinner, but I was six & I didn't mind. He had been one of my favourite bearers. I enjoyed watching him cavort in the garden, laughing whilst he juggled bananas with a bucked-tooth smile, his turban going askew. I don't know why he died, but Yasmin told me he had become a dragonfly, & that she kept some of his ashes in the moonstone urn to keep her company. I understood only later that he was probably her husband.

I ate my dinner & pondered what part of Vikram I might be ingesting. I thought of his pierced earlobe, his misshapen little toe & his hooked nose. It was possible that Yasmin's pinch of ash had merely captured a bit of his shroud, but I hoped not. I wanted to eat something of Vikram because I missed him.

Do you find me monstrous, Adela?

When we moved from our small house to the big one on Garden Reach Road, Vikram was one of the bearers who escorted Mother & me. I moved the curtain of our palanquin to inhale the street smells of India – smoke & spice & something else I could not identify – & for the first time, I wondered what comprised that distinctive odour. Later, standing inside the gate of our new house, I looked up at Mother & twitched my nose. She pursed her stingy lips & gave a wag of her head. 'Squatting,' she said with a twist of distaste. 'Women squatting in the dirt over their cooking.' She sniffed at the offending air. 'You should understand by now that these people prefer to live in the street.'

But Adela, it was not only the smell of food cooking, it was burning cow dung & funeral pyres – the odour of poverty & grief. I saw the biers trotted daily through the streets, laden with thin, brown corpses surrounded by fresh flowers. Father turned away from the funeral processions. 'Poor wogs,' he said with a grim smile. 'No point in their living terribly long anyway.'

Don't you find that sad? They lived & died & we paid them no heed. We didn't even notice them in our food. But they knew! Since I've been back in India, I've heard of cooks putting ground glass into the sahib's food. They knew.

I put Yasmin's 'joke' out of my mind until I came back to India & sat down one evening to a dinner of partridge stew. With my first taste, the memory of another stew seasoned with human ashes surfaced with visceral impact. I looked around the room & saw our bearers, one standing behind each of us, erect & impassive. One sees nothing in their faces, even when Father goes on & on about politics – the religious feuds & the malcontent sepoys.

*Well, Father can boil his head. I love India & intend to
live here on my own terms. I shan't marry; I shall make
myself useful. I have my annuity, & when we go to the hills I
shall hire a simple bungalow near Masoorla. My Hindoostani
is coming back, & I shall go so thoroughly jungli Mother will
want nothing to do with me.*

I cannot wait!

Your sister in joy,
Felicity

The letter had never been mailed. I laid it down, thinking
. . . human remains in the stew? I remembered a *National
Geographic* article about ritual cannibalism, which concluded
that it was deeply spiritual, involving a belief in transferred
power and continued existence. Only cannibalism for
survival entailed reluctance or regret. Of course, Yasmin's
behaviour didn't truly qualify as cannibalism, but something akin, for which I had no name. Apparently, human
ashes in the stew were simply the Indian equivalent of a
slave spitting into the massa's mint julep.

Cannibalism or not, the belief that what we ingest tran-
scends the physical has deep roots in the human psyche.
Ritual cannibalism attests to a primal human urge to consume what we love or covet – an atavistic pull like the sound
of the sea – and religions that symbolically eat the body and
drink the blood are an echo of those primitive and literal
customs. It is not unnatural to wish that we could simply
ingest power, love, redemption and all things desirable. It
occurred to me that if Martin were to die, having a pinch of
his ashes in my food might even be comforting. I murmured,
'You weren't monstrous, Felicity.'

I searched my mental archives for India in 1856. Tension

between Hindus and Muslims was longstanding, but 'malcontent sepoys' triggered a fuzzy memory from a world history class, some incident having to do with anti-British sentiment, but the details eluded me.

I went to the vacant space in the brick wall and peered into the dark recess, checking for anything I might have missed.

Nothing.

I examined the wall for another loose brick.

Nothing.

I stood in the middle of the room, holding the letter and staring out of my sparkling kitchen window. The sun was beginning its westward plunge behind the white-capped Himalayas, and in a few hours the icy peaks would turn copper and then dim to lavender. I loved to watch that, but it was always over in a couple of minutes. Night descends swiftly in India. On any other day the brief spectacle might have made me think about impermanence, the fleetingness of life, but not that day, with my Victorian letters flying in the very face of impermanence.

I refolded and retied the packet of letters and thought about stashing it in a kitchen cabinet, but that felt too casual, almost disrespectful. I considered the drawer of a side table in the living room, but that seemed somehow too public.

There had been a time, before the war, when I would have left the letters scattered on the kitchen table, eager to show them to Martin. I remembered when we had shared joy as easily as breathing, and that was how I thought our marriage would always be. But since the war he'd become so intractably sullen that my first thought was to hide the letters from him. I didn't want him to cast a pall on my excitement. To be in his presence was to be sucked into a dark place by a magnetic pull; I was tired of him extinguishing my enthusiasm, and exhausted by the effort of fending off his gloom. It was fertile ground for a seed of bitterness to sprout, and though I tried to resist, it flowered. I found myself becoming as secretive as he was shut down, and I fell into the irrational habit of keeping things to myself to balance his withdrawal.

In the end, I tucked the letters into my lingerie drawer, pillowed between silk panties and satin bras. They belonged with my intimate things. I didn't yet know who Felicity and Adela were, but I wanted to keep them close, to protect them. I patted my secret cache and closed the drawer. Martin could go boil his head. They were *mine*.

Chapter Three

1844–5

EIGHT-YEAR-OLD Felicity Chadwick clung to the deck rail and watched India recede. She stared down at Yasmin, standing on the chaotic dock, dabbing her eyes with a corner of her white sari.

Before boarding, she had clung to Yasmin's legs while Lady Chadwick tugged at her. 'For heaven's sake, child. Stop that this instant.' When Felicity could not stop sobbing, Lady Chadwick bent down and took firm hold of her little chin. 'You cannot grow up in India. You would become weedy and delicate. You would acquire that chee-chee accent.' Her face kinked up. 'We can't have that, can we?' But Felicity continued to cry until Lady Chadwick grabbed her shoulders and shook her hard. 'Stop this now. It's for your welfare, and sentiment must be pocketed.' Felicity did her best to stifle her sobs as her mother handed her over to her chaperones for the journey, the Perth-Macintyres, who were returning to England.

Now, Mrs Perth-Macintyre stood at the railing beside Felicity, trumpeting assurances that Felicity would *love* England. It was *home*, after all, even though Felicity had never been there because her entire family served the East

India Company. A foster family in England was the commonly accepted solution for a child like Felicity. 'Don't worry, my girl,' said Mrs Perth-Macintyre. 'We'll get India drummed out of you soon enough.' As the ship moved off, Felicity kept her gaze fixed on Yasmin, now sobbing openly and growing ever smaller on the dock.

That night Felicity slept in a hammock wrapped in an old quilt made of sari fabrics, patches of worn silks and soft cottons, with a fanciful border of birds and flowers. Its scent of patchouli and coconut oil conjured Yasmin and the soft clash of her bangles as she walked barefoot around the house in Calcutta. Felicity dreamed of India, but the next morning, she walked out on deck and discovered it gone. It had been a dusty world, but beloved, and now, finally, she knew she would not see the red tulip on the silk tree bloom again.

After months of boredom, disgusting food, seasickness, and a terrifying storm that threw Felicity out of her hammock, the ship neared England's shore in March. Felicity stepped out of her cabin into a raw blast of wind sharper and colder than anything she had ever known. Excited passengers gathered at the rail as they sailed into port, and Felicity, blue with cold, strained to see something of the fabled isle through a murky fog. As she shivered in the damp, a vision of green rice paddies, waving under a brilliant sun, ambushed her; she remembered sunlit mountain picnics with sweet, round watermelons cooled in icy streams, and violet tints on distant snow-covered peaks. When the foghorn sounded, she buried her face in her Indian quilt and inhaled.

The Perth-Macintyres handed Felicity over to her guardian, Mrs Winfield, and in that moment she exchanged a sensual world rich in colour and freedom for the mannered, gas-lit world of nineteenth-century England, where children were seen and not heard. The Chadwicks had been a dedicated East India Company family for generations, and employing a guardian to oversee a child's English education was a time-honoured tradition.

Felicity had heard her father describe Mrs Winfield as 'A decent woman. Perhaps one who assumes you probably hold too high an opinion of yourself and intends to pull you down, but decent.' Of Dr Winfield he had said, 'A common medical man, but respected.' Her mother had said, 'It is a proper family, they are willing to take her, happy to have the stipend, and they have a daughter just her age.'

That seemed to be enough to recommend the Winfields as guardians and so it was settled. But now, standing on the Royal Albert Docks in Liverpool, Felicity did not know what to make of this pale, long-faced lady in a fur-trimmed pelisse, reaching for her hand. Mrs Winfield gave Felicity a tight smile and hurried her into a waiting carriage, but she did not speak during the entire ride to Yorkshire. The carriage sped away from the docks, through the city and into the countryside, and Felicity stared out of the window at this place everyone wistfully called home. At rest stops, her breath puffed in the frosty air and steam rose off the sweating horses; Felicity thought it very strange to be so cold in March, the beginning of the hot weather in India. Dark forests gave way to rolling moors, tidy and pleasant, but after India it seemed impossibly empty.

At Rose Hall, named after Mrs Winfield's prize-winning garden, eight-year-old Adela waited on the front steps with her father. She stretched her neck and stood on tiptoe, eager for her first glimpse of the girl from India. Would she speak strangely? Would she dress in bizarre costumes? Adela had seen pictures of India.

But out of the carriage stepped an appropriately clad girl with wide-set blue eyes and an ordinary bonnet. Still ... there *was* something different about her face. Her skin was unfashionably burnished, as if by sun and wind, and her look was ... what? A thought crashed through Adela like a wrecking ball through glass. Her look was deliciously insolent.

Mrs Winfield did not tolerate insolence, and Adela did not break the rules. But here stood a girl with an impertinent look, coming from the fantastic Orient to enliven their staid home. The possibilities were terrifying and wonderful. Adela held her breath as this marvellous girl hopped down from the carriage and stood there, hands on her hips, appraising her new home as if she owned the place; she pulled off her bonnet and a mass of rose-gold hair tumbled around her face. When Adela took her next breath, the air smelled sharper, the green lawn and the blue sky blurred, and she felt the first stab of a romantic longing that would afflict her for the rest of her life.

As solitary children of cold parents, the girls both found comfort in sisterhood. The terms of their friendship crystallized the day Felicity and Adela skipped along the second-floor hallway while Felicity sang an old Hindu lullaby. Mrs Winfield came up behind them and seized Felicity's arm. She squeezed the arm as she spoke. 'In the first place, you do not *skip* indoors. And in the second place, I will not have heathen jingles sung in my home.'

Adela knew that expression on her mother's face and she froze. Felicity simply said, 'My ayah is not a heathen.'

Mrs Winfield's eyes narrowed. 'Are you contradicting me?'

'Well, you're wrong, aren't you?'

Mrs Winfield seized Felicity roughly and hauled her on to the banister, balancing her precariously on the edge, two floors up. She said, 'You will not contradict me, young lady. You will watch your mouth or I might push you off.' She made a sudden jerking motion that made Adela's stomach lurch.

Mrs Winfield had once perched Adela on that same banister and made the same threat. Whenever Adela thought to defy her mother she remembered the terror of looking down to the cold stone floor she would fall on, the sick sensation in her stomach and the way she trembled for an hour afterwards. She would be an adult before she fully understood that it was merely a scare tactic; it had worked with her because she was frightened to death of her mother.

But Felicity called the woman's bluff. She looked Mrs Winfield in the eye and said, 'No, you won't. That would be murder and then you would be hanged.' Felicity tipped up her chin, gloriously defiant.

Mrs Winfield's mouth made a perfect circle, and Felicity slid easily off the rail to safety. Mrs Winfield took a step towards her, but Felicity stood her ground and the woman looked suddenly confused. 'Why, you cheeky little . . .' They stared at each other, the woman and the girl, and the woman looked away first. She gave Felicity's shoulders one mean shake, then stalked off, muttering. 'Doesn't care what anyone thinks. Not a whit. Bad. Very bad.'

Stunned, Adela watched her go. She had never before seen her mother bested, even by her father. The girl from India had performed a miracle, and Adela's affection for Felicity became, from that day on, tinged with awe.

As much as Adela loved Felicity's brio, Felicity appreciated Adela's fascination with India. No one else wanted to hear stories about Yasmin, and guava chaat, and the boys who followed them around with yak-tail fans to keep the flies off. Adela said, 'India sounds like *The Arabian Nights*.'

'The what?'

'Scheherazade, silly! Surely you know.'

But she didn't, and so Adela told her. Adela's great love was reading, another disappointment to her mother. Mrs Winfield warned, 'Keep that up and you'll end up completely unmarriageable.' But a good book was the one thing for which Adela would ignore her mother. Felicity described fantastic Indian festivals, glittering bazaars, and the notoriously soft-hearted, white-clad ayahs who offered end-less treats and crushing hugs when the memsahibs were not watching. For her part, Adela read Felicity *The King of the Golden River* and stories from Hans Christian Andersen.

Felicity said, 'Oh, Adela, you're so clever.'

Adela shrugged. 'I just read made-up stories. Your stories are real.'

Throughout the spring and summer, Mrs Winfield tended her roses while the girls traded tales and came to inhabit each other's worlds. Adela recorded the stories Felicity told her, and Felicity made simple sketches of Yasmin and the palanquin in which she used to ride, carried by four bearers while properly curtained and insulated from the chaos of Calcutta. Adela had never felt she belonged to her mother's world, and Felicity felt neither English nor Indian, but now they had each other.

In September they were sent to St Ethel's, an elite board-ing school of half-timbered Tudor buildings with cupolas and turrets set around a quadrangle of well-kept grass and elderly trees. The Chadwicks paid Adela's tuition as part of their arrangement with the Winfields, and both sets of parents consigned their daughters to the mercy of St Ethel's, trusting the girls would wear neatly starched pinafores and become proficient in riding, needlework, basic maths, read-ing and calligraphy.

But when the girls at St Ethel's ignored timid Adela and ridiculed Felicity for calling breakfast *chota hazri*, the pair took to eating breakfast by themselves at a corner table. Things got worse after a lecture about London women known as bluestockings who were thought to be excessively intellectual and a bit mannish. The St Ethel girls immediately began calling bookish Adela 'the dowdy little bluestocking'. Adela ignored them, usually by keeping her face in a book, but Felicity generously passed out dirty looks and rude gestures.

No matter. Felicity and Adela occupied themselves by plotting their futures as Indian princesses or famous authors. By their tenth birthdays they talked of becoming spies or famous courtesans, and by twelve they had discovered memoirs in the library and came to admire women like Emma Roberts, who edited her own newspaper in Calcutta, and Honoria Lawrence, who marched around India with her husband, a surveyor, having babies in tents and riding elephants through uncharted jungles. But their favourite heroine was the outrageous Mrs Fanny Parks, who travelled in remote areas of India with no one but her servants. The girls read Fanny's memoir by candlelight, shocked when she wrote that her husband went mad in the cold season and that it was her duty to herself to leave him and wander about.

'Imagine that,' said Adela. 'Not her duty to her husband or the Empire. Her duty to *herself*.'

'She's marvellous.'

Fanny Parks killed scorpions with her hatpin, she loved the spicy native foods, and when she had a headache she took opium. Fanny even chewed paan, which Felicity explained was a betel leaf wrapped around spices and tobacco. 'But it stains the teeth red,' she said, wrinkling her nose. And then they were quiet for a moment, adjusting their picture of Fanny Parks to a woman with red teeth. Fixing this image in their minds, they read on, learning that Fanny kept a pet squirrel named Jack Bunce, and had once spent a month gossiping in a zenana.

'That's a harem,' Felicity whispered, and they giggled.

But the enthralling Mrs Parks also wrote about mind-erasing heat, cholera epidemics, snakes in her bedroom, and partially burned corpses floating down the Ganges. Felicity put the book down and gazed out of the window. 'I wonder how Fanny could do all those astonishing things and keep her spirits up in the face of such hardship.' She thought of Mrs Winfield, carefully pruning her roses – a serious business – and her own mother angrily forcing castor oil into the mouth of an errant kneeling servant. Felicity rested her chin on her fists, thinking hard. 'I believe she did not judge,' she said slowly. 'And she had joy.'

Adela recalled her mother sucking sourly at a thorn-pricked finger. 'I think you're right. I'm not sure I've ever seen my mother genuinely happy.'

Felicity gave Adela her wide, sudden smile. 'Let's be like Fanny. Let's scrap the rules and live a life of joy, no matter what the price.'

'Yes!' Adela took Felicity's hands. 'Come what may, we shall not judge and we shall be joyful.'

After that, both girls made a point of calling breakfast *chota hazri* and laughed when the others snubbed them.

Chapter Four

1938

I FIRST SAW MARTIN on campus, studying under the grizzled elms, history textbooks scattered around him like fallen leaves. We looked at each other one beat too long, but neither of us spoke.

At first glance, Martin struck me as swarthy, probably because of his untamed dark hair – a mass of careless ringlets completely out of sync with the times – or maybe it was his olive complexion and sable eyes. But his features were too fine to be called swarthy. His clothes were more collegiate than stylish, and his glasses gave him a scholarly look. Still, I found him fatally glamorous, and I often went out of my way to walk past the elms. The chemistry between us percolated silently, but in the 1930s 'nice' girls never made the first move. Add to that the fact that Martin was a shy, bookish fellow, and we passed each other in fraught silence.

Freshly released from a girls' school called the Immaculate Conception – I called it the Inaccurate Perception – I had never been in love. In college, I hobnobbed in platonic groups, but at night, in the ebb and flow of erotic dreams, the *objet du désir* was always that elusive dark-haired fellow under the elms.

I had a scholarship – Da could never have afforded the University of Chicago – and I intended to study astronomy, eager to probe cosmic mysteries. I had been called 'gifted', which made me feel a responsibility to perform flawlessly, but it wasn't a burden, it was a privilege. I wanted to learn and contribute, and my life seemed to be opening in every direction. I would have liked to move into a jazzy little apartment with interesting room-mates, makeshift bookshelves and Art Deco posters. I'd stencil the walls and hand-paint the lampshades. I'd comb thrift stores for green glass bookends and conversation pieces – maybe an old French barometer or a Bakelite fan dancer. I might even find an affordable geometric rug. The pipedream was a bohemian apartment, or a *cave*, in the college argot of the day. But all that would have been expensive, and Da would have worried, so I commuted.

Da became overprotective after Mum died. I was eight when she passed away, but I remember her auburn hair, her velvety scent of Ponds hand cream, and her wheezy voice, crooning 'Danny Boy'. I also remember her lying dead in her bed with her eyes open in surprise, and the dark squall of emotions that gripped me. We never dreamed that asthma could kill her, even while we watched her suffocate to death. I don't remember the wake or the funeral, but that moment when they put her in the ground, down in that deep hole, I cried myself blind. Da did too.

Her death forged a new bond between Da and me, as if by clinging to each other we could somehow keep her alive. So I commuted to college and took a part-time job near the campus at Linz's German Bakery. After my classes I switched off the budding scientist in me and assumed the role of docile *Fraülein*, a worker bee dressed in a frilled white apron, one of four young women buzzing around the *Bienenstich* and *Apfelstrudel*, our menses flowing in tidal synchronization, our conversation limited to neighbour-hood gossip and *schwartzwalder Torte*.

Linz's bakery had something of the harem and the convent about it, and in that environment, smelling of baker's yeast and sugar, I pined for the dark-haired guy under the elms, until one day I looked up from the cash register to see him standing there, pointing at a Jewish rye. I felt a blush spread over my face and splash my chest. I said hello, and he said hello, and we both stood there like idiots. Then lame brain Kate said, 'That'll be ten cents, sir.' He dug out his wallet and paid, and then he sort of *had* to leave. But he came back the next day and then every day and, really, no one eats that much rye bread. Every time he came in I just about broke my neck getting over there to wait on him, and eventually we exchanged names. He said, 'Evaleen? That's unusual.'

I shrugged. 'It's Irish.'

'It's beautiful.' He pushed his glasses up on his nose. 'And it suits you.'

I felt the blush surge to my face. God, I *hated* that. Then he asked me out on Saturday night, and I was struck dizzy.

That Saturday, I wore a soft dove-grey dress that moved with me and complemented my coppery hair; bright colours with my flaming hair and blue eyes made me feel like a tropical fish. When Martin saw me he stared with a dopey, smitten look and then smiled with his whole face.

We went to a movie and held hands and, yes, I know how dull that sounds now. I know that kids today think they invented sex, and feel free to indulge with cheerful abandon. Simply holding hands has gone out of style as a form of fore-play, but I think it's a shame. Having to sit for hours with only hands touching, fingers moving suggestively, watching a stray wisp of hair curl over a collar, trying to follow the movie while hearing the whisper of fabric shifting, curious minds whirring away, enduring that forced restraint while pressure builds . . . now that's foreplay.

I don't remember the movie, but we laughed at the same scenes and tensed up at the same moments. When the lights came up, we looked at each other with a stir of recognition – so *that's* who you are.

Afterwards, we went to Darby's pub, where Da played his fiddle every Saturday night, and I introduced my two men. Martin, earnest and polite, shook Da's hand and pulled a chair out for me. Da hugged me and assessed Martin with flinty eyes. When Martin went to fetch our beers, Da asked, 'Who are his people?'

I said, 'He's Jewish, Da.'

Da stared at me, weighing Martin's foreignness against his status as a college man. Even though Da didn't know the difference between a social historian and a whirling dervish, he knew Martin was the sort of educated fellow he had wanted me to meet at my fancy university. He just hadn't figured on Jewish.

That night Da got up to play and did not sit with us again. He played his heart out, stamping the hollow boards, singing passionate songs about fighting the English and rowdy drinking songs punched up with whistles and shouts. Da's music always made me see fiery colours, Irishmen jigging, and heels clicking in the air. I grew up on that music and I loved it, but I wondered whether Martin, who liked Bach, might find it slightly raucous.

Depending on how you looked at it, Martin and I appeared either perfectly balanced or wildly unsuited. Martin, with his dark good looks and mildly brooding nature, said I had a mercurial presence and runaway laughter, and that when I smiled the dimple in my left cheek changed me from innocent ingénue to slightly dangerous coquette. I was breezy and he was serious; I was quirky and he was traditional. Learning that he was Jewish made me think his face and temperament had been forged by ancestors dressed in black, scuttling through the ghettos of *Mitteleuropa*. In fact, his face took me even further back, all the way to the Levant; his smoky complexion conjured handsome nomads crossing the desert in camel caravans.

I imagined that Martin's home must reek of ancient and enduring persecution and I pictured gloomy rooms cluttered with dark furniture and strange Judaica, an embedded smell of boiled cabbage, a silent mother, labouring over her gefilte fish, and a balding, bearded father wrapped in a prayer shawl and hunched over his Torah.

I knew nothing about Jews except the half-baked suspicions absorbed from Old Testament stories force-fed us at the Inaccurate Perception. I imagined a slightly furtive religion of skullcaps and veils, wailing and keening over piles of mouldering scrolls, bloody rituals involving baby boys and goats – and all of this on Saturdays when Catholics are playing baseball and mowing the lawn. I knew my fierce Celtic ancestors were, at the time of Moses, painting their faces blue and howling at the moon, but that had nothing to do with Da and me. We were normal; Jews were mysterious.

So Dave and Rachel astonished me. I met them one Sunday in their sprawling Highland Park home with its wall-to-wall carpeting, oyster-white furniture and views of a yawning front lawn. They had decorated their home with souvenirs picked up on their travels: a bronze Degas ballerina from Paris in the study, a hand-painted etching from Italy in the powder room, a Wedgwood cigarette box on the coffee table . . .

Rachel taught painting, and her winsome watercolours

hung, tastefully framed, all over the house. The walls vibrated with gentle landscapes and serene seascapes, all as assured as the woman herself. Rachel had a graceful habit of looping her ash-blonde hair behind one ear, and her smart cashmere twinsets never wrinkled when she sat with her ankles neatly crossed.

Dave, greying elegantly at the temples, was strong-boned and clean-shaven. He had a formidable chin (ah, that's where Martin got the Cary Grant cleft), the chin of a man to be reckoned with. He had family money and a manner that made my own dear Da seem like a throwback. Dave greeted me with a peck on the cheek that took me by surprise, and he frequently clapped Martin on the back for no apparent reason. Dave was a Columbia man who tolerated the Midwest so that Rachel could teach at the Art Institute. He taught Middle English literature at Northwestern.

They were upbeat people who kept a small Chris-Craft in Burnham harbour because they liked to celebrate sunny days. Martin's shadowed temperament, which would sour into sulking, the sensitivity that would warp into paranoia, and the self-awareness that would become self-loathing, all the dark subtleties that the war twisted into nightmares – those were purely Martin.

Dave and Rachel were polite but cool, and it occurred to me that my Catholicism might seem as arcane to them as their Judaism did to me. For me, the pageant of Byzantine robes and chanting in a dead language, the drama of tortured martyrs, virgin birth and crucifixion had been worn thin and made bland by repetition. Even the cannibalistic implications of eating the body and drinking the blood were lost on me. Sunday Mass left me glassy-eyed with boredom, all the esoteric rituals drained of mystery by familiarity. I wondered whether the same mistrust that Da subsumed in boisterous Irish music also lurked behind Dave and Rachel's impeccable manners.

Rachel had prepared dinner, and I still half expected a mudgy lump of chopped liver, but she served a roast capon, plump and succulent under crisp skin scented with tarragon, and a fresh green salad with pine nuts. After dinner, Dave poured Grand Marnier into pear-shaped snifters, and Martin played the piano, a sleek, black Steinway, the like of which I'd never seen in a private home. Martin sat on the piano bench like a man preparing to pray, with a straight back and bowed head. He hesitated with his hands hovering over the keys, seemingly overwhelmed at the prospect of touching them. Then he played Mozart and, I think, Chopin. He had a wonderful touch, light and profound, and there was a tender, searching quality about his playing.

After Martin played for me, I wanted to share my passion with him. I doubted that his heart would melt over a lecture on gravity, but I believed I could touch his soul. One day in early May, we arranged a rendezvous in Pulaski Park. I said, 'Come to the sundial behind the field house at ten o'clock tonight.' I struck a sassy pose and smiled.

He touched my dimple. 'What are you up to, you copper-top minx?'

'Just be there.'

Chicago winters are bitter and long, but by the end of April the last crusts of grey snow have melted and spring rains have begun the greening of the city. May evenings are balmy; the wind has lost its icy bite, and silky breezes bring a sense of luxury and reprieve.

I arrived at the park early and stood in the clearing behind the field house, enjoying the soft air. Inside the field house, a kid was taking a cello lesson, and painful amateur squeaks sawed through the spring night. I hoped the noise would stop before Martin arrived.

The weather-beaten sundial bore blunted stone numerals furred with lichen, and a thicket of myrtle bushes encircled the clearing. The space felt like a Druid temple open to the sky, with the moon and stars looking down like a billion sparkling gods. Leaning against the sundial, I thought about the way moonlight enfolds the world in a unifying glow. While we're down here beating the hell out of each other, the old moon hangs there, knowing and silent, bathing us all in the same cool light.

Martin came up behind me and whispered, 'Sweetheart.' I loved his scent of shampoo and fresh ironing, the slightly abrasive feel of his cheek against mine, his arms crossed in front of me, pulling me close, and his fine, talented hands on my shoulders. For a moment, I forgot why I'd asked him to come. He did that to me. Then he said, 'Full moon tonight,' and I remembered.

'I want to show you the moondial.'

'I thought it was a sundial,' he said, stepping up to look.

'When there's a full moon, like tonight, it's a moondial.' I pointed. 'See.'

He leaned over and saw the lean wedge of moon-shadow at ten o'clock. He said, 'I'll be darned.'

'I used to come here as a kid,' I said. 'This thing fascinated me, and I wanted to know everything about how it worked.'

'My *Wunderkind*.'

'No.' I wanted him to understand. 'It's *wonderful*. You know? Full of wonder.' I made a sweeping gesture at the night sky. 'There are so many more questions than answers. See?' I pointed. 'There's Ursa Major. And there's Orion. It's exciting. It's what's *next*.' Then I gasped. 'Look! A shooting star!' It was the best thing that could have happened.

After the star streaked away, I turned to Martin and saw astonishment on his face. I said, 'Wasn't that breathtaking?'

'Yes.'

'Do you know what a shooting star really is?'

'I didn't see the star.'

'What?'

'I was looking at you.' He turned his head and pretended to scratch the side of his nose so he could wipe the corner of his eye.

I whispered, 'Martin?'

'You're luminous.'

'You missed it?'

'I didn't miss a thing.' He rolled the back of his hand down my cheek and pulled me in close, and a little moan escaped from deep in my throat. Moonlight sparked in his black hair, all mussed and sprung, and in his wet eyes, and we clung to each other. It seemed important to remain still, to leave the moment undisturbed so that it could sink deep into the clay of our being. Just then the cello teacher in the field house must have taken over because a heartbreaking Bach suite wafted out on the spring air, and I closed my eyes and saw amber lights, melting and mixing. Martin said, 'I *love* you,' and I said, 'I love *you*,' and that was the beginning of us being smashed and remade with something of the other in each of us.

Two weeks later, we rounded up Da and Dave and Rachel, and we grinned through a ten-minute wedding ceremony in City Hall. No priest, no rabbi, nobody really happy except us. The guy with the power vested in him said, 'I pronounce you . . .' We kissed like we meant it, and then Dave treated everyone to Chinese. Da held up his end of a strained conversation, while Martin and I shared an order of Lovers' Nest Shrimp.

By combining our stipends, we were able to rent a two-room basement apartment near the university. We declined Dave's offer of help because we wanted to create our own world beholden to no one. On the first night in our new place, Martin brought home a fistful of moon daisies. He said, 'Moon daisies don't close up at night like ordinary daisies. They're brave, like you.' I put the daisies in a glass and set it on the old Formica table, for which we had no chairs. Then we heated canned soup in our one pot and sat cross-legged on the floor to eat out of mismatched bowls from Goodwill.

We made up the mattress on the floor with hand-me-down sheets and scratchy, brown wool blankets from the Army Surplus store. It wasn't the first time we'd slept together, but it was the first time in our own place, our own bed, and we held back. We faced each other from opposite sides of the mattress and shed our clothes like shy butterflies struggling out of cocoons. Martin was lean and angular; his soft jumbled hair and strong cleft chin made me think of a perfectly balanced equation.

We knelt on the bed and leaned into each other, and then he touched the hollow at the base of my neck. He said, 'I love this spot. I can feel your heart beating there.'

After we moved in together, people at school speculated about whether or not I was pregnant; those who didn't know we were married wondered if we might be communists, starting a commune. But we did not feel shunned, we felt unshackled. We were Adam and Eve before the fall, innocent and alone and full of grace. In that time and place, love was all we needed, and that is not only rare and special, it is every bit as fleeting as Buddhists say it is.

Everything was easy in our closed little world. Even when

we argued, it never amounted to much because Martin always let it go. I didn't know that sometimes he let things fester. If I'd understood that, I might have been better prepared for my post-war husband. I was naive enough to think we were just that special.

Once in a while I wondered whether our love was really so unique that it rendered us immune to ordinary problems, but I didn't want to examine the question too closely for fear of jinxing us. I didn't know then that love is not only something you feel, it's something you do. In that time and place, feeling it was enough, and it seemed ungrateful to question it – until after the war.

Chapter Five

1941–7

I GOT PREGNANT during our first year of grad school. Martin and I had agreed on no children because we thought all babies were alike. We found it absurd to have to rhapsodize over other people's infants, those identical, pallid, frog-legged, sticky, bald, cartoonish screaming *things*.

But in 1941 a rabbit died and my career in astronomy went with it. Killing rabbits with the urine of pregnant women sounds downright medieval now, but that was then, and of course I dropped out of school because in 1941 pregnant women simply didn't belong in school; they barely belonged in public. There was something vaguely embarrassing about it. Yet, in spite of having to leave school, and in spite of our aversion to babies, the godlike magic of making another human being stunned us, and soon enough we were ridiculously excited. I remember one sweet night, not long after I'd felt that first astonishing kick, Martin and I lay in bed batting around baby names. Martin wrapped his leg around mine and ran his hand over my swollen belly. His eyes filled and shone, sweet sentimental fool, and he said, 'This is my family. Right here. Blooming in my arms like a hothouse flower.' Then he kissed me with fresh appreciation.

A few months later, we bathed our new son together. We inhaled his innocence, lathered the peach fuzz on his head, marvelled at the perfect whorls of his tiny ears, his starfish hands, the tender flush on his round, wet, baby belly. Martin cupped one wee foot and growled, 'Arrgh-arrgh-arrgh. Oooh, I'm gonna eat him.' He kissed each pink toe. 'Oooh, he's delicious.' Afterwards, we lay in bed chuckling at our new-born, who lay snoring like an old man.

We called him our glorious boo-boo, which in time evolved into BoBo, one of Billy's many nicknames. He was also known as Cutlet, Noodle, Sweet Pea, Peach, Rascal, Peanut, Chicken and Pickle. He was Wee One to Da, Big Guy to Dave, and Little Man to Rachel. The many-monikered child said 'Mama' at ten months. At a year, he dropped a plastic rattle from his crib and said 'Nuts'. At fourteen months, my milky babe shuffled around with his hands in his pockets as if he had car keys to jingle. I watched him sleep and wondered how anything could be so sweet. I thought I might die from insulin shock.

Whenever I mourned my lost future as an astronomer, Billy made me feel better. He had loopy blond curls, coppery in the sun, an elfin face, pewter-blue eyes, and a plucky dis-position. Whenever I felt I was impersonating a wife or mother, I looked at Billy and felt less like a fraud. If I had to choose, I would choose Billy again and again.

We were improbably happy until Martin was drafted in 1943. The army gave him two months of boot camp followed by three months at officer training school, and he emerged as yet another Ninety Day Wonder. Like everyone else, he was in for the duration.

I started smoking Raleigh cigarettes and wearing slacks and sensible shoes, and I enjoyed taking long sure-footed strides down the street. I learned how to drive our round-fendered Chevrolet, rolled bandages for the Red Cross, counted ration coupons, and watched the tragic gold stars appear in the front windows of my neighbours' homes. Every time an official car rolled down our street, I held my breath.

When Billy was three the war ended, thank God, and Martin came home. I knew, right off the bat, that we were in trouble. By then, he was smoking, too – he preferred Chesterfields, although in Europe he had smoked whatever he could get – but that was all he did. He didn't want to go anywhere or see anybody, not even Dave and Rachel. He had a hunted look. He'd stare vacantly out of a window or at the fringe on a rug, with a cigarette burning down close to his fingers, and when I whispered his name, he'd startle and blink at me with moist, frantic eyes. Sex? Forget about it. Once, I brought Billy into bed with us to cheer him up. Billy snuggled under Martin's arm and kissed his cheek – a soft, sloppy-sweet, open-mouthed, baby kiss – and Martin started to cry.

In 1945 they called it combat fatigue, but in the First World War they had called it shell shock, which is more accurate. Martin wasn't simply tired of combat, he was shocked by the barbarism skulking in men's souls. After Vietnam, they started calling it Post Traumatic Stress Disorder. Stress? Please. The names for this mental illness become more sanitized with every war.

My combat-fatigued, shell-shocked, stressed-out husband surprised me by accepting a monthly cheque from his father to supplement the government funds available to veterans who wanted to complete their education. So Martin went to graduate school full time, while I took care of the house and took charge of the chequebook. I didn't particularly enjoy handling our finances, but later, in India, I had reason to be thankful that Martin had left the money management to me.

In those early days after the war, Martin studied, smoked, ate and slept, but he didn't smile and he didn't play the piano. His new hobby was reading *Crime and Punishment*. He carried around an old paperback edition whose cover was creased, curled at the corners and worn soft as cloth. The pages were stained, dog-eared and scribbled over with cryptic marginal notes. He kept the thing in his back pocket like a talisman.

Martin was impotent at first and one night, exhausted by his repeated attempts, I pushed him away, saying, 'Forget it. It doesn't matter.'

He snapped, 'It fucking *does* matter.' Then he turned his back to me and shrugged off the hand I laid on his shoulder.

The impotence ended abruptly one night when I rolled over to kiss him goodnight and he attacked. That's the only word for it. He didn't become aroused, he became enraged; he fought his battles on my body. He pushed my legs apart and held my shoulders down and pounded into me. I started to cry, and he went still. He said, 'Oh, God,' and fell on my breast with a strangled sob. I wept with him, and we held each other, naked and weeping.

Every night after that, he gave me a chaste goodnight kiss and turned his back to me. We lived like polite room-mates until one Sunday morning in 1946. Martin had just poured a cup of coffee and sat down to breakfast with the *Chicago Tribune*. When he found the announcement on page two, he held the paper up and read Senator Fulbright's words aloud:

'The prejudices and misconceptions which exist in every country regarding foreign people are the great barrier to any system of government. If however the peoples of the world could get to know each other better, live together and learn side by side, maybe they would be more inclined to cooperate and less willing to go off and kill each other.'

When Martin put the paper down, he was smiling.

The first Americans were awarded Fulbright Fellowships in 1946 and Martin, the History Department's most promising star, was among them. He would meet his contact at the University of Delhi, Dr Chiranjeev, and then continue north to Simla to document the end of British rule in India. The university arranged office space for him in the telegraph office used by Reuters in Simla, and a colonial bungalow for us in the nearby village of Masoorla. The salary for a family of three was small but adequate.

Excited, I went to the library and discovered that Simla was the official summer capital of the British Raj, and had long been popular with British families seeking respite from the oppressive heat of the plains. But after Gandhi's Quit India campaign gained momentum, Britons began to find India less welcoming, and by 1947 half of the colonial bungalows in Masoorla were empty.

That suited me just fine. I imagined we'd have India all to ourselves; we'd be outsiders in a setting so alien we'd have only each other to cling to, and we'd return to our early days of blissful isolation. I envisioned smiling brown people in white dhotis and colourful saris, cave temples lit by butter lamps, picturesque old railways snaking around green mountainsides, painted elephants and sacred cows, smells of jasmine and charcoal fires, bazaars alive with cobras and flutes . . . and us. Our cracked marriage would be mended with exotic glue, and we would rediscover the charmed world we had shared in the beginning.

Well, what can I say? I was young. After three months in India, we had merely succeeded in exporting our unhappiness. Martin and I shared only the dry logistics of day-to-day life, moving around each other as if we existed in parallel universes.

The day I tucked Felicity and Adela's letters away with bitter stealth, Martin came home from work in a flurry of high energy. I saw his animated face and felt a surge of hope. It was usually the morose, haunted Martin who slouched through the door and asked what deadly species of curry he'd be enduring that night. He barely responded when I talked about my English lessons for village children – their shy, sweet faces, their open minds and delightful accent – and he glanced with disinterest at any new photos I might have had developed.

But when he burst through the front door with his dark eyes blazing, I allowed myself a moment of optimism. Maybe something wonderful had happened. Maybe I could share the letter with him. Maybe, after I put Billy to bed, we could drink a bottle of wine and embark on a tipsy treasure hunt, tear the house apart hunting for more letters and, find them or not, end up in a tousled bed. He looked alive and excited, and I remember wishing I had worn a dress instead of slacks that day. I flicked a wisp of hair off my forehead. 'Martin—'

'There's trouble.'

Oh, it was *that* kind of excitement.

Billy, on the floor playing with Spike, stared at us, his emotional radar pulsing. He said, 'Mom?'

'Not now, Noodle.' I patted his head.

Martin said, 'All hell's breaking loose.'

'What—'

'You and Billy have to get out of here.' Martin threw his briefcase down, and the clasp burst open and papers spilled out over the floor. His face went livid and he shouted, 'God *damn* it!'

Billy pulled Spike close to his chest and his chin began to quiver.

Martin bent down and cupped his chin. 'Hey, BoBo. Did I scare you? I'm sorry, son.' He picked Billy up and kissed him, not realizing that he radiated panic. Gently, I prised Billy away and carried him to his bedroom.

Billy, who was not subjected to Habib's curries, had already eaten a bowl of chicken ginger soup and chased it down with a sweet mango lassi. I dressed him in his favourite cotton pyjamas, the ones with the Little Engine That Could chugging merrily across the chest, and I tucked him into his narrow bed. Lying there with a nimbus of flaxen curls ruffled around his face, he stared up at me with adult gravity. 'Is Dad mad at us?'

'No, Cutlet. Dad's just tired from work.' I snuggled Spike under his arm and stroked his forehead while I hummed 'Danny Boy'. After a few minutes, he murmured, 'I can't hold up my eye covers,' and I passed my hand over his small face, saying, 'Sleep, baby.' I gave him a light, lingering kiss, closed the mosquito netting around the bed, and left his door ajar.

In the kitchen, Martin sat at the table with his head in his hands; his glasses lay discarded at his elbow. I placed my knuckles on my hips – my pugilistic stance. 'Will you please tell me what happened?'

'Jesus, Evie, don't start.' He looked at me, and I felt a jolt. Distress had blasted his face clean of its normal stoniness. His soulful brown eyes seemed stripped and unguarded without his glasses. He said, 'This country's getting ready to blow. You and Billy have to get back to the States.'

I sat across from him. 'What happened?'

'I shouldn't have brought you here. And Billy . . . Jesus, what was I thinking?' He massaged his forehead.

I leaned across the table and touched his arm. 'Martin, what happ—'

'Throw a few things in a suitcase. Don't be too fussy. I want you both on the eight o'clock train to Kalka. From there, you can get a train to Delhi.' He lit a cigarette; it trembled between his fingers. 'The university in Delhi can get you to Bombay. Then you can get a ship for London, and then another to the States.'

'Martin, do you hear yourself?' I sat back and folded my arms. 'The eight o'clock train is twelve hours away. Calm down and tell me what's going on.'

Martin took a drag of his cigarette and blew smoke out in a long whistling breath. 'OK, you're right. I just heard about this, but . . . all right.' He held up his palms, a truce.

I said, 'I'll get us some dinner.' I took down two plates and began ladling out rice and an evil-looking mutton curry. Suddenly I yearned for a grilled cheese sandwich. I put the plates of curry on the table and asked, 'So what's going on?'

'Mountbatten has moved up the date for Britain's with-drawal.' Martin crushed out the cigarette and stared at his plate.

'To when?'

'August the fifteenth.'

'Of *this* year? But that's only two months away.'

'Exactly.' Martin took a mouthful of curry and fanned his mouth, but I could tell it was mostly for show. He said, 'And Partition is still going to happen. Before they leave they're going to draw imaginary lines through this country and divide it between Hindus and Muslims.'

'But Gandhi is fighting Partition.'

'Well, Gandhi is losing.'

'But August? That's . . .'

'Insane.' He put his fork down. 'India will be Hindu, and a new country called Pakistan will be Muslim. Millions of frightened, angry, confused people will be pushed out of their homes and rushing to cross new borders. Mountbatten is saying anyone who wants to stay put will be protected, but how? By whom?' He put his elbows on the table and something like a smile, but not a smile, played around his mouth. 'Imagine the British, or anyone, telling Americans that since we have problems with race relations, the east and west coasts of America must be black and the middle of the country must be white, and that we have to get it done in two months.'

'Dear God.'

'And then imagine black and white extremists running around stirring up antagonism.' Martin took my hand. 'It's going to get ugly, especially near the new borders and in big cities – Calcutta for sure, and maybe Hyderabad. I don't want you and Billy here when it does.'

I squeezed his hand, to let him know I appreciated his wanting to protect us. But the idea of Partition wasn't new, only the date for British withdrawal had changed. What might happen after the Union Jack came down was pure speculation, and Martin's hysteria didn't really make sense. With the British Raj finally over, Indians were getting what they'd wanted for a long time. They welcomed the end of the Raj and had no more quarrel with Westerners. Partition was an issue between Hindus and Muslims, and we lived a thousand miles from both Calcutta and Hyderabad. I said, 'We're out here in the middle of nowhere, and I've never seen the slightest hint of animosity between the people here.'

'Don't minimize this.'

'I'm not. I just don't see how it could affect us up here. We're not Hindu or Muslim, or even British.'

Martin slapped the table so hard his plate jumped. 'God damn it, Evie. Don't argue with me about this. You don't know anything about war. I do.'

So that was it. Mountbatten's announcement was surprising, but this panic was Martin's post-war paranoia in high gear. It was futile to argue when he was like that. I pushed rice around on my plate and said, 'Fine.' I put a good dose of exaggerated patience into it. 'We'll leave in the morning. But I want you to come too.'

'I'll go with you to Delhi. The university will take care of you from there. But I have to come back; surely you can see that. This is actually great for my thesis. I'll be able to document it as it happens.'

'But if it's so dangerous—'

'For *you*. I know how to take care of myself. I only hope—'

'We both hope.' This was stupid. I didn't want to leave, didn't even believe it was necessary, and it felt good to cut *him* off for a change.

After dinner, Martin threw a few things into a suitcase, and then sat at his desk in a corner of our bedroom, sorting papers. I took our cash out of the tea tin in the kitchen and zipped it into the side compartment of my purse. Unable to take everything at such short notice, I took what was practical. I took slacks and sensible shoes, but left my nice black dress with cap sleeves and my sexy heels. I bid a sad farewell to the lemon-silk sari I'd imagined wearing to cocktail parties in Chicago, and I tiptoed in and out of Billy's room with miniature shirts and stacks of cotton underwear. As I folded pyjamas embroidered with blue teddy bears, I asked, 'What were Indian politics like in 1856?'

'1856?' He cocked his head at me. 'Why?'

'Um . . .' Those letters were *mine*. 'Nothing really. I sort of remember something from a history class . . .'

'By 1856 things were pretty tense between Indian soldiers, sepoys, and their British superiors. The Sepoy Rebellion broke out in 1857. Well, that's what we call it; Indians call it the First War of Independence. The sepoys mutinied, and it turned into full-blown war. There were atrocities on both sides.' He bit his lip. 'There always are.' Then he snorted, suddenly angry, and asked again, 'Why?'

'Nothing.' I patted the pyjamas into the suitcase and picked up a pair of small tan overalls. How could an un-married Victorian girl live alone in India during an uprising? Did she survive? I said, 'Imagine how terrifying it would be for, well, a bystander to be caught up in something like that.'

Martin looked at me. 'Yeah, that would be bad.' He came across the room and took hold of my shoulders. 'Like now.' He paused, as if his words might take for ever to sink in, as if he was waiting patiently for the sluggish, underutilized cogs in my stagnant brain to engage. 'Like right now,' he repeated. 'Civil war is coming to this country, and you and Billy are the bystanders. Now, for Christ's sake, pay attention.'

Chapter Six

1846–51

A T ST ETHEL'S, FELICITY and Adela had become accustomed to sleeping in the same dormitory and so, when they returned to Rose Hall each Christmas, they shared Adela's big four-poster bed, a custom that would continue through the years. If they had had separate rooms Adela would not have been able to pet Felicity's hair while they talked of Fanny Parks. In the morning they would not have been able to share the tea tray Martha brought, laden with boiled eggs and rashers and toast and Cook's special marmalade. They would not have been able to conspire while Martha built up the fire and, outside, triangles of snow collected in the corners of the wavy windowpanes.

Martha made a Christmas kissing ball: a double hoop covered with evergreen boughs and decorated with holly, apples and ribbons. A sprig of mistletoe hung from the centre and anyone who wandered under it had to pay the price of a kiss. On Christmas Eve, Felicity and Adela walked under the kissing ball and Adela covered Felicity's face with soft, urgent kisses. Felicity laughed and said, 'Enough, Adela. That's enough.' That Christmas, Adela often caught Felicity beneath the kissing ball; it almost seemed as though she was lying in wait.

Felicity was voluptuous by fourteen. Her voice had deepened to a smooth and womanly tone, while her complexion remained radiant and her rose-gold hair had grown thicker and more lustrous. Her school uniform strained across the bosom, nipped in at the waist and rounded over her hips.

Adela was not beautiful in the ordinary sense, but intelligence and striking green eyes animated her expression. Her body, however, remained all bones and knobs. Her dresses fell as flat as glass on her chest, and her hands and feet grew large and ungainly. Her lack of femininity was compounded by the fact that Adela remained abnormally bookish. Mrs Winfield lifted a lock of her daughter's limp brown hair and let it fall with a sigh. She said, 'A man doesn't like a girl who thinks herself more clever than he.'

Adela sniffed. 'Then let him read a book or two of his own.'

This was the year Mrs Winfield engaged a young lady's maid to look after the girls during the holidays and otherwise help around the house. She was a plain Irish girl, Kaitlin Flynn, who smelled strongly of lye soap. She had coarse, ruddy skin and curly black hair escaping from a white mobcap. Mrs Winfield handed Kaitlin her uniform, saying, 'See if you can't do something with poor Adela's hair.'

'Yes, madam.' Kaitlin curtsied prettily and gave the girls an arch smile that seemed to say she was on their side. After she disappeared up the servants' stairway, Adela said, 'I don't think Kaitlin is much older than we are.'

'No,' said Felicity. 'And I think she has a touch of mischief about her.'

They smiled at each other and said in unison, 'Thank God!'

Amid the flurry of Christmas preparations, only Adela

and Kaitlin noticed that Felicity seemed listless. When Felicity began coughing, Dr Winfield spent half an hour in her room with his black bag, thumping her back and asking questions in a low murmur, then came out and sombrely diagnosed consumption. He touched a knuckle to his moustache and bowed his jowled head like an undertaker. Adela rushed to Felicity's side and crawled into the sickbed with her, but her parents pulled her away, saying she must not expose herself to the illness. Still Adela sneaked back whenever she could, youth and love making her reckless.

Felicity lay in bed for weeks, limp, hot and coughing, with pink spots burning high on her cheeks. Adela would wait until her mother was occupied with visitors or gardening, then she would creep into Felicity's darkened room with a cup of beef tea, which she spooned between the patient's parched lips with great patience. When Dr Winfield visited Felicity, Adela hovered at the door, pressing him for assurances he could not give.

Kaitlin, however, walked boldly in and out of the sick room at will. While Dr Winfield listened to Felicity's chest, Kaitlin waited nearby with a washbasin and towels, humming an Irish ballad under her breath. When he had finished, Kaitlin sat on the bed to sponge Felicity's face and arms, saying 'Here we go, Miss. You'll feel ever so much better once I freshen you up.' One day, as Kaitlin leaned across her patient to adjust the pillow, Felicity said, 'You shouldn't come so close, Kaitlin.'

'Don't you go worryin' about me, Miss.' Kaitlin plumped the pillow with her characteristic good cheer. She squeezed out the washcloth with strong, chapped hands and swabbed Felicity's neck and shoulders with practised movements. Kaitlin had been in service since she was twelve, and before that she'd been her mother's right hand at home, cooking and cleaning for a family of eight, making meals out of wilted cabbage and old potatoes, and carrying back-breaking loads of peat to warm their two-room stone cottage. Hard work was all she knew and she took pride, even pleasure, in being useful. Adela watched Kaitlin minister to Felicity, marvelling at the girl's unfailing good nature, sure that she herself would be bitter to have been born into similar circumstances. Felicity said, 'Really, Kaitlin. At least cover your mouth and nose when you come near me.'

Dr Winfield, putting his instruments in his bag, said, 'That might be a good idea, Kaitlin.'

'Now I said you're none of you to worry about me and I meant it.' Kaitlin smiled. 'Me brother had the consumption, and I tended him for a year before he passed.' She pushed a stray wisp of hair off her face with the back of her hand, adding, 'I'm a hearty one.'

Dr Winfield nodded as he snapped his black bag shut. 'You're one of the lucky ones, Kaitlin. Some people seem to have a natural immunity.'

Adela, standing in the doorway, suspected she might also be one of the lucky ones. Even Felicity didn't know how often she sneaked into the sick room to kiss her friend's fevered brow – Felicity was often asleep and sometimes delirious – but Adela had never coughed once.

Felicity grew gaunt and when the fever threatened to consume her they called the Bishop. While he ministered to Felicity's soul, Adela locked herself in her room and balled herself up on the floor, in a corner, trying to come to grips with the idea of a world without Felicity. It would be like a world without light, without the possibility of joy.

When Felicity's fever broke, Mrs Winfield allowed Adela to bring morning tea into the sick room. Adela pushed Felicity around in a squeaky wooden bathchair, first around the room, then out in the hallway. When Felicity tried to stand, her legs, weak from lying so long in bed, buckled and gave out under her, but Adela caught her and held her up. After that Adela came daily to wrap her arms around the patient and walk her around the room in a sort of clumsy dance. They did this every day, then twice a day, and soon the girls were able to walk about together, hand in hand. In time, the sound of girlish laughter once again echoed through the house, and the doctor pronounced Felicity cured.

On Christmas Eve the following year, when the girls were fifteen, they were allowed a cup of wassail with dinner. Cook's recipe called for hot ale mixed with hard cider, sugar, spices and clove-studded apples. The girls thought it tasted bitter and much too strong, but they drank it anyway, suppressing grimaces, to show how grown up they were.

Later, in their shared room, they undressed for bed as usual by candlelight. Adela watched Felicity, in her white cotton bloomers and silk chemise, sitting in front of the oval mirror as she brushed a sheaf of lustrous hair over one shoulder. Felicity still wore her pearls, lambent in the candle-light, and the sight of her – it might have been the wassail, or Felicity's small breasts rising under the silk, or the pearls glowing on her bare skin – made Adela's knees go weak. She felt confused and upset without understanding why, so she slipped on her nightdress and slid into bed, pretending to fall asleep immediately. Felicity thought it must be the effect of the wassail, and she eased into bed quietly, trying not to disturb her friend. The punch had indeed been strong, and she fell asleep very soon herself.

That night Adela watched Felicity sleep, and for the first time she acknowledged the true nature of her feelings. She held a trembling hand inches above her friend's sleeping form, moving it over the contour of Felicity's shoulders and along her arm, dipping at the waist, rising over the hip and down the length of her leg. There seemed to be a warm prickling current between her hand and Felicity's body, which made Adela feel tingly and a little sick in the pit of her stomach. She took a long shuddering breath, then lay down and pulled the covers up to her chin. She wept as quietly as she could.

But she wasn't quiet enough. Felicity woke to the rhythmic shaking of the bed and heard Adela's stifled sobs. She didn't have to turn and ask what was wrong. In a cloudy, half-understood way, she knew. She had noticed the soft-eyed way Adela looked at her and it was not the way girls normally looked at one another. She had felt Adela's hand lingering longer than necessary on her neck when she fastened the clasp on her pearls, and she had puzzled over the pressure of Adela's thigh against hers when she sat close on the settee. She had only an imprecise grasp of what it all meant, but she knew Adela loved her differently from the way she loved Adela. She also knew Adela was good, Adela was her friend, and Felicity would not judge her.

Chapter Seven

1947

MARTIN AND I LAY under a limp sheet with our backs to each other, scrupulously avoiding contact. Two suitcases sat at the foot of the bed. I kept my eyes closed, but I knew that Martin knew I wasn't asleep. I didn't care. *Pay attention?* His condescending tone had made me furious, and how dare he imply that I would be cavalier about Billy's safety?

After he had told me to pay attention, he'd said, 'You haven't seen war, Evie. You live in blissful ignorance.' Not only ignorance – *blissful* ignorance. He used to call me his *Wunderkind*. Now I had apparently become a blissful ignoramus.

Sure, I had seen his bafflement when I'd asked about 1856, and I could have told him about the letters, but by then the habit of holding back was entrenched. I had slipped the letters into my suitcase when he wasn't looking.

I tugged the pillow into the curve of my neck. How appropriate, I thought, that our bed had come furnished with virginal white sheets. In the three months Martin and I had been in Masoorla, we'd never once made love.

An itch prickled my ankle, but if I scratched it I'd have to abandon my pretence of sleep. Even though I knew he knew I was awake, and even though I knew he knew that I knew he knew, there were rules. I moved my foot in a small arc, trying to rub the itch with a motion that would seem natural in sleep. It helped for a second, then the itch bit like a wasp. I gritted my teeth and moved my foot again. The itch was going to derail my charade of sleep as sure as World War Two had derailed my marriage. It spread up my leg, and I carefully moved my foot back and forth on the sheet. Soon I'd have to scratch.

There had been a time when I would have sat up and scratched my ankle with all ten fingers, oohing and aahing, and Martin would have said, 'Faker,' and we both would have laughed. But the happy connection between us had died, and my efforts to resurrect it only irritated him. Once, I suggested we sit cross-legged on the floor to eat a dinner of curry and rice by candlelight, and he gave me a look so saturated with contempt it took my breath away. He'd said, 'Grow up, Evie.'

When I couldn't stand the itch any longer, I reached down and scratched as if my foot was on fire. My cover blown, I turned to see Martin's strong profile in the dark room. Indian moonlight outlined his high forehead, the noble nose that lent his face authority, and his sensitive mouth, precisely contoured without being feminine – the perfect mouth for an articulate man. I wanted to touch his cheek and ask what had happened to us. But – *Pay attention . . . blissful ignorance* – I couldn't.

Martin said, 'You're awake.'

'You knew I was.'

'Yeah.'

'You too. Are you worried?'

He snapped, 'Of course I'm worried. Jesus, Evie.'

'I'm sorry. I know—'

'No, you don't know. You think war is just ration coupons and flag-waving.'

'What? No.'

'The smell is so thick you can taste it. You can't get rid of that taste. It's the one thing I hate about India, the constant smell of smoke and burning. Makes me gag.'

'Calm down.'

'Don't tell me to calm down. You do *not* know. And I don't want you to.' Martin pressed his thumb and forefinger into his eyes, then he propped himself up on one elbow. 'I'm sorry, Evie. This isn't your fault. I should never have brought you and Billy here.'

I pushed up on my elbow to meet his eyes. 'I didn't give you much choice.'

I remembered the day I had forced the issue. The university had offered him a bungalow, and he told them he only needed a small flat or a room because he would be going alone. When I heard that, I stood nose to nose with him and said, 'You've been gone for two years and now you want to leave again?' I planted my hands on my hips. 'This is a chance to share something unique and put the war behind us. We're going together or I *promise* you won't hear the end of it for the rest of your life.'

'But—'

'They wouldn't send you if it was dangerous. India will be under British rule for another year and a half, Martin. Safe as going to London.' I took his face in my hands. 'They're offering us a *house in India*, an adventure, and I want it. I want it for *us*. Remember *us*?'

He raked his hair and said, 'Oh, Evie.' Poor guy never had a chance.

I moved closer to him in bed. 'Martin?'

'Go to sleep, Evie.'

'It's not your fault. No one expected Mountbatten to bring the date forward by a whole year. And we didn't want Billy growing up thinking the entire world is nothing but white middle-class Americans. Remember? That was good, right?'

He snorted. 'Right now, middle-class America sounds swell.'

'We'll leave in the morning.' I touched his face. 'It'll be all right.'

Martin slid his arm under me and pulled me close. I nuzzled into his chest, took in his familiar scent and shape, the texture of his skin. In that moment, I wanted to share Felicity's letter with him. I said, 'Martin—'

'You smell good.' He buried his nose in my hair.

'Martin, today—'

'Don't worry. I'll get you both out of here.'

I reached for his face. 'But Martin—'

'I know. It's upsetting. But you should try to get some sleep.'

He turned away and the rare window of emotional intimacy slammed shut. Who was this man who wouldn't even let me finish a sentence?

'Right, I said. 'Let's get some sleep.' I turned my back to him, and convinced myself it would have been embarrassing anyway – admitting to pulling the brick out of the wall, dusting off the old letters and getting excited, like a little kid with a shiny penny. He might have told me to grow up.

Eventually, I drifted into a restless sleep, wondering why Felicity had never sent her letter.

We arrived at the train station around seven, sleep-deprived and edgy. Billy, a little frightened by our sudden departure, sat in the crook of Martin's arm, quiet and watchful. He held

Spike clamped tight to his little chest. Martin had worried that the train might not be running, but the dilapidated thing was there, rusting in the sun and ready to leave more or less on schedule. In Masoorla, the eight o'clock train was considered on schedule if it left before ten, but at least it was there. Martin said, 'Thank you, Jesus, Krishna, Allah and all the rest.' We stood our suitcases on the platform and sat on them to wait.

Other passengers began to arrive and I watched them covertly, feeling invisible behind my sunglasses – beaked and weathered faces etched with hardship and creased by sun, dusty turbans, women with bundles on their heads, skinny children, chickens, a sweet-faced goat. One family dragged along a steel trunk that held everything they owned, a common custom. The woman took out a teapot and cups, then squatted in the dirt to prepare a small coal fire in a brass brazier. Her daughter lowered a clay pitcher from the top of her head and poured water into the teapot. The family sat on their heels and waited for their tea.

Around seven thirty, Edward and Lydia Worthington arrived by rickshaw. Lydia, a birdlike woman with sharp features, had a nasal voice that reminded me of a donkey braying. Her husband, Edward, was a tall, slim man with a vain little moustache. He had an odd tic, a habit of showing disapproval by darting the tip of his tongue over his lips at remarkable speed. I once tried to move my tongue that fast, like a hummingbird's wing, but I couldn't do it. Edward must have started disapproving of things very early in life to have developed such dexterity.

The Worthingtons, who had business interests in London and Nairobi, had been touring India the way people tour a zoo. Lydia seemed to think Gandhi's significance lay mainly in the fact that it was becoming more expensive to buy handmade rugs. Edward fancied himself a sahib and always wore a wrinkled linen suit and pith helmet. They'd been staying in a British hotel in Simla, and three more rickshaws followed them, carrying two steamer trunks and four pieces of shiny black luggage. Martin watched them arrive and mumbled, 'Here comes the Empire.'

Edward alighted and held out his hand to Lydia. She stepped down from the rickshaw in a gabardine suit with squared-off shoulders, and quickly turned away from the emaciated rickshaw wallah, pulling a veil down from her hat to keep flies off. Edward pulled a few coins from his jacket pocket while the other rickshaw wallahs wrestled trunks and luggage to the ground. Lydia noticed us and came running. 'Darlings, isn't this a dreadful nuisance?'

Martin stood up with Billy in his arms. 'Good morning, Lydia.'

Billy peered at her from under his curls. 'We're going on a train ride.'

'Good morning indeed.' Lydia tutted. 'Honestly, Evie, I can't imagine what you were you thinking, bringing a child to a place like this.'

Billy laid his head on Martin's shoulder and mumbled, 'Meanie.' Embarrassed, Martin and I laughed too loudly, and I hurried to say, 'Good morning, Edward.'

He touched the edge of his pith helmet, and his hummingbird tongue made an appearance. 'Devil of a thing. Couldn't get a car or even a tonga. It's always something here. No better than Africa, really.'

Martin and I murmured indefinite sympathy, glanced around for escape and saw James Walker, a British journalist with Reuters, pushing through the crowd. Martin waved and called out, 'Walker! Over here!'

Walker returned the wave as he trundled towards us. For

such a big, solid fellow, he was surprisingly nimble, with wiry grey hair and a full beard. His face was agreeably tanned from years in Asia, and his friendly blue eyes always looked alert, if a little tired. An unruly lock of hair flopped over his forehead, and he always wore the same frayed khaki safari vest equipped with first-aid basics and iodine tablets to purify water. A flask bulged out of one pocket, and some-times he smelled of cigars. As Walker joined us, he called out something to a loitering bus wallah who responded with a red, paan-stained smile. Walker winked at Billy and said, 'Figured I'd find you lot here.'

'Of course we're here,' said Lydia. 'We must get out of this blasted country before the trouble starts.'

'The trouble started quite some time ago, Lydia.' Walker chucked Billy under the chin. 'How are you, little sahib?'

'Good.' Billy grinned.

'Don't be difficult,' Lydia brayed. 'You know what I mean.'

'I do.' Walker nodded. 'Nevertheless, it's too late. Everyone has heard about the new date for Partition and they're already panicking. They're frightened and angry and rushing to get from here to there, or wherever they need to be, as quickly as possible. There is sure to be trouble. You simply can't get on that train.'

Billy brightened. 'Let's go home and have *chota hazri*.' He'd only bolted a piece of toast and a glass of buttermilk before we rushed him to the train station.

'*Chota hazri*?' James Walker laughed. 'The little fellow is going native.'

'Oh, come now, Walker. Don't encourage that.' Edward's tongue darted. 'It's breakfast, young man, not *chota hazri*.' He turned back to Walker. 'I don't know what's got into Mountbatten, but this changes everything. We need to get out of here now.'

Martin handed Billy to me. 'What have you heard, Walker?'

The big fellow made a calming gesture, like pushing air down. He said, 'Think for a minute. Simla's a British hill station. Now that the Raj is packing it in, they have no quarrel with us. They've won; we're leaving. If there's trouble it will be between Hindus and Muslims, and it will happen mostly in the cities and near the new borders. Masoorla is a quiet backwater. It'll be safer here than on the road, where you'll surely encounter refugees.'

'That makes sense.' I kept my voice casual but I privately gloated. I knew Martin had been overreacting.

Martin said, 'It's different for you, Walker. You're on your own.' He jutted his chin at Billy and me. 'I want my family back in the States. Once this gets going it can flare up anywhere.'

'But,' I shifted Billy's weight in my arms, 'James has been here a lot longer than us. He knows these people.'

Martin, the mule, shook his head. 'I want you out of India.' Absently, he passed the back of his hand over Billy's cheek.

'There's the rub, old boy.' Walker kept his voice neutral. 'Your concern for your family is clouding your judgement. I'm not sure you *can* get them out just now. I've been in India almost twenty years, and I'm telling you you're better off staying put.'

Martin shook his head again. 'From Delhi, the university can fly them to Bombay, where they can get on a ship.

'Delhi?' Walker barked a laugh. 'Good luck. The Delhi train might not be running at all. These rattletraps run like a network of hardened arteries. Can't be sure when they'll run at the best of times, and now they'll be loaded with refugees. Train travel is the most dangerous thing you could do.'

'Bloody India.' Edward sniffed.

Walker continued as if he hadn't heard Edward. 'Hell, man, I've been on trains that stopped in the middle of nowhere just to ensure they'd be late.' He flashed a good-natured, nicotine-stained smile. 'Damn things stand baking in the countryside. People get off to stretch, cows park themselves on the tracks, and when the old bucket starts moving again – with no warning, mind you – everyone runs alongside clamouring to get back on. And that's when all is well.'

I said, 'I don't want to get stranded.'

'That *would* be inconvenient.' Edward's tongue darted again.

Martin hooked his thumb on his belt loop. 'Maybe we could hire a car.'

Walker shook his head. 'You've got Muslims rushing one way and Hindus rushing the other. The roads will be jammed with frightened, angry people. Any kind of travel is just too damn risky.'

'Well, you've convinced me.' Edward held out his elbow for Lydia. 'Didn't fancy getting on that filthy train anyway. When all this settles down we'll have time to take our leave properly.'

Lydia said, 'Oh, Eddie, our rickshaws have abandoned us.'

'We'll manage, my dear.' He tipped his hat, saying, 'Cheerio,' and they walked towards a rickshaw wallah sitting on his heels smoking a bidi. Billy said, 'There goes the Empire.'

'Billy!' I stifled a smile.

'What?' He looked surprised. 'Dad said it first.'

I glanced at Martin. 'You know he imitates everything.'

'Jesus, I'm sorry.' Martin shrugged one shoulder. 'I shouldn't have said that, son. It wasn't nice.'

Billy shrugged one shoulder. 'Jesus, I'm sorry.'

I glared at Martin, but he pushed his glasses up on his

nose and turned to Walker. 'I don't like it, but you have a point. It would be hell to get stranded.'

'Now you're talking sense.' Walker patted Billy on the head. 'Enjoy your *chota hazri*, little sahib.'

'My Mom makes the chai really sweet.'

James gave the little chin another manly chuck then ambled off. I said, 'Lucky he found us. We might have gotten ourselves in a real pickle.' I canoodled a kiss into Billy's neck and he giggled. 'OK, rascal, let's get some chai in that tummy.'

Martin looked bewildered. 'You're happy?' He shook his head. 'I swear to God, Evie, sometimes I don't understand you.'

Chapter Eight

I HEATED WATER on the old cooker, opened a can of sweetened
condensed milk and gave Billy a handful of pistachios to
nibble while the tea brewed. He held a nut to Spike's
miniature muzzle and made chewing sounds. I poured a
splash of tea into Billy's cup, filled it to the brim with thick
sweet milk, and we sat at the table sipping and munching
while a bamboo wind chime on the verandah clapped in the
breeze. I noticed that yesterday's garbage was gone and
realized that Rashmi must have arrived to find the house
empty, perhaps done a few chores, taken the garbage and
left. There had been so much emotion and so little time the
night before that I had not sent a message to the village. But
having told no one of our departure meant that Habib
would arrive as usual, later in the afternoon, to prepare
dinner. With this strange arrangement of having a kitchen
attached to the house, and the even stranger penchant we
had for eating in the same room where he cooked, it was uncomfortable for Habib to be there unless he was working.

After breakfast, Billy played rickshaw on the shady verandah, carting Spike around in his Red Flyer wagon, weaving
between potted plants and faded wicker chairs. Now and

then he shouted 'Cheerio!' or 'Namaste!' to a passing monkey. I called out, 'Don't touch the monkeys,' and he answered, 'I knooow.' His piping voice made me smile as I returned our household cash to the tea tin and unpacked, tucking Billy's cotton undies back into drawers and hanging his little shirts in his almirah.

I ran a fond hand over my lemon-silk sari, once again imagining myself floating around a faculty cocktail party, the returned expat, holding forth on Hindu temples, painted elephants and colourful customs. I blessed James Walker for saving me from having to leave too soon as I slipped the old letters back under my bras and panties, enjoying a sense of danger averted. Martin would calm down in a few days.

After getting up at dawn, the hurried snack before leaving, and then the tense hour at the grimy train station, Billy was drooping by tiffin. He usually loved to wait by the front door for the tiffin wallah, lumbering along, his bullock cart heaped with deliveries. The tiffin basket was like a treasure trove for Billy. He would open the stacked steel compartments, never sure what to expect, shouting, 'Oooh, raita! Oooh, chickpeas! Oooh, pakoras! Oooh, lychees!' He whooped with delight when tiffin included *phirni*, a light pudding scented with cardamom and sprinkled with ground pistachios. But that day, he almost fell asleep over his *phirni*, so I carried him to bed, drew the mosquito netting around him and closed the blue shutters. After I switched on the slow overhead fan, Billy flipped on to his side and tucked his hands under his cheek, falling into untroubled sleep with a swiftness that adults can only wish for. I reached into the netting to loop a fine blond curl around my finger and kissed it before creeping out of the room.

In my bedroom, I took the packet of old letters from my drawer and stared at them. There were only four, but they spanned many months and if those women were close enough to call each other sisters, there should be more. I laid them on my dresser and marched into the kitchen to search for another loose brick. I ran my hands over the bricks, pushing against the mortared seams, but the wall appeared to be as snug and tight as the day it was built. I expanded my search to other walls in the house, tapping and listening.

The plaster walls descended to high wooden skirting boards and a plank floor that glowed with a patina acquired from a century of wax and wear. I ran a butter knife behind wooden mouldings and unzipped the cushion covers on the old brocade chair with wooden arms. One of the chair arms looked as if a small animal had gnawed it – tiny teeth marks that reminded me of the teething marks Billy had made on his crib railing. Those marks made me wonder about rats, but I had never seen any droppings.

The old bungalow had high ceilings and exposed beams, but the Victorian furniture made it feel more English than Indian. I had hung jewel-toned sari fabric for curtains: emerald in the living room, sapphire in the bedrooms, and topaz in the kitchen. In Billy's room, I hung a string of orange and purple sequinned camels under his mosquito netting, and in the living room, I replaced the old mantel clock with a jade sculpture of the elephant god, Ganesh, with his ears flared out wide and trunk raised high. Ganesh is the god of good luck, remover of obstacles, and I figured it couldn't hurt. On the mahogany dining table, I kept wild red poppies in an old pewter water pitcher, a study in contrasts.

The only furniture we had brought with us was a phonograph, our cherrywood Stromberg-Carlson, sitting on a table in the living room next to a stack of vinyl records that I had packed with fanatical care. Since Martin's ability to play was another casualty of war, the lack of a piano was a small mercy – it would have stood there like a rebuke – but I enjoyed a bit of music in the evening while Martin lost himself in *Crime and Punishment*. I liked playing the phonograph, the way I liked cleaning my little house, and teaching English to village children, and taking photos; I liked anything that distracted me from the detritus of my marriage.

With the weather already hot, I also liked having a ceiling fan in every room. Before electricity, colonials had servants who did nothing but sit in a corner and pull a cord to wave long reed or cloth fans back and forth – punkah wallahs. I could see the punkah rod still in place on the ceilings of every room and it made me think of those Egyptian paintings of slaves fanning the pharaoh with peacock feathers and palm fronds. But the Indian people weren't slaves, and I wondered how they'd been persuaded to play such a menial role in their own country. I had an idea that their acquiescence had to do with the way they had quietly survived waves of invaders by bending rather than breaking. The Aryans, the Turks, the Portuguese, the Moghuls and the British had all swept through the subcontinent, and yet India remained Indian. They kept their heads down and outlasted everyone.

When Gandhi started his Quit India campaign, Indian landowners, zamindars, started buying up British bungalows. Our zamindar was a Sikh who bought the place fully furnished and rented it to foreigners by the month. He had a reputation as a clever man who had taken his family's silk fortune and tripled it with his savvy business sense.

I walked from room to room tapping the walls, searching for traces of Felicity and Adela, and ended up on the verandah steps looking out at pine forests and green terraces carved into the Himalayan hillsides. In the distance, jagged white peaks rose, enormous and powerful and shrouded in clouds. Martin said that at higher elevations clouds invaded people's houses and children played with them. I loved that!

I could see why Simla had become the official summer capital of the Raj – ancient temples and bustling bazaars, the gentle chanting of pandits floating on apple-crisp air, red bougainvillea and vast cerulean skies. I watched a bony white cow nibble mimosas at our gate and felt every bit as safe as James Walker said we were.

Back inside, I checked behind marble-top side tables and the undersides of chairs; I knocked on the back panels of old oak cabinets and searched for hidden compartments in the bedroom wardrobes. I even shook out an antique afghan, a throw crocheted in hot coral and cool turquoise shot through with gold. I found nothing, not even much dust. Rashmi must have swept up with her acacia branches while we were at the station.

Rashmi, blithe spirit, spoke a charming pidgin English and Billy adored our small, round ayah. Her ruby nose pin flashed when she talked, she always included Spike in their games, and she sang to Billy while she brushed his blond curls. Every day, she brought Billy a piece of fresh coconut, hidden in the folds of her Himachali headscarf, and slipped it to him behind my back. She would say, 'Come, *beta*,' and they would disappear together. I didn't mind him snacking on coconut, but I pretended not to know so they could have their secret ritual.

Rashmi helped me set up an informal school by convincing a few farmers that their children would benefit from learning English. I fashioned a makeshift classroom out of burlap and bamboo poles, making an awning under the spreading canopy of a venerable banyan tree in the village. One side of the tree had sent so many aerial roots into the

83

ground that the original trunk was lost in a wall of secondary trunks. I found a used blackboard in the bazaar, which I nailed to the massive trunk, and Rashmi contributed a box of pink chalk. She stayed with Billy while I bicycled into the village to teach English vocabulary to eight barefoot children with serious dark eyes.

On the first day, the children filed under the awning and peered at the blackboard with suspicion. They sat on the ground, clustered close together, some holding hands, and stared up at me – the water-eyed foreign lady with fire-hair who wore slacks like a man and rode a bike. I moved among them under the sagging canopy, smiling and speaking softly.

That first day, they learned my name, and I learned all of theirs; next time, I started on the alphabet, and they dutifully parroted letters, but I could see it was meaningless, so I drew pictures with the pink chalk while birds and monkeys chattered overhead. I drew generic pink trees and simple pink houses and rudimentary pink camels. The children repeated the words after me, nudging each other knowingly. I learned more than I taught, including the fact that those children did not know they lived in poverty. One-room huts without running water and two small meals a day was simply the way of things. They weren't sure whether school was supposed to be work or play, and their earnest faces occasionally flashed incandescent smiles. They were all per-fectly beautiful, with large black eyes and drooping lids and cheeks that glowed like burnished copper.

The sense of my expanding worldview seemed almost physical, like being stretched on a rack, and I welcomed it. I was grateful to Rashmi for letting me into a little corner of India.

After I had searched the entire house, I stood in the

middle of my living room with my lips scrunched up to one side. More information about my Victorian ladies would have to come from the letters I already had, so I brought them out from under my panties, spread them over the kitchen table and chose the letter with the greatest number of legible words.

> From . . .   Ad . . . Winfield
> . . . shire, England
> September 1854
>
> Dear Felicity
>   . . . last night . . .   . . . a chinless little man . . .
>   . . . bored . . .
>   . . . a good cry . . .
> . . . duty to yourself . . .   but your health . . .
>   . . . intrepid Fanny Parks . . . not consumptive . . .
> . . . worry about you . . .

I blew on the bottom half and raised a small puff of dust, which exposed two more words. Encouraged, I fetched a pastry brush, and tickled away flecks of dirt. A couple more words emerged, and I held the paper up in a shaft of after-noon light.

>   . . . Mother . . .   . . . utterly
> determined . . .
>
>   . . . Katie . . .   . . . consolation . . .

The third letter provided a bit more:

October 1855

Dearest Felicity,
   . . . most terrible . . . most wonderful . . .
. . . Mother . . .
. . . Katie & me . . .   . . . India . . .
   Poor Katie . . . I do not know where . . .

     . . . long hearty cry . . .   . . . wrote Katie . . .

. . . so sudden & so bittersweet
   Tears course down . . .   . . . even whilst a smile . . .
               . . . feel quite mad . . .
  I will . . . after all . . .

               . . . sister in joy,
               Adela

I refolded the letters and stared out of the window. Now who was Katie?

Chapter Nine

1853–4

AT SEVENTEEN, Felicity and Adela left school. The time had come to introduce them into society, and the Chadwicks, still in Calcutta, sent a great deal of money to Rose Hall for gowns. Mrs Winfield giggled nervously when she saw the cheque – more than her husband made in a year – but she lost no time buying fabrics and hiring dressmakers. She supervised fittings with a forced nonchalance, as though she were used to spending such huge sums on clothes. She held swatches up to the girls' faces to see which colours suited them best, and pored over drawings of matching shoes and reticules.

The girls pooh-poohed the pageantry and bother, but Felicity found she rather enjoyed wearing the silvered gown that set off her golden hair, and the parchment silk train that made an oddly satisfying swishing sound when she walked. She ran her hands down her bodice and felt a shiver of pleasure at the richness of the embellished brocade. Adela struggled into a green silk bustle-gown, chosen to bring out the colour of her eyes and give her some curves, then she stared into the cheval mirror with a big-knuckled hand on her bony hip and sighed.

At their first ball, Adela lurched around the dance floor until her frustrated partner asked, 'Does dancing bore you?'

'Yes,' she said frankly. 'Some of us prefer more intellectual pursuits than the dubious art of shuffling about in mindless, predetermined patterns.'

Felicity danced gracefully and often with Percy Randolph. He was tall and broad-shouldered and comely, with wavy blond hair and a straight nose. Felicity thought he looked distinguished in his fine wool jacket and wide gold cravat, and she liked the smell of pipe smoke on his clothes and the feel of his muscles moving under his upper arm.

Adela stared over the shoulder of her own partner, her green eyes sweeping the room. She didn't like the way Felicity leaned her head back to gaze up at Percy, the exposed curve of her throat, all that excessive smiling. She hated to see Felicity's tapered fingers resting so comfortably on his shoulder, and his wide hand on her narrow waist. Twice, Adela excused herself and retreated to the terrace, where she stood, breathing through flared nostrils and slapping a tightly furled silk fan against her palm. 'Well,' she whispered to herself in the dark, 'you knew the day would come.'

Later, in their shared room, Adela watched Felicity brush her hair and said, 'He doesn't deserve you.'

Felicity stopped brushing. 'What?'

'Percy.' Adela stared, hawk-like, ready to strike. 'He doesn't appreciate you.'

Felicity's back stiffened. 'I have the impression he appreciates me very much.'

'His intentions are dishonourable.'

'Adela!'

'I see the way he looks at you.'

'I like the way he looks at me.'

'I'll wager he's never noticed the small bones in your wrists.'

'My *wrists*?'

'When you smile at him he's self-satisfied. He should be grateful.'

'Adela, what's got into you?'

'He doesn't love you.'

'Are you *jealous*?'

Adela pulled herself up and wrapped a shawl tightly around her shoulders.

Felicity reached for her, but Adela pulled away.

Percy Randolph often came to tea, and after the chaperoned pouring and sipping, he and Felicity walked in the garden. Felicity twirled her parasol as they admired Mrs Winfield's roses, and then they wandered on to the lawn, where Percy spread his coat on the grass for Felicity to sit. He sat an arm's length from her and when she leaned closer he moved back. He would have been shocked to know how much his careful propriety annoyed her.

Felicity watched him taking pains to avoid any physical contact and couldn't help but wonder what sort of life she'd have with a man who held his little finger out when he drank tea. She thought of her mother, running a household with its tiresome round of daily duties and social obligations, and Adela's mother, whose world extended no further than her garden and her rules. It all seemed so dull compared to Honoria Lawrence crashing through jungles on her elephant, and Fanny Parks chewing paan in the zenana. But she was in England, not India, and Percy was no different from any of the other young men who came to the dances. At least he was good-looking. Perhaps she could inject some spice into his world, bring out the carefree in him, assuming there was some to bring out. As an experiment, she ran to the hedge maze, laughing and daring him to follow her. Hidden in the maze, with which she was completely familiar, she would ambush him with a kiss. She would unearth the passion she believed must be in him . . . somewhere.

But he failed to follow her to the maze, beckoning her back and offering to read from a book of poetry by Robert Browning, which he produced from an inside pocket of his jacket. Apparently he had planned an afternoon of poetry and she would not be allowed to spoil it with silly, girlish games.

Adela watched them from a window; at that distance they looked the perfect picture of a courting couple. When Felicity came in, Adela met her at the door. 'Tell me,' she said. 'Do you love him?'

'For heaven's sake, Adela, what's got into you? You look as though you'd like to throttle me.'

'Do you?'

'He's a nice enough fellow. But I don't like your tone.' Felicity untied her bonnet while Adela waited for more, but there was no more. Felicity hung her bonnet on a peg and walked away.

Adela interpreted Felicity's evasive answer as an attempt to hide her true feelings. It was no secret that Adela didn't like Percy, and no doubt Felicity simply didn't want a scene. Adela felt surer than ever that an engagement would soon be announced, and that certainty made her feel desperate and abandoned.

In her room, Adela paced back and forth until she thought she might scream. She sat down with a book, but she could not concentrate, so she tossed the book aside and brushed her lank hair for a minute before throwing the brush down in disgust. Then she went back to pacing. At dinner she watched Felicity pick at her food and sigh – sure signs, Adela believed, of lovesickness – and for the first time she did not want to be around her.

After dinner, Adela called Kaitlin to walk out with her, and the soft evening air combined with Kaitlin's funny stories about the other servants proved a tonic for Adela. They went out again the following evening and the one after that. In time, they would hold hands and sing while they walked, and their evening stroll would become a welcome ritual. Sometimes they were gone for hours, but when Mrs Winfield asked where they walked, the girls just shrugged. Adela said, 'Here and there.'

One such evening, Adela and Kaitlin stopped to sit under a chestnut tree. Kaitlin leaned against the trunk to peer up at the leafy canopy, and Adela noticed her breasts straining against her uniform. Hesitantly she touched Kaitlin's hair, and then lightly stroked her face. Kaitlin froze, and the air became charged with something weighty and unsettling, something that had been lurking and growing in the shadows. Adela's hand wandered down Kaitlin's neck and over her breast. Kaitlin's nipple stiffened and showed through the fabric of her dress, and the two young women stared at each other. Adela held her breath, sure she had committed an unforgivable sin, but the look on Kaitlin's face told her otherwise. Kaitlin said, 'Your eyes are a beautiful shade of green, Miss.'

'Please call me Adela.'

'Will you call me Katie?'

'Katie.' Adela smiled and Kaitlin blushed. Seconds lengthened, a breeze ruffled through the chestnut tree, and their lips came together, natural as birdsong. Kaitlin pressed her mouth into Adela's neck, and their hearts galloped against each other. Searching hands found their way through hooks and laces and bloomers, kisses became more urgent and Adela moaned. Kaitlin seemed to know just how to touch her, spreading fire up and down her body. Pressure built and intensified until Adela lost herself utterly and gasped as if she'd been stabbed.

When they returned to Rose Hall, their dishevelment and the flush on their cheeks seemed a bit more than one would expect from a quiet walk, but the household, waiting with baited breath for an announcement from Felicity and Percy, didn't notice. The couple had been seen holding hands in the gazebo and all talk was of them – what sort of wedding gown Felicity would wear, how soon might the wedding take place, and who would host it if the Winfield house were deemed not grand enough?

Even Felicity was beginning to think that marriage to Percy was inevitable, if only she could coax a hint of fire out of him. Weren't men supposed to be lustful? Adventurous? Surely he had it in him, buried beneath those respectable manners, but she needed to see it before she could commit herself to him.

One evening in the summerhouse, Felicity leaned into Percy with a coquettish arch in her back, and tipped her face up to his with her eyes closed. She licked her lips and allowed them to part slightly, and she waited. At first nothing happened and she felt a combination of disgust and disappointment. Then his hand slid around her waist and rested on the small of her back. She moved closer until she felt his warm breath on her face and smelled his freshly laundered shirt. Her dress rustled as he pulled her body tightly to his. This was it! She closed her eyes and angled her face slightly to the right and then – nothing. He released her and she opened her eyes to see him turning away, smoothing his twill waistcoat and straightening his cravat. He said, 'Forgive me. It will not happen again.'

Felicity straightened up and stared at him. This man would be bound by the letter of the law for the rest of his life, and he would bind her to it as well. 'No,' she said. 'I think it will not.'

Later, in their shared bedroom, Felicity said to Adela, 'Can you imagine? The prissy old thing refused to kiss me.'

'No,' said Adela. 'I can't imagine.'

'Well, so much for dishonourable intentions.'

At this Adela gave Kaitlin a quick, meaningful look. Kaitlin blushed violently, dropped the dress she was mending and hurried out of the room. Felicity said, 'What's wrong with her?'

'Kaitlin? Oh, I think it's her time of the month.' Adela picked up the dress, shook it out and carried it to her armoire.

Felicity wondered how Adela would know such a personal detail about Kaitlin, but some instinct warned her not to ask. Silently, she watched Adela hang up the half-mended dress.

Adela, unperturbed, sat on the edge of the bed and folded her hands in her lap. 'So now that you've broken off with Percy, what will you do?'

Felicity felt a strange relief at the change of subject. She said, 'Well, as you know, if a girl isn't engaged after her first two seasons, she is looked at askance.' Felicity took the pins out of her hair and let it tumble. 'I think I shall save myself the boredom of another season and simply join the Fishing Fleet straight away.'

'The Fishing Fleet? You mean go to India? Somehow I can't see you amongst a troop of desperate girls sailing halfway round the world to fish for a husband. Unless you think a British military man would be more interesting than the lot Mother has been parading past us.' Adela's face lit up with her sudden realization. 'Or unless the Fishing Fleet is merely an excuse to get back to India.'

'Well, how else does a young woman get to India alone? I don't want a husband, but I love India. Perhaps I'll be a teacher. They do have schools there, you know. And orphanages. My Hindustani will come back to me. I'm sure I can be of use.'

'And will you not marry?'

'I think not. Then I would have to be a proper memsahib.' Felicity shook out her hair. 'I've seen how the boredom eats up my mother. No. I don't wish to marry.'

'Ever?'

'Perhaps not. Percy has made me think. To my mind it would be awfully dull to live all my life with one man. I feel sure I'd want to change husbands at least every year or two.'

She took Adela's hands in hers and sat next to her. 'Think of Fanny Parks doing her duty to herself. That's what we both must do.'

'But—'

'I'll telegraph my parents immediately, then sail in September, and join them by January, the height of the season in Calcutta. Now that I've come of age, they'll think I've come looking for a husband and will be delighted to assist. I'm sure there are a number of alliances they'd like to see. I'll bide my time until March. That's the start of the hot weather, when everyone goes to the hills for six months.

'Of course, March to September will be an endless round of dances and dinners at the Club in Simla, all designed to throw hopeless cases into each other's arms. But, you see, when they go back to Calcutta in the autumn, I'll stay on in Simla and find myself a lovely bungalow out in the *mofussil*

– that's the countryside. It's beautiful, Adela, with terraced tea plantations, mountain streams and wildflowers, and looming in the distance the mighty Himalayas. Out there I can do what I please, just like Fanny and Honoria. Oh, Adela, come with me.'

'Me?' Adela raised her eyebrows. 'In India?'

'Why not?'

'India.' Light flashed in Adela's eyes. 'Wouldn't that be just ... oh, my. The two of us, together in India.' Then the light went out. 'My parents would never allow it. The expense alone ...'

'I could ask my father—'

Adela laughed. 'Can you imagine my mother's face if I announced out of the blue that I was sailing for India? The Fishing Fleet is fine for girls who have had two or three failed seasons, or girls like you who have your family there. But me? Never. Mother thinks Company men are chopped up to give a secular flavour to missionary croquettes. Thanks to our blathering about Fanny Parks, she thinks memsahibs are enticed into harems. Imagine me in a harem,' she said drily.

Felicity didn't answer. Somehow, she found the idea of Adela in a harem comical and at the same time disturbing, but she wasn't sure why.

Adela stroked the fine bones in Felicity's wrist and said, 'It's only been one season, and Mother still has hopes for me. She's lining them up like a firing squad. Perhaps after a few failed seasons she'll let me join the Fishing Fleet out of desperation.'

'But that could take years.'

'How else can I manage it?' Adela put her head in her hands and groaned. 'Oh, Felicity, what will I do without you?'

Felicity closed her eyes as if suppressing a headache. 'I won't go. I'll stay until you can come with me.'

'No!' Adela's head shot up. 'I couldn't let you do that. Imagine all the proposals you'd have to fend off. No. You go, and I'll join you when I can. We must each do our duty to ourselves, remember?'

'Do you mean it?'

'Yes.' Adela kept her voice lighter than she felt. 'We each have our own path, and I have Kaitlin for company now. Did you know I'm teaching her to read?'

Felicity sighed. 'Oh, how I shall miss you.'

'We'll miss each other.'

One month later, with a brisk September wind whipping their skirts, Adela and Felicity stood on Liverpool's Royal Albert Docks casting about for last words and finding none. The crowd on the deck grew noisier and people streamed up and down the wide gangway. Cabs loaded with luggage rattled up to the docks perilously late, and the arm of the great steam-crane swung load after load high in the air and lowered it into the hold. Military wives, returning after a sojourn at home, could be recognized by a certain look of resignation as they trudged up the gangway.

A small group of steerage-class missionaries dressed in drab clothing took up a position near the front of the ship; they opened their little black hymnals and began to sing a dismal song about dangerous voyages, and long, lonely exile. Felicity said, 'What idiots they are. As if they couldn't find anything cheerier to sing but that.'

Adela said, 'How I shall miss you.' She threw her arms around Felicity and they held each other. Kaitlin stood at a discreet distance, watching Felicity's boxes and trunks being hauled aboard by ropes and pulleys. When it seemed the girls would never quit their embrace, Kaitlin shouted, 'There goes one of your little tin-lined boxes!'

They pulled apart and Felicity promised to write from every port: Gibraltar, Alexandria, Colombo; they made the same time-worn arrangements everyone makes, simply for want of something to ease the parting. The whistle blew and Felicity went up the gangway of the *Cambria*. She shouldered her way to the railing and leaned over, blowing kisses shore-ward. Adela and Kaitlin waved as the great ship moved off, and when Adela sobbed softly, Kaitlin squeezed her hand.

Chapter Ten

1947

MARTIN CAME THROUGH the door like a storm front. Months of riding around with the Packard's top down had tanned him darker than some of the natives, and when I mentioned it he laughed and said he was blending. He'd also given up socks and his brown wingtips and started wearing airy leather sandals, which made sense in that climate; I'd bought sandals for Billy and me, too. They made us look like adaptable tourists, but with Martin's black hair and darkening complexion his ethnicity was becoming ambiguous.

He put down his briefcase, giving off a contagious tension that stiffened my neck and made Billy go quiet, but I kept my voice light. 'Anything new?'

Martin picked Billy up. 'Later.' He kissed our boy. 'How are you, BoBo?'

'Good.' Billy put his little hands on Martin's cheeks. 'Are you sad, Dad?'

'Sad? I can't be sad when I'm with you and Mom.'

'Yes, you can.'

Martin smiled sadly.

After we put Billy to bed, Martin and I sat down to plates

of mustard curry, lumpy with something that looked like chicken but had the texture of old leather. Habib had also left us a bowl of raita – chilled yogurt mixed with chopped cucumbers – a culinary fire extinguisher. Martin took a mouthful of curry, and I waited for the customary gasping and moaning, but he barely winced as he reached for his water. I said, 'Raita is better than water for cooling the spices.'

'I've tried. I just don't like raita.' He filled his mouth with water and swished it around.

I sighed. 'What happened today?'

Martin took off his glasses and rubbed his eyes. 'Riots in Lahore, arson in Calcutta. Dozens dead. God only knows how many injured.'

I stared at my plate. 'In the name of religion?'

Martin made a cynical sound through his nose. 'I wired the university. Thought I should remind them I have my family with me. Hell, I don't know what I expect them to do. They can't stop the riots, and I chose to bring you here.'

'*We* chose.'

'Telegraph wires have been cut.'

'Oh!'

'Not around here.'

'Thank God.' The wires out of Simla were our lifeline to news and assistance, and money. Martin's paycheque arrived by wire, and we lived on a budget. The thought of being cut off made me feel unmoored and queasy. I said, 'I'm sure that won't happen here. Masoorla is a backwater, like Walker said. We're safe here.'

Martin eyed me as he swallowed. 'Walker didn't say we'd be safe. He said we'd be *safer*. Anything can happen anywhere.'

Safe, safer, safest. I wanted to be patient. The adventurous man I had married would not have been so determined to worry, and I believed he was still in there somewhere – I could feel him behind the gloom – but this intractable pessimism was *wearing me out*.

Martin rose early the next morning and left without break-fast. I listened to the front door click shut, then ran my hand over his side of the white bed while I stared at the ceiling fan. It moved lazily enough for my eyes to follow the circuit of a single blade, and that rote activity kept my drowsy mind from starting up. I followed the fan blade, around and around, enjoying a semi-hypnosis that kept the world at bay.

Billy woke soon enough, running into my bedroom and jumping through the mosquito netting to snuggle up – our morning rite. I prepared his usual breakfast: a soft-boiled egg and a warm roti. Rashmi had showed me how to make roti, and I loved the idea of making fresh bread in two minutes – just roll out a small lump of dough and roast it quickly in a pan. Native women cooked roti on hot, flat rocks and it only took seconds to puff up and speckle golden brown. I slathered it with butter and jam and rolled it up. Billy was eating noisily when Rashmi poked her smiling, round face through the back door. Billy waved Spike's paw. 'Namaste, Rashmi.'

'Namaste, *beta*. Namaste, Speck.' Her nose pin glinted, and she rocked her head from side to side. She offered me her praying hands and said, 'Today, to the temple I am going to make puja.' She raised her plump arm to show me the holy red yarn that the pandit had tied around her wrist, and then she pointed at the orange tikka on her forehead.

'Very nice, Rashmi.'

'Puja I am making for Madam and Sir.'

'You're praying for us?'

'Every day I'm checking Madam's bed.' The head waggle

turned serious. 'There is no good sexy time in your bed, isn't it?'

'What?' I could feel the blush rising.

'Not for worrying, Madam. I am making puja to Shiva.' She winked as if I knew what she was talking about. 'Shiva you are knowing, isn't it?' She did a wicked little shoulder shimmy, and suddenly I understood why I'd seen so many phallic sculptures in Shiva temples. Shiva is the god of creation and sex.

'Oh, my God.' Maybe the Brits weren't all wrong about maintaining distance from their servants.

'Shiva is one hundred per cent excellent first class.' Before I could say any more – not that I knew what to say – Rashmi said, 'Come, *beta*,' and she swooped Billy into her chubby embrace and bundled him off to the living room to sneak him his coconut.

I dreaded getting a lusty wink every time Rashmi caught my eye, so I grabbed my purse and told her I had errands, which wasn't completely untrue. All churches kept records, and I hoped Felicity and Adela might have left some trace of themselves at Christ Church in Simla. Billy loved going into Simla – the costumes, the colours, the smells – and clutching Spike and a pillow he ran out to hop into his Red Flyer wagon.

I grabbed my sunglasses and camera and we set off down the road, passing tidy colonial bungalows nestled in the green mountainside. In the nineteenth century, this would have been the agrarian *mofussil*, countryside made up mostly of plantations and small farms. When Simla became the queen of hill stations, more bungalows popped up and by 1920 it was a fully fledged colonial district. The ancient village of Masoorla, in true Indian fashion, took no notice.

The bungalows sat far back from the road in a luxuriant

tangle of flowering shrubs and old trees. Each had its idle group of swarthy servants awaiting commands from the shadowy interior. Here and there I saw a servant sweeping a verandah with a bundle of branches or another clipping a hedge. The houses had their identities painted on their gateposts: Monsoon Villa, Morningside, Tamarind House.

It was mid June and hot, and yet half of the bungalows stood vacant. Twenty years earlier, every bungalow would have been occupied by the first of May, but now only those officials involved in the handover of India to the Indians were there, and most of them would leave the country for good after August.

When I had first arrived in Masoorla, the wives of those officials, smiling English ladies in sedate dresses, had welcomed me with an afternoon tea at Morningside, the bungalow of horsey Verna Drake. The scones had been oddly shaped, but the clotted cream was perfectly luxurious, and why not? Clotted cream – *malai* – has been made in India for centuries. The jam had come from Fortnam & Mason by way of the local import shop, and the ladies had been polite, but I didn't fit. I wore my tan slacks and a pretty tunic I had found in the bazaar. Always wary of bright colours, I had rummaged through a pile of vivid tunics until I found a champagne-coloured *kameez* of raw silk with silver embroidery and bits of amber glass around the neck and hem. I put on my straw hat and sunglasses and sandals and bicycled over, feeling pleased with myself until I walked into a room full of chintz cabbage roses, floral summer dresses and pearls. I'm not sure that all the women were shorter than me – they were sitting – but I felt as conspicuous as a giraffe in a Victorian drawing room. I smoothed my *kameez*, wrinkled from my bike ride, while a roomful of ladies with careful finger curls smiled over their teacups. When I took off my hat, someone said, 'My husband has a topi like that,' and I wasn't sure whether it was a compliment or a criticism.

A bearer served the tea and, in the time-honoured way of bored memsahibs passing time in the hills, we chatted aimlessly. At some point, Verna invited me to the services at Christ Church, saying, 'Reverend Locke gets high marks for his wit.' I had once seen the tall, loose-limbed clergyman while shopping in Simla. He had waved, beaming a gap-toothed smile, and seemed like quite a pleasant fellow, but church did not interest me. Stained glass and sermons induced flashbacks to the Inaccurate Perception.

The ladies also invited me to join them at the Club for bridge and gin pegs. Verna said they played bridge every Tuesday and Thursday, and went to Annandale for cricket and polo at the weekend. The ladies of the floral-print dresses lived in a carefully transplanted corner of England, dining at the Club or at the Hotel Cecil, ordering cakes from the Willow Bakery, enjoying amateur theatricals at the Gaiety Theatre, and teaching their Muslim cooks to make roast beef and blancmange. They were perfectly nice and had gone out of their way to welcome me, but I didn't want to spend my limited time in India watching cricket and playing bridge. I had not made an effort to see them again.

I pulled the Red Flyer past Morningside and down the hill to Kamal's fruit and paan stall in the village. Kamal always sat cross-legged on a table to roll his paan in fresh betel leaves; he displayed the triangular green packets on a woven tray under a hand-lettered sign that read: TENSION-FREE PARKING. For three rupees Kamal would happily watch Billy's wagon while we took a horse-drawn tonga or a bicycle rickshaw into Simla. He said, 'For nothing I would be watching, Madam, but I know white people want always to be paying, isn't it?' Indians often pretended not to want their wages and accepted them as if being forced. It seemed to be a well-established game, so I insisted on paying, and Kamal nodded with seemingly pained resignation as he palmed the three rupees.

But that day, I wanted to take the little red wagon with us because I intended to climb the steep street up to Christ Church, which would be too much for Billy. I bought two coconut slices from Kamal – I had to give him his three rupees one way or another – and I heaved Billy's wagon into a tonga.

Outside the colonial district, it felt more like India. The road through Masoorla was lined with squat, one-room Himachali houses with slate roofs, and the air hung heavy with smoke. Two men strolled along in white kurta pyjamas, their arms slung over each other's shoulders, and a stooped woman in an orange sari sold limes under a droopy awning. Billy giggled at a complacent cow standing in the middle of the road, forcing people and tongas and bull carts and rickshaws to go around it. I saw no hint of the danger that so worried Martin. We munched our coconut slices and bumped happily along the rutted road.

On the outskirts of Simla, the housing deteriorated into a slum of makeshift shelters. Rags strung over ropes and poles like filthy laundry served as walls and roofs, and the air smelled of sewage and humid vegetation. Workhorse women herded children and cows while carrying bundles on their backs or on their heads. One woman stopped to look at me as we passed. She had a gold ring in her nose and I began to raise my camera, but her eyes caught mine and we both stared, wondering what each other's life was like. I needed no photo. The bleakness in her face took root in my memory, and I knew that if I had to scratch the earth for my food and raise Billy in a dirt-floored hut, I would resent the rich foreigners I served. But what could one person do? I averted my eyes.

An endless stream of people trudged along both sides of the road – walking, carrying, sitting on their heels waiting, herding goats, cooking over dung fires, selling vegetables, urinating, selling fruit, talking, sleeping, eating . . . Women in diaphanous saris fluttered through the dust and smoke, and bull carts competed with cars and rickshaws, and tongas, and flat-bed trucks that rocked under loads of canvas-wrapped cargo, bulging off either side. Children begged, dogs scavenged, and sacred cows ate garbage. A temple bell rang, and the mid-morning call to prayer floated out of a minaret like a rumour of God.

We passed a small patch of land with a cross poking through the weeds, and I called to the tonga driver to stop. I'd noticed the little graveyard before, but that day, maybe because I had Felicity and Adela on my mind, I felt an urge to explore. The driver pulled on the reins and I asked him to wait. Billy said, 'What are we doing?'

'Snooping.' I lifted him out of the tonga, and we walked into the weeds. The old place was overgrown and appropriately quiet, a peaceful abode. A stone monument at the entrance read: 'They are young and old. No question, no answer, all silent.'

I've always found cemeteries soothing, reassured by the reminder that, eventually, we will lay down our cares. I held Billy's hand and poked around crooked tombstones girdled by scruffy shrubs, and headstones half buried under moss and mud. This wasn't Simla's main cemetery and I found only about twenty graves, but they all told tales of colonial hardship, of babies and young people felled by cholera and smallpox, typhoid and brain fever. They affirmed that, without anyone lifting a finger, Mother India herself could boot us out whenever she pleased.

There was one tombstone for a couple known only as John and Elizabeth, buried with their six infants, lost one after the other over six years. Another told of a girl who died giving birth in 1820:

> Just fifteen years she was a maid
> And scarce eleven months a wife.
> Four days and nights in labour laid,
> Brought forth and then gave up her life.

Other stones were more cryptic but equally telling.

Reginald Townsend
1856–1859
Our Dimpled Boy

Billy asked, 'What are these big stones for?'

'Well, Chicken . . .' How much could a five-year-old understand about death? 'After people die, we bury them and put up markers with their names. It helps us remember them.'

'You mean there are *people* buried here?' His eyes widened.

'Only their bodies.' I stooped down and rubbed his back. 'They can't feel anything. The thing that made them alive and who they were went away when they died.'

'Where did it go?'

'I don't know, sweetie. People have lots of different ideas about that.'

Billy looked thoughtful. 'Why do people have to die?'

'They just do.'

'Do they ever come back?'

'I'm afraid not.'

'Are you and Dad going to die?'

Oh, dear. 'Not for a very long time.'

'I don't want you to die.' His chin began to quiver.

'Hey, nobody is dying.' I gave him a firm hug. 'And Spike is *never* going to die.'

'That's good.' He rubbed his cheek against the fur muzzle. 'I love Spike.'

'I know, Peanut. And you'll have him for ever.'

Billy put Spike's ear to his lips and passed on the news of his immortality.

We wandered through the tumbledown cemetery until we came to a small, weathered granite headstone that made me stop and blink.

Adela Winfield

1836–1858

A Good Woman

But Adela had not accompanied Felicity to India – her letters all came from England – and shortly after Felicity left, the Sepoy Rebellion broke out. I searched the other graves for Felicity, but she wasn't there. I went back to Adela's headstone and read it again, wondering what on earth could have induced a young woman to come to India during an uprising.

Chapter Eleven

1854

FELICITY WATCHED THEM cast off the ropes and felt the *Cambria* move off. As the great ship slipped away from the wharf, the cheering crowd surged forward, Adela and Kaitlin with it, drowning out the singing missionaries with hearty hurrahs. Soon the figures on the wharf dwindled to specks and barefooted lascars in red turbans climbed among the ropes like a circus act.

She wandered into the dining saloon and sat down in a revolving chair, where she watched a fat ayah singing a baby to sleep on the floor. She thought of Yasmin and the sorrow she had once felt at leaving her and India, yet now she was ambivalent about leaving England. It was really Adela she regretted leaving, but in any case there was, once again, a sense of loss. She watched the baby pat the ayah's face and play with the gold hoops in her ears as the ship throbbed down the river to the sea.

In Gibraltar, Felicity rode in rattletrap conveyances through the twisted high-walled streets, out past the Spanish market, where everyone bought figs and pomegranates. Then she trotted through the sand and the short grass round the mighty grey foot of the Rock to look up and marvel. Afterwards, she strolled through the roses and verbenas of the Alameda Gardens and drank strong black coffee on the boulevard. Here she posted her first letter.

Gibraltar 1854

Dearest Adela,

My cabin mate, Miss Stitch, is going out to India to marry a military man she's met once. There is nothing wrong with her apart from her unrelenting virtue & obsessive neatness. She asked, in a pained voice, whether I might take care to keep my things to my own side of the cabin, & whether she might have the room to herself for an hour every morning for her private devotions. One feels someone should warn her fiancé.

Then, of course, we have the Fishing Fleet – anxious, not-so-young things imagining a sandy land fringed with coconut palms & filled with eligible men. Poor dears. There is also a dashing young Maharaja – very handsome – with a posh accent & rumoured to have, somewhere deep in the bowels of the ship, an army of servants, starching his collars & preparing his favourite dishes. None in the Fishing Fleet give him more than a polite nod, but I would think the life of a Maharanee would be more interesting than that of a memsahib like my mother, who expends all her energy keeping India at bay.

The most imposing passenger is a military wife known as the burra mem, meaning that she is married to the most senior officer in her set; the wives of lesser rank revere her. She is a tall, thickset woman with crinkly steel-coloured hair & the bearing of a commandant. Wherever she sits, she creates a hallowed space, & the other military wives hover around her like court ladies round the queen. The imperious burra mem takes it as her due.

One day, in the antechamber of the bath, she made to step in front of me as I waited my turn at the door, expecting me to say, "After you, Madam." But I neatly blocked her with a quick sidestep & a sweet smile. When the door opened & a freshly bathed woman stepped out, I gave the burra mem a cordial nod as I closed the door in her formidable if surprised face. I saw my assertion as a duty to myself, like Fanny, & it made the cold saltwater shower ever more pleasant.

It promises to be an amusing voyage. I will write again from Alexandria & Colombo. I wish you were here.

> *Your sister in joy,*
> *Felicity*

Alexandria 1854

Dearest Adela,
I've been under the weather because I took the advice of some philanthropic lunatics who go about giving information they don't have to people who don't want it. Old Hands, they call themselves. They advised I eat plenty of meat to fortify myself for the voyage, & I did, even though I suspected it had gone off. Foolish of me, but they have a worldly way of expressing themselves that makes one think they know what they're talking about. At one point, I felt so sick, & the weather became so oppressive I lay in my hammock in nothing but a chemise, wondering whether I would walk off the ship in Calcutta or be carried.

On a voyage such as this, whose purpose is only to get from here to there alive, there are only two things to write about: the people on board & the weather. I have already mentioned the Fishing Fleet, Miss Stitch & the burra mem, but the weather is far more interesting. The passengers can only affect our sanity, but the weather can kill us. It can do so in many ways, but it really only comes down to this: too much weather, or too little. We have had both.

Last week I survived a gale that frightened & thrilled me. It took us by surprise, one afternoon whilst all who were not green with seasickness strolled the deck, grateful to be out of our cramped quarters. At first, the sea swelled in glorious white-crested peaks & a refreshingly cold spray spattered the deck. Then the sky slowly darkened & it began to rain. At that point, most passengers went below, but I opened my parasol, knowing it would do no good in the slanting rain but enjoying the feel of fresh water on my face. I was a free woman now; I could stand in the rain if I pleased.

My first pang of fear came when the benign waves rose up like sea monsters, each one bigger than the last, until they virtually blocked the sky. My parasol was whipped from my hands, & I watched it spin away in the grey rain. I climbed into a giant coil of rope & held on as we rode up the side of a mountainous wave. When we dived down the other side I screamed, half in terror & half in a sort of wild joy. A deckhand hauling a thick rope saw me & shouted, 'Get below!' I paused, only for a second, marvelling at the courage one must possess to undertake this voyage over & over, knowing the dangers full well. He shot me an angry look & shouted again, but his voice was carried off on the screaming wind.

As I made my way below, the ship tossed me to & fro & I have a fearsome bruise on my left shoulder. I found Miss Stitch, wide-eyed with fear, pulling the sides of her hammock around her as if to wrap up in a protective cocoon. After a few lurching attempts, I managed to climb into my hammock

& the two of us swung violently back & forth, crashing first against each other & then against the walls. We could not talk above the ferocious din of the sea, bashing the ship as if trying to crush it. I wondered whether cold water might begin to seep in through the walls or drip from the ceiling – how horrible to watch one's death approaching drop by drop – or perhaps a merciful torrent would break down the door & the sea would swallow us whole.

Trying to be calm, I reminded myself that hundreds, if not thousands of Englishwomen had made this voyage before me, & then, baring my secret pagan soul, I invoked the protection of Neptune. When it was over I felt that the sea gods had baptized us & that they would now watch over us for the remainder of the voyage. Trounced & shaken but feeling almost unbearably alive, I washed my face & hoped for another storm.

A fortnight later, we suffered the other weather disaster – no wind. The ship sat in water smooth as glass, the sails limp & useless in the still air, with the crew passing each other nervous glances as they went about their work. They gave the passengers ugly looks, as if we had brought them this bad luck. Miss Stitch prayed, the Fishing Fleet sat in tight clusters, whispering, & the burra mem stared fiercely at the sky as if to demand a good strong gust.

On our fifth motionless night, I fell asleep wondering whether the Cambria & all of us on it would become another tale of mysterious loss at sea. But the next morning, I awoke to a familiar rocking & swaying of my hammock. Miss Stitch & I exchanged a cautious smile & we crept up to the deck to see the sails billowing in a high wind. We laughed & clapped our hands at the happy sight, & even the most hardened deckhand joined his mates in a cheerful sea shanty. Everyone remained in high spirits until the sea once again became too choppy & all *but the Old Hands retired to their cabins to suffer in privacy.*

One peaceful evening, I stepped out on deck to see Alexandria, looking very gay, the Egyptian bazaar flaming with lights & lively music coming from the gambling houses. But I stayed on board to nurse my stomach with Jamaican ginger-root. I believe I may have lost as much as a stone & my dresses simply hang on my bones. Old Hands!

Next we will travel by land to pick up another ship that will take us to Calcutta. The Old Hands have told me the warm waters of the Indian Ocean are full of fantastic creatures – I imagine King Neptune's court – & they have described silver fish darting & streaking near the surface whilst whales & porpoises gambol alongside the ship as if to escort us. I cannot wait to see it!

I will post this letter by way of the Old Hands going ashore to drink and gamble. Why do they never get sick?

Your sister in joy,
Felicity

Calcutta 1855

Dearest Adela,
After almost three months at sea, gulls were sighted, an indication of land, & within a day villages & coconut palms appeared along the coast of Ceylon. At Colombo, bumboat men rowed out to sell coconuts & bananas & a deckhand shouted, 'Look at them come! Like bees to the honey pot!' The crew lowered baskets bearing money, & then pulled them back up laden with tropical fruits. Little brown boys dived for the gold coins we tossed overboard & came up holding them in their teeth.

The smell of India is in the air & I have come alive. I find myself dragging steamer chairs about for old ladies & borrowing pulpy white babies from their brown ayahs to dance up & down the deck whilst I sing 'Camptown Ladies'. Do dah, do dah.

Some time after Madras we slipped, finally, into the wide brown mouth of the Hooghly River, which took us into India. On the Hooghly, the ship slowed to a shuddering stop & word went round in the cool of the evening that we would lie there till the tide came in with morning. There, in the darkness, we listened to the gurgling river whilst a heavy tropical wind blew in from the jungle. I heard stories of the famous quicksand of the Hooghly that has dragged down more than one ship, & I had the queer idea that spiteful genii opposed to the Raj sat like spiders in a web, waiting for any Britons who came too near.

But the morning tide took us away & eventually we came to Calcutta. On the wharf, a rainbow-coloured crowd greeted us, a few staid Europeans in their pith helmets scattered here & there like common mushrooms in a field of exotic flowers. The vibrancy of India makes England look like a faded water-colour, & my first glimpse of it made my heart leap, its gorgeousness & its great seething masses. I remembered the distinctive smell, a mixture of spices & burning cow dung & decay. Perhaps it is a smell that only one born to it can love.

When I first set foot on land my knees buckled as though I were still balancing on the rolling deck. I staggered around for a while, quite disorientated, until I found Mother, who had come with a palanquin to take me home. I climbed in whilst mangy yellow dogs slunk around my skirts, I had forgotten about the pariah dogs in India; a proper hound is a rarity here.

As soon as I settled into the palanquin, Mother closed the curtains & buttoned them down. The Calcutta I will inhabit is English & cloistered, all grand Palladian villas, palm-shaded gardens, & a multitude of turbanned domestics. I will live secluded in a replicated piece of England until we escape to the hills. I truly wish you were here.

Your sister in joy,
Felicity

Adela put down Felicity's letter and looked at Kaitlin. 'Doesn't it sound exciting? I've written to Calcutta, and when Felicity settles in she'll find my letters waiting for her, not that I have anything half so wonderful to report.'

'Wonderful?' Kaitlin raised her eyebrows. 'It sounds a bit frightenin', if you ask me.'

'Yes, actually, I suppose it does. Still . . .' Adela sighed. 'Perhaps it's just easier to leave than to be left behind.'

Kaitlin busied herself, laying out Adela's clothes. 'You should be gettin' dressed to meet the young gentleman your mother has comin' to dinner.'

Adela stared at the dress Kaitlin held up for her approval – russet silk with gigot sleeves. She said, 'I'm sick to death of this pointless charade.'

Kaitlin spread the dress on the bed and laid a whalebone corset next to it. 'Budge up now, darlin'. There are worse things than a lovely dinner, even if you don't think so.' She warmed a cotton chemise in front of the fire. 'The sooner we get you dressed, the sooner you can have it over with.' She walked towards Adela, waving the chemise.

Adela sat on her dressing chair and crossed her arms. 'I will refuse them all, you know. In the end you and I will grow old together in some cobwebby townhouse in London, a dotty old spinster and her Irish maid. I'll write little books that no one reads, and we'll drink weak tea and eat blanc-mange. Perhaps we'll even have cats.'

'Well, isn't that a charmin' picture.' Kaitlin rustled the che-mise at her. 'And still you must get dressed.'

'Yes, I know.' Adela slipped off her dressing gown and raised her arms.

'Ah, it's not so bad as all that.' Kaitlin dropped the chemise over Adela's head. 'You'll finish your puddin' and come back up, and sure I'll be waitin'.'

Adela smiled. 'Katie, dear, you are my joy.'

'And you are mine, love.' Kaitlin smoothed down the chemise, and Adela gave her an affectionate smile. Kaitlin cupped Adela's compact breast and planted a kiss on her lips. They had not heard the doorknob turn.

'Sssaphisstsss!' Mrs Winfield stood in the half-open door-way, one hand on her cheek and the other at her throat.

Kaitlin screamed, and Adela instinctively crossed her arms over her breasts.

Mrs Winfield's face contorted into a mask of disgust. 'Sssaphissstsss!' It sounded like the strike of a match.

Kaitlin covered her face, and Mrs Winfield pointed at her. 'Vile creature! Get out!'

Kaitlin doubled over, hugging herself.

'I mean now! Leave this house immediately.'

'Mother—'

'Do not speak, Adela. I cannot bear to look at you.'

Kaitlin lurched out of the room, and Mrs Winfield followed to shout abuse after her. Adela stumbled for the door, but her mother slammed it in her face and locked it.

That evening, the young gentleman dined with a pale set of parents who apologized repeatedly for their daughter being indisposed. He ate quickly and made a neat escape directly after pudding.

Dr Winfield touched a napkin to his moustache. 'Well, that was awkward.'

'Never mind him. What shall we do with her?'

Dr Winfield rubbed his forehead. 'I think the Fishing Fleet might be the thing.'

'India? But Alfred—'

'By God, she's unnatural, woman.' He whipped the napkin off his lap and threw it on the table. 'The best thing is to marry her off as quickly as possible. We can't let this . . . this aberration set in. British men outnumber British women in India at least five to one, and the Fishing Fleet is all normal women seeking husbands. Everything is organized to get as many as possible engaged. I say we put her in among them. She'll meet plenty of dependable military bachelors.'

Mrs Winfield looked at her lap and murmured, 'She'll meet women too.'

'Damn it, what do you want to do? She'll meet women, no matter what. At least the Fishing Fleet will get her away from this damn maid and keep her busy with parties designed to throw her together with eligible men. The memsahibs are all respectable married women who will assume, like everyone else, that she's there to find a British husband and they will oversee her every move. For heaven's sake, that's what the Fishing Fleet is *for*.' He leaned forward, disgust clouding his face. 'Good God! Surely you're not suggesting she would initiate a liaison with an *Indian* woman?'

'Well . . .' Mrs Winfield looked up and when she saw her husband's face she whispered, 'No. No, of course not.' She dropped her eyes and stared at her own fingers, fidgeting in her lap. 'Still, Alfred, to ship her off with the Fishing Fleet after only one season? It will look as if we didn't even try.'

'Well, what do you want to do? Hire another maid for her to corrupt? She's afflicted!' He looked at the ceiling as if appealing for help. 'Who knows, perhaps the rigours of India will burn this . . . this defect out of her. In any case, she'll be constantly chaperoned, and there's nothing else for a young woman to do in India *but* marry a British man. I suspect she'll end up with a military man who's more interested in horses and battle drills than domestic bliss.'

'It's a long voyage, but I should like to see her married.' Mrs Winfield stared at her centrepiece of white roses. 'A child might settle her.'

Dr Winfield lit a cigar and his wife asked, 'Are you going to smoke that in here?'

He puffed angrily. 'I think we have more serious things to discuss than smoke in the curtains.'

'Yes.' She smoothed the cool white tablecloth with her palm. 'We wouldn't see much of her any more if she married in India.'

'And does that disturb you terribly?'

She hesitated. She did not look at her husband and her voice, when it came, was small and sad. She said, 'Not really.'

'That's what I thought.' He took another angry puff. 'I'll make the arrangements.'

October 1855

Dearest Felicity,
The most terrible, most wonderful thing has happened.
Mother discovered Katie and me in a compromising position.
Do you understand me? If not, I will be able to explain
because they are sending me to India with the Fishing Fleet!
I sail almost immediately.

Poor Katie has been turned out, & I do not know where
she has gone, but I've given Cook your address in Calcutta in
case she returns. After a long hearty cry, I dried my face &
wrote Katie a glowing letter of recommendation. I put money

in the envelope as well – my entire allowance for I cannot bear the thought of her in want. I left it with Cook, who promises she will do her best to see Katie gets it. I don't know what else I can do for her.

It is all so sudden & so bittersweet – I find myself weeping for Katie, then suddenly smiling at the thought of joining you. Tears course down my face even whilst a smile plays around my mouth. I actually feel quite mad, when I feel anything other than shock.

I will join you, after all.

> *Your sister in joy,*
> *Adela*

Chapter Twelve

1947

L IFE IS VERTICAL in Simla. It perches on the sides of mountains, and getting up to the broad pedestrian street called the Mall means riding up a steep, pine-shaded road in a horse-drawn tonga, or being hauled up by three panting rickshaw wallahs, two pulling and one pushing. The road to the Mall frightened Billy the first time we took it – it even scared me a little, climbing unsteadily on a dirt road full of hairpin turns – but after three months, India had seduced us and we simply sat back at a forty-five-degree angle while the horse panted and strained against the harness as it pulled us up the long curving road.

At the top, I paid the tonga driver and sat Billy in the Red Flyer with Spike. As always, the Mall teemed with people, and the air smelled of pakoras, bobbing and browning in cauldrons of boiling coconut oil. Narrow stone steps branched down to the native quarter, a cramped warren of lamplit shacks and stalls, temples and mosques. Hawkers hawked and buyers haggled, and I adjusted my sunglasses. My Brownie camera swung by a leather strap around my neck, ready to do what no one had ever managed – to capture India. We blended into the moving crowd, the dust, the noise, the polychromatic chaos, and it took me so far from my problems that I loved it.

From the Mall, I could see Simla spread out below me – houses and market stalls set into the mountainsides – and above me, high on the ridge, the butter-coloured spires of Christ Church poking into the heavens. I pulled the red wagon past the Krishna Baker's and a shoebox-sized tobacco stall called the Glory Palace, then turned up the steep road to the church. It was a long haul, and I arrived at the tall, arched church door sweating and panting. Billy said, 'Aw, nuts. Do we have to go to church?'

'Just for a minute, Peanut.' I pulled on the iron handle, but the door didn't budge. A woman in an apricot sari lolled on the doorstep, playing with the bangles around her ankles. I bent down, smelling the coconut oil in her hair, and asked, 'Is it closed?'

'It is closing, Madam.'

'All day?'

Head waggle. 'Church is all day closing, Madam. In two hours coming back.'

'Um, is it all day, or two hours?'

Head waggle with irritation. 'All day closing, Madam. Back in two hours.'

'Right.' I turned to Billy. 'Cheer up, BoBo. Apparently we're not going to church.' I nodded to the woman, and she fiddled with her toe ring.

I went around to the rectory, but that door was locked too, so I rummaged in my purse for a pencil and wrote a note on the back of an old receipt from Masoorla's import store.

Dear Reverend Locke,
At your convenience, I would appreciate having a look at the
church records from the mid nineteenth century. Thank you.
Evie Mitchell

I folded the note, slid it under the rectory door, and then I wheeled the wagon around and headed for the square stone library next to the church. That door was open, but the place was deserted; the planks squeaked under my feet, and the dusty stacks bulged with serious-looking old books. Billy said, 'This is worse than church.'

'Let's find you a book. I just need a few minutes.' I found a book with fanciful pictures of Moghul emperors, onion domes and fierce armies with scimitars raised. Billy turned the pages with fainthearted interest while I located the history section. A thick volume titled *The Raj* looked promising, so I slid it off the shelf and leafed through, scanning for the word 'sepoy'. I found it beneath a picture of a cocky young Indian in a plumed turban, tight white trousers and a red military jacket studded with brass buttons. He held his English rifle like a trophy.

I turned the page to a grisly drawing of dead and dying Indians in a walled enclosure. Hundreds of bodies lay heaped along the base of the wall and some hung over the side of a well. Corpses lay in piles, their eyes still wide in terror, and women in blood-soaked saris held dead children. The caption read: 'Massacre at Amritsar'.

The article on the facing page explained. In 1919, after thousands of Indians had assembled for a spring festival in Jallianwalla Bagh in Amritsar, British troops under Brigadier General Reginald Dyer marched on the park and opened fire. Political tensions had been simmering for weeks, but no one expected an attack on unarmed families. Dyer instructed his men to shoot into areas where the crowd was the thickest, and they continued to fire until all ammunition was exhausted – 1,400 rounds. An armoured car blocked the only exit, and people tried to climb the walls, where they were easily cut down. Some jumped into a well to escape the bullets – 120 corpses were recovered from that well. Dyer left more than fifteen hundred dead and wounded. The youngest victim was a six-week-old baby.

Churchill later said: 'The Indians were packed together so that one bullet would drive through three or four bodies; the people ran madly this way and the other . . . and then was seen the most frightful of all spectacles, the strength of a civilization without its mercy.'

A court found Dyer guilty of massacre, but Parliament reversed the verdict and cleared his name. The House of Lords passed a motion commending him as 'the Saviour of the Punjab'. The *Morning Post* established a sympathy fund for Dyer, and they received £26,000. The following year, Gandhi instituted his Quit India movement against the British, and thus began the end of the Raj.

I closed the book slowly, trying to absorb what I had read, and jumped when Billy tugged on my arm. He said, 'Spike is tired of that book.'

I fought for control of my voice as the image of someone gunning Billy down in a park came unbidden. I cupped his chin and said, 'You bet, Peach. How about we explore the bazaar?'

'Sure!' He dashed out of the door and I left the book open on the table. Billy hopped into his Red Flyer and shoved Spike between his legs. He said, 'The bazaar beats the pants off that book.'

I walked along the Mall feeling battered, wanting to replace the images of death at Amritsar with life in Simla, but I could not help imagining the cold terror of seeing a tank roll up the street and a machine gun trained on Billy and me. How *could* they? How could *anyone*?

Billy wanted to follow the sound of drums and trumpets, which led us to a wedding procession. He pointed excitedly at the dashing bridegroom astride a white horse, his turban flashing with bits of green glass. I was more taken by the bride, smiling bashfully on her palanquin behind transparent curtains. She wore a red wedding sari, and gold dripped from her ears, dangled from her nose, and encircled her neck, arms and ankles. An intricate henna tattoo covered her hands, like gloves of orange lace, a scrollwork of flowers and butterflies that spoke of the complicated web between living things, the ups and downs between a man and a woman.

Billy said, 'Is that a prince and princess?'

I nodded. 'They are today, Sweetpea.'

As they passed, the bride lifted the curtain of her palanquin to peek at me, and I saw her teenaged face – her kohl-lined eyes and plump mouth. She looked like the embodiment of untroubled love, in spite of the fact that her marriage was undoubtedly arranged. I struggled with a bitter mix of nostalgia for that warm feeling and disdain for such naivety. Why do we insist on believing in the impossible? That young couple were positively luminous with the belief that their worlds were now complete. I remembered how that felt, and my throat constricted, aching. I had to swallow and blink and turn my face away from Billy. He always registered changes in my mood, and I wanted to protect him, at least for a while. I wanted him to enjoy the magic while he could and to give him a soft launch into a hard world. I put on a smile and pulled the wagon away from the wedding party, saying, 'Wasn't that pretty?'

'Will they live in a palace, Mom?'

They would probably live in a one-roomed hut with a dirt floor. The princess would collect cow dung for fuel, haul wood and carry water pots on her head for the rest of her life. She would lose almost half of her babies in infancy. The dashing young prince would probably pull a rickshaw until his health gave out, or he might wrest his food from the stubborn earth and watch his children die while he begged the gods for the right amount of rain. I said, 'Not a palace, sweetie. They're just ordinary people, but today is their big day.' I did not add that because they were Indian their resilience would probably save them, unlike the rest of us poor fools.

With Amritsar and the wedding procession hurting my heart, I walked through the dusty, unpaved lanes watching for signs of the unrest that so worried Martin. Two men sat on a rooftop contentedly chewing paan, and the ground beneath them glistened red where they spat; a barefoot man in a white skullcap strolled by, cracking sunflower seeds in his teeth; a little girl with an enchanting smile sat on her heels, holding a white rabbit, and, slowly, India worked its soporific magic on me. Life went on.

People wore the same saris, dhotis, chadors, salwar kameez, dupattas, kurtas, skullcaps and turbans they'd worn for centuries. These street scenes had probably not changed much since Felicity and Adela walked there. I imagined Victorian parasols and sun-struck pith helmets amid the saris and kurtas, and I felt a sense of continuity. It was a congenial scene, except for the beggars, especially the children.

There were too many of them: thin, ragged mites with matted hair and bony legs and small hands thrust out. I couldn't resist the tiny brown palms, tough as paws, and the lean little faces. They made eating motions, putting their dirty fingers into their mouths, their dark eyes desperate. No child should look like that. I knew the moment I placed a coin in the hand of one, ten more would come swarming, quick as rats. Many were no older than Billy; some were younger. They tried to touch my clothes, as if I was a saint with curative powers, and I felt ashamed of my wealth and powerlessness. I had been warned to resist them. James Walker had said, 'Giving them money compounds the problem.'

The problem was slavery. Walker said the children were often sold to slavers by relatives who could not afford to feed them – earthquake victims from Bihar, war orphans from the Punjab, refugees from West Bengal – and the money they begged would be used to buy more children. They were thin, filthy and vulnerable, and yet those children were some of the luckier ones; having masters gave them the means to stay alive.

When the children became too old to beg, they would be sold into domestic service or prostitution. I knew all this, and I didn't want to perpetuate it, but if the children didn't bring in a daily minimum, they would be beaten. There was no way to win, so I carried lots of small change and gave them each one pice – less than a penny. I salved my conscience by thinking: *It's not enough to buy another child and maybe today this one won't be beaten for bringing in nothing at all.* Billy didn't ask why the children begged, but he watched them with a solemn expression. I walked quickly, trying to distract him.

I pointed out an astrologer giving consultations from a wooden chair under a tall, fringed umbrella, and let Billy snap a photo. We took another shot of a shoemaker fashioning sandals from old bicycle tyres. People spoke Hindi, Urdu, Telugu, Bengali and a jumble of other languages, all of which created a babble as impenetrable as the culture. All we could do was stare and take pictures. In my viewfinder, I framed up tea stalls packed with baskets of fragrant leaves – *snap* – spice merchants standing behind open sacks of cumin seeds – *snap* – and an incense shop swathed in gauzy smoke – *snap*.

I found the perfume vendor especially seductive and always stopped to sniff his samples – patchouli and musk, tincture of myrrh, roses and smoke. I'd often felt tempted to buy a small, stoppered bottle of something, an ounce of India just for me. I didn't normally wear perfume, but I thought it would be nice to take some back to Chicago, where, on a grey, sub-zero day in January, I could hold it to my nose and remember. But we lived on a budget, and I knew exactly how much we had in the tea tin, even if Martin didn't. Anyway, I had never mastered the art of haggling, so I just smiled at the vendor, snapped a picture of his elegant cut-glass bottles, and moved on.

We came to a stall where an old man with wide, flat Mongolian features sold Tibetan turquoise, and I stopped to watch him manipulate an abacus with flying fingers. He had skin like cured leather, and his polished stones, in shades of mottled aqua, were set into elaborate silver earrings, complicated necklaces and thick bracelets, all hung around him like a rattling curtain. One moment too late, I saw Edward and Lydia rummaging through a basket of loose stones.

'Evie, darling!'

Edward touched the edge of his topi, a polite greeting. 'Thought we'd do a spot of shopping, as long as we're stuck here.'

'Those are beautiful.' I nodded at the loose turquoise.

Lydia passed a hand along the curtain of necklaces. 'Have you ever seen anything so vulgar?' She gave me a con-spiratorial smile and lowered her voice. 'But the loose stones are magnificent.' She held up a turquoise the size of a quail's egg. 'I can bargain this ignorant fellow down to nothing, and have it set in London.' She beamed, and Edward nodded his approval.

'Mom?'

I turned to Billy gratefully. 'What, Peanut?'

'Me and Spike are learning how to belch. Wanna hear?'

'Um . . .'

'BUUURRRP.'

'Wow. Sounds like the real thing.'

'Thanks.' He smiled with shy pride.

Lydia looked as though someone had handed her a still-beating heart on a plate. 'Really, Evie, what were you thinking, bringing a child to India? Such a lovely boy. Honestly, how could you?'

I nipped the tip of my tongue to bite off the salty retort sitting there. I said, 'I've recently heard an interesting bit of history, and I wonder if either of you might shed some light.'

'Of course, darling.' Lydia switched to gossip mode. 'What have you heard?'

'It's an episode in Indian history involving Great Britain.'

Lydia's eyes wandered back to the turquoise. 'I should say all Indian history involves Great Britain.'

Edward mumbled, 'Indeed.'

I forced my mouth into something I hoped passed for a smile. I said, 'This happened in 1857. The Sepoy Rebellion?'

'I'm sure I don't know anything about it.' Lydia foraged through the turquoise. 'That sort of thing depresses me.'

'Ah, yes, the sepoys.' Edward assumed the voice of imperial authority. 'Natives in British service caused all sorts of devilment. You'd think they'd appreciate the uniform and proper training, but no, they kicked up a bloody fuss. Cheeky ingrates. Plenty of British lives lost in that one, I can tell you.'

'What upset them?'

'Some superstitious rot about the grease on their rifle cartridges.' Edward snorted. 'Cow fat or pig fat, or some such. Who knows?'

'Please don't bother yourself, dear.' Lydia turned a concerned face to me. 'We came to India to get away. London's all rubble, you know. The war . . .' She frowned, trying to find adequate words. 'Well, you can imagine our disappointment when we got here. The good parts are English, only not as good as England, and the rest is just a sprawling slum. Of course, I feel sorry for them, as far as that goes, but honestly . . .'

The tip of Edward's tongue made its appearance. He said, 'Don't misunderstand. We pity them, poor buggers. But they don't help themselves, now do they? Reminds me of Africa. Those Kikuyu, I can tell you stories.' He raised one eyebrow.

'Eddie, you don't want to go on about that. You'll only bother yourself.'

I felt heat building in my face, but I forced my voice to remain even. 'I think Gandhi has been trying to help the Indians to help themselves. But first they must be allowed to govern themselves.'

'Gandhi.' Edward pronounced the name with a flat A, like candy. 'A politician dressed up like a prophet.' Pink splotches on each of his cheeks deepened to the colour of raw pork. 'Look here, Mrs Mitchell, it's easy for you Yanks to flounce over here and be terribly democratic about every little thing, but we Britons have had to put up with a damnable responsibility in this godforsaken place.'

Billy had registered the rise in Edward's voice as well as the strain in my face. He stopped his belching practice and leaned forward in the red wagon, eyes wide and mouth slightly open. He held Spike close to his chest.

I asked, 'What responsibility would that be, Edward?'

'Keeping the peace, of course.'

Lydia sniffed. 'I should think that would be painfully obvious, especially now.'

'Yes,' I agreed. 'The peace isn't being kept very well just now, is it?'

Edward stepped closer. 'You can't blame us for this Hindu–Muslim muddle.'

'Oh? I thought Great Britain favoured Partition.' I could feel colour rising. I *hated* that.

'Of course we do! The bloody wogs can't get on together. Never have.'

'They seem to be getting along just fine here in Simla.'

Lydia appeared to have lost interest in the turquoise. 'Really, Evie, I don't see how you can claim any moral high ground when you've brought an innocent child into this . . .' She flapped her white gloves around at the bazaar. 'A child. Your little boy, your baby . . .' Lydia's voice cracked on the word 'baby', and her face went rigid.

Edward put an arm around her shoulders. 'All right, my dear. Steady on.'

Billy stared at the Worthingtons, his mouth slightly open and his eyes wide. I knew he shouldn't be hearing this, but having just read about Amritsar I couldn't stop myself. 'Maybe you're right, Edward. I guess I don't have your refined sense of moral responsibility. I've read about how well you kept the peace at Amritsar.'

Noises receded. The bazaar blurred. Time slowed. We stared at each other in cold stasis. My reference to the massacre had pushed us beyond the bounds of polite conversation. I felt lightheaded, realizing I'd gone too far. After all, Lydia and Edward had nothing to do with Amritsar. I heard the quick click of the abacus, the running murmur of strange languages, and I caught a swirl of movement in my peripheral vision. Then the noon bell from Christ Church broke the spell, and normal sounds and movement resumed.

Edward touched the brim of his topi. 'Lovely running into you, Mrs Mitchell.'

Lydia tugged on her white gloves. 'Good afternoon, Evie.'

As Edward and Lydia walked away, I felt a grim satis-faction. Good, I thought, maybe now they'll avoid me and save me the trouble of ducking them.

'Mom?' Billy's face made me think of a worried cherub. 'Spike is tired. Let's go home.'

But I needed to walk off the Worthingtons. I bent down and planted a good, solid kiss on his cheek. 'Why don't you and Spike take a little nap?' I fluffed up his pillow and petted his hair. 'When you wake up we'll have masala chai.'

Billy consulted Spike, and then curled up on the pillow with the toy dog under his arm. I took a deep breath and started walking, but I feared that walking off the Worthingtons might require trekking clear over the Himalayas. *Amritsar*. My hand tightened on the wagon handle at the thought of it, but why take it out on Lydia and Edward? It wasn't at all rational. My face still felt hot from the encounter.

I looked back at the wagon and saw Billy asleep, curled peacefully around Spike, so I stopped under a neem tree and sat in the lacy shade, watching a silk merchant mist rose water over the dusty ground outside his shop. I smiled at him and he salaamed like a Moghul prince.

Sunlight dappled through the neem leaves, and I remembered Martin saying that villagers brushed their teeth with the frayed twigs of neem trees. I'd often seen cut branches with leaves still fresh and supple for sale on street stalls. Impulsively, I reached up and broke off a twig. The pale-green centre leaked clear sap and I chewed one end until it softened, then rubbed it over my teeth. It tasted bitter and astringent, but it was pleasantly uncivilized to have a twig in my mouth, and I liked the feel of the fibres massaging my gums. Suddenly I laughed out loud at the absurdity of a redhead from Chicago, morally outraged and sartorially confused, brushing her teeth in public with a mashed twig, and I'll be damned if laughing at myself didn't purge me of the Worthingtons.

I breathed in the mountain air, picked up the wagon handle and headed for a tobacco stall to buy a pack of Abdullah cigarettes. I hadn't smoked much in Chicago – a Raleigh after meals, maybe one at night – but I liked those short, oval Abdullahs with gold, rose-scented tips. Verna had offered me one at her tea party and now I smoked them all the time. I had tried one of Martin's bidis, the thin native cigarettes wrapped in a leaf and secured with a thread, but I found them hot and harsh. The bidis were another thing that made Martin appear Indian, but he said it established a rapport with the people he interviewed.

After buying my cigarettes, I turned down a street behind the Chinese shoe shop and found myself in a quiet cul-de-sac that ended at an old temple – yellow brick built on top of the stone ruins of an earlier structure. Two wooden doors stood open and appeared welcoming. They were carved in a filigree of birds and flowers, and a string of faded prayer flags fluttered above them. I peeked inside and, in the dim light of oil lamps, I made out the figure of a large stone Buddha.

I knew I could not enter a Hindu temple without taking off my shoes, and mosques had rules about ritual washing and head coverings. I didn't know the protocol for Buddhists, but I poked my head inside the door and glanced around the empty space. I wondered, isn't Gandhi Buddhist?

No, he's Hindu. Or is he Muslim? I suppose he could be Christian. Then again he could be Parsi or Jain. The Jains were fanatical pacifists, who sometimes wore masks to prevent them from inhaling microscopic insects; they weren't even willing to kill hair lice. India was a spiritual carnival complete with sideshows, but whatever religion Gandhi had been born into, he had become a humanist espousing all religions and none.

Everyone admired Gandhi for forcing the British out, but I secretly marvelled at the backbone of the colonials who had managed to establish themselves in this land of conflicting taboos, killing heat, medieval kingdoms and a plethora of exotic diseases. They had transplanted a pocket of England into one of the most confounding places on earth with nothing but mules and determination. It must have been a terribly hard life, especially for the women, and I wondered whether any but the most dedicated empire-builders were really happy here. They had grit – you had to give them that – but like all imperialists, they sowed the seeds of their own demise.

It was all too complicated, the sun was too hot, and I'd been out too long. I felt drawn to the shadows and serenity of the Buddhist temple, and when I stepped over the threshold, a sense of calm came over me. The place transcended the Worthingtons, politics, even India. In the end, the pull of tranquillity won out over caution. I left my shoes at the entrance and crept inside, pulling my sleeping munchkin in his red wagon behind me.

Chapter Thirteen

1856

F ROM THE journal of Adela Winfield:

March 1856

When I disembarked in Calcutta, grey-haired porters on the docks fought with younger men to carry my trunks. They shouldered each other aside, thrusting their hands out at me whilst holding each other back with sharp elbows. I had no idea what to pay them or how to choose; they all looked the same to me – brown & dusty, barefoot & anxious.

Out of the chaos, a man came running at me, both arms aloft, holding up a brilliant orange cape. When he came closer I saw that it was not a cape but rather long strings of marigolds affixed to his arms; I later learned they were sold for temple offerings, but why on earth would he think I wanted to buy temple offerings? Ah, but this was India: all questions, no answers. I backed away, unnerved by him & by the porters, not knowing how to put any of them off.

I looked around the teeming wharf, beginning to panic, & then I saw a man holding up a placard with my name hand-lettered on it. Lord Chadwick stays in Calcutta to work through the hot weather, as do most Company men, & he kindly sent his bearer, Kasim, to collect me from the dock & bring me to their home on Garden Reach Road.

Kasim frightened me a bit – tall & dark with a proud bearing, a glaring white turban, & a red sash round his waist. He seemed the embodiment of all the tales Felicity had told me about this alien place, yet he gestured to a waiting palanquin in a most gentlemanly manner. I climbed into the curtained enclosure, & Kasim buttoned the curtains down securely; after the intense sun & swirling turmoil of the wharf, spots danced before my eyes, making me blink in the dim, well-cushioned interior.

I found the palanquin confining, but I dared not walk in this bustling & unruly place. I contented myself with undoing a few buttons & holding open the curtain to catch my first glimpse of Calcutta.

An endless stream of people, all carrying loads on their backs or heads, walked along dirt streets lined with shacks & stalls & wretched huts. We passed vendors selling fish, fruits, towers of flat bread, & many more things I did not recognize. The vendors without stalls sat on their heels, holding a cat or talking to a pet bird in a bamboo cage, their wares spread out before them on large cloths.

The heat was unlike anything I'd ever felt, the air stifling & heavy, as if it were a thing one could hold in one's hand like a wet sponge. Sweat beaded on my upper lip & slid down my back & my underclothes stuck to my skin. I dabbed my face with a handkerchief, resolving to buy a fan at the first opportunity.

I leaned my head out the side of the palanquin, as much for air as out of curiosity, & a bearded old man with deep-set eyes & high cheekbones caught my eye. His costume & the gravity in his face reminded me of an Old Testament prophet. As my palanquin approached the spot where he sat cross-legged on the ground, I started to smile, but his dark eyes hardened in response. He held up a basket from which the head of a King Cobra appeared, yellow & black, its scaly hood fanned wide & its forked tongue flickering. I drew back in surprise & fear, & then the old man smiled.

I dropped the curtain, withdrawing into the cloistered dark, & before I could collect myself enough to look outside again, something changed. Street noises diminished & I had the pleasant sensation of passing beneath shade trees. I peeked out & gasped at the opulence of Garden Reach Road. The houses reminded me of pictures I had seen of the world's most intimidating architecture – the Taj Mahal, the Parthenon, St Peter's Basilica. It was a shock to see this grandeur juxtaposed with the squalor I'd observed on my way in from the wharf, & I gazed up at the stately white buildings in awe, exactly as I, & everyone else, was meant to do.

Calcutta is divided between Black Town & White Town, & having entered White Town we eventually halted in front of the Chadwicks' palatial home. I emerged from the palanquin, bedraggled & begrimed, & had a general impression of being surrounded by soaring white pillars & spacious gardens.

Lord Chadwick greeted me in the porte-cochere, saying, 'Welcome to our bit of England in India. You're amongst civilized people now.' He told me Felicity & her mother had left for Simla more than a month earlier.

March 1856

The house rambles in every direction, & the high ceilings are not enclosed; the bare rafters are covered with a vast white cloth. At one point, I heard scratching overhead, & looking up, I saw something scuttling in the cloth. I realized with a start that either very small rodents or very large insects must be creeping round up there, & the cloth was meant to keep them from falling on our heads. I know now that this is a common arrangement in the grand villas of Calcutta. At first I thought it silly to go to so much trouble over a few ants & moths, but the insects here are not like the appropriately bug-sized ants & bees in England. Once, in my bedroom, I saw a beetle the size of a crabapple!

The floors are cool stone & animal head trophies decorate the walls. There is plenty of fine heavy furniture, marble tabletops & Japanese vases full of flowers. Curiously, it's all quite English, & yet not.

On my first day here, a line of bearers carried my luggage on their heads & a barefoot young woman in a white sari accompanied me to a bedroom with a four-poster bed swathed in mosquito netting. I looked around the spacious room with its high wooden mouldings & massive oak almirah, & I might not have known I was in India but for the perspiration trickling down my back, the mosquito netting, & the woman in the white sari, pouring rosewater into a brass basin.

A large reed fan – a punkah – creaked back & forth overhead, churning the sultry air, & my gaze followed a rope down to the hand of a little brown boy sitting in the corner – the punkah wallah. I later learned that in some homes, holes are drilled into the walls so that the punkah wallah can operate the fan from outside the house, but folks who have been long in India are no more incommoded by servants sitting in the room than by so many chairs or footstools. Dark forms glide about silently on bare feet, coming into one's presence unexpectedly, & no one takes any notice.

I sat on the bed, not quite knowing what to do next. The bearers had left my cases on the floor, but would the young woman unpack them, as a lady's maid would do in England? I reached down to unlace my boots but the young woman – my ayah, I now realized – appeared at my feet with her basin of scented water. She smiled up at me, gently pushed aside my hands & finished removing my boots. I tried to imagine dear, high-spirited Katie being so obsequious & had to smile.

The girl shooed off the punkah wallah & gestured for me to stand. She helped me undress down to my chemise so that she could refresh me with rosewater, & I was so hot, so weary, so lonely for Katie & heartsick at having missed Felicity, I moaned when the girl touched my face with the cool sponge. When she finished bathing me, she bowed, as if I had done her some honour, took up her basin & backed out of the room.

I climbed on to the bed, closed the mosquito netting & lay down with legs & arms spread out. After months in a hammock, a real bed seemed absurdly luxurious, & I wondered how it could be that I'd never sufficiently appreciated it. At some point, the punkah wallah must have returned for I felt the air shifting rhythmically over my body. I thought I might die from pleasure, but . . .

Oh, Katie.

I stared at the net canopy sagging above me, grateful to have arrived safely as well as for this comfortable haven, but I could not shake off the sensation of movement, as though the bed rocked on ocean waves or on the poles of a palanquin. Neither mind nor body knew where it was.

March 1856

England indeed. Every evening we eat variations of the same dinner: soup followed by fish, chops, overcooked vegetables, & then puddings & port. As an Old Hand, Lord Chadwick believes that great quantities of meat & wine are the best measures one can take to preserve health. I wonder why no one seems to have noticed that Hindoos in this land have thrived on sparse meals of rice & vegetables for a thousand years without keeling over from the diseases that fell most Englishmen.

Last night, I picked at my lamb chop, its rind of fat beginning to whiten and solidify like a strip of lard, & Lord Chadwick leaned towards me to offer a conspiratorial wink. He said, 'Hearty meals are important. The Dutch say that if we could exchange our blood *for native blood, we would be proof against all their diseases, but don't believe it.' He nodded sharply. 'Meat & wine are the ticket. Now tuck in, my girl.'*

He asked whether, after spending the hot weather in the hills, I would be returning with Felicity to Calcutta. If a girl does not find a husband in the hills, she comes back to Calcutta for the cool season to attend balls & entertainments, always fishing for a proposal. Knowing that Felicity did not intend to return, I answered that I would go wherever Felicity went.

After dinner I like to walk in the garden & often catch whiffs of intriguing cooking smells coming from the godowns. When I join Felicity in the hills, she will educate me in the native diet, for surely these ponderous English meals were never meant for this climate, no matter what the Old Hands say.

March 1856

Usually we have English entertainments in the evening – harpsichord or piano concerts – but last night Lord Chadwick arranged a native entertainment in honour of a local Nawab with whom he has business.

A girl no more than thirteen years old appeared before us swathed in yards & yards of turquoise silk trimmed with a wide gold border. Bearers threw back a curtain and she stood in the doorway, holding the corners of her garment up at shoulder level, making me think of a giant butterfly. On her left, a very black man sat cross-legged, thumping tablas with his fingertips & the heels of his palms. On her right, another black man sawed away at a sitar. The musicians were nondescript bookends, mere appendages to the dazzling creature between them.

Filigree gold earrings framed her copper-coloured face, but she never smiled or looked directly at any guest. She wore no kohl on her eyes, no colour on her lips, & her glossy-black hair had been parted in the middle & brushed back into a sleek chignon. Her young face was deliberately downplayed so as not to distract from the spectacle of her dance. In the candlelit room, her body was a blur of colour & motion. She moved with sensuous grace, seemingly unrestricted by bones or joints or even gravity. I have never seen the like of it.

At first, the strange music sounded dissonant & grating, but the girl drew me in with her serious face & hypnotic dance; I became mesmerized by her serpentine movements & the whisper of whirling silk. That night, I began to fall in love with India.

April 1856

We set out for the hills yesterday. They say 'hills', even though they refer to the mighty Himalayas. Lord Chadwick told me, 'If we said "We're going to the mountains," one might think we were going to Switzerland.'

It will be more than a thousand-mile journey from Calcutta to Simla, first by water up the Hooghly & Ganges & Yamuna by budgero – a sort of cross between a barge & a houseboat – & the final bit by land. I say 'we' because I am travelling with a chaperone, Mrs Daisy Crawley, also off to the hills for the hot weather. Simla is known as the queen of hill stations & is the preferred destination for the hot season. There will be many entertainments at the Club (most of them designed especially for the girls of the Fishing Fleet) & Mrs Crawley & I have four large trunks apiece with our clothes packed in wax cloths. There are more cases filled with cooking implements & another large case carrying my books & journals & some new sketching paper for Felicity. Mrs Crawley, who has made this journey before, has hired an army of servants who, I understand, will work for little more than their daily food. We each have an ayah to tend to our personal needs, a dhobi to wash our clothes, two sweepers to keep things tidy, a cook, a server, & a number of coolies to row & carry.

*I paced the slippery banks of the Hooghly, eager to be off,
watching the sweating coolies load the two budgeros, one for us &
a cookboat for the servants. Later, after getting underway, I sat on
a small rattan chair tied to the deck. From my perch I saw women
bathing in the brown water, their cotton blouses soaked through &
their wet skin glistening in the sun; they smiled & waved unself-
consciously as we poled by.*

I sense Felicity coming closer, & India looks green & bountiful.

April 1856

*When we left the Hooghly & entered the Ganges, I noticed a
different odour to the water, something swampy & ancient.
Now & then, we caught cooking smells wafting from riverside
villages, & once a huge flock of crows flapped out of a tree & fled
over us, blocking the light like an ominous black cloud. The superstitious servants pointed & threw grains of rice into the Ganges for
protection. Mrs Crawley laughed at them.*

*The sinewy men pole us past yellow mustard fields & small rice
paddies dotted with bursts of red, gold & blue – the saris of raven-
haired women who stoop & stand, stoop & stand, tending delicate
green shoots. As I record this, I wonder whether Felicity made
sketches when she came this way. It would be a pleasant thing to
match my writings to her drawings.*

May 1856

*After three weeks on the water, we have embarked on the final leg
by land. We walked through a jute field to a narrow path that
curved up into the hills & disappeared in a distant stand of trees.
The coolies loaded our trunks & cases on to hackeries, rude carts
pulled by thick-necked bullocks, & Mrs Crawley said, 'Now we
shall go by dhoolie.' She pointed to two long contraptions lying on
the ground. The dhoolie is a kind of one-person palanquin but
more like a covered pallet. Instead of a chair or bench it holds a*

thin mattress with straw poking through the muslin & it is completely enclosed by a cloth roof & curtain down the sides. I crawled
in & as soon as the bearers picked up their bamboo shafts, I fell
flat on my back & stayed there. Since the journey was uphill &
lurching it is impossible to sit comfortably, & I was horrified at the
prospect of lying on my back in the claustrophobic dhoolie for six
days. It is like travelling in a coffin, but without the benefit of a
corpse's insensibility. The bearers, sure-footed as goats, jolt & bump
us along whilst we listen to the wooden wheels of the hackeries, &
I wonder how many women have travelled in this preposterous
apparatus.

We stop in the evening & camp in simple tents or in dak
bungalows, which are travellers' huts equipped with rope beds.
'Those back-breaking charpoys,' Mrs Crawley calls them. It is good
to climb out of the dhoolie at the day's end & stand upright,
stretching whilst the servants make camp. Night descends
suddenly in India, dropping down like a curtain on a stage, & we
light lamps to eat with three-tined steel forks worn down to
dagger points. Dinner seems always to be rice & moorghy, which
is some sort of freshly caught fowl, but this is no civilized English
bird. The moorghy stalks up & down India, strengthening his
muscles, & eating him is like chewing wet paper. Still the cook
manages to season him ingeniously & the tough flesh is at least
rendered tasty.

I have noticed that when we camp near a village, morning finds
us with the same number of servants, but they are not the
same individuals. Mrs Crawley says this is typical and sees no
reason to object as long as nothing is missing & we are
not left short-handed. 'They're all the same,' she said, waving me
off.

After dinner, I sit in the cool, soft dark, listening to the night –
crickets & the occasional hoot or scuffle in the trees – whilst I write
my diary. I enjoy the smell of wood smoke in the thin mountain

air, Mrs Crawley's peaceful snore & the low voices of the servants huddled round their fire – not so difficult, I think, to find joy in this land.

May 1856

On the third day, I abandoned my dhoolie, much to the dis-approval of Mrs Crawley & the bewilderment of our bearers. It was not only claustrophobia & boredom that caused my rebellion, but the absurdity of my well-shod feet never touching the earth, whilst barefoot 'boys' carried me uphill.

Mrs Crawley tutted & mumbled as she buttoned herself in for the day, & her bearers looked on enviously as my 'boys' picked up their empty dhoolie. After about an hour they began trading jibes in their foreign tongue, & I did not need to understand the words to catch the sense of their exchange. The four of them who were frowning bore a heavy burden whilst the four who were smiling carried naught but straw & bamboo. Was it an injustice that must be righted or was it simply a twist of fate that must be borne? One bearer patted his backside as he nodded at Mrs Crawley's dhoolie, no doubt making an indelicate reference to her generous figure. But soon they were taking good-natured turns, nimbly relieving each other at regular intervals.

I walked along a path shaded by pines & spruce, admiring the profusion of wild rhododendrons, crimson patches scattered amongst the wild grasses & lichen-covered rocks. Mischievous monkeys scampered through the trees & the air tasted rarefied & delicious. Poor Mrs Crawley, entombed in her dhoolie, would never know what she was missing.

May 1856

Today, straight ahead, at the top of a ridge, I glimpsed the in-credible sight of an English village at seven thousand feet above sea level.

Simla!

Monkeys scrambled over half-timbered cottages & I saw the pale spires of a church, poking through a thick copse of deodar trees. Wave upon wave of blue hills surrounded us, & peeps of snow gleamed in the distance. We skirted the covered stalls of the Indian bazaar clustered lower on the hill, & then we veered left to Masoorla.

May 1856

I arrived in Masoorla yesterday. Mrs Crawley has gone to Simla, & I am here in the countryside – the mofussil – in Felicity's charming bungalow. The bearers set my dhoolie down under a handsome sandalwood tree, & I beheld a thatched-roof bungalow wrapped in a verandah overgrown with flowers & creepers.

It was a tonic & a shock to see Felicity, insolent & joyful as ever, come dancing out of the vine-clad verandah, barefoot in a raspberry sari & wearing gold hoops in her ears. Her complexion is much darkened by the sun & her hair has lightened, as she refuses to wear a pith helmet – a topi, as they call it – preferring simply to pull the end of her sari over her hair when the sun is high. I must say I have never seen her looking healthier. Mrs Crawley was scandalized, & I have no doubt she is at this moment telling her compatriots in Simla about the young woman in the mofussil who has gone irretrievably jungli.

But Felicity & I had no time for Mrs Crawley's opinions. We ran, shrieking like children, into each other's arms. After a long, hard embrace, she stood back & looked me up & down: my bonnet askew, my crushed skirt, & my boots coated with red dust. She said, 'Adela, please tell me you are not wearing stays.' Mrs Crawley huffed as well as any woman can huff in whalebone stays, & Felicity said, 'Thank you for bringing my dear friend to me, Mrs Crawley. May I offer you refreshment?'

We were much in need of a wash & a cup of tea, but Mrs

Crawley eyed the bungalow as if she suspected it to be full of idolators. 'I must be getting on to Simla,' she said, pleasantly enough. Felicity replied, 'Safe journey, then.' We helped Mrs Crawley back into her dhoolie & Felicity waltzed me into her home whilst the bearers followed with my trunks.

We passed through the shady verandah, which is almost entirely enclosed by climbing vines & hanging plants, & entered a high-ceilinged room with bare rafters, much as I'd seen in Calcutta, but smaller. The floor is laid with woven bamboo matting & covered by blue striped dhurrie rugs, which go well with the blue window frames & shutters. Each of the two bedrooms has a large almirah for clothes & linens, & the windows are hung with soft ivory saris. Books are kept in glass cases to protect against white ants, & the plaster walls are tinted a cool grey. Felicity said, 'Sit, Adela. You must be exhausted,' & she plopped herself into a wicker chair beside an oval-backed sofa.

I sat in the other chair, a brocade with heavy teak arms, remarking on how much cooler it felt inside than out. Felicity pointed to reed screens covering the windows. 'Grass tatties,' she said cheerfully. 'The servants keep them wet during the hot weather, & the breeze that comes through is exquisite.'

I said, 'You look well, Felicity,' & she gave me her wonderful sudden smile. 'But your dress . . . & you have no shoes. And where is your mother?'

'Of course I have shoes, you goose. But I don't need them in the house, do I? And you'll soon see how lovely it is to wear a sari, elegant as any ball gown & one hundred times more comfortable. As for Mother . . .' She laughed lightly. 'Mother is the wife of a governor & would never live in a humble bungalow like this. You saw our grand house in Calcutta.'

'But where is she, then?'

'She has a lovely suite of rooms in Simla, where she can eat fancy pastries at Peliti's & play whist & watch cricket with the *other ladies from the Club. She plays tennis, enjoys her gin pegs in the evening & carries on harmless flirtations.'*

'Do you see her at all?'

Felicity lost her smile. 'When I arrived in Calcutta I stood on the dock a long time waiting for her. In fact, she was standing quite nearby, but we didn't recognize each other until almost everyone had cleared off. It had been ten years, after all, & we really don't know each other.' She shrugged. 'Mother is appalled at the way I choose to live, but I have my allowance & she has hers, so . . .'

Her voice trailed away, but before I could respond, Felicity looked past me & called out, 'Come along, Lalita. Meet my good friend, Memsahib Adela.' I turned to see a girl in a white sari, about twelve or thirteen years old, glide into the room. The child offered me a salaam & then backed away with praying hands.

Felicity said, 'Lalita is my ayah, something like a lady's maid, & she will attend you as well.' At this my face must have clouded over, for Felicity hastened to say, 'I'm so sorry about Kaitlin. It must have been dreadful for you to lose her.'

'There was nothing I could do. I think about her every day.'

We were quiet then, & a man in white kurta pyjamas & a blue turban brought in a tray with tea & mango slices on a plate. Felicity said, 'Thank you, Khalid.' She nodded at the tray. 'Please refresh yourself. The water bearer is drawing your bath, & afterwards you shall have a long lovely nap. Your room is aired & ready.' She poured hot creamy tea from a chipped pot. 'This is Indian tea,' she said. 'Masala chai.' She handed me a cup, & I was delighted by the sweet, spicy taste.

I sat back in my chair, suddenly exhausted. No more budgeros or dhoolies, no more Mrs Crawley or stuffy Calcutta drawing rooms, & Lady Chadwick happily tucked away in Simla. It was perfect. I rested my head on the chair back whilst a bandy-legged water bearer fetched my bathwater from the well, heated it outside over an open fire, & hauled it in to fill the zinc tub, four gallons at a time. At a nod from Felicity, Lalita knelt at my feet & took off my boots.

June 1856

Truly I saw nothing of India in Calcutta except the inside of palanquins & English dining rooms. But here itinerant vendors come to the door – box wallahs carrying an eclectic miscellany of goods on their heads – & farmers drive bullock carts up & down the road outside our compound. The godowns are located so close to the house, it feels almost as if we live with the servants. We ride to the village every morning for exercise, & in the afternoon monkeys cavort in the sandalwood tree in front of the bungalow, sometimes scampering along the window ledges & swinging into our verandah to sit in the wicker chairs as if waiting for tea. Sometimes Felicity stands under the sandalwood tree & tosses sweetmeats up to them. Hindoos consider the sandalwood tree holy & judge it auspicious to have one in front of the house.

We are surrounded by wild purple heliotrope & red bougainvillea & white rhododendron. Felicity has planted beds of fiery Indian marigolds beneath the sandalwood tree & along the verandah simply because she finds them cheerful. The natives, too, favour marigolds for garlands & temple offerings, & I have decided that their sunny hue is a universal symbol of joy. Other flowers wax & wane with the weather, but the sturdy marigolds bloom tirelessly through hot & cold, simply to keep our hearts glad.

Chapter Fourteen

1947

THE MUTED SQUEAK of the Red Flyer's rubber wheels echoed in the vaulted silence of the Buddhist temple, and I was glad Billy had fallen asleep; his high, sweet voice would surely ricochet off the walls. The stone floor was cool under my bare feet, but I felt like an intruder and I suppressed an urge to walk on tiptoe.

It was much smaller than Christ Church, more like the gaily painted little Hindu temples that I saw everywhere, but simpler. A calligraphy scroll hung on one wall, and a multi-coloured thangka depicting Indian myths hung on another. As in Hindu temples, there were no chairs, but instead of Ganesh or Hanuman, a massive stone Buddha sat under a gold cloth canopy, and at his feet, an array of butter lamps flickered amid a scattering of offerings: marigolds, a bowl of rice, browning apple slices, bidis and the odd item – a curling leaf, a black and white photo, a beaded bracelet – whose significance was known only to the supplicant and Buddha.

The relative emptiness of the place felt foreign. I was accustomed to stained glass and pipe organs, gilded saints, silver candelabras, and ceilings covered with naked cherubim.

By comparison, the Buddhist temple felt stark, and there was a sense of waiting.

A man in white kurta pyjamas padded through a side entrance, his bare feet softly slapping the stone floor. I realized this was no tourist attraction and said, 'Excuse me . . . I was just going.'

His shaved head shone bronze in the candlelight, his eyes were coffee-bean brown, and his skin was like dark honey. He was not handsome, not at all, but his face was likeable – his forehead seemed too large, almost bulbous, and his features were compressed into the centre of his face. His eyebrows slanted down at the corners, giving him a look of ironic patience. The man put his hands together in an attitude of prayer and said, 'It's quite all right, Madam. I'm an interloper myself.'

His British accent caught me off guard. 'You're English?'

'Eurasian. Born in Delhi of an Indian mother and English father who, amazingly, didn't try to hide me. That would make me a very fortunate Eurasian. I read law at Cambridge.'

I felt excitement rise in my chest like bubbles in champagne. Here was an Indian who might be a bridge between East and West, a source of understanding. I said, 'May I ask why you came back to India? ' I thought he looked disappointed and hurried to say, 'I don't mean you shouldn't have.'

He smiled. 'Many would wonder why anyone would leave the comforts of Europe. I came with some of my colleagues to assist Gandhi three years ago and rediscovered my mother's spiritual roots in Ladakh. At the moment I'm attempting a meditative retreat at an ashram, but frankly it's not going well. I find the silence quite unbearable, and I tend to sneak out every day. I walk around town just to hear the sounds of life, and I end up here.'

'Well, that's honest.' I offered him my hand. 'My name is Evie Mitchell.'

He did not shake my hand, but stepped back, pressing his praying hands firmly to his nose and bowing deeply. Later, I would learn that while on retreat Buddhist men refrain from physical contact with women. He said, 'A pleasure, Mrs Mitchell. My name is Haripriya, but you can call me Hari.' He looked slyly amused. 'Harry, if you like.'

I'd been dithering around trying to understand India for months, and here was an Indian who truly spoke my language. I saw the heavy, opaque door to that inscrutable country swinging open, and I returned Harry's bow. 'Please, call me Evie.' I gestured at Billy, still asleep in his wagon. 'This is my son, Billy. We were out for a stroll and I saw the temple. I couldn't resist coming in.'

'I understand. It's human, don't you think? To be drawn to places of transcendence.'

'Is that it? Transcendence?'

'I think so.' He chuckled. 'Or in my case, escape. We get up so bloody early, every day seems endless.' He shook his head. 'I have a long way to go.'

'Well, since we're being honest, I came out today sleuthing for information that's probably none of my business, but I've become intrigued. I'm living in a house where an English lady lived about ninety years ago. I've found her letters, and her friend is buried in a graveyard in Masoorla.' I stopped short, amazed to hear myself talk so freely about Felicity and Adela for the first time, and to a stranger. But it felt good. 'I believe they were here during the Sepoy Mutiny, and I'd like to know what happened to them. But . . .' I shrugged. 'Ninety years . . .'

Harry smiled, more with his eyes than his mouth. He said, 'In India, ninety years is nothing. The monks at the ashram have records from before the Moghuls. Almost every-thing that has happened here has been written down somewhere by someone. When did your elusive ladies write their letters?'

Gentle excitement swelled in my chest. 'The letters are dated from 1854 to 1856.'

'And their names?'

'Adela Winfield and Felicity Chadwick.'

He nodded, committing the names to memory, then said, 'Two young women living alone in the *mofussil*? That would have been highly unusual. Girls came out to India to find husbands, and if they didn't succeed in a year they went back home. Poor things were called "Returned Empties".' He shook his head. 'But you've made me curious. I'll check our records.'

'Wonderful.'

'Sad to say, you can find me here every day about this time. I'm sure they think I'm in my cell communicating with my inner self. Unfortunately, I've discovered that my inner self is rather a bore.'

I laughed. 'I'm sure that's not true.'

Billy stirred and sat up in his wagon. Bleary with sleep, he looked soft and defenceless, his eyelids pink and puffy. Harry and I watched him rub his eyes. I said, 'Hi there, sleepyhead.'

'Hi.' Billy looked at Harry, then at me, then back at Harry. He said, 'Who the heck are you?'

'Billy, that's rude.' I turned to Harry apologetically. 'He's only five.'

Harry smiled and bent down with his hands on his knees. 'I was just talking to your mother.'

Billy scowled at me. 'I thought we're not supposed to talk to strangers.'

'*You* are not supposed to talk to strangers. This is Harry.'

Harry bent down further and put his hand out. 'Glad to meet you, Billy.'

Billy's little hand shot out, quick as thought, and he squeezed Harry's nose between the knuckles of two fingers. He said, 'Gotcher nose!' He stuck the tip of his thumb between his fingers and wiggled it, laughing. His cheeks glowed like waxed apples.

'OK, Peach.' I shrugged another apology. 'My father taught him that.'

Harry laughed and said, 'A child's mind. How enviable.'

'We should be going. But I'm happy to have met you.' With the awkwardness of a novice, I pressed my palms together, saying, 'Namaste.' I hesitated, and then, 'I hope to see you again.'

He said, 'I'll see if our records say anything about your English ladies.'

'You're very kind.' I wheeled the wagon around, and Billy wiggled his thumb. 'I still have your nose.' I threw a sheepish grin over my shoulder, and then another question made me turn back. 'One more thing.'

'Yes?'

'What do you think about Partition?'

Harry looked at me with a kind of weariness. 'I think that when you create borders based on ideology you create a reason to fight. When you live side by side, you create a reason to get along.'

'But we're safe in Simla, aren't we? Someone told us we'd be safe here.'

'Perhaps, or perhaps not, but there are many things more important than safety.' Harry's demeanour of ironic patience deepened. 'Anyway, is anyone ever safe?'

Chapter Fifteen

1856

FROM THE journal of Adela Winfield:

June 1856

Beyond our little compound, cows wander at will. The roads are full of ox carts & camels & elephants & people, always people. Women collect cow dung from the road & take it home to make cakes of it to dry in the scorching sun for cooking fuel.

I cannot keep the servants straight. We have at least two dozen, although there are always more in the godowns than we have hired. The extras are the caste-brothers who come by for a daily gossip & whatever bit of patronage might fall their way.

Ours is considered a small staff. It takes a multitude to accomplish anything because caste & custom complicate the simplest task. For example, a server cannot let the sweeper's shadow fall on him, & a Hindoo cannot enter the cookhouse or even touch our plates, which are polluted. As foreigners, we are Untouchables. Mohammedans are preferred as servants, as worshippers of one God & people of the book, but I cannot yet tell them apart from Hindoos.

Our bearer, Khalid, assigns daily chores in the bungalow, but how do they manage all these rules whilst living together in the godowns? Only the syce – the groom – is on his own, living in the stable with the ponies, & Lalita, who lives in the village & walks to work.

We have our own cow, which the servants consider even more auspicious than the sandalwood tree. To buy milk from unknown sources is to pay a high price for cholera & a plethora of other diseases, which is absurd since they can easily be had for free. The cowherd, who would disdain to bring water to a horse, is honoured to live within range of the cow's sacred odour. I have seen our cow wearing a string of blue beads around her horns & contentedly munching hay poached from the pony.

The cookhouse is separate from the bungalow, & Felicity has gone to great lengths to befriend the cook, Hakim. I wonder whether she is compelled by her memory of food defiled by human ashes or by her democratic inclinations. Felicity took me into the cookhouse to meet Hakim, & I'm afraid I could not disguise my distress at the dirt-floor shack they call a kitchen. There is a shelf of questionable condiments dear to Hakim's heart, a table for chopping, & a stove precariously constructed from scavenged mud bricks. A hollow in the top was full of glowing charcoals, which Hakim fanned with a palm frond; he has a tin box to serve as an oven. I suggested the possibility of sending to Calcutta, or even to England, for a proper cooker, but Hakim sees no reason to afflict himself with the complicated ways of the foreigner. Felicity, too, is content with this arrangement, which is familiar to her from her childhood.

But I saw leftovers crusty with mould & milk stored in an old kerosene can. I lifted a kettle & a family of cockroaches scattered in a panic. The day's market basket sat on the table heaped with cauliflower, beans & potatoes, but a feeble squawk revealed a live pigeon with its wings twisted round one another, snuggling next to a joint of raw mutton. Mohammedan law forbids the killing of pigeons, but encourages the eating of them. The solution appears to be to allow the poor creature to expire on its own.

At seven every morning, Khalid delivers chota hazri to Felicity & me in our bedrooms. I take only toast & tea, but I would enjoy a serving of kedgeree if I could face the prospect, first thing in the morning, of fish & eggs prepared in that squalid shed. In spite of Hakim's satisfaction with his domain, I hope to persuade Felicity to build a proper kitchen. I believe it is the only thing lacking to make this place perfect. I marvel at my own lack of fear in this place steeped in strange sights & smells & customs. Every day is a new adventure, a new revelation, & I have acquired a taste for embracing the unknown. My life has achieved new dimensions & I feel richer for them. Apparently English roses and roast beef are not necessary for my happiness.

July 1856

The monsoons are supposed to commence on June 15th, & on that day everyone looks at the sky full of expectation & shorn of patience. After months of punkahs, & hot winds, & dust coating the trees, it is necessary to define the exact limit of one's endurance; after June 15th it is simply not possible to go on enduring. So when the sun marched across the sky on June 15th without winking, we broke.

Felicity & I lay about the bungalow in a stupor, servants failed to appear when called, & one of our ponies dropped dead. By the following week, rickshaw wallahs refused all fares until sunset, the water bearer constantly drenched the grass tatties & then himself to little effect, & I woke irritable in the night & rose stealthily to shake the sleeping punkah wallah.

The dry earth split, heat lightning crackled in the sky, & the sandalwood tree hung limp & grey under a coating of powder from the road. Crows hopped about with beaks agape, & evil odours from the river wafted up to us. Sealing wax melted, books curled up in protest, & always the punkah stopped in the night. Day after day the sun set in an angry red glow, & the natives wondered how they had offended Lakshmi.

Finally, on June 28th, clouds gathered over the mountains & everyone stared but dared not speak. The first rain roared down like a solid wall of water, & Felicity & I ran outside to dance barefoot in the downpour. Farmers dropped to their knees in the mud to give thanks.

It stopped abruptly, & the air was so heavy it felt like breathing through wet cotton. But when sunshine broke through, the landscape sparkled as though newly washed, & the sandalwood tree echoed with birdsong. The sodden earth steamed gently until new clouds gathered sulkily over the mountains, & the monsoon resumed with renewed strength.

It has rained for a week without stopping, & pernicious green mould creeps over paper, cloth & leather. Fishtail insects feed on my books, & the house grows a pelt. White ants tunnel up from the ground to devour the bamboo matting whilst stink beetles, caterpillars & centipedes invade the house. Some of the insects fascinate us with their delicate beauty: moths with diaphanous green wings, blood-red flies & woolly caterpillars with orange stripes. We have begun a collection of oddities in jars.

At night the moon peeks through the clouds & glimmers in pools of rainwater, twinkling like a field of fallen stars around the verandah. We fall asleep to the croaking of frogs & the patter of rain on the thatch roof.

August 1856

Yesterday morning I heard Felicity coughing in her room, but she insisted it was nothing. I have heard of consumptives who enjoy a respite only to be stricken again months or even years later, but she assures me she feels fine. Fortunately, I brought along a goodly supply of pulmonic wafers, which seemed to help during her last *illness. I was also required to bring tremendous quantities of quinine, ipecac, Eno powder, iodine, castor oil, mercurial salts & tartar emetic. Mother simply could not stop talking about cholera, blackwater fever, typhoid, dysentery & malaria. She would be tragically aggrieved if I were to perish unmarried. I felt tempted to tell her that according to Fanny Parks, all one needs to cure anything is a big black ball of opium in a hubble-bubble, but I did not want to discourage her from sending me to India.*

In the afternoon, we bought odds & ends from an itinerant box wallah who came to the door clad only in a turban & loincloth, carrying a large tin box on his head. He spread his wares on the verandah & we bought lead pencils, carbolic soap, hill honey & ribbons. I almost bought a toothbrush, but Felicity warned me that these were always secondhand, pilfered from the rubbish or the home of another sahib. We shall continue to use neem twigs to polish our teeth, & I am beginning to enjoy the sharp, bitter taste. Felicity bought a pair of Persian morning slippers – plum velvet with gold embroidery – whose turned-up toes delighted her.

August 1856

When we fancy an outing we ride through the village. Felicity has had the durzi – that's what one calls the tailor – fashion ingenious riding skirts that are split up the middle so that we can ride astride rather than sidesaddle. It felt quite improper at first, but I'm used to it now & cannot help but smile at the scandal we would cause if either of our mothers saw us riding thus. It would seem we enjoy being wicked women.

In the village, we meander in the small bazaar, where merchants sit on the ground in front of their open stalls smoking a hookah whilst they await customers. Sometimes we buy small roasted gourds stuffed with fennel & browned onions or hot vegetable fritters that leave their leaf cones slick with grease.

Felicity takes these opportunities to deliver lentils & Mother

Bailey's Quieting Syrup to a small orphanage run by Scottish missionaries. Last week, on our way to the orphanage, a woman set a naked toddler down in the dirt directly in our path. We called to the woman as she ran off, but she did not look back. We watched the little one cry weakly until she fell over in an unnatural sleep. Felicity dismounted & went to her, & I watched her face darken as she examined the child's distended stomach. Felicity said her mother probably could not feed her & left her here for us. We brought the child to the orphanage..

Felicity says the children become 'rice Christians', willing to pray to whichever god you like for a meal. But she has no quarrel with the missionaries, saying, 'Better Jesus & a full belly than the slave market. A four-year-old girl is worth two horses in Peshawar.' I'm sure she's right. Still I wonder how I'd feel if a group of Indians came to England to make Hindoos or Mohammedans of us.

She brings the children sugar cane, which they peel with their teeth & chew to a pulp, leaving their faces & hands smeared & sticky. I have seen Felicity kiss children with crusty eyes & scabby legs. Sometimes she gathers a few waifs under a pipal tree in the mission compound to teach them a word or two of English, which everyone finds quite jolly.

I fear she will contract some loathsome disease, but she says she was born here & is immune. Once, when I glanced uneasily around the bare, dusty compound full of scruffy children, she touched my arm gently & said, 'No judgement. Only joy.'

'Not judgement,' I answered. 'Caution.'

'Adela, dearest. In India, one can be full of life at noon & buried before dinner. If I must choose between joy & caution, I choose joy.' With that she swooped up a mangy, half-naked child & danced away singing that silly American ditty, 'Camptown Ladies', with a tattered band of urchins clamouring happily after her.

September 1856

Hallelujah! She has agreed to build a proper kitchen. Hakim mutters & sulks in his fetid hut, as bewildered at the idea of cooking inside the house as my mother might be at keeping oxen in the bedroom. In a foreign kitchen not entirely his own, he cannot be sure a pigeon mightn't be killed or even, Allah forbid, the odd pork chop find a way in. When he threatened to quit, Felicity agreed to leave his cookhouse standing, assuring him the new kitchen would only be for our amusement. At this he was slightly mollified, but he eyed us with suspicion, fearing the new arrangement might reduce his income. If we begin buying our own foodstuffs, he will lose the customary commission he takes at the market stalls. I suspect that Hakim cooks nothing better than his books.

Coolies arrive daily with loads of brick & timber, & we have sent to Calcutta for a beautiful modern cooker.

September 1856

Invitations to dances & amateur theatricals come from Simla with assurances that there will be six men to every woman. Thus far we have begged off, but we did accept an invitation to tea with Felicity's mother. Apparently she wanted, at long last, to meet her daughter's companion & perhaps to verify whether Mrs Crawley's undoubtedly alarming report was entirely accurate. Felicity thought it best to put her at ease so that she might leave us in peace.

We wore demure dresses & crinolines, which smelled of camphor from disuse, & hired a tonga to take us to the Ladies' Club in Simla, where we took a room for the night.

Simla is an oddly distorted version of an English village set in an Indian landscape – prim, half-timbered cottages amidst Himalayan pines & terraced hills, misty blue mountains, & the smell of dung fires rising up from the labyrinthine native quarter below. It is built around a wide central street known as the Mall, one of the few semi flat stretches in the area, & along the Mall one finds scores of English shops with pots of red geraniums at their doors, a proper hotel with good mahogany bedsteads & Peleti's tearoom, where one drinks tea from fine china cups. It seems as if someone had lifted a whole English village – house by house, shop by shop, custom by custom – & transplanted the whole lot to the Himalayas. The Mall is full of Britons in tongas & rickshaws, but no Indians apart from servants. There are signs that read 'No Indians or dogs'. Memsahibs in bustles sip tea at outdoor cafés & small white children in miniature pith helmets romp about freely. There are none over the age of six or seven, at which time they are sent to England, as was Felicity.

Looking up, one sees Christ Church high on the ridge, an edifice which, with its soaring spires & magnificent stained glass, would not seem out of place anywhere in England. Looking down, one sees long flights of crooked stone steps leading into the native quarter, a dark warren of cramped streets crowded with tiny shops & stalls & temples.

About two miles from the Mall one comes to Annandale, the spot for cricket & polo. On weekends, genteel crowds sit in folding chairs to watch men wheel ponies in tight turns amid triumphant yelps & pounding hooves.

We met Lady Chadwick & others in her circle – they call themselves the Exiles – at Peliti's. As the burra memsahib of the group, Lady Chadwick sat at the head of a linen-covered table set with heavy silver & fresh flowers; she ordered the servants about with imperious flicks of her wrists. Felicity was uncommonly quiet, but she looked charming in a high-collared, slightly outdated pink taffeta she bought at Swan & Edgar. We even carried parasols.

But I fear our disguise was inadequate to fool the memsahibs in their wide-brimmed topis & starched dresses. They could smell the camphor on us, & they already regarded Felicity as an incorrigible woman of inexplicable tendencies. I, of course, am guilty by

*association. Although polite, they spoke around us about polo &
cricket & the fashions in their six-month-old catalogues. They did,
however, ask us when we might return to Calcutta for the season
& we skirted the question with a trumped-up story about a sick
servant. Lady Chadwick & her friends will leave next month.*

*We were relieved to return to our jungli little bungalow. That
evening, Felicity wrapped herself in her favourite lavender sari, &
we sat on the verandah with our shoes off, listening to doves coo
& watching a breeze stir the sandalwood tree. Easy talk dwindled
as the moon rose, & we put our feet up whilst we smoked Felicity's
pretty brass hookah with the carved ebony mouthpiece.*

September 1856

*Some evenings we light a lamp & take our needlework to the
verandah, crocheting or embroidering decorative pillow casings.
The indigenous designs are flamboyantly beautiful & I am quite
pleased with a coral & turquoise afghan I have crocheted. Hot
colours shot through with gold. I used yarn made from the hair of
baby mountain goats from Kashmir, soft & voluptuous & dyed in
vibrant hues appropriate to this lush place.*

*Felicity is utterly content here, with her sketching, her charity
work, her pony & her hookah, but I feel increasingly off balance.
For one thing, I miss Katie & wonder daily what has become of
her. I have sent letters to Cook, but have had no reply. When I
return to England – for this is no place for an Englishwoman to
grow old – I will look for her. Even if she were not already on my
mind, the sensuality of this place would remind me of her. Men
glisten with perspiration, women sway along in gossamer veils, &
the lush landscape burgeons, wild & fleshy. Even religion here
seems fraught with eroticism – Hindoo carvings of dancing girls &
carefree fornicators, & Mohammedans making one think constantly of sex by keeping women sequestered in purdah behind the
high walls of the zenana.*

I have given up my corset & crinolines & must say it has been a revelation. At first I felt soft & naked & even a bit slovenly without my corset, but the ease of movement & the joy of taking a deep breath without strain soon put vanity in perspective. The crinolines always struck me as a silly nuisance & I was instantly happy to be rid of them. So I go about in simple cotton dresses & minimal underwear, but I have not gone so far as to wear a sari – yet – & I simply cannot walk about without shoes, even indoors. The great variety of creepy crawlies discourage me, but I admit my leather boots are a bit much for the climate. I compromise with native slippers woven of jute.

As for India, the novelty is wearing off & my thirst for adventure is waning as well. Even as it becomes more familiar I sense that this place is too big, too old, & too confusing for me ever to feel that I belong. It's like trying to grab hold of a single image in a kaleidoscope whilst it changes.

This week the punkahs will come down.

Chapter Sixteen

1947

RASHMI ARRIVED, smiling as always, with a garland of marigolds that she hung on the cane headboard of our bed.

'What's that, Rashmi?'

'Good luck, mala. You can see? I am making puja for you and sir.'

Christ, not again. 'Thanks, Rashmi, but you really don't have to.'

'Not for worrying, Madam. Mala very good for Shiva.'

'OK. That's great.'

'I am knowing other white lady from Australia. She is telling me like charm mala is working.'

'OK.'

'You know Australia?'

'Yes.'

'Nice village in England.'

'In England?'

'All white people there. Verrry rich, but not so happy in bed.'

'OK. Thanks for the mala.'

'Working one hundred per cent for Australian lady.'

'The one in England.'

'Yeeess.' She gawked at me as if I were slow. 'Very happy in bed now. Verrry haaappy your good self too.'

'Right.'

The curry that night was lurid pink; it was thick with potatoes and peas and cauliflower, but the meat was un-identifiable; Martin guessed water buffalo. Tired of trying to convince him to counter the spice with yogurt instead of water, I had mixed the entire bowl of raita into the red curry, and the damn stuff turned the angry colour of a skin rash. It resembled a plate of lumpy Pepto-Bismol, but it wasn't spicy. Martin took a bite and shoved out his bottom lip. 'Not bad,' he said. 'You finally got through to Habib about the peppers.'

'I guess I did.' No point in being smug. 'Is that a new kurta?' Martin had begun wearing white cotton tunics, the top half of a native's kurta pyjamas. They were cool and loose, and he said dressing like that made the natives more comfortable around him. By now the only Western thing about him were his incongruous gabardine slacks.

He said, 'Walker showed me a cheap place in the Lakkar bazaar. That guy has been here so long he pays the native prices for everything.' He looked down at the loose white tunic and smiled. 'Thiry cents!'

'Just stay away from skullcaps and turbans. You don't want to be mistaken for a Hindu by an angry Muslim, or vice versa.'

He laughed. 'Fat chance. My Hindi has the most awful American accent you can imagine.'

'Any news today?'

Between bites, Martin told me Reuters had reported more riots in Calcutta and Lahore. 'Gandhi is running around trying to quell the violence but . . . well, Walker says they love the old guy, but when they're pissed they don't listen to him.'

'How human of them.' I pushed pink rice around my plate. 'Have any more wires been cut?'

'A couple.'

I tensed, and he quickly added, 'Not here.'

'Are the telephones working?'

Martin chewed a second too long before he said, 'More or less.' He applied himself to the curry and his face shut down; I knew there was no point pressing for details. I said, 'I took Billy for a walk today.'

'Oh?'

'We ran into Edward and Lydia.'

'Lucky you.'

'They're unbearable.'

Martin chewed thoughtfully. 'In a paradoxical way, their kind of arrogance kept the peace.'

'You've got to be kidding.'

Martin loaded his fork with pink curry and said, 'British imperialism united Muslims and Hindus against a common enemy. But now that the Brits are pulling out, all those ancient religious feuds are boiling over.'

'And so Partition.'

Martin nodded. 'A lot of Muslims like the idea of having their own country – especially Jinnah, who would be the top dog. But August is too soon. Everyone is confused and scared, and extremists on both sides are stirring them up.'

I stared at my plate. 'Why can't the Brits just hand the country over and let the Indians sort themselves out?'

'There is no central government to hand it over to. The British have ruled here for centuries. Gandhi has the Indian National Congress, which is mostly Hindu, and Jinnah has the Muslim League, but they don't want the same things.' He spoke around a mouthful of curry. 'Compromise is difficult because Hindus and Muslims are completely committed to their religions. It's their identity.'

'Speaking of religion, Rashmi is making puja for us.'

'What?'

I hadn't planned to tell him, but I wanted to see his reaction. Would he apologize? Would he be embarrassed? Would he laugh? 'She says there's no "sexy time" in our bed. She's praying to Shiva.' I fiddled with my curry, wishing he would reach for my hand.

Martin put down his fork, disgusted. 'That's great.'

'Don't you think it's funny? A little funny?'

'Yeah, hilarious.' He rubbed his forehead as if the subject didn't bear thinking about. As if the idea of sex with me was *offensive*. Hurt and confused, I couldn't get away from the subject fast enough.

I said, 'Today we met a guy on retreat at an ashram. Billy grabbed his nose like Da does.' I smiled at the memory. 'Harry something. Interesting man.'

Distracted, Martin said, 'There's an ashram in Masoorla?'

'Oh, no. We met him in town.'

'What?'

'In Simla. That's where I saw Edward and Lydia.'

'You went into Simla with Billy?'

I raised my eyebrows. 'Why not?'

Martin pushed his plate away. 'I don't believe you, Evie.'

'We just went for a walk.'

'Riots and protests all over the place, and you decide to take Billy out for a walk?' He tapped his head to indicate that *someone* was not playing with a full deck.

'Oh for God's sake, Simla was as peaceful as a lake. You expect us to stay in the house like prisoners?'

'Things blow up in an instant.' His voice inched up a

couple of decibels. 'I expect you to keep yourself and Billy out of harm's way.'

I put my fork down and drilled him with my eyes. 'We used to live in a big, crime-ridden city. We went shopping and to the movies. We went downtown. We rode buses. We went to restaurants and to the lake. We never considered pulling down the shades and hiding in a corner. The terrible things we read in the paper didn't stop us from getting on with our lives. And now that we've come halfway around the world to this fascinating place, *now* you want me to stay home?'

Martin slapped his napkin on the table. 'Big-city crime and civil war are not the same.' His voice got louder. 'I didn't think I had to say this, but I'm telling you now – do not go into town.'

'What about my English classes?'

'That's the village. You can go that far.'

Somehow, a specific boundary made it worse. You can go as far as the harem wall, as far as the barbed-wire fence, and not one step further. I gripped the table edge as if that would keep me from flying apart. I shouted, 'You're being ridiculous. There's no war here. Your war is over, Martin. For God's sake, it's *over*.'

Martin stood up so fast his chair unbalanced and toppled backward. I flinched at the crash, and Martin loomed over me; the muscles in his neck knotted and bulged. Just then, I heard a whimper and turned to see Billy coming towards us, rubbing his eyes and dragging Spike by the tail. 'What are you guys yelling about?'

'Perfect.' I released the table edge and hurried to Billy. As I picked him up, he laid his cheek on my shoulder.

Martin righted his chair and mumbled, 'Sorry, son. Everything is OK.'

I carried Billy back to his bedroom and laid him down. He stared up at me and said, 'I don't like it when you and Daddy yell.'

'I know, Peach. I'm sorry we woke you.' I tucked Spike in next to him.

'Yelling is scary.'

'Don't be scared. It's OK.' I kissed him and drew the mosquito netting. 'No more yelling, I promise. Go to sleep now.'

Billy curled around Spike, and I walked out of the room and stood outside his door. If I went back to the dining room it was a good bet there would be more yelling, so I marched to our stark white bedroom and closed the door. Only the thought of Billy sleeping nearby kept me from slamming it.

The next morning I found Martin on the sofa, where he'd spent the night wrapped in the coral and turquoise afghan. I studied him, snoring and unshaven, and noticed a half-empty glass of Scotch on the side table. How long, I wondered? How long can we go on like this?

Reverend Locke was a lanky Englishman whose long, pale face and clerical collar concealed a waggish personality. When I opened the door to him that morning, he executed an exaggerated bow, and displayed his gap-toothed smile with disarming unselfconsciousness. He said, 'Mrs Mitchell!' It sounded like an announcement.

'Reverend, good of you to come.'

I swung the door wide, and he flourished my pencilled note as he walked in. 'Want to investigate us, do you? Looking for skeletons?'

'Not at all. I've taken an interest in Indian history.'

'I dare say you'll find skeletons, whether you want to or

not. People, you know.' He waved circles in the air, as if the subject was simply too bizarre for him.

'Would you care for tea?'

'Splendid!' He dropped into the green wingback chair, and I popped my head into the kitchen to ask Rashmi to serve tea. When I returned to the living room Reverend Locke said, 'Well, what d'ya think of us? Don't say you haven't been here long enough to form an opinion. The first thing everyone does here is form an opinion; it can't be helped.' He shook his head, suddenly disappointed. 'It was once quite original, you know. In 1800 we had chartered accountants in full mufti, lying about on pillows, smoking hookahs, and Scotsmen wearing tartan turbans and sporting Sikh beards. But all that was over by 1830. Now everyone is *respectable*. Damn shame.'

Rashmi waddled in with the tea tray and set it down. She stood there, appraising this man who had come to visit a married lady in the middle of the day without her husband present. I had to say, 'Thank you, Rashmi,' and raise an eyebrow at her. In the end, I think Reverend Locke's clerical collar must have exempted him from suspicion because she said, 'Come, *beta*,' and Billy followed her out to the verandah.

I said, 'Colourful as 1800 sounds, it's not the period I'm curious about. Recently I heard about the Sepoy Mutiny of 1857.' I poured tea and offered him a cup.

'Ah, the Sepoy Mutiny.' He took the cup and sipped. 'Well, we call it a mutiny; Indians call it the First War of Independence.' He crossed his legs and balanced the cup and saucer on his knee. 'By 1857 there'd been years of bad feelings about caste violations, arrogant officers and zealous missionaries. It all blew up when the Crown issued the sepoys cartridges greased with cow or pig fat. Not clear which. Possibly both.' The gap-toothed smile flashed without warning. 'No sense offending only Hindus or Muslims when you can offend the whole lot at one go.' The smile disappeared and he inspected his tea. 'You see, the sepoys had to put the cartridges between their teeth to break the seal. Completely taboo. The Crown denied everything, of course. Told the sepoys to make their own grease from beeswax if they didn't like it, but it was too late. The sepoys believed it was part of a plot to make them break caste and convert to Christianity and . . . well, they rose up.'

'Did the trouble reach Simla?'

He took a sip of tea thoughtfully. 'After the massacre at Kanpur, British troops were dispatched from the cantonment here as well as other places; they swept through most of northern India.'

'Do you suppose the church records say anything about it?'

'They might. I think our records go back to 1850. There were often gaps between clerics and records were kept by anyone willing to take the time, so they tend to be patchy. But there are all sorts of things about the trials and tribulations of colonial life. Come along any time.' He drained his cup and stood. 'Excellent tea, Mrs Mitchell.'

I set my cup on the tray. 'I always ask Rashmi to use Assam in the afternoon, but I think this was English breakfast tea.'

He nodded amiably. 'Glad to know the Empire is still spreading civilization.'

At the door I asked, 'Would this afternoon be convenient?'

'Splendid!'

That day, Rashmi took the garbage and left early on some mysterious mission, and an hour later, Habib came through the back door carrying his ominous wicker basket. He began unloading onions and chilli peppers and an assortment of other-worldly vegetables. Habib always came into the kitchen looking suspicious of what he might find; his eyes were inky and his face buttoned up. Unlike good-humoured Rashmi, he moved around silently, as if cooking was only an excuse for espionage. He responded to my greetings with a cautious head waggle.

But that day, I said hello, and he smiled. It was a quick and guarded smile, but I counted it as a small victory. Then it was down to business as he piled onions, carrots, eggplant and a small hunk of bloody meat on the chopping block. Out came the heavy knife and the big pot, and that night's culinary ordeal got underway.

I didn't want to take Billy to Christ Church, fearing another scene with Martin. Rashmi was gone, and although cooks were accustomed to having the sahib's children around I didn't want Billy to get underfoot. I gathered odds and ends from the house and arranged everything on the living-room floor – my opal earrings, a silver necklace and a gold bracelet (he liked to pretend they were pirate treasure), a sack of pistachios (his favourite), the jade elephant god (which he wasn't normally allowed to play with), a small box of crayons (taken out only occasionally to make them last), the plastic buttons that he used for tiddlywinks, the boar bristle hairbrush we used to groom Spike, a box of Billy's favourite cookies (a shameless bribe), a round bar of sandalwood soap (he loved the smell), and one of Martin's cheap kurtas, for playing dressing up like Dad.

Out on the verandah I asked, 'How would you and Spike like to play bazaar?'

His face lit up. 'Are we going to town?'

'No, Pickle. I made a bazaar for you in the living room.'

Billy came in and stared at the cookies, the crayons and his father's kurta. He said, 'Why does Dad dress like the people in the bazaar?'

'It's comfortable. So do you want to play bazaar?'

He whispered to Spike and the little cowboy hat tilted forward. He said, 'Can we buy stuff?'

'Absolutely. And when Habib starts cooking, it will even smell like the bazaar.'

Billy whisked his thumb and forefinger together as he had seen people do in the shops.

'Money? You bet.' I dug around in my purse and came up with a handful of pice. Handing them over, I had the passing thought that the rent would be due before Martin's next pay-cheque, but I knew there was enough to cover it in the tea tin. I snapped my purse shut. 'I'm going now, baby, but don't pay too much for those cookies. I'll be back in an hour.'

'How much is an hour?'

I led him to the kitchen wall clock and showed him where the hands would be in an hour. I said, 'It won't be long, and Habib will be here, cooking, like always.'

Billy looked at Habib, and the man nodded. I'd noticed that he and Billy seemed able to communicate, and I wondered how they did it.

'Take your time,' Billy said magnanimously. He took Spike to the miniature bazaar, and I watched him head straight for the cookies while he whispered and Spike answered like a ventriloquist's dummy. There were not enough foreigners in Masoorla for Billy to have playmates, and we didn't have enough servants to have any native children around. Could Lydia be right? Should we not have brought him to India?

I squared my shoulders and presented myself to Habib, ready for a game of charades. I pointed to myself, and then to the front door; then I pointed at Billy, patting the table in a stay-put gesture. Habib gave me an abbreviated head wag and a riddle of a smile, but he seemed to understand and motioned me out the door with a wave of *noblesse oblige*.

In Simla, I left my tonga on Cart Road, below the Mall, and, irrationally, looked around for Martin. Of course he wasn't there, but what a scene there would be if he saw me in Simla so soon after he had emphatically told me to stay at home. I knew his intentions were good; he was playing the protector, just doing his job. But I would not be sequestered against my will, especially since I believed his fear to be exaggerated by his chronic paranoia.

I set off along Cart Road, enjoying the scent of incense drifting out of a tiny pink temple. Without Billy, I planned to hike up the narrow winding path to the Mall and get a few photos on the way. At the end of Cart Road, I stopped at a stall where a young man was selling some kind of mysterious red snack out of a brass vessel. I snapped a picture then paused, trying to work up the courage to try some, when . . .

BOOM!

The ground shook and my hearing shut down. Men ran past me on Cart Road, their mouths stretched open, apparently shouting, but I heard nothing. Ridiculously, I thought of a silent movie with Keystone Kops running every which way with no sound but a frenzied piano in the background. I remembered Martin talking about the temporary deafness that came after bombs and mortar blasts.

I smelled oily smoke, my throat burned, and heavy black clouds billowed into the sky. I pushed through the crowd and saw a car on fire, a blackened shape barely discernible in the flames. Smoke surged, blurring my vision, and the green lenses of my sunglasses added to the sense of unreality. My ears began to recover, and I heard the roar of the giant fireball. It was too shocking to be instantly believable, and again I thought of movies because no one sees things like that in real life. I felt I should run, but I couldn't look away. I stood still, trying to understand.

The crowd shouted at two men who dragged a third out of the smoke; he was burned and unconscious and their three shapes materialized like heroic figures marching out of hell. I thought, thank God they got him out. Then they threw him down and the crowd fell on him. Bamboo sticks appeared and they beat the burned man viciously. The air thickened with the iron smell of fresh blood as the mob worked hard, sweating and panting, their faces skewed with rage.

I moved backward, tasting the bile that rose in my throat. *No. Do not vomit.* I swallowed and kept moving until I cleared the crowd, then I ran past abandoned rickshaws and tongas whose drivers were watching the beating. I ran, stunned, zigzagging up the mountain towards the Mall, my Brownie swinging from my neck. When I came to a stepped street I took the steps two at a time until a stitch in my side made me stop and bend over, gasping.

On the Mall, far above it all, life moved with surreal normality. I could see smoke roiling below, but from so far up it could have been just another pile of burning rubbish. I sat on an iron bench to catch my breath while a few people, having heard the blast, stood at a rail, staring down. But others ignored it, buying and selling as usual, even strolling along, casually eating ice cream. I realized then that although there had been no riots in Simla, growing tension had probably provoked minor incidents in the native quarter every day, and people were learning to live with it.

After my heart slowed and my hands stopped trembling, I climbed the road to Christ Church, already knowing I would not tell Martin what I had seen. If told him I'd had a brush with violence he'd try again to keep me at home like a Muslim wife in purdah, and I couldn't allow that. Martin and James Walker, Felicity and Adela, and millions of other people lived every day with uncertainty and danger and they did not surrender their freedom. Why should I?

Reverend Locke welcomed me to the rectory with a resounding 'Splendid!' But his smile faltered as he looked at me more closely. 'Are you all right, Mrs Mitchell?'

I was sweaty and dishevelled from running, and there was soot on my clothes from the explosion. 'I walked up,' I said, whisking my hand over my slacks. 'It's awfully steep, and hot. I sat by the side of the road to rest and . . . please excuse my appearance. I'm fine.'

'I see.' He looked doubtful, but showed me into his wood-panelled study. He offered me one of two comfortably overstuffed chairs and sat across from me in the other. Antique duck decoys sat on the carved mantel, and a well-worn Queen Anne chair stood behind a Victorian writing table. Books packed an entire wall of shelves all the way up to the crown moulding. It was a comfortable English room with no hint of India; the room conveyed a sense of complete insulation, and this time I was grateful.

Reverend Locke said, 'Thought I heard some sort of explosion earlier. Did you hear anything?'

I hesitated. 'Yes, but I was on the Mall. It seemed to have come from below.'

'Oh, dear.' He touched his collar. 'I hope the troubles haven't found us.'

I examined a fingernail. 'The Mall was as peaceful as a lake.'

'Good. Perhaps a lorry backfired down there.'

'Are the records in here?'

'Every one of them.' He went to the wall of books and pulled out a thick volume. 'I believe this is the first. Should be 1850 to 1857.' He blew dust off the top then ran his finger along a row of books on another shelf, a collection of old black Bibles with pebbled leather covers. 'These are family Bibles, some with a spot of history here and there. Feel free to look at them as well. They came to the church whenever the last family member passed on. Happened rather too often, I'm afraid. Cholera, yellow fever, war.' He handed me the heavy record book and said, 'Tea?'

I imagined having tea with him, breaking down and blubbering – the fire, the beating, my shock – but I didn't want anyone to know I had been there. I said, 'No, thank you. I had some on the Mall.'

'Splendid.' He tapped the book with a finger. 'I'll leave you to it, then.'

Chapter Seventeen

1856–7

F<small>ROM THE</small> journal of Adela Winfield:

October 1856

Lady Chadwick has gone home to Calcutta, which will be quite busy & gay with balls & dinner parties until next March. She sent word, offering to escort Felicity & me downriver for the season, but we declined, & she did not press us. It is only a matter of time before Mother & Father get wind of my refusal to participate in the husband hunt, & I don't know what they will do. If they suspend my allowance I shall be completely dependent on Felicity.

The new kitchen is almost finished & we have decided to mark it somehow as our own. We rejected carving our names into a wooden beam, sharing a horror of people who visit interesting places & disfigure them with their own uninteresting names. But this is our kitchen – even Hakim wants no part of it – & it seems right to put some personal element in it.

Last night Felicity came out to the verandah with some of the letters that have gone between us, including one she did not post after hearing that I was en route to join her. She also showed me an amusing sketch she had made of me riding astride in my split skirt, & she suggested secreting all these papers in the kitchen's half-finished brick wall. I liked the idea immediately. It pleased me to think that part of our unconventional story would be preserved in our unconventional kitchen. Like cave paintings left by early humans, a simple message – we were here – left without fanfare, not knowing who might stumble upon it.

We prised a brick out, placed our ribbon-tied packet behind it, & replaced the brick with a bit of fresh mortar. Not the most professional job, but it will hold. We were quite pleased with ourselves & went out to the verandah to smoke the hookah.

At night, lying under my mosquito netting, I thought about this bungalow standing here in the mofussil, under the sandalwood tree, long after Felicity & I have departed. It came to me that death steals everything but our stories, & I felt the urge to leave a fuller account of ourselves, here, in this house where we have been happy. Fanny Parks & Honoria Lawrence left stories that have meant much to Felicity & me. I shall do the same & leave it to Fate to determine whom my words might touch.

I'm not yet sure how to accomplish it, but I will keep it in mind as I write.

November 1856

Through her activities at the orphanage, Felicity has met an Indian chap who shares her affinity for the downtrodden. That is fine, as far as it goes, but it seems he has led her to unsavoury parts of the native quarter, even into bustees, to offer blankets & laudanum to the old & infirm. This seems a dangerous enterprise for a young white woman, especially now when we hear reports of rising tension between the sepoys & their British commanders. These sepoys are well-trained, well-armed Indian soldiers & if they, in their great numbers, should rise up against a handful of Britons, we should find ourselves in dire straits.

Add to this all the old resentments against the Raj, the simmering bitterness that causes cooks to defile the sahib's dinner, & water bearers to slide a snake into the bathtub. One sometimes wonders whether the servants, sitting quietly round their fires in the godowns, are hatching revolution. And in the midst of this, Felicity fraternizes with an Indian as if they were intimate friends. It is worrying.

They see each other at the orphanage, but messages come & go & she does not show them to me. She says they are notes of thanks from the missionaries, but when she reads them, I see a light in her face that no missionary could inspire.

This familiarity is perilous for both of them, but she dismisses my concern as she dismisses all my worries. This difference of opinion has occasioned a subtle rift between us. We endeavour not to speak of him, but he is much on my mind.

November 1856

Diwali is the Festival of Lights & never have I seen India more enchanting. Diwali means 'rows of lighted lamps', & for five days every stall, every house, every rickshaw & every tree is ablaze with small clay oil-pots set with cotton wicks. Crowds of people dressed in their finest make puja to the light, which symbolizes victory of good over evil within the individual.

During Diwali, the sun god, Surya, is worshipped, but Hindoos define God as the Unknowable, their many gods being only symbolic intercessors, much like Christian saints. They greet each other saying, 'Namaste,' which means, 'The god in me bows to the god in you,' & I find the reverence of this custom more affecting than the most sincere handshake. Diwali celebrates the inner light that dispels ignorance & brings joy.

How I wish Katie could see this. I recall the delight on her dear face every time she learned to read a new word. She would run her work-hardened hands through her black hair, her curls bouncing wildly. Sometimes she would laugh, & I never failed to be charmed by the lightness of her voice, like a bell, always coming as a surprise, juxtaposed as it was against her rough exterior.

I will always love Katie & Felicity, but one is lost to me & the other can be naught but my sister. Still, I have love in my heart; that is a gift, & I am grateful.

Felicity & I hung lanterns & fire-pots inside & outside the house, & when the servants brought us baskets of carrot halwa & almond cakes, we gave them baksheesh in exchange.

Felicity's Indian friend brought us a basket that reminded me of treasure from a shipwreck, an elaborate affair heaped with fresh fruits, chutneys, glazed lotus seeds, Persian dates & bunches of marigolds in leaf cups. Well, he is a wealthy man. I thanked him as I thanked the others, but Felicity held his hand in both of hers, & I had the impression that something unsaid passed between them.

At night, we sat on the verandah with marigolds in our hair, & watched fireworks breach the night sky, spitting like fat in a fire, & I was touched. On the darkest night of the year in one of the most destitute countries in the world, people celebrate the light. We retired to our beds humbled by their indefatigable hope.

November 1856

Felicity's cough has worsened & she has expressed a wish to go up to Pragpur to take the pure, high country air. But when I asked Lalita to begin packing for us, I was shocked to hear that Felicity intended to go alone. She made light of it, saying, 'Someone must stay to keep the servants from absconding with the house,' & she kissed my cheek sweetly. 'I promise to make sketches of everything,' she said, '& I shall return fit and kicking.'

But there is something evasive in her demeanour. I do not understand.

December 1856
I miss her.

December 1856
Felicity returned in the pink, & all my fears have vanished.

The air has gone frigid & we shiver luxuriously in the snapping cold. There is nothing more delightful than to sit in the sunshine, wrapped in an Indian shawl, & admire the distant peaks. Those mountains! When God gave us speech, he did not expect us to talk about the Himalayas. They appear like a mirage, a hallucination painted on the sky & at the sight of them one can only babble foolishly or remain silent. In the evening the drawing room looks cheerful with a fire crackling in the grate.

The moon on these clear winter nights is startlingly bright, & it is a pleasant novelty to embroider our pillow covers by moonlight. Can this crisp white moon be the same one that hides behind grey clouds in Yorkshire? A local woman with bangles on her arms, bells on her ankles & a ring in her nose sells us goose feathers to stuff our pillows. These bejewelled women in their vivid saris look like tropical birds fluttering through a dusty landscape, & I believe the earth gods must have conceived the notion of gold when first they beheld brown skin.

December 1856
Christmas! We have decorated the bungalow with pine boughs & Lalita created a rangoli on the tea table, a marvellous display of red poinsettias & wild orchids arranged in concentric circles. We sat on the verandah singing 'Adeste Fideles' & the servants once again came bearing baskets of fruits & cakes, & we again gave them baksheesh.

Felicity's Indian friend visited, this time with a surprising basket filled with tins of mincemeat, sardines & smoked oysters, a bottle of tawny port & a wheel of genuine Stilton, all nestled in a bed of marigolds. He must have sent to an import shop in Calcutta months ago to accomplish this Christmas miracle. His largesse was surprising, but Felicity gushed on & on like an excitable girl. It made me uncomfortable.

Felicity & I went to the bazaar & bought heaps of sultanas & raisins for the plum pudding. At the spice merchant's stall, we bought cinnamon & nutmeg scooped from sacks & weighed on a copper scale. We also purchased plenty of raw sugar to make the golden syrup for treacle tarts.

While Hakim roasted a peacock, which he later carved like an Oriental assassin wielding a sword, we made pudding & tarts in our new kitchen. As I set the breadcrumbs to soak, Felicity coughed a hoarse, bleating cough & my back stiffened. She assured me she only had something caught in her throat, but I don't believe her.

January 1857

An element of secrecy has come over Felicity. Her silences are weighted, as if she verges on revealing some momentous thing, but when I ask, she shakes her head & wanders outside to feed her pony an apple. It is a puzzling new aspect to her & I cannot say I like it. I feel left out.

She is coughing again & has discontinued her work at the orphanage lest she infect someone. I would not be surprised to learn that her charity work in foul hovels has caused her to relapse. I never liked the idea of her going to noxious bustees infested with beggars & lepers. I fear the air in those quarters is contaminated with zymotic poisons.

The servants are talking about arson in Calcutta. It would seem some sepoys are seriously disgruntled.

January 1857

Felicity has taken a dramatic turn downward. It is a wrench to see her glide, oh, so slowly, through the house with a handkerchief pressed to her mouth. She is pale & her lovely hands look like twigs.

Surely this is a recurrence of consumption, & yet it is different from the last siege. I am feeding her up on beef tea & buttermilk, but she continues to languish. I pray it is only consumption, which she has already survived, & not one of the dreadful afflictions common to this land.

I proceed as I did in England, hanging the camphor ball over her bed & insisting on a daily dose of tartar emetic to strengthen her blood. But her body does not respond, & I am baffled. In the mornings she vomits. She is chronically fatigued, & often lies abed in her chemise for hours. Her monthly courses have stopped as they did when she was ill in Yorkshire, & she moves around as though under water.

I sent a message to her mother, & to the station doctor, who arrived that night, drunk & stumbling. He staggered up the veran-dah steps, asking where he might find the patient. I said, 'Don't you usually find them in bed?'

As he held Felicity's wrist, he belched. Then he asked, stupidly, 'How are we feeling, young lady?' When she said, 'Perfectly fine,' he seemed relieved. 'Very good then,' he said. 'I'll let your sister know you've recovered.'

'I think you mean her mother,' I said tightly.

He shot me an irritated look. 'Rest tonight & if you're not up & about tomorrow, I'll come back & bleed you.'

'Lovely.' Felicity treated him to one of her wonderful smiles.

I saw the useless blighter to the door, & he asked, 'Shall we have a peg for the road?' I gave him a short whisky just to be rid of him, & then went in to Felicity, who seemed to think the drunken fool quite comical.

The next day Lady Chadwick arrived in a smart victoria pulled by a sleek black pony. She picked her way through our overgrown verandah with distaste, & filled our doorway with her crinolines. She swept through our little drawing room, making it appear suddenly small & shabby, & went to the foot of Felicity's bed. 'I hear you are once again on the road to recovery.'

'Yes, Mother. Thank you for coming.'

It was a ten-minute visit, but awkward enough that it seemed to last for hours. Now Felicity says the only visitor she will receive is the Indian. Thank God we live out in the mofussil where there are no prying eyes to make something ugly of their innocent, if ill-advised, friendship.

The Indian. I am reluctant to use his name, as if relegating him to the anonymous masses will make him disappear, or at least seem less important. When speaking to him, I call him Sir, & he bows politely & calls me Madam. Our exchanges are brief & cold & it is I who keep them so. Heartless, I know, but there it is. I was happier when it was only Felicity and me.

At least the man is not lowborn. He speaks the Queen's English, having lived in London & studied at Cambridge, & he comes from a family of wealthy landowners – silk, I believe. Still, he is Indian, & we represent the Raj, & no good can come of their association at this volatile time.

The flap amongst the sepoys revolves around some new cartridges for their rifles. Apparently, the grease on them is profane, cow fat or pig fat, or so they believe. Whether the grease is profane or not, religion is no thing to trifle with in this land of many gods.

Chapter Eighteen

1947

I HEAVED THE RECORD book open near the centre and checked the date – 1855 – then leafed through pages of church trivia until I came to 1856. I read endless lists of births, christenings and deaths, a note about a parishioner suffering from consumption, details of the acquisition of new rattan chairs for the Club, and a description of a swanky ball at the Viceregal Lodge.

I turned the page and saw a heading penned in graceful calligraphy – *New Arrivals, January to June 1856*. The list included dates, names of officials and family members, military personnel with their ranks, and halfway down the page, *May 1856, Miss Adela Winfield, Companion to Miss Felicity Chadwick*. No more doubt. It was my Adela in the graveyard.

I flipped through the book to January 1857. Ordinary parish business followed a dismissive remark about malcontent sepoys. In March, an entry fairly seethed on the page, the handwriting an angry scrawl.

March 1857
More rubbish about those damnable cartridges being a plot to

corrupt their faith. General Anson says he will never give in to their beastly prejudices. Hear, hear.

That sounded pretty bloody-minded for a cleric, but Reverend Locke had said that records were often kept by anyone willing to take the time. Whoever took the time to record the mutiny seemed to speak for the majority.

April 1857
<u>Mutiny!</u> *A sepoy in Barrapore, one Mangal Pandey, actually shot & wounded a British officer. The community is outraged. This cannot stand.*

April 1857
Pandey has been hanged, but there have been protests.

May 1857
Disaster in Meerut. Sepoys have slain the entire Christian population! Now they ride for Delhi to enlist the Moghul Emperor in their cause. Bahadur Shah Zafar will never give his blessing to these malcontents. He is too shrewd a fellow to defy the Crown. He will put them down for us.

May 1857
Bahadur Shah Zafar has given the sepoys shelter in his palace. Surely he was coerced. In any case, it is war.

June 1857
The sepoys have taken the Red Fort in Delhi. British citizens, women & children included, roam the countryside seeking shelter. It is a bloody rebellion, but the Indians are calling it a War of Independence.

Thus far, we in Simla have been spared, but there have been ominous incidents, gatherings that approach the character of mobs. The mood is threatening, & we venture out of our homes infrequently. We watch our servants for signs of subversion. Even some of the children carry sticks, which they brandish with an air of menace. God help us.

June 1857
The Tytlers are safe in Karnal, God knows how, but Vibart is missing. The Clarke family was slaughtered in their home, but Morely could not describe the scene. Mrs Clarke was far advanced in her pregnancy.

July 1857
Kanpur! Our women & children dismembered & thrown down a well! Unspeakable. God curse their black souls. They will pay. One hundred of theirs will die for every one of ours. Wagentrieber has called for annihilation. Canning has asked for restraint & has been dubbed 'Clemency Canning'. He is roundly ignored. It is agreed that we must avenge Kanpur in a way that sends a clear message. Never again!

Strangely, the next pages listed only births and deaths, a wedding, and a cricket match with multiple exclamation points after one of the scores. It read, *'Cracking match!'* It seemed that rebellious sepoys, however troublesome, were not taken as a serious threat to the Empire; they were, after all, only employees. I saw one more mention of consumption, and then a description of British revenge for Kanpur.

August 1857
Nicholson has been disarming regiments of sepoys with great success & hanging their leaders. He has abandoned the practice of

blowing mutineers from the mouths of cannon because he believes that the powder expended might be more usefully employed.

August 1857

Canning says we go too far, but he is a lone voice. Our army of retribution sweeps across the north & entire villages are put to the torch. Loyal Sikh troops have been allowed to torture captured insurgents. Sepoys have been made to lick clean the floor of the massacre site at Kanpur, after which they are ritually outcaste by having pork & beef & everything that could possibly break caste stuffed down their throats. Then they are sewn into pigskins & hanged. General Neill has ordered that, contrary to both faiths, the Hindoos are to be buried & the Mohammedans burned. Distasteful, but as Mackenzie said, 'We would be less than men if we did not exterminate them like snakes.'

The Indians are calling our revenge the devil's wind, but it is our right, enshrined in the Bible. Wallace bayonets sepoys whilst chanting the 116th psalm.

The bile that I'd swallowed at the sight of the burning car rose up the back of my throat again. I pushed away from the desk, imagining a British officer, crazed by revenge, chanting psalms like an angel from hell while he waded through the blood and gore with his bayonet raised. My sense of sarcasm kicked in, and I thought, poor God, six thousand religions in the world and everyone claiming that He is on their side; what a headache.

September 1857

British troops have retaken Delhi. This Sunday we will give thanks as a community united in gratitude. Dalhousie, the dim-witted scoundrel, has been chastised & there is talk of reorganizing the East India Company. The need for a stricter rule of law has been impressed upon us at great cost. But rebellion will not be tolerated and reprisals will continue for some time.

September 1857
How fortunate we are to enjoy the cool climes of Simla. Newcomers report that the humid heat in Calcutta & Delhi is oppressive &, for some, even fatal. But comfort can breed moral laxity, as we have seen recently with the Singh scandal. It is disconcerting to imagine . . .

But the next page had been torn out. I wondered why the record book in an Anglican church would mention a scandal in an Indian family, so I leafed through the book, hoping the page had been placed elsewhere, but it had not.

I stared at the wooden duck decoys on the mantel. Britons would not take any notice of a scandal in an Indian family unless one of their own was involved. Of course Englishmen often took Indian mistresses, but after 1830, when missionaries began to arrive en masse, interracial relationships were condemned along with pagan idols and harems, and they would certainly not be mentioned in a church record.

As for a relationship between an English woman and an Indian man, well, that would have been beyond scandal, simply impossible. The man would have been lynched if he lived long enough to get a rope around his neck. Even in the twentieth century, when an Englishwoman in the Punjab reported being bothered on the street by an Indian man, the governor ordered all Indians using that street to crawl its length on their hands and knees.

A relationship between a Victorian woman and an Indian man was unthinkable. But what could have happened in an Indian family that would be recorded in church and then torn out?

The record ended in December 1857, and it was time for me to go home. As I replaced the volume on the bookshelf, the row of old-fangled Bibles drew my attention, and I ran my hand over the cracked leather spines imprinted with names in an ornate gold type: Chilton, Braithwaite, Marlowe and – yes – Winfield.

When I opened the Bible, a folded sheet of paper floated to my feet. I picked it up as the church bell began to chime the hour, and I imagined Billy staring at the clock whose hands indicated that I should be home. I imagined Habib watching the door. Quickly, I scanned the top line.

February 1857
She is expectorating blood & I begin to despair. My best efforts have failed.

It appeared to be a journal entry. I fanned the pages of the Bible to shake out any other loose sheets, and breathed a quiet 'Holy Christ' when several more folded papers wafted down in a swinging drift. I stooped to gather my windfall, wanting to read them immediately, but I had to get home. As I shoved them into my purse, I thought I heard footsteps and glanced at the door. Tricked by guilt, the word 'stealing' came to mind and I mumbled, 'Only borrowing.' I clicked my purse shut and replaced the Bible. I had the irrational idea that my hair must have gone messy, and I patted it down before I let myself out. I slipped away without seeing the splendid Reverend Locke, and I was glad. My purse felt heavy with ill-gotten loot, and I wouldn't have been able to meet his eyes.

I hired a tonga and on Cart Road we passed the burned-out car, scorched and skeletal and still smouldering. But there were no bamboo sticks to be seen, and feet and hooves and wheels had already churned up the dirt where there might have been blood. In time, they would haul away the wreck, leaving no hint of what had happened there. A cow stood nearby, grazing on a pile of refuse, and I was struck by how such a thing could happen and leave no trace. Oceans of blood had been shed in India, but the only evidence left was in books. It seemed wrong, yet at that moment I, too, wanted only to forget.

Chapter Nineteen

1856

W HEN FELICITY FIRST met him at the orphanage, he avoided her eyes, and she thought him cold. The children and the missionaries made her feel needed, but he made her feel like an intruder in his world. She wondered if he held her responsible for the subjugation of his people, but she thought that would be unfair. After all, he didn't know her. Still, his presumed judgement made her quiet in his presence.

Sometimes she watched him from the corner of her eye and admired the way he swung along, dignified and self-confident. He had a well-groomed black beard, and his turbans always matched his sash – he was Sikh, and he carried a ritual dagger at his waist, a symbol of his willingness to defend the weak. She found this at once gentle and courageous and a little dangerous. She wondered how he looked without his deep-blue turban.

She had no idea how much she frightened him; one word of accusation from a white woman could get him killed. He found it astounding that the British still didn't understand that Indian men found white women unattractive – unfinished, like uncooked dough. But he had to admit that the young woman who came to the orphanage had an appealing delicacy about her face and a fluidity of movement. Her hands were long and slender and she had exceptionally fine bones in her wrist – he wondered how a henna tattoo might look on those creamy white hands. Although he usually found blonde hair wanting, hers was warm, with a touch of the sunset in it. She was different from other white women in many ways, wearing strange clothing, riding astride, covering her head with a veil instead of a topi. It was all very unsettling.

Once, she stepped into his path and said, 'Pardon me,' in a low, buttery voice that terrified him. He couldn't shake the feeling that she had done so deliberately. But why would she do that? He tried to avoid her, but she kept turning up at the orphanage he sponsored. He didn't mind that the missionaries were Christian. As a liberal and educated man, he believed religion was a matter of karma and everyone had his own path.

Felicity liked his smoky dark eyes, but every time she caught his glance he seemed angry. Strange. Apart from his chilliness towards her, he did not behave like an angry man. He played easily with the children, bringing them strings of sequinned elephants and soft blankets from his silk plantation near Pragpur. He had a wide, white smile – but never for her.

One morning, Felicity and this man helped the two Scottish missionaries fill bowls with sweetened rice porridge. The children waiting to be fed watched the ones who were already eating; their eyes tracked the food from bowl to mouth, and when they were served they ate slowly, carefully, as if the food were a sacrament. The room fell quiet while they ate, nothing to hear but the pulpy sound of chewing. While the children ate, the man glanced at Felicity, and she caught him. He looked away immediately and she stared at his profile, trying to make him look at her again, but he wouldn't.

Another morning, she walked into one of the makeshift huts in the orphanage compound to comfort a little boy with a broken arm; she carried an embroidered feather pillow and a vial of Mother Bailey's Quieting Syrup, and she stooped at the low entry, blinking as her eyes adjusted from sun to shade. The cold man squatted next to a little boy sitting on a woven mat with his back against the wall, cradling one arm in a rag sling. The man was peeling an apple with his dagger and feeding the boy, slice by slice, murmuring something she couldn't make out, but the boy was smiling. They both looked up when she entered, and the boy stared, but the man lowered his eyes and went back to peeling the apple. She watched him slice the fruit, his concentration and precision, his tender mouth moving as he spoke to the little boy. Felicity thought he must belong to the warrior caste, having the gentleness of the truly strong.

She waited, bent over in the low doorway, with her pillow and her brown medicine bottle. It was a cramped space, and the man seemed to fill it completely. Finally, she stepped forward and knelt beside the little boy. It seemed to her that her split riding skirt rustled too loudly and her hands moved clumsily. Felicity manoeuvred the pillow behind the boy's back and the man tried to help without jostling the injured arm. In trying to position the pillow, their fingertips touched, and he pulled away so fast she gasped. She said, 'Pardon me, I—'

'No, Madam, pardon me.' He handed the boy the rest of the apple and abruptly left.

After Felicity had given the boy a dose of Mother Bailey's, she walked out to the compound and saw the man chatting with Reverend MacDougal. The tall, lean missionary and his wife had come to India with a light in their eyes and one desire burning in their hearts – to educate and sanitize the baboo. They lived on rice and ideals and received funds from this wealthy Indian now standing in the compound and some obscure source in America. Felicity approached the men and saw the Indian's expression change from calm to dread, but she stepped right up to him and said, 'Sir, it isn't polite for people to encounter each other so often without speaking.'

'I beg your pardon, Madam.' He bowed. 'My name is Singh.' His British English had no Indian lilt.

Reverend MacDougal said, 'Mr Singh keeps our doors open.'

'In that case, I'm honoured to meet you. I am Miss Chadwick.'

Mr Singh bowed stiffly, and then strode out of the compound to his buggy.

Reverend MacDougal said, 'How peculiar. He was about to tell me when to expect the next rice delivery.'

The following week, they arrived at the orphanage at the same time, and while Mr Singh stepped down from his buggy, Felicity wheeled her pony around to block the entrance to the compound. Mr Singh shaded his eyes and noticed how her coppery hair blazed against the blue sky. Her pony stamped and snorted and she said, 'I don't see why we can't speak to one another like civilized people.'

'Indeed.' He paused, then said, 'The weather has been exceptionally mild this year.'

A laughing dove burst out of a pipal tree and the pony's head shot up. Felicity said, 'Please don't patronize me, Mr Singh.'

His face remained blank. 'I don't understand what you want from me. But I would like to enter now. I have rice.'

Felicity pulled on the reins and steered the pony out of his way.

A week later, he arrived at the orphanage in time to see her walking into the compound. His horse whinnied to a halt, and he wondered how she had managed to teach a *durzi* to make those split skirts she wore. He'd never seen another Englishwoman in such a bizarre costume, but then he'd never seen another Englishwoman riding astride or working at the orphanage. She was strange; she was trouble, yet he thought about her all the time. He sat in his buggy, wondering whether he should wait for her to leave before he went in. But if she saw him sitting here, waiting, it might offend her. Damn woman. He'd even dreamed about her. He dropped the reins and jumped down.

She was sitting under a pipal tree with orphans crowded around. Teaching them English. For what? But they all loved her; that was obvious. After finishing his business with MacDougal, he walked across the compound, looking neither left nor right, but she called to him and waved. Now he would *have* to say hello.

He walked towards her, and Felicity watched him approach. When he reached the shade of the tree she got up, saying, 'I'm finished for today. Will you join me for a cup of tea?'

The breeze moved the small hairs at the back of her neck, and something cold twisted in his stomach. He said, 'Thank you, Madam, but I don't think that would be wise.'

'Oh, for heaven's sake.' Her mouth set itself in a firm line. 'It's only a cup of tea.'

What was she doing? Would it be more dangerous to accept, or to refuse? And how could she still be so pretty with that stubborn look on her face? He heard himself say, 'It would be an honour.'

They walked to a local chai stall and pretended not to notice everyone staring. A group of turbanned men sat on the ground, drawing perfumed smoke from a hookah, and even the smoke seemed to pause in a static blue haze while the brown and white couple sat down at the one small wooden table. They sat opposite each other on rickety three-legged stools, and he ordered masala chai.

As the chai wallah stirred milk and tea and spices into a tin pot and set it over a coal fire to boil, Felicity said, 'It's really quite silly, you know.'

'I beg your pardon?'

'Trying to avoid me. I don't bite.' She snapped her teeth at him and he jumped.

'Madam—'

'Stop that. My name is Felicity. Haven't you wondered why I live alone in the *mofussil*?'

'Do you?'

'Well, with a companion. But I'm not like other memsahibs.'

'I can see that.'

The chai wallah served them tiny porcelain cups of steaming tea, and she took a sip. He cleared his throat. 'Why do I see you so often at the orphanage?'

'I wish to be useful.'

'Commendable.' He sipped his tea and rubbed a damp palm over his knee.

'And you? Why an orphanage?'

He shrugged. 'It was needed, and the Scots were willing.'

She finished her tea and set the cup down. 'So. That wasn't so difficult, was it?'

They did not make plans to meet again, but they both

went to the tea stall on the same day at the same time the following week. He ordered tea and they spoke of the orphanage, of India, and of England. He learned that she had been born in India, and she learned that he had been educated in England. They sat staring at each other for a full minute before they got up and left.

The next time they met they could no longer pretend it was a simple coincidence to have found each other at the tea stall. Their conversation came out halting and self-conscious, and they cleared their throats and toyed with their teacups. When she coughed and then dropped her handkerchief, he retrieved it and she blushed. It was the silly ploy of a coquettish woman and she wanted to tell him it had been an honest accident; she had become a bit clumsy in his presence. He handed her the handkerchief, and their hands touched again, but this time, for the briefest moment, she rested her fingertips on his palm and a shiver ran up her spine. He murmured, 'I am married.'

Felicity straightened her spine and looked him squarely in the face. Knowing marriages in India were arranged, she asked, 'Do you love your wife?'

He looked away and she knew he was considering how honest he could be. Finally he said, 'In India we do not marry for love. Marriages are alliances formed for social or political or financial reasons. I met my wife for the first time on our wedding day.' He crossed his arms over his chest and his eyes hardened. 'Our system is clearly understood by everyone and it has worked for a long time.'

'You didn't answer my question.'

He sighed and his shoulders sagged. 'Love is problematic.'

'Indeed. But what a shame it would be to marry a stranger and then fall in love with another. One has a duty to be true to oneself, don't you think?'

He stared at her and she sipped her tea. They sat in silence, disconnected from the life moving around them. Men chatted and smoked their bidis, tea bubbled in the pot, and people walked in and out, yet they were alone. Eventually, he said, 'You are different.'

'Yes.'

They finished their tea and made their way through the cramped lane, squeezing past vegetable carts and dhobis with bundles of laundry on their heads. She paused to admire a gold-eyed mynah bird in a bamboo cage, poking her finger through to stroke the bird's blushing breast. She said, 'India is dirty and poor, and I love it. Is that odd?'

He smiled. 'You're asking an Indian.'

She gestured at the people pushing through the narrow lane. 'Your people seem to ask little of life, but their gentleness has made them easy prey for conquerors.'

He looked away. 'Perhaps it is wiser to bend than to break.'

'But you—'

Her voice stalled at the sight of Tyra MacDougal running straight towards them through the crowded lane. Her topi was gone and her thin dishwater hair flew around her panicked face. A group of young toughs with bamboo sticks followed hard at her heels. They caught her by the arm and threw her to the ground, and one tore the silver cross from her neck and threw it in the dirt. Tyra kept her head bowed in prayer, and that seemed to enrage them more. One young man kicked her side, and she fell over, clutching her ribs. Another struck her head with his stick and a trickle of blood scribbled down her face.

Felicity moved towards her, but Mr Singh held her back and ordered the young men to stop. The authority in his voice stilled one fellow, his stick frozen in mid air, then Mr

Singh stepped forward and they all reverted to petulant boys, grumbling under their breath as they backed away. Felicity went to Tyra and knelt in the dirt to cradle her head. Blood smeared her white riding blouse, and Tyra stared at her with watery eyes. Felicity appealed to the young men. 'How could you?'

A truculent young fellow shouted, 'She wants to make us outcaste.'

'No.' Felicity shook her head. 'She means you no harm.'

'Then let her go back where she came from.' He broke his stick in half with a sulky snap and walked away. The others followed.

They helped Tyra back to the mission, and when she collapsed into her husband's arms, Mr Singh watched MacDougal tend to his injured wife and said, 'If India ever stops bending . . .' He shook his head and looked away.

The following week at the tea stall, Felicity cleared her throat and said, 'I have heard you have a silk plantation near Pragpur.'

'I do indeed.' Mr Singh put his cup down.

She leaned across the small, scarred table. 'Pragpur, like Simla, is another popular summer retreat for my country-men.'

'I've heard that.' He tried to read her face.

She lowered her voice. 'There is a British hotel there; I used to go there with my parents when I was a child. If I were to go next month, it would be deserted, with everyone at home for Christmas. Only a small staff would be there to see the place doesn't fall down, and of course they sleep in godowns apart from the main building. I plan to go there next month to enjoy complete privacy.'

'And how long must you journey for this blessed seclusion?'

'It is four days by buggy and dhoolie.'

'That is a long journey to take on impulse.'

'Not if you yearn for privacy as much as I do.' She moistened her lips. 'Do you?'

He sat straighter, swallowed hard, and then gave a barely perceptible nod.

She continued as if it was settled. 'I will take a room facing east. Those rooms have balconies overlooking the valley and high mountains. It is magnificent at any time, but under a full moon, it will be unforgettable.'

He murmured, 'Pragpur at the full moon?'

'Yes. It is December the tenth by my calendar.'

He leaned across the table and his voice became husky. 'It will be cold, and you must bring warm clothing. But in spite of the chill, I suggest that on the first night, you forgo having a fire.' His expression was blank, but a bit tense, she thought. Or was that only her? He said, 'The better to enjoy the moon-light on the mountains.'

'And how far is this hotel from your silk plantation?'

'About six hours on horseback.'

'That's a long ride.'

'No, Madam. It is nothing.'

Like the Club in Simla, the hotel in Pragpur had been decorated in the Indo-European style. Kashmiri rugs covered polished teak floors, Indian screens stood behind chintz sofas, and stuffed animal heads stared down from the walls with glass eyes. The ground floor offered a high-ceilinged dining room, and a sweeping stairway led up to the bedrooms.

Porters carried in Felicity's luggage while she waited in front of an abandoned reception desk. After putting down one of her cases, a porter hurried behind the desk and smiled – the reduced winter staff doing double duty. He said, 'Unexpected you are coming, memsahib. Christmas, neh?' He rocked his head from side to side.

She said, 'I trust you have a room available.'

'Yes, memsahib. All rooms are being available.'

'I would like a room facing the mountains to the east, please.'

'Yes, memsahib.'

'And I don't want to be disturbed.'

'Yes, memsahib. Only one servant will be laying the fire, isn't it?'

'No fire.'

He raised his eyebrows. 'It is cold.'

'No fire.'

'Yes, memsahib.'

'But please draw a hot bath for me after dinner.'

'Yes, memsahib.'

In the dining room, she pushed curried lamb and rice around her plate, trying to give the impression that she was eating, and then climbed the wide, curved staircase to her room. In typical colonial fashion, the bedroom and bathroom were large, with high ceilings and wide teak moulding. The bed, piled with quilts, faced a cold fireplace; an oak almirah stood in one corner and a wingback chair in another. In the white-tiled bathroom, a cast-iron claw-foot tub full of steaming water waited, tendrils of steam rising in the chill air.

She bathed slowly, squeezing the sponge to watch rivulets of water run down her arms and sheet her breasts. When the tremulous voice of a muezzin snaked into the room, she lay back and listened, then she took a deep breath and slid under the water, her hair floating on the surface like a tentacled sea creature. She stayed under as long as she could and came up smiling.

She dried herself with care, as if she would never touch that body again. She wondered what she would feel like in the morning, whether her transformation would show. She towel-dried her hair and pinned it loosely.

The porters had unpacked while she dined, and she stood in front of the open almirah deciding what to wear – the pink taffeta or her pale lavender sari. Who would she be? She settled on the sari. She slipped on the tight little blouse and tied the simple petticoat beneath her navel. Then she gathered up the opulent fabric, yards and yards of shimmering silk with a wide silver border, and wound it around her body. She carefully made her pleats and draped the sari over her shoulder. It seemed to take an intolerably long time.

Felicity sat in the wingback chair to wait, and after a while she found herself unable to draw a full breath. With no corset to loosen and her breathing becoming shallow, she went out on the balcony with a cashmere shawl wrapped around her shoulders. The brisk air shocked her lungs into a deep breath, and she watched the full moon rise over the mountains. Ghostly light laid blue shadows on the white peaks while Indian ragas and coils of smoke rose up from the godowns. As always, the air smelled charred.

With the full moon well risen, she spotted a figure on horseback racing along the base of the mountains. She held up an oil lamp and watched him ride. She admired the way he sat on his horse – high and straight and in control. When he came near enough for her to hear the pounding of hoof beats, he reined the horse in and slowed to a canter. He looked up and she moved the lamp in a small arc, and the horse reared up in salute. She blew out the lamp and shivered, then pulled the shawl tighter around herself. When she heard a whinny and snort close by, she went inside and sat on the edge of the bed with her back to the balcony.

She heard a scrabbling on the vine-covered wall outside, and she sat very still. Riding boots dropped on to her balcony, but still she did not turn. He came in, shutting the door behind him, and crossed the room to stand before her. Under one arm he carried a carved wooden jewellery box, and moonlight flung his shadow up against the wall. They did not speak. When he opened the box, the gold hinge gave a faint creak, and for a moment nothing happened. Then a soft explosion of pale-green silk moths erupted from the box and poured out into the room. Felicity gasped at the rush of flickering wings, and he said, 'In this place, in this moment, we are free.'

Silk moths filled the room, fluttering and darting, casting nervous shadows on the wall. They flitted and danced in the moonlight, alighting on a bedpost then a chair, but only for the briefest moment. They filled the room with magic, but if there had been a fire, they would have flown towards the flames and been incinerated.

He stood so still that a moth alighted on his shoulder. It flew off when he knelt before her to unwind his turban, and she watched thick glossy hair fall in black ringlets around his face and on to his shoulders. They stayed like that, not touching, not speaking and not quite smiling, while silk moths flashed around them. When he grazed his lips on her cheek, her lashes brushed his brow and he groaned. With two fingertips, he caressed the back of her neck, while his other hand slipped the lavender sari off her shoulder.

Chapter Twenty

1947

I FOUND BILLY'S MAKESHIFT bazaar ransacked, the cookies gone and the coins lying in their place. In the kitchen, Billy sat at the table with Habib, munching cookies and drinking creamy Indian tea. Billy said, 'Hi, Mom,' and Habib gave me a full smile, revealing an entire row of square, white teeth. I wondered whether my entrusting Billy to him had broken the ice. Had he distrusted me because he thought I distrusted him? Would I ever understand India? Billy pointed to the clock. 'You're late, but that's OK. Spike is playing with Habib.'

'Well,' I said, 'how about that.'

The kitchen was redolent of coriander, and while Habib packed his basket, I peeked into the pot he'd left on the stove and saw big juicy chunks of eggplant in the curry. I said, 'Oh, I love eggplant.'

Habib shocked me by saying, 'Eggplants are being the king of vegetables, isn't it?'

'You speak English?'

'Eggplants are being good for the senses, madam. I am wishing health for you and sir.'

I was dumbstruck. 'You speak English,' I repeated.

'Good day, Madam. Namaste, *chota sahib*.'

I looked at Billy. 'He speaks English.'

Billy shrugged and said, 'Namaste, Habib.'

As Habib opened the back door to leave, I had a flashback to the burning car in Simla, the bamboo sticks rising and falling. I said, 'Habib!'

He turned with his hand on the door. 'Madam?'

'You live in Masoorla, don't you?'

'Yes, Madam.'

'You're not going into Simla today, are you?'

His eyes questioned me. 'No, Madam. You are needing something?'

'No. Thank you. We'll see you tomorrow.'

He left without another word, and Billy said, 'We're glad you're home, Mom. Can you read us a story?'

I could almost hear the stolen pages in my purse clamouring to be read, but . . . that cherubic face was irresistible. 'Sure, BoBo.'

We had just finished reading *The Little Engine That Could* when Martin came home early. The sight of him irritated me immediately, because I wanted to tell him what I'd seen in Simla and couldn't. I'd lost my best friend and I missed him like fire.

I went through the motions of an ordinary evening – Billy's dinner of ginger chicken soup with Indian plums and buttermilk, then bathtime, pyjamas and an Irish lullaby.

Martin and I sat down to the mustard-coloured curry, surprisingly mild, and Martin said, 'There was an incident in Simla today.'

My fork stalled briefly. 'Oh?'

'A mob set a car on fire and beat the driver to a pulp.'

It all came back: the fireball, the smell of smoke, the

blood-spattered sticks, the angry faces. I said, 'Why did they do it?'

Martin shrugged. 'No one's talking. According to the locals, no one saw anything.' He shook his head. 'Whatever the guy did, I suspect his real offence was being Muslim when he did it.'

'You don't know that.'

He tilted his head at me. 'An educated guess.'

I glanced at his kurta pyjamas – he was wearing the whole outfit now, long tunic top and baggy pants. I said, 'My educated guess is that you're looking for trouble dressing like that.'

He looked away and said, 'Let's not go through that again.' He took another helping of curry. 'This stuff isn't bad, but it would be better without the eggplant.'

Just as well to change the subject. 'Habib speaks English.'

'Great. Tell him to lay off the eggplant.'

After the dishes were washed and put away, Martin buried himself in *Crime and Punishment* and I put a record on the turntable – 'Is You Is Or Is You Ain't My Baby'. The title had jumped out at me, and the snappy rhythm seemed to dare anyone listening not to join in or at least tap a foot. I lay on the camelback sofa, singing along with the exuberant Andrews Sisters, while heat lightning flashed outside, but Martin never even looked up from his book. I stared at the ceiling, surprised at how easily I had lied to him. Then I wondered how he could not have seen it in my eyes. A crack of thunder rolled over the house, and I asked myself, for the first time, whether it might be better for everyone if we just got a divorce. The thought took my breath away.

The record ended and I put it away, trying to think of someone who was happily divorced – but I didn't know anyone who was divorced, happily or otherwise. It wasn't done much. Dave and Rachel would be disappointed, and Da would be devastated, but they'd get over it. They'd have to. What was the point of this sham, and what would it do to Billy to grow up with parents who didn't even speak to each other? Wouldn't it be better to be apart and amicable than together and miserable?

Around ten o'clock, Martin and I wandered into the bedroom more or less together. I remember a goodnight peck and then, as usual, he turned his back to me.

I waited until his snoring hit the rhythmic stride of deep sleep, then I slipped out of bed, unhooked my purse from the bedroom doorknob and crept through the dark house with my stolen papers. It was cool by then, and I took the crocheted afghan off the sofa and wrapped it around my shoulders. I didn't want light to seep into the bedroom or even, irrationally, to be seen from outside. Guilt really can make you crazy. I took a flashlight from a kitchen drawer, sat down at the table with my cache of notes and unfolded each sheet, careful not to damage the fragile paper. In the narrow beam of light, I arranged the pages in chronological order, February to June. They were journal entries, and in my eagerness to read them, I didn't stop to wonder why someone had torn them out and put them in a Bible.

February 1857

She is expectorating blood & I begin to despair. My best efforts have failed. Could this be a different malady? In Yorkshire, she grew skeletal, but this time her face & body bloat unhealthily in spite of her lack of appetite. Even the smell of food makes her nauseous. The coughing is the same, but all else is different.

I have confined her to her bed, & today I turned the Indian away from our door. But when I went to her, after she had heard his voice, she turned her head on the pillow & would not look at me. I am wounded. I only want what is best for her.

There have been more protests amongst the sepoys regarding those cartridges. General Anson says he will not appease their stupid superstitions. Rather stupid of him, I think.

February 1857

Our world has ended & a new one has begun. Felicity is with child & the Indian (now must I use his name?) is the father. I need time to digest this & cannot bring myself to sit with them when he calls. He knocks on our door, & Felicity hobbles out of her room, her face mottled with blushes that flare & fade with every step. She is too weak to stand for very long & leans on a bamboo walking stick. I sit alone in the kitchen whilst they converse in the drawing room.

With such widespread tension across this land, I sometimes wonder whether he is using Felicity to make some sort of statement amongst his people. But when I suggest it, she accuses me of jealousy. She is not wrong. I admit to some resentment – a hard cold thing lodged in my heart – at having our closed & idyllic world breached by him. I did not stop loving Felicity when I fell in love with Katie & we have made a life here, Felicity & I, platonic but warm & companionable, just the two of us. He has ended all that & I am grieving. I suppose this is selfish of me & I must overcome it, but I am also frightened. Tensions between Britons & Indians are running high & I go about with a feeling of dread. Jealousy, fear, confusion . . . I want our quiet life back, but now – a baby!

I also wonder what the Indian's wife must make of this, if she knows. Mohammedans are allowed multiple wives, but this man is a Sikh & can only have one wife. He is an adulterer and this makes me question his character. In England this would be scandalous, but here, with race & class & politics thrown in the mix, it is quite dangerous. This is a volatile moment in history, what with the sepoys carrying on. We could all be in grave danger.

March 1857

This morning, I rode into the village to watch the natives celebrate Holi, the spring festival of colours. Holi is an invitation to abandon all inhibition, & the natives dance wildly in the road, throwing dye powders at each other & even at the goats & cows – pink, green, blue, yellow & every mixture they can make. The children splash tinted water on each other & everyone ends up drenched & painted. They eat coconut fritters laced with bhang, which is a mild narcotic, & the day ends with faces splotched green & pink, black hair streaked with blue & yellow, & everyone twirling & singing lustily to long reed trumpets & thumping tablas.

I met an English planter & his wife, also come to watch the natives play Holi. He was red-faced & rather silly; I suspect he had indulged in some bhang fritters. She was a glum, mousey little thing, slumped on her pony & quite disinterested in the festival. I asked whether she was enjoying it, & she said, 'My baby died from a miasma that came up through the floor.' I told her how sorry I was & galloped home straight away to tell Felicity about the planter's poor wife. It made Felicity cry & she said, 'We must put in a new plank floor.'

I think it's a splendid idea. The white ants have made a perfect sieve of our bamboo matting, & we want no miasmas seeping up to kill our baby.

March 1857

Today the sun was shining, & I spread the coral & turquoise afghan under the sandalwood tree for Felicity to take the air. She napped whilst I wrote my journal. As the air warmed I, too, began to doze until a loud drilling woke us. I looked up to see a crimson-headed woodpecker attacking the tree with his long pointed bill. I wanted to shoo him off, but Felicity said the tree was more his than ours, so we watched the bird's industrious red head hammer away as he worked for his meal.

Higher on the trunk I spied a neat oval hollow, & it struck me that it would be an excellent ready-made place to stow some of my story. It's a capricious notion, I know, with nothing practical about it, but that is part of the appeal. I know no one in England who would read my account without judgement, & the idea of leaving it to Fate pleases me. I can buy tin-lined boxes & hot-water bottles of vulcanized rubber in the village, which should protect it through a good number of monsoons.

There has been an incident in Barrapore. A sepoy has been arrested, but I do not know the details.

March 1857

I have had a message from Mother. After learning that I had not returned to Calcutta for the season, she could not wait for her response to reach me by ship. She went to the extravagance of a telegram, & a post bearer brought it this afternoon. I read it aloud to Felicity.

> *Return home immediately stop*
> *Chadwicks will assist stop*
> *Behaviour unacceptable stop*
> *Obey or we wash hands stop*

Felicity said, 'No matter. My annuity is enough for us both.' She stroked her slightly rounded belly & stared out of the window, placid & content. But I felt a disturbing intermixture of joy & fear.

This week the punkahs must go up.

April 1857

This morning the servants appeared in an excited state. Lalita told us news had come to the village that the sepoy who was arrested is one Mangal Pandey & his name is on everyone's lips. He attacked & wounded his British officer. He has been charged with mutiny & sentenced to death.

I'm quite sure the profane cartridges must come into this somehow, but the servants profess to know nothing more. They affect to be shocked & disgusted, but the tension in the air is as thick as pudding, & I detect an element of triumph in their eyes.

Lady Chadwick will not come to the hills this hot season, as travel is too risky right now. I am glad not to have to deal with her interference at this time.

May 1857

Pandey was hanged on April 22nd. After his execution, riots & fires broke out in Agra & Ambala. General Anson is untroubled enough to have left for Simla during the hot weather, but I think he is underestimating the significance of Pandey's death. I fear he may have created a martyr.

May 1857

Felicity continues to enumerate her lover's good qualities in an effort to elevate him in my eyes. She says he cares for the poor (but he is wealthy & they are his own poor), she calls attention to his strong-boned face (but it is a brown face with a warrior's beard & topped by a blue turban), & she makes much of his fine manners – English manners!

If their relationship became public, she would be disgraced, but he . . . well, Indian men would question his taste in women, & certain of our military men might not hesitate to hang him. Their child will be an outcast, no matter where he goes. They must be terribly in love to disregard all this, but that makes it no less problematic.

I think of Katie & know I have no right to judge forbidden love, but this man has deceived his wife & put Felicity at risk. How can I trust him?

A solitary life in the mofussil might be the most joyful way to live in India, but perhaps not the most prudent. I think of the safe, insulated drawing rooms of Calcutta & I see now that the life we have chosen is lonely & dangerous.

Lalita tells us that eighty-five sepoys have been court-martialled in Meerut. This is not over.

June 1857

Mutiny! The sepoys have risen en masse & slaughtered hundreds of Europeans in Delhi. A messenger has come from Simla with an invitation for Felicity & me to take refuge at the Club, but Felicity insists the villagers are friendly & we are safe here. I did not argue, because I believe she is too weak to travel, as well as unmistakably pregnant.

Felicity is pale & peevish, her once lustrous hair is lank & dull, & she complains of headache. I cannot separate the symptoms of consumption from the symptoms of pregnancy. My lovely friend lies abed, coughing weakly, & still her belly swells with this new life. I believe the little creature inside her is surviving at her expense.

On bad days she becomes delirious & mistakes her bedpost for the Grim Reaper. She shouts at it to stay away from her baby, & then falls into a fit of coughing. Khalid pads to the door with the tea tray, leaving it on the floor, & the water bearer passes basins of tepid water through the window. I have instructed Lalita to pull her veil over her mouth & nose when she enters the room.

The servants are uneasy, but it is not the possibility of death that disturbs them. Death is common & swift in India, a promise of paradise for Mohammedans & a brief interlude between incarnations for Hindoos. It is this strange memsahib who is not wholly English & not wholly Indian, dying in the mofussil whilst rumoured to be carrying a half-caste child, even as Europeans in Delhi are slaughtered in their homes & sepoys fight Britons to the death in Benares & Allahbad. It is confusing for them.

It is confusing for me.

I clicked off the flashlight and sat still in the dark kitchen. Felicity was not buried in Masoorla and she sounded too sick to have returned to England. What happened to her and her baby?

I pulled the afghan tight around my shoulders and a shock of recognition rippled through me . . . *'I spread the coral and turquoise afghan under the sandalwood tree'* . . . I pressed my face into it, smelling wool and dust and a faint whiff of camphor. It must have been stored in a tin-lined trunk. I ran my hand over its soft surface, marvelling that Adela's fingers had made it and that it had once rested on Felicity's shoulders. They were *real*.

I had never noticed a hollow in the sandalwood tree, but I had never looked. I crept out of the house and down the verandah steps, and stood under the tree in the moonlight. But it was too dark to make anything out through the dense leaves and deep shadows, so I went back inside. I'd look again in the morning.

I refolded Adela's journal pages and tidied them into a neat stack with a sense of ownership. No – I corrected myself – stewardship. I considered tying the bundle with a pretty ribbon, like a proper Victorian, and stashing them with the letters under my lingerie, but that would be an admission of my intention to keep them. I put them back in my purse, a comfortably ambiguous hiding place. I knew the next time I went to Simla I'd feel obliged to return the pages I had taken, and I also knew that I wouldn't do it. Felicity and Adela's story resonated with me; I wanted more.

My eyes wandered over the shadowed curves and planes of the kitchen: the old cooker where Adela had made her beef tea, the blackened brick wall – it would have been new then, with only a whisper of smoke damage – and the wall clock whose modern art-deco style suggested that it had probably been hung quite recently. The kitchen table looked as if it had come from a cottage in the Cotswolds, hewn from sturdy English oak, with a trestle base and surrounded by ladder-back chairs, a style popular in the 1930s. The set must have been shipped from England, between the wars.

I stopped fussing with Adela's papers: where was the rest of Felicity's furniture? The camelback sofa and the brocade chair with the teeth marks on the arm were Victorian, but almost everything else was newer. The breakfront in the dining room had the same simple lines as the china cabinet I'd left in Chicago. There was a 1920s style lamp on a side table in the living room, and a *fin-de-siècle* mirror above the mantel.

Old journal pages might have been used to line the drawers of a chest that had been carted off to an export store in Bombay. There could be letters in a desk or wardrobe sitting in the home of our Indian landlord, who would have had his pick of things when he bought the place. The messages that Adela said came and went between Felicity and her lover might not be hidden at all, but simply forgotten in an almirah now sitting in some antique store in Kensington. The rest of their story could lie scattered almost anywhere across two continents. But hopefully Adela's journal, or some part of it, would still be in the sandalwood tree.

I draped the afghan over the back of the sofa, hung my purse on the bedroom doorknob, and slid back into bed.

Martin had stopped snoring and looked relaxed; no dreams tonight. In sleep, I could see the untroubled face I had loved during our early days. His waking face was a little frightened, a little angry and habitually tense, but asleep . . . I stared at him. The love of my life was still there. How could I divorce the post-war Martin when the real Martin, my Martin, was still in there?

Chapter Twenty-One

THE NEXT MORNING, I went out to the sandalwood tree and peered up into the leaves. I squinted against the sun and walked around the trunk, trying to see through the canopy, but it was too dense. In a hundred years the tree must have grown tremendously; did tree hollows eventually close up? Even if they didn't, anything left could have long ago been dragged away by an animal. An animal small enough to nest in a hollow probably couldn't move a tin-lined box, but a monkey could.

I shaded my eyes and watched a monkey dangling from a branch. It showed off, hanging by one hand and scratching its hairy chest, baring its long teeth in a disturbingly human smile. It swung from branch to branch like a trapeze artist, shrieking when one branch bent unexpectedly low under its weight, far enough for me to see above it. I spotted something in the trunk, a dark, oval depression, more than twenty feet up. It *could* be a hollow, but was much too high to reach. The monkey leaped to a sturdier branch, and the hollow disappeared in the bouncing canopy. I had never climbed a tree in my life; I would need a ladder.

They might have one at the import shop, and I planned

to go there anyway because Martin had invited James Walker to dinner; I thought it would be a nice gesture to serve Walker an English meal. I felt sure the big fellow must enjoy his meat and potatoes. After Rashmi arrived, I would bicycle down to the village, where I could find everything I needed for an English dinner; only the meat would be tricky.

Butchers were always Muslim, so it was impossible to buy pork. Beef was risky, since cows were protected, and you could never be sure what might be passing for steak. Goat was terribly ordinary – and I didn't know how to prepare it anyway – and chicken was always unaccountably tough. Lamb roasts were usually sold in unidentifiable chunks that tended to be mutton, so I settled on baby lamb chops. I was pretty sure I could recognize a lamb chop, and mint jelly would make it English. I didn't realize at the time that mint jelly is basically anglicized chutney.

I was searching for my sunglasses when Rashmi came in with a fresh tikka and a conspiratorial wink, which I pretended not to notice. I said, 'I'm going shopping after my class.'

'You will buy buffalo milk?'

'Um, no.'

'But your good self must buy buffalo milk. For Sir.'

'He doesn't drink milk.'

'I knew it! He must be drinking buffalo milk, yes.'

'No.'

'What is it, you're not enjoying buffalo milk?'

'We've never had buffalo milk.'

'I knew it! From here is your problem coming.'

'OK, I'll buy buffalo milk.'

'Pinch your neck and swear.'

'What?'

'Do it!'

'Fine.' I pinched my neck, feeling like an idiot. 'Shall I get some for you, too?'

'I don't like buffalo milk so much.' A lascivious smile split her face. 'And I am not needing.'

I bicycled down to my banyan-tree school, and we did Bs that day. I drew a book, a basket and a backbone, which presented an opportunity for touching the children's spines and tickling them. I got a finger between Timin's ribs and the poor child jumped as if I'd pulled a knife on him – the upturned face, the frightened eyes. I hadn't realized they were still afraid of me. I spent most of the hour cajoling the children into letting me hug them. In the end, shy smiles turned into giggling fits, and eight pairs of enormous black eyes crinkled with mirth. They didn't learn Bs that day; it was much better than that.

Afterwards, I pedalled to the shop of a butcher with an orange henna beard and I shopped the way I taught English: pointing, miming and drawing pictures. I sketched a fluffy cartoonish lamb and said, 'Baaa.' I felt like a fool and the drawing actually made me a little uneasy: living among vegetarians sometimes gave me pause, and I didn't like connecting an appetizingly grilled chop to an adorable animal. But I showed the butcher my sketch and ruthlessly held up seven fingers.

While the butcher wrapped the meat, I realized that this man would very soon have to decide whether to stay in a Hindu country or move across the new border to Pakistan. I looked around for signs of packing up, but everything looked normal. Flies buzzed around a bloody haunch of meat on a hook, ducks honked in a bamboo cage, and the butcher offered me a pleasant salaam when I signed his chit.

Like the other merchants, he would send it to my bungalow at the end of the month.

Outside, I hooked the basket on to my handlebars and glanced back to see the butcher tipped back on his wooden chair, smoking a bidi and telling his beads. If a Muslim in Masoorla could be that relaxed on the eve of Partition, I'd be damned if I'd let Martin spook me into staying at home.

Pedalling up the hill, I stopped to buy potatoes and peas from a woman in a watermelon-coloured sari sitting by the side of the road. I pointed, and she deftly wrapped the vegetables in newspaper while balancing a limp baby on one arm. She wore the end of her sari pulled over her head and had no tikka on her smooth brown forehead. I assumed from this that she, too, was Muslim, and yet there she sat, bold as day, with her baby.

I laid the peas and potatoes on top of the chops in my basket and pedalled hard uphill, ignoring the looks provoked by my speed, my slacks, my sunglasses and my flaming wind-whipped hair. I parked in front of the import shop run by Manesh Kumar, an enterprising Indian who stocked digestive biscuits, marmalade, Earl Grey tea, tinned sardines and all the other necessities of colonial life. Inside, I poked around the congested shop until I found mint jelly for the lamb, canned milk for the tea, a box of English toffee and a dusty bottle of French Burgundy. I couldn't find a ladder, and I wondered whether I'd have to go to Simla for it. At the last minute I added a fifth of Scotch to my basket; I'd noticed that the bottle at home was getting low.

Manesh had a round head, round face and round body, all of which gave him an agreeable Falstaffian bulk. Instead of the more common orange tikka, he usually wore three horizontal white stripes drawn across his forehead with sandalwood paste, which made him look oddly tribal. I plopped my purchases on the little counter and Manesh waggled his head. 'English food and French wine you are buying. You are having a party?'

'A small one. How are you today, Manesh?'

'A-OK, first class.' Then his smile drooped. 'Even though my wife's mother from the city is coming.'

'I'm sure your wife will be happy to see her.'

He shook his head sadly. 'No. Even wife is not liking. From Calcutta old woman is coming because too much crazy fighting is there.' Without warning, the smile broke his round face open. 'But is good karma, neh?'

'Excellent karma.' And I wondered – did karma, the Great Leveller, keep this man smiling? Was that his secret? I said, 'Karma makes it all come out even in the end, doesn't it?'

He wagged his head happily. 'Maybe yes, maybe no. But no use wanting what is not, neh? Wanting is suffering. Accepting is peace.'

'Indeed.' I stared at him a moment longer than was polite, this biscuit-importing philosopher. Accepting is peace? I'd have to think about that. But for the moment, I wasn't ready to accept not getting up in the sandalwood tree. I asked, 'Do you have any ladders?'

'Not having, Madam, but can get.'

'Great. How long will it take?'

And there it was – the dreaded head waggle. 'Soonly, Madam.'

'Um, a few days or a few weeks?'

'Oh, yes.' Waggle. 'Some days only.'

I wanted to ask how many days, but I remembered the woman in the apricot sari who had said the church would be closed all day but open in two hours. 'OK,' I said. 'Please order a ladder and send it to my house as soon as it arrives.'

Manesh smiled as I signed my chit. When I hopped on my

bike he called, 'Not driving fastly, madam.' He beamed at me and waved.

I waved back, thinking how much Manesh reminded me of Rashmi. He had a small house next to the store and a bunch of kids – I never did figure out how many – but he managed to keep them fed and that seemed to be enough for him. Now his apparently unpleasant mother-in-law would be living with him and he still smiled. Like Rashmi, he expected little and accepted much. Maybe I could learn acceptance from these people. They even accepted their arranged marriages. Ninety-five per cent of the marriages in India are arranged, and yet they have the lowest divorce rate in the world. Life is temporary, so why not accept it all as transitory and get through the day the best way you can? Maybe it was too much to expect romantic love to go on for ever. Maybe it was unreasonable to expect Martin to come back from the war and pick up where we left off. Maybe we'd both be happier if I could just accept the change in him.

Chapter Twenty-Two

A WESTERN, SPICE-FREE MEAL sounded as tempting as a balmy oasis in a burning desert, and I knew Martin would appreciate the break from incandescent sauces, no matter how authentic they were. I laid the dining-room table, using the china and glassware that came with the house – Rosenthal porcelain with a blue floral design, and heavy Waterford crystal, both of which would have been unaffordable in Chicago. I held a glass up to the light to admire the rainbows in the facets, then went outside to cut fresh red poppies for the pewter pitcher. The flowers looked vibrant and spontaneous between staid, antique candlesticks, and the whole lovely effect made me smile. Acceptance seemed attainable.

Habib arrived as I finished the table. He saw the lamb chops and peas in the kitchen and stood there, scowling. I began unloading his basket for him. 'Go ahead with dinner,' I said. 'I'm just making a few extra things for a guest.' Habib counted on his small wages, and it would be crummy of me to deprive him of them. He moved the chops out of his way and began to dice onions – it seemed every Indian dish began with dicing onions – and I watched him busy himself, chopping, grinding and seasoning. He lined up chickpeas, spinach, cumin seeds, coriander buds and, as always, a pile of hot, hot chillis. I decided to serve his curry and raita as witty side dishes, but when he pulled out an eggplant I said, 'Oh, Mr Mitchell doesn't care for eggplant.'

'Of course not, Madam. Eggplant is a useless vegetable.'

'What?'

'A mistake I am making with this vegetable. I will take back. The merchant should not even be selling such useless vegetables, isn't it?'

'But last night you said eggplant was the king of vegetables.'

Habib regarded me with pity for not understanding something so simple. 'Madam,' he said, 'for you I am working, not for the eggplant. What good would it be doing *me* to be disagreeing with you and agreeing with the eggplant?'

I watched Habib put away his eggplant and saw a bamboo stalk bending without breaking.

James Walker rang the bell as I set a pot of potatoes on the stove, and I wiped my hands on my apron as I hurried to welcome him. The big man seemed to fill the doorway, and I was surprisingly happy to see him. India had turned out to be so lonely. When Walker presented me with a six-pack of Kingfisher beer, I couldn't stop myself from throwing a glance at the open bottle of Burgundy I'd left on the sideboard to breathe. He followed me into the kitchen, where I put his beer in the wooden icebox and turned up the flame under the potatoes.

Walker peered into the pot and said, 'In the land of perfumed rice you're boiling potatoes?' I decided to take his surprise as a compliment. Then he lifted the lid from Habib's curry pot and inhaled the spicy steam; he closed his eyes and purred. Had I miscalculated? He was English. Wasn't he mad for roast beef, fish and chips, mushy peas, steak and kidney pie, kippers and bangers? Verna had showed me the memsahib's bible, *The Indian Housekeeper and Cook*, and there wasn't a single Indian recipe in it. Was James Walker some kind of culinary aberration?

But of course! He'd been in India for almost two decades. Thank God I hadn't thrown out Habib's curry. I said, 'Care for a Scotch?'

Walker glanced at the icebox, saying, 'Have you tried the local brew?'

I opened two bottles of beer, and Walker took one by the neck. 'Don't bother hunting for a glass,' he said. 'This is fine.' He clinked his bottle against mine and took a swig. I took a timid sip and found the rich brassy taste surprisingly pleasant. The perfect counterpoint, I realized, to a spicy curry.

Billy noisily slurped up his bowl of lentil dhal. He ate his rice the way Rashmi had taught him, rolling it into little balls that he popped in his mouth. I made a mental note to speak to him about that. Walker said, 'So, little sahib, have you learned to converse in Hindi yet?'

Billy peered at him with a dhal moustache. 'Don't need to,' he said. 'Mom's teaching them all English.'

I smiled over my shoulder. 'Not all of them, Noodle.'

Walker clamped a hand on his little shoulder. 'What say we learn some Hindi?'

Billy nodded, serious in spite of his lentil moustache. 'Maybe I better.'

While I arranged chops on the grill, Walker taught Billy to say 'please' – *kripya* – and 'thank you' – *shukriya*. Billy scrunched up his little face and did his best, and Walker pronounced him bilingual.

After Martin arrived, I opened another beer for Walker,

and we excused ourselves for the bedtime ritual. Billy said, 'Namaste, Mr Walker,' and I carried him into his room. Martin and I sat on opposite sides of Billy's narrow bed, and Martin tucked the blanket up to his chin while I settled Spike under his arm. We kissed him and Billy said, '*Kripa*,' then waited for a reaction.

Martin laughed. 'Rascal.'

I blew into Billy's neck and he giggled. 'It's not *kripa*, BoBo. It's *kripya*,' I said.

'Nuh-uh.'

'Uh-huh. I learned it from my students weeks and weeks ago.'

Billy regarded me with infinite patience. 'I know, Mom. But I learned it *tonight*.'

His earnestness made me want to laugh and cry, and I could see that Martin felt it too. A look of shared understanding passed between us, and I thought again that my exercise in acceptance wouldn't be terribly difficult.

I kissed Billy one more time and said, 'Go to sleep, Peach.'

In the dining room, I repeated Billy's remark to Walker and he smiled indulgently. I knew Martin and I were thinking the same thing: Walker simply didn't understand how *special* Billy was. It was amazing how many people missed that; only Martin and I got it. Remembering how Martin's face had relaxed in Billy's bedroom, it occurred to me that our son was the only reason Martin smiled at all any more. Would we even have lasted this long without our son? I quashed that thought and busied myself with serving spoons.

Walker spread his arms wide at the table. 'Evie, you're a wonder.'

I demurred, 'Well, Habib—'

'She sure is,' said Martin. 'She was studying astronomy when we met.'

'Actually,' I said, 'we met in a German bakery. I worked behind the counter and—'

'No we didn't.' Martin poured wine into Walker's glass.

'Sure we did. You used to come in for rye bread.'

He poured wine for me. 'We met on campus.' He filled his own glass and shook his head at Walker as if to say, 'The little woman is confused.'

I felt an angry flush spreading down my neck. 'I can't believe you don't remember.' In fact I *didn't* believe it. There was no way he didn't remember Linz's. He was denying it, but why?

Martin continued as if I hadn't spoken. 'She was studying astronomy, and you should have heard her go on about con-stellations and galaxies.' He patted my hand. 'Ours was a cosmic love.'

I slipped my hand out from under his and listened to the idealized version of myself, the pre-war *Wunderkind* that Martin had loved, someone very different from the little *Hausfrau* with the bad memory. But we *had* met at Linz's. I felt the tightness between my eyebrows and realized I must look as confused as I felt.

Walker said, 'I'm glad you two met, wherever it was, or I wouldn't be enjoying this marvellous dinner.' He had heaped his plate with Habib's vegetable curry and ladled on a small lake of raita. He stabbed one lamb chop off the platter, like an afterthought, and ignored the mint jelly altogether. Walker shovelled in a mouthful of curry and dipped his head with an appreciative hum. 'This masala is excellent. Kudos, Evie.'

Martin and I exchanged another quick look. 'Actually,' I said, 'our cook made the curry.'

'Ah, you have a cook. I saw you in the kitchen and I thought . . . well, of course you have a cook, and a good one.

Ask him to make you some aloo aur gobhi ka salan. Terrific local dish.'

'I'll do that.' I noticed that he had not yet touched his lamb chop and wondered, with sudden horror, if twenty years in India had made him a vegetarian. I should have asked.

'So,' I said, cutting into my chop, 'you're not married?'

'No. I'm not marriage material.' He talked around a mouthful of curry. 'When I see a little one like Billy, I'd be a liar to say I have no regrets. But I suppose one can't have it all.'

'That's true.' I took a sip of wine, thinking about how Martin had forbidden me to go into Simla. 'But I think that's the first time I've heard a man say that.'

Martin snorted the most eloquent snort I'd ever heard, as if to say, 'You're a wife and mother, you wanted to come here, and you got your way. Now you have a nice house with servants.' In 1947 this was known as having it all.

'Excuse me,' I said, standing quickly. 'I think I left a burner on.' I hurried away from the table, away from Martin, and paced back and forth in the kitchen. *Acceptance.* I dumped English toffee on a platter and when a piece fell on the floor, I picked it up and ate it on the spot. I stood very still and took deep, regular breaths until my heart slowed down.

When I walked back into the dining room, Martin was talking about the university. 'I know they're not going to swoop out of the sky in a fighter jet to rescue my family, but I don't think they should simply abandon us in a war zone.'

Walker listened without comment, sucking his teeth and tapping a fingertip on the table. Bored. I set the platter of toffee on the table and Walker immediately took a piece and crunched into it. He seemed pleased, and I thought at least I'd chosen the dessert well. Then he said, 'Have you tried the

Indian desserts? They do miraculous things to custard with fruit and spices.'

I sighed. 'You're a man of the people, James. Not like some of your countrymen here.'

He leaned forward, amused. 'Are you suggesting that Lydia and Edward are arrogant?'

I inclined my head as if to indicate, *You said it, I didn't.*

'Ah, they're not so bad.' He sat back. 'And I should warn you whenever an American gets on an egalitarian high horse, the English start bashing on about the Red Man and Negroes.' He raised his shaggy eyebrows and looked suddenly challenging. 'No comeback, eh?' His eyebrows relaxed and he looked his friendly self again. 'Most of us here muddle along without causing too much harm. We've even done some good along the way – schools, roads, hospitals. I say live and let live.'

'Hear, hear.' Martin downed his wine and poured the last of the bottle into his own glass. I thought, *For God's sake, Martin*, and then – *acceptance.*

Walker said, 'We left a few good things in Africa, too. And when I served in Burma—'

'You served in Burma?' Martin straightened up, alert as a startled deer.

Walker nodded. 'At the end of the war. At first I served here in India. We had a POW camp for Italian prisoners in Dharamsala, but there wasn't much to do – all mountains and jungles and no place for them to go. We simply had them check in every night. When they got drunk on arrack and slept on someone's verandah we locked them up for a week. But it all seemed rather pointless. I thought I could do more good as a foreign correspondent where the war was actually happening. I volunteered for Burma.'

'I served in Europe.'

Walker suddenly deflated. He looked bone tired. 'Ghastly mess,' he muttered.

'I'll say.' Martin gulped down his wine in one go and I winced. He said, 'I was there at the end. Helped liberate one of the camps.'

I stared at him. 'You what?' He had never told me that.

Walker played with a piece of toffee and said, 'Which one?'

'What difference does it make?' Martin looked defensive.

'None, I suppose. But I've heard stories about some of those liberations. Messy is what I've heard.'

'You have no idea.'

Walker's piece of toffee stalled in mid air. 'Burma was not exactly a walk in the park.'

Inexplicable hostility crackled between them, and I had no idea why, but I didn't like it. It was never a good idea to bring up the war with Martin. 'Oh come now,' I said. 'The war is over, and surely not fit for dinner conversation.'

'Sorry, Evie. Old soldiers, you know.' Walker stared at Martin a second too long. 'So you were a hero then. Liberating that camp.'

'I never said that.'

I tapped an Abdullah out of my pack and lit up. What was going on?

'Oh, don't be modest. All those poor souls starved and tortured. You were a hero to them.'

'Just doing my job.'

'I heard they were beside themselves with joy when the Allies rolled in.'

Martin's face was a thundercloud. I said, 'What on earth—'

'All right, Walker.' Martin got up and poured himself a Scotch. 'Yeah. They were half dead. It was lousy. Really shitty.

We sprung 'em from the Krauts and they were grateful. What else do you want to know?'

'Martin, what's going on?' Everything felt out of control and I had a ridiculous urge to start clearing the table and washing dishes.

'Stay out of this, Evie.'

'Stay out of what?' The cigarette trembled between my fingers. They both knew something about those camps, and it didn't look as if anyone was going to tell me about it.

Walker played with his empty wine glass. 'You Yanks didn't waste time on protocol with the Krauts in those camps, did you? Especially Dachau. I've heard stories about Dachau.'

'You don't know what you're talking about.'

'Enlighten me.'

Martin's hand tightened around his glass and the muscles in his neck bulged. I stood up. 'That's enough. I don't know what this is about, but the war is over, thank God. Why on earth are we talking about concentration camps? It's obscene.'

They stared at each other; neither moved. Then Walker said, 'Forgive us, my dear. Of course you're right.' He appeared chastened, but Martin looked fierce, ready to throw a punch. The glass in his hand trembled.

I said, 'Let's have coffee in the living room.'

Feeling like a referee in a game I didn't understand, I got them seated at opposite ends of the living room and set a record on the turntable – Debussy, light as a Degas ballerina. I would ask Martin about the camp later, after Walker left. I smoothed my apron, feeling like a junior memsahib, but I didn't care. I had a sudden appreciation for how those women had carried the burden of keeping civility alive amid uncertainty and violence. I asked, 'Coffee or tea?'

'How about Scotch?' Martin said.

Walker nodded. 'Sounds good.'

I went into the kitchen to make myself a cup of tea, and as I waited for the kettle to boil, I wondered how many women had served whisky pegs to angry men in this house. I didn't understand what had just happened, but when I went back to them with my tea, they were talking Indian politics. I settled into my wingback chair and said, 'You were right about staying in Masoorla, James. Manesh told me his mother-in-law is coming here from Calcutta to escape the violence. We're lucky to be here.' I threw Martin a quick, pointed look. 'Things couldn't be quieter.'

Walker swirled the Scotch in his glass. 'Well, there have been some disturbances in the native quarters, coolies brawling – of course you wouldn't be going there anyway – but there was also an incident on Cart Road. A spot of caution wouldn't be out of place.'

Martin shot me a look, unbearably smug, and I tensed. I said, 'But that was hardly a riot. We don't even know why it happened.'

'True. But this country goes from doldrums to maelstrom in the blink of an eye.'

I knew Martin was gloating, and I dreaded the self-righteous tirade he would launch after Walker left.

Walker said, 'It's bad in the Punjab. Last week an entire Hindu village committed ritual suicide to avoid being cast out or converted. There'll be more trouble when Muslim refugees start pouring into Lahore.'

Martin said, 'I want to talk to the refugees in Lahore.'

'I wouldn't advise it.' Walker sipped his drink. 'Dicey situation.'

'Not for whites.'

Walker laughed. 'Sorry, old man, but you're not looking

particularly white these days. If mayhem breaks out, you think they'll stop to ask for your passport?'

Martin set his glass on the table very carefully. 'I don't need you to tell me—'

'OK.' Once again I played the good memsahib. 'I think that's enough ugly talk for one evening.' This was not what I'd had in mind when I had brought up our relative safety. I said, 'James, you seem to know a lot about Indian food. We're having trouble getting used to it. What would you recommend?'

I nursed my tea while Walker compared the grilled kebabs of north India to the tongue-cauterizing vindaloos of the south. Martin slouched on the sofa and guzzled Scotch.

When we heard the late-night prayer call of the muezzin, Walker checked his watch, downed the last of his Scotch and hauled himself out of his chair. He said, 'Thanks for a marvellous dinner, Evie. Excellent curry.'

Martin mumbled, 'Yeah, thanks for coming.' He didn't get up, and I felt like slugging him. I saw Walker to the door, considered apologizing for Martin, then decided an oblivious smile would be more comfortable for both of us. I closed the door after him and leaned against it, relieved to have the evening over.

Martin peeked around the side of the sofa and raised one eyebrow. He looked sickeningly triumphant, and infuriatingly bleary-eyed. He said, 'Can I say I told you so?'

'No, you can't.' *Acceptance?* I tried to inject some gentleness into my voice. 'He didn't say I shouldn't go into town.'

'Well, he sure as hell didn't say you should. But that's why you brought it up, isn't it? To make me look bad.'

'You do that very well by yourself. You're drunk, and you humiliated me. And what was all that about concentration camps?'

'You're changing the subject.'

'I want to know.' Anger expanded in my chest and acceptance dwindled to an abstract concept. If we kept going we'd start shouting and wake Billy again. Abruptly, I said, 'Forget it. You're drunk.' I pushed away from the door and headed for the dining room to clear the table. 'We'll talk tomorrow.'

Martin got up and followed me. 'Oh, come on. So I had one too many. So what?'

I picked up a stack of plates and carried them into the kitchen with Martin tagging along. There had been a swagger in his voice that infuriated me. I wanted to say, 'Who *are* you?' I bit my lip and stacked dishes in the sink. I said, 'Tomorrow.'

I turned on the tap and clenched my teeth while I sprinkled soap powder into the basin. I could feel my jaw muscles working as Martin came up behind me and kissed my neck. 'Come on,' he murmured. 'Don't be like that.'

'Stop it.' I pushed him away with a soapy hand.

'Oh, come on. It's been a helluva long time . . .' He cupped my breast, and I whirled around and slapped his face.

Martin's mouth fell open, and his glasses hung cockeyed. He touched his face where soapy water dripped from a red mark on his cheek, and we stared at each other. I had never hit anyone before in my life. I said, 'Martin—'

'I'm going to bed.' He backed away. 'You're right. I'm a little drunk.'

'But, Martin—'

He held his palms up, a warning, and then he wheeled around and walked out of the kitchen.

I closed my eyes, but he was imprinted on the inside of my eyelids. I saw him swaying on his feet, the wet hand-print on his face, his mouth hanging open, glasses askew, eyes shocked. I walked around the kitchen in tight circles, hugging myself. I felt blasted apart and cornered at the same time. In the living room, I wrapped myself in the crocheted afghan, trying to imagine the isolated, unloved life of a divorcee, and cried myself to sleep on the sofa.

Chapter Twenty-Three

THE NEXT MORNING, Martin bent over the sofa and squeezed my shoulder. 'Evie?' he whispered. 'I'm sorry.'

I lay facing the sofa back and woke instantly at his touch.

He said, 'I was drunk, but there's no excuse for the way I behaved.'

The evening rushed back and I mumbled, 'We were both awful.' I twisted to look at him. 'Why didn't you ever tell me you liberated a concentration camp?'

He withdrew his hand. 'I don't want to talk about that. But I'm sorry for last night.' He backed away and went out of the front door, shutting it quietly behind himself.

I closed my eyes and remembered fragments of a dream about struggling to clip on my opal earrings. I had pressed them hard on to my dream earlobes only to have them slide off, over and over, and I had woken in the middle of the night, grinding my teeth.

After breakfast, I started cleaning – the dishes, the table, the floors. I was polishing the jade Ganesh on the mantel when Billy tugged my sleeve. 'Mom?'

'Hmm?'

'You and Dad mad again?'

'No, BoBo. Everything is fine.'

'You look mad.'

'No, Peach. Nothing to worry about.'

Billy slunk out to the verandah with Spike. He climbed into a wicker rocker and I heard him say, 'She's lying.' He sat there staring at the mountains, rocking like a little old man, and I wanted to run out there and crush him to me. I wanted to apologize for bringing him to such a lonely place, for my crippled marriage, for his damaged father, for my inadequacy as a mother. But he was *five*. I went out to the verandah and pulled him on to my lap. We sat together quietly, staring at the sandalwood tree.

Rashmi came through the back door with her winking nose pin and her hidden coconut, calling, 'Come, *beta*.' I kissed Billy goodbye, got on my bike and cycled down to the village. I went through the motions of drawing pink cartoons on the blackboard, but I pressed so hard the chalk broke. The children's mispronunciations – which I usually found charming – irritated me and I rushed through the lesson, willing myself to be patient. I hadn't taken my camera along, and had no interest in dallying in the village.

Masoorla seemed leached of colour that day, and the smell of burning rubbish filled the air. The cows looked neglected, and the ubiquitous monkeys annoyed me. I cycled back at top speed, pushing myself on the incline, huffing and puffing. When I swerved around pedestrians or rickshaws I rang the ear-piercing handlebar bell like a woman with her hair on fire.

Shortly after Rashmi left with the garbage that afternoon, a post bearer came to the door – a barefoot, bare-chested, turbanned little fellow with red teeth. He placed his palms together and bowed, then handed me a cylinder of paper. It was one of those long narrow sheets of grainy paper which Indians write on horizontally and then roll up like a scroll. I gave him a few coins and returned his bow, then I unrolled the paper while he trotted down the steps. The sheet opened to about six inches wide and bore a brief message in English. The handwriting was formal and graceful.

Dear Evie,
I have found a reference to your English ladies in our records.
You can find me in the temple today at three o'clock.
                                                    Your friend
                                                    Harry

Curiosity reared up, fresh and clamouring, and I rolled up the paper feeling eager to see Harry. India was so damn lonely. But, of course, I would no longer take Billy into Simla. It was almost two thirty and Habib would arrive to start dinner around four, but the note said 'today at three o'clock'. Was he going away? Was his retreat over? I imagined Harry waiting for me, glancing at the door, maybe going out into the street to look for me. I needed a babysitter.

Most of the memsahibs in Masoorla made careers out of killing time, and of all of them, Verna Drake of the horsey smile and misbegotten scones lived the closest to me, at Morningside. Verna didn't have children, but she had always been friendly. Whenever I ran into her at the import store she gave me a blinding smile and repeated her invitation to the Club.

I put Harry's letter in my purse, sat Billy in his wagon, and set out for Morningside. As we walked up her verandah steps, Billy asked, 'Isn't this where the lady with the big teeth lives?'

'Yes.' I pinched off a smile. 'But don't say that in front of her. It would hurt her feelings.'

Billy looked at Spike as if they had both been insulted. 'We know that, Mom.'

'I want you and Spike to behave for Mrs Drake while I run an errand.'

'Why can't we come with you?'

'It's a grown-up errand.'

'Aw, nuts.'

When Verna opened the door, surprise danced across her face, but she recovered quickly and smiled. 'Why, Evie Mitchell! Come in!' Her speech was clipped and imperious, developed over many years as a burra memsahib surrounded by servants and underlings. She bit out each word and came down hard on the Ts. The woman smiled continuously, and I have never seen such large teeth on another human being. Verna said, 'We never see you and Martin at the Club. Where have you been hiding?'

'Oh, just busy. You know.' I nodded towards Billy, as though his existence made any life apart from him im-possible. I counted on childless Verna not to know any better.

Billy crawled into a chintz chair with Spike, and I sat on the edge of a period sofa upholstered in pink brocade. I thought about Felicity's missing furniture and suppressed an urge to open a drawer in the side table. I said, 'You have lovely furniture, Verna. Is it Victorian?'

'I believe some of it is. Would you care for tea? My bearer is outside.'

'No, thanks. I've come to ask a favour.' I realized I was clutching my purse with both hands. Lying to Verna was more difficult than lying to Martin, and that seemed wrong for so many reasons. 'I have to take something to

Martin.' I patted my purse. 'He forgot it. This morning. And he needs it.'

Verna shifted in her chair. 'Can't you send it with a servant?'

'It's important. I really should give it to him myself.' I patted my purse again.

'Well, do be careful.'

'Of course. But could I possibly leave Billy with you?'

'Billy?' Verna smoothed the skirt of her floral dress. She gaped at Billy as though he were a bug-eyed Martian, disembarking from a spacecraft in her living room. 'Well . . . I suppose . . .'

'Thank you, Verna. I won't be long. There and back in a shot. I promise.'

Verna stared at Billy, and her smile floundered. 'Well, if you must . . .'

'I appreciate this. I really do.'

When I folded Billy in a bear hug, I noticed a black Bakelite telephone on a low marble-topped table next to his chair. I said, 'Verna, you have a phone?'

Verna was already standing at the front door, fidgeting with her pearls; I imagined her thinking the sooner I left, the sooner I'd be back. 'Yes,' she said. 'Some of the bungalows have phones.'

'Does it work?'

Verna shrugged. 'Like everything else here – when it wants to, and then not very well. One can't really count on anything here, can one?'

I joined her at the door. 'That's why I don't want to take Billy with me. The troubles, you know.'

'Quite right, my dear.'

I had inadvertently struck the right note – civilized Westerners sticking together against the unruly Asiatic hordes. Verna nodded sharply as though she had, that moment, decided to die for a cause. 'Bully for you, not trusting your child to an Indian servant just now. Some do, you know.' She raised a disapproving eyebrow, as if the natives were headhunters who picked their teeth with human bones.

I considered Billy, dwarfed in the oversized chair, his baby legs, soft as taffy, barely reaching the end of the seat cushion. Subjecting him to Verna Drake – her curt manner, that attitude, those *teeth* – seemed almost cruel. But Billy saw me looking at him and misinterpreted. He said, 'You can go, Mom. We'll be-have.' He said 'have' with a long A, splitting the word 'behave', and something caught in my throat. I flipped on my sunglasses, thanked Verna, and hurried out before I could change my mind.

Chapter Twenty-Four

I ENTERED THE VILLAGE of low-slung, slate-roofed huts, alert to signs of unrest: tension in a face, hostile eyes, mumbling . . . But it was so quiet that I heard a cow urinating beside a house. I smiled at a woman in a strawberry-coloured sari and she nodded pleasantly. I hailed a rickshaw and by the time I arrived at the Buddhist temple, I was convinced the beating had been an isolated case of random violence. It could have happened anywhere.

I kicked off my sandals at the temple doors and found Harry inside, sitting in meditation. Shivering candlelight made the scene hallucinatory, like an image in wavy amber glass. I took off my sunglasses and hung back, reluctant to disturb him. He sat cross-legged with his feet on top of his thighs rather than tucked under; his hands lay open, palms up, resting on each knee – the lotus position. He held his back straight and his shoulders square as a T, yet he appeared relaxed. He sat so still I couldn't detect the rise and fall of his breath. His eyes were half closed, but appeared to focus on a point just beyond his knees.

Perhaps Harry heard me come in or maybe he felt my eyes

on him. He untangled his legs, rising in one fluid move that seemed to defy gravity. He pressed his palms and held them up in greeting. 'Namaste.'

'Namaste, Harry. I'm sorry to disturb you.'

'Not at all. My inner self is as boring as ever.'

'You sit so still. I couldn't even see you breathing.'

He shrugged. 'It's only a matter of practice.' His face opened, and he laughed. 'They actually call it that – practice.'

'Oh?' I smiled, but I didn't get it. 'I brought the letter I told you about.' I handed him Felicity's letter and said, 'Apparently, as a child, Felicity had an ayah who put the ashes of the dead into their food. I wonder if it was simple resentment or if there is some custom I'm not aware of.'

Harry read the letter and handed it back. He said, 'People are interesting, aren't they?' It reminded me of Reverend Locke's airy reference to the inexplicable eccentricities of the human race. He said, 'I have no idea what the ayah thought she was doing, but there's nothing like death to inspire the imagination. Have you ever seen an aghori?' He simulated a shudder. 'Death-obsessed sadhus who live in the cremation grounds and smear themselves with the ashes of the dead.'

'How ghoulish.'

'People get very creative in the pursuit of life everlasting. Moksha, nirvana, enlightenment, heaven – we have all kinds of names for it, and everyone wants it, yet no one wants to die.' He smiled and his eyebrows slanted down at the corners.

I said, 'What if there is no life everlasting?'

Harry reflected for a moment. 'I'm not sure it matters. I have an idea the only thing that makes this life bearable is the beauty we create out of chaos – music, art, poetry, but most of all, living a beautiful life, however one might define that.'

'It can be difficult to live a beautiful life. Other people can make it difficult.'

He almost smiled. 'We can only attend to our own lives. I think it's like a symphony. Each musician plays his own part, and if everyone plays well, the result is harmony. But each of us can play only our own small share. If we reincarnate, we will eventually play all the parts, but only one at a time.'

I considered that. 'If Felicity's ayah believed in re-incarnation, she might have thought she could dictate what part the sahibs played in the next orchestra. Cause them to be reborn as servants.'

'Well, I don't think that's how it works, but . . .' Harry's high round forehead wrinkled at a new thought. 'Hindus believe that having their ashes fed to the Ganges ensures a human reincarnation, and Buddhists think that twirling a prayer wheel shortens the cycle of rebirth. Personally, I don't think there are any magic rubrics, but who knows what the ayah thought? Some people can't resist the urge to meddle in other people's lives.'

'Yes. I wonder why we do that.'

He paused. 'Are we still talking about the ayah?'

I gave a little start. 'We've gone off on a tangent, haven't we?'

'I don't mind. It's nice to meet someone who listens. Hindus say knowledge is talking and wisdom is listening.'

'That's beautiful.' But I remembered what I'd come for. 'You found something in the ashram records?'

'Yes. The records tell of two young Englishwomen who came to Simla and lived alone in the *mofussil*. Apparently they were quite unconventional and there was a scandal.'

'Felicity became pregnant by an Indian.'

'Ah, you already know!' He shook his head. 'I'm not very useful, after all.'

'I only discovered it recently. But does it say what happened to them, or to the child?'

'No, although I'm afraid many, many children died in infancy. Mothers too. But there's a specific reference to Adela Winfield.'

'Oh?'

'Her name appears in a different passage written in Urdu. We have many languages in India and countless dialects. The monks write in whatever language is most familiar to them. I'm afraid don't speak Urdu very well, but I can have it translated.'

'I wonder why there would be something about Adela but no more about Felicity and her baby.'

'No idea. But I'll get the translation and maybe we can figure it out.'

His generosity, coming in the middle of my stand-off with Martin, brought a lump to my throat. I swallowed and said, 'How can I thank you?'

'No need.' Harry inclined his head and smiled. 'Just be kind to someone.'

It was as if he *knew*. I was seldom kind any more. I said, 'Of course.'

I left the temple and wandered through the bazaar, inhaling smoke-scented air, listening to the thump of thumbs on small round drums, the winding wail of finger flutes. I watched saris swirl and blur in the moving crowd and the effect was mesmerizing.

An old woman, shrunken amid the folds of her banana-coloured sari, scuffed along the lane, rubber sandals flapping on the hard-packed earth. I caught her eye and she put her hands together and offered me a wide, toothless grin. I smiled back, and we understood each other because everyone smiles in the same language. Martin and Verna could huddle in their paranoid world without me. I felt something free and hopeful wake up and blink in the sunlight. This place *was* as peaceful as a lake.

I passed the tent of the henna artist, curious as always. Other stalls and shops were open to the street; even people's one-room huts were often open on one side, and it was common to see men sleeping, children eating and women grooming themselves. Life is public in India, but the henna artist needed privacy to ply her trade. Bashful brides were dressed and decorated in secrecy, prepared like sacrificial lambs for the day when they would wear the red sari and their husbands would see them for the first time. I never heard a sound from within the tent of the henna artist, and I imagined a shadowy interior with shrouded women whispering tantric secrets to a frightened virgin.

As always, I stopped at the perfumer's stall and sniffed his samples. My head filled with sandalwood and patchouli and I had visions of Maharanis with henna tattoos and moonlight on the Himalayas. At that moment India was the fantasy I had dreamed about in Chicago – the bazaar, the people, that day in Simla, that moment in June. I felt happy!

I selected a perfume that smelled like India – smoky, sensual and mysterious – and the perfumer extracted a syringe full of amber liquid from a tall bottle and squirted it into a smaller one of diamond-cut glass. I had not asked the price and I didn't want to. I knew that I would probably pay more than I should, and I didn't care. I found the business of haggling over pennies with poor people morally repellent and, remembering Harry's suggestion that I be kind to someone, cheerfully handed the perfumer a handful of rupees. He offered me change and I waved it away, feeling generous and kind. The perfume would be my personal memento of that perfect moment in India; the cost didn't matter.

Rumbling home in a rickshaw, I sniffed my perfume and thought about Simla. Fun, I realized. That day I had had fun. It had been the sort of day I had imagined when we first came to India. Simla was safe and fun and I felt satisfied and vindicated. I would have loved to show Martin the pretty diamond-cut bottle of perfume and tell him how lovely everything had been. Of course, I might as well meet him at the door wearing boxing gloves. I would hide the dainty bottle in my lingerie drawer – plenty of room in there for one more secret – and in that moment, I determined to live my own life and let Martin live his. If I couldn't have tenderness, if I couldn't have intimacy, I'd accept perfume and a truce.

My rickshaw bumped up the hill through a landscape shimmering in waves of afternoon heat; cows lowed, saris fluttered in a light breeze and flies buzzed. I felt as torpid as a bee drunk on pollen when I mounted Verna's front steps, and the memory of the slap in the kitchen blindsided me. I held on to Verna's bannister and paused a moment for the sudden ache in my chest to subside. I took the perfume from my purse, pulled out the stopper and dabbed it behind each ear as if it were medicinal. The heavy, complex scent took me back to the whirling bazaar, the pleased perfumer, the smiling brown faces, and just like that I decided to apologize to Martin and show him my secret stash – Felicity's letter and the pages from Adela's journal. If I wanted to be closer to him, it was the right thing to do. I should have done it sooner.

Verna's face bore the expression of a woman whose feet

hurt. The horsey smile soldiered on, but she did not invite me in. She brought Billy to the door and gently shoved him towards me.

I said, 'Thank you, Verna. You've been a lifesaver.'

'You're quite welcome. We'd love to see you and Martin at the Club.'

'Thank you. I'll keep it in mind.'

'It's one of the few civilized places in Simla. And don't worry, my dear, the bearers are always made to wear gloves.'

'I see.' I couldn't be polite much longer. 'Well, thank you again.' I heard the door close behind us before my foot hit the first step.

With only a few words, Verna had breached my pleasant mood. I muttered a prissy impersonation. 'The bearers are always made to wear gloves.'

Billy said, 'What?'

'Nothing, baby.'

'Mom?'

'Hmm?'

'Next time, can we go with you?'

'Wasn't Mrs Drake nice?'

'I guess.' Billy slung Spike over his shoulder. 'But we'd rather go with you.'

I didn't feel like defending Verna Drake. Harry had said, 'Be kind to someone,' and it had been easy with the perfumer, but it seemed that I didn't want to be kind to anyone I actually knew. Well, that would all change when I apologized and showed Martin what I'd been up to. Adela's journal might even be relevant to his thesis, and I imagined how pleased he'd be about that.

I fondled the perfume bottle in my pocket, feeling deep pleasure, then a surge of panic. I'd spent too much money. I squeezed the cut-glass bottle, and the edges bit into my palm. I tried to remember how much I had in the tea tin, knowing I couldn't return perfume that had come out of a syringe. I didn't even have a receipt; I wasn't even sure how much I had paid.

'What's wrong, Mom?'

'Nothing, cutlet. Mommy is a little silly sometimes.' But it would be all right. Tonight, I thought. Tonight I'd make everything all right.

Chapter Twenty-Five

THAT EVENING, I gave Billy an extra portion of rice pudding, followed by a boisterous bubble bath with his octopus squirty toy, a slow shampoo that involved a unicorn horn fashioned out of thick white suds, a bedtime story – *The Rooster and the Pearl* – and two Irish ballads. The extra attention assuaged my guilt for having left him with Verna, and it gave me time to screw up my courage to face Martin.

I intended to apologize right up until the moment he had walked through the door; the sight of him brought a rush of conflicting feelings. I'd told him I'd eaten with Billy and that he should go ahead without me, then I hurried away from him with Billy clinging to my neck like a baby monkey.

By the time I came into the living room, he had taken off his sandals, put his feet up on the coffee table, lit a bidi, and his head was buried in *Crime and Punishment*. He didn't even respond when I walked past and touched his shoulder. Apologize? I wanted to slug him again. But . . . I took a deep breath. 'How was your day?'

He started as though he had thought he was alone. 'It was OK.'

'Martin, I've been thinking.'

'Yeah?' He pushed his glasses up and waited.

I tried to remember how Harry had put it. 'I want to live a beautiful life.'

'What are you talking about?'

'I'm sorry I slapped you. I want us to—'

'Forget it, Evie. I had it coming.'

'No—'

'I don't want to talk about it. Please. I've got a lot on my mind. I'm taking the train to Lahore next week.'

'Lahore? But Walker said—'

'I know what Walker said. But that's between Hindus and Muslims. I'm an American. An academic. Harmless.'

I studied him, sitting there in his kurta pyjamas and sandals, with his mussed black hair, his tan darker than ever, and the bidi smouldering between his fingers. I said, 'Are you trying to get yourself killed?'

'Please, don't be melodramatic.'

'So let me get this straight. I'm not supposed to go to Simla, the queen of British hill stations, but you can go to Lahore with a bunch of refugees, looking like an Indian.'

'It's my job.' Martin took a drag of his bidi and went back to his book.

This was new. This was worse than post-war withdrawal. This was masochism or a death wish, and I didn't know what to do with it. But I couldn't face another fight, knowing it would go nowhere.

I marched into the bedroom, where I stripped down to my underwear and slammed my clothes into the wicker hamper. I crawled into bed and lay there watching the ceiling fan go around and around.

*

Strips of morning sun slanted through the shutters, and I woke to see that Martin's side of the bed had not been slept in. I listened for splashing sounds from the bathroom, but didn't hear any. I glanced at the clock on the bedside table and realized he had already left for work.

I lugged myself to the bathroom and studied my reflection in the mirror. I saw a tense face, years older than it had been three months earlier. I scrubbed hard with a rough washcloth and splashed with icy water, but the angry old woman still glared back at me.

That afternoon, right after tiffin, Billy said, 'Can we go into Simla today?'

'How about we build a fort with your blocks?'

'Nah. Let's go to Simla.'

'We could make another pretend bazaar.'

'Nah, the real one's better.'

'We could read a book.'

'Let's go to Simla.'

'We can't go into Simla, Sweetpea.'

'How come?'

'Tell you what,' I said. 'You and Spike can hop in the old Red Flyer, and I'll give you guys a ride down the hill, but only to the first little houses in the village.'

'Why can't we go to the bazaar in Simla?'

I whisked a blond curl off his forehead. 'Only as far as the little houses.'

Billy said, 'Aw, nuts.'

'Come on, BoBo. We can take pictures of chickens and cows, maybe a camel. We can bring a carrot for that baby goat you like.' I folded my arms and sat back. 'It's a good deal. Take it or leave it.'

Billy consulted Spike, then said, 'Okaaay.'

After Rashmi left, I put the camera strap around Billy's

neck and we set out merrily, Billy and Spike in the wagon and me leading an off-key rendition of 'Old MacDonald Had a Farm'. Billy threw his head back and belted out the chorus while Spike danced jerkily on his lap. Starting down the hill, we left the colonial district behind and began to see our little corner of India – slate roofs against pine-green hills, jagged peaks piercing the clouds, and a bull cart carrying two women in peach- and plum-coloured saris, ripe human fruit. Our voices carried in the thin air, and people smiled at us. We entered the familiar neighbourhood of Himachali houses just as I ran out of farm animals and launched into an improvised verse: 'And on this farm he had a yak, e-i-e-i – Oh, my God!'

Crude graffiti scrawled across the side of a house stopped me in mid phrase. The wall had been defaced with garish red paint, violent against the dull grey wood. Huge, reckless letters in an alphabet I couldn't read, the paint still wet and dripping like bloody drools. A knot of people milled around the house, muttering and edgy, and the air felt weighted with ancient grievances. There were no friendly grandmothers in that crowd; a few women and children shuffled among the men, but their faces were closed and bitter. One man sat slumped on the ground with his back against the vandalized wall. He looked dazed, and his kurta pyjamas were spattered with red, which could have been paint or blood. I couldn't tell who was Hindu and who was Muslim, and I didn't care.

Spike had stopped dancing. Billy said, 'Mom?'

'We're going home.' I pulled the wagon around sharply.

A half-naked little boy with thin legs and matted hair detached himself from the crowd and glared at Billy. The child's ribcage stood out on his thin torso. His mouth was set in a hard line, and his eyes were dead black. He held his arms stiffly at his sides, his hands balled into blunt little fists. I wondered what had to happen to a child to make him look like that, but I didn't hang around to think about it. I started back up the hill, towards home, but the ragged little boy followed us. I remembered the remark in the church record about children brandishing sticks, and thought, *Oh, no. Please.*

I walked faster, but when I looked back, the little boy had shortened the distance between us, and three or four more urchins had joined him. They straggled along, stopping now and then to pick up stones, which they weighed menacingly in their palms. I threw a stern glance over my shoulder, hoping that an adult stare of disapproval might stop them, but they kept coming. The wretched little boy in the lead had taken on a belligerent swagger. I ordered Billy out of the wagon, thinking I could carry him if we had to run.

When we stopped for Billy to get out, the woebegone little boy stopped too. He stood a few paces away with his bony legs braced apart, and the other children clustered behind him. Then I saw that the boy was not staring at Billy, but at Spike.

I took the camera off Billy's neck and looped the strap over mine, thinking how ludicrous it was to be carrying it around like some carefree tourist. I tried to walk fast, holding Billy's hand and pulling the empty wagon, but Billy's short stride slowed me down. I could hear the children coming closer, their feet scuffing the dirt close behind us. I felt damp under my arms and my heart thudded in my ears. I was trying to decide whether to pick Billy up and run when a tonga clopped over the hill ahead and halted in front of us. Edward Worthington jutted his head out of the side. He took in the children's malicious little faces, the stones in their hands, and he pulled his topi down in front with an air of challenge. 'What's going on here?'

Lydia leaned across Edward. 'Can we be of assistance?'

I felt foolish admitting that I was afraid of a band of small children. 'I, um . . .' I spoke in stops and starts, finally saying, 'It's nothing, really. They're only children.'

Edward eyed them, his tongue darted, and he said, 'They're bloody niggers.'

'For God's sake, Edward!' A shiver of revulsion rippled between my shoulder blades. I saw, by his face, that Billy had heard the despicable remark. I hated the idea of climbing into a tonga with that foul-mouthed bigot. On the other hand, he was the only help in sight.

Billy glanced back and forth between the tonga and the boy, who sidled closer while I told Lydia and Edward about the graffiti and the restless crowd. The little boy reached out a scrawny arm to touch Spike's cowboy hat. Billy said, 'Cut it out,' and the boy pulled back.

'This is no good,' said Edward. 'You'd better let us give you a lift home.' I cast a glance at Billy's wagon, and Edward added, 'Leave the blasted wagon.'

One more look at the children's faces made me say, 'OK, sure.' I turned to Billy just in time to see the ragged boy grab Spike by the head. Billy yelled, 'No!' But the boy wrenched Spike away and ran.

I lunged for Billy's arm, but he was too fast. He took off after the boy, but the other children cut him off and knocked him down. They scuffled as I hurried over, and there were childish shouts and petulant faces as I pulled them off and tossed them aside like rag dolls. Billy lay curled and weeping on the ground, and I knelt beside him while the others ran off in a fit of what sounded to me like demonic laughter. Billy's face and hands were smeared with dirt, his shirt was torn and his elbows were scraped and bleeding.

I tried to pick him up, but he fought me. 'Let me go,' he screamed. 'I gotta get Spike.' Tears streaked through the dirt on his face, and I held on to him as the little mob dispersed in the village. Billy clenched a baby fist and shrieked after them, 'You bloody niggers!'

I clapped a hand over his mouth and bundled him into the tonga, but I couldn't stop his flailing. A glistening mask of tears and snot sheeted his face; his innocent eyes burned with outrage. Edward heaved the red wagon into the tonga while his tongue darted furiously, and Lydia sat straight and silent, staring at nothing. Her face had gone pale and terribly, terribly tight.

I asked Edward to take us to the telegraph office. In spite of the tension between us, in spite of the fact that he would be angry that I had taken Billy out at all, I needed Martin. At that moment, only the sight of him could comfort me, only his voice could steady me and calm Billy. Our bond might be maimed, but it wasn't dead. The horse snorted and cantered towards Simla, the tonga rocked, and Billy's angry screams shrank to frustrated sobs.

At the telegraph office, Edward helped us out of the tonga, then hopped right back in and put his arms around Lydia, who had not moved or said a word. He seemed instantly to forget about Billy and me. He held Lydia like an invalid. He enveloped her, whispered into her ear, and ordered the driver back to their hotel with a curious urgency in his voice. I remembered Lydia's habit of crit-icizing me for bringing Billy to India. She always seemed so afraid for him, and now that something had actually happened she appeared catatonic. In that moment, I knew there was more to Lydia than met the eye, but with Billy sobbing in my arms I did not pause to think about it further.

I stood in the doorway of the telegraph office, holding Billy, still crying with his face buried in my neck. The office buzzed with normal, workday bustle – men talking, a type-writer clacking, a phone ringing. I located Martin near the back of the room, sitting in a corner, bent over an open book with a blizzard of handwritten notes scattered over his desk. He had a pencil behind one ear, another between his teeth, and he wrote with a third.

As I stepped over the threshold, my presence caused a wave of awareness. When Martin saw me, his face registered instantaneous rage. Billy saw his father and screamed, 'The bloody niggers took Spike!'

The typewriter stopped, conversations halted, and the pencil dropped out of Martin's mouth. He walked towards us with an angry stride, took in Billy's dirty, tear-stained cheeks, and pulled him from me without a word. He examined the miserable, wet little face and quailed at the bleeding elbows. He looked at me and said, 'What happened?'

I whispered, 'Martin, please—'

'What. Happened.'

People pretended not to listen, watching us with quick, sidelong glances.

I said, 'We only went into the village, but . . .' Martin's face hardened as he listened. After I finished, he gave me a look that I felt in the pit of my stomach. He wiped Billy's face and said, 'It's OK, son. Stop crying. Dad's here.'

'D-dad. The b-bloody niggers took Spike.'

'Stop saying that.'

Billy blubbered, 'D-dad, will you get Spike back?'

'We'll see. Calm down now.'

'Will you b-beat 'em up?' His little chest heaved spastic aftershocks of grief. 'Will you get Spike and beat up the bloody niggers for me?'

Chapter Twenty-Six

BILLY HOWLED LIKE a demon being ripped limb from limb while I painted his elbows with Mercurochrome. 'I WANT SPIKE!' He knocked the bottle off the sink and rusty red liquid bled all over the white tiled floor. I mopped it up with a towel, but it had permanently stained the grout, another battle scar on the old house. I knew we'd have to pay the landlord for the damage and that reminded me of the money I'd spent on perfume and also that the rent was soon due. Too much, too much.

Martin had driven us home, and while I struggled to paint Billy's elbows with Mercurochrome, he stuck his head through the bathroom door to say he was going to the Club for dinner. That was fine with me.

I warmed up some chicken soup, but Billy refused to eat. I made him a sweet lassi with pistachios, his favourite, but when I held it to his lips, he squeezed them shut, slipped off the chair and crawled under the table. He sat there, legs crossed, crying, with pudgy fists pressed into his eyes. I got down on my hands and knees, dragged him out, screaming, and carried him to his room. I took pyjamas out of a drawer and he said, 'I don't want pyjamas.'

'You can't sleep in your clothes.'

'I don't want pyjamas!'

'Your clothes are dirty.'

'I don't want pyjamas.'

'You can't sleep in dirty clothes.'

'I don't want pyjamas.'

I wrestled him into the pyjamas and wondered why I was forcing him. Would it kill him to sleep in dirty clothes? Would it kill me to let him? But I'd gone too far down the road of parental insistence; it had become a power struggle and I had to get the damn pyjamas on him or he'd think that tantrums worked. He fought and screamed and tried to pull the pyjama top off, and I had a shocking urge to smack his bottom. I had never spanked him, never even considered it. I held his shoulders and shouted, 'Billy, for the love of God, stop crying. *Stop it!*'

His eyes opened wide. I had never shouted at him before in such anger. He held his breath, and I put my arms around him.

'OK,' he said in a small voice. 'I won't cry any more.'

'I'm sorry, baby. I shouldn't have yelled at you.'

He sagged on the bed and wrapped his arms around my hips. I felt stifled sobs shake his small body, and I eased his head on to the pillow. He pulled the sheet up over his head and balled up underneath. I watched the bulge under the sheet heave rhythmically, but he didn't make a sound. I said, 'I love you, Billy.' But it sounded feeble, even to me.

His muffled voice came from under the sheet. 'I'm not crying.' I sat on the edge of the bed and stroked the bump that was his head. Eventually his silent convulsions subsided, and after he lay still, I peeled the sheet back to see his swollen red eyes closed in an uneasy sleep. One more silent sob convulsed his chest and ripped my heart out.

I put Habib's curry into the icebox and fixed a cup of tea, but it went cold while I sat at the table, staring at my cheery yellow curtains. I dumped the cold tea in the sink and went to check on Billy. He had pulled the sheet over his head again, but at least he was still asleep.

In the bathroom, I took off my dusty, sweat-soaked clothes. I didn't feel like waiting for the big claw-foot tub to fill, so I took a sponge bath at the sink, working up a good lather and washing off the terrible day. I rinsed my dusty feet in the tub, dried off with a fresh towel and put on my blue chenille robe.

I poured myself a glass of wine, pulled a book off the shelf and then sat in the wingback chair facing the front door. I hadn't looked at the book when I grabbed it; I only wanted something to do until Martin came home. It was the poetry of Rumi, and I opened it at random and read two lines:

> *You can't quit drinking the earth's dark drink?*
> *But how can you not drink from this other fountain?*

Why did everything in India have to be so abstruse? I read it again, and then again, but I couldn't concentrate. I kept reading the same two lines, over and over, and soon even the individual words had no meaning. Still I kept reading them.

I wondered whether Martin was doing that with *Crime and Punishment*, reading meaningless words with his mind off somewhere else. Maybe that book was just a way for him to fill his spare time until he could lie down and die. I sat there with the open book on my lap, not understanding.

Around ten thirty, Martin lurched through the front door. I closed the book and stood up. I began carefully. 'Please let me explain . . .'

I stopped when Martin stumbled on the edge of the rug

and fell back against the door jamb. He offered me a vapid smile that made my throat constrict and my ears heat up. I'd expected him to have a beer or two – it had been a rough day and I'd had my glass of wine – but I didn't expect *oblivion*. I'd never seen him so drunk, and it disgusted me. It had been a horrible day for all of us, not only him. I stepped up to him, and we faced off in the doorway. Martin rocked on his feet, grabbed at the doorknob for support and missed. I said, 'You're drunk?' I felt my jaw clench.

He mumbled, 'Oh, yeah.'

His breath stank of arrack, and I knew then that he'd been drinking in the native quarter, not at the Club. I thought, *You can't quit drinking the earth's dark drink? But how can you not drink from this other fountain?*

'Where have you been?' I heard myself ask, loud and demanding.

He said, 'Don't start.'

'We needed you.'

'Oh, really?' He stared at me, bleary. A sneer stretched his mouth, and he shouted, 'You need me when Spike gets stolen. You need me when Billy is hysterical. But *you*—' He put a finger in my face. '*You* don't need *me*.'

I pushed his finger away and my voice rose to meet his. 'I can't talk to you when you're like this.'

'Then don't.'

'You should have been here. You know what Spike meant to him. You saw him.'

'Yeah, I saw him. But I'm not the one who took him out.'

Billy said, 'Mom? Dad?' He stood behind the sofa, rubbing his eyes. 'Are you guys fighting about Spike?'

'Ah, Jesus.' Martin reached for the doorknob, missed again and fell against it.

'What's wrong with Dad?'

'Sweetie.' I went to him and picked him up.

'I'm sorry.' Martin hung his head. 'Really, I'm sorry.' He looked at me with begging eyes, but I didn't understand. He needed more than forgiveness for getting drunk, for shouting, but I didn't know what. We stared at each other for a moment – sad, just sad – then he wheeled around and staggered across the verandah and out to the road.

I picked Billy up and cupped the back of his head. 'Let's get you back in bed, Sweetpea.'

'Is Dad sick?'

'Dad's OK. He's just very tired.' I carried Billy back to bed, laid him down gently and pulled up the sheet.

His chin quivered and he said, 'Dad's mad about Spike. If we get Spike back, will you guys stop fighting?'

I had to press my lips together for control. 'I'm sorry we woke you, Peach. Sometimes grown-ups argue, but this has nothing to do with you or Spike and there's nothing for you to worry about.'

'Will Dad come back home?'

'Oh, baby.' I gathered him in my arms. 'Of course Dad will come home. Of course he will. You go back to sleep.'

A half-hour of stroking his brow soothed him back to sleep, and then I crawled into my white bed and watched the fan. At two in the morning the front door opened, and I sat up. Martin bumped into something in the living room and muttered, 'Son'va bitch,' then stumbled into the bedroom and pitched on to the bed without taking off his clothes. He reeked of sweat and arrack, and within seconds he began snoring so loudly I wanted to smother him with a pillow. I kicked the sheet off, flung aside the mosquito netting and stomped into the living room to sleep on the sofa.

*

ELLE NEWMARK

In the morning, I heard him in the bathroom, the toilet flushing, the shower running. I caught the smell of sandalwood soap drifting out to the living room on wisps of steam. Drawers opened and closed in the bedroom, the hinge on the almirah door squeaked, and finally a hairbrush thumped on to the dressing table.

I lay on the sofa as if nailed to it. When Martin came through to the living room, he walked past me and went out of the door without a word. I stared at the ceiling fan – around and around. Around and around we go.

The sound of wooden blocks being thrown at a window told me Billy was not about to launch himself through the air to smother me with kisses. I pulled myself off the sofa and trudged to his room. Standing in the doorway, I watched my angelic little boy pick up a block, cradle it in two hands and crook one leg like a baseball pitcher, then let it fly at the closed blue shutter. It landed with an impotent thud and fell on the pile of blocks on the floor beneath. He was getting ready to hurl the next one when I picked him up. He stiffened for a second, then wrapped his arms and legs around me.

Billy didn't want to take off the pyjamas that he hadn't wanted to put on the night before, and I wasn't going to force him again. I slipped a pair of moccasins on his feet and let it go. I prepared his roti, boiled his breakfast egg and put it in the chicken-shaped eggcup he liked. I cracked it with a knife and lifted the top off while reciting 'Humpty Dumpty', but Billy just stared. I offered him a spoonful of yolk, his favourite part, and he said, 'I'm not hungry.' His face was blotchy, his eyes puffy.

'But you didn't eat your dinner last night.'

'I'm not hungry.'

I put the spoon down. 'I'll get you another doll, BoBo.'

264

He set his scraped elbows on the table and perched his chin on pint-sized knuckles. 'Spike isn't a doll. I want Spike.' His lip quivered, but he said, 'I won't cry.'

'You can cry, Cutlet.' But he didn't. I put my arm around him and we stared at a drizzle of yolk clotting on the shell. Then Billy started kicking the table leg. I tried to ignore it, but *thunk, thunk, thunk.* I said, 'Stop kicking the table, Chicken.'

Thunk, thunk, thunk.

'Billy, please stop that.'

Thunk, thunk, thunk.

'OK. If you're not going to eat, go to your room.' Billy sloped away, and I fixed a cup of tea, listening for the thud of blocks being thrown, but no sound came from Billy's room. No blocks, no crying, nothing. I went in and found him balled up tight on his bed, his knees jammed into his chest. I said, 'Billy, are you OK?'

'Uh-huh.'

I touched the back of my hand to his forehead. No fever. 'Are you sure?'

'Yeah.'

It wasn't until I tried to straighten his legs that I realized his clenched muscles were trembling. 'Billy, honey . . .'

'I'm trying not to cry.'

Oh God. I watched him tremble and said the one thing I shouldn't have. 'Baby, I'll get Spike back.'

'You will?' His little face opened with hope. 'Promise?'

'I'll try.'

Billy considered that, then, 'You're not gonna get Spike back.'

'Oh, sweetie, we'll fix it. Somehow. I promise.'

Billy sat up and wrapped his arms around my hips. He didn't cry, just hung on with his face in my stomach. I laid him back down and he immediately curled up in a foetal position. I sat next to him and stroked his hair. After a while, his breathing slowed and he fell asleep. Emotionally exhausted, I thought, like everyone else in this whole lousy world.

I stared at his crimped little body, so like an embryo, and touched his rounded back, feeling the pitiful buttons of his spine. It had been so long since I'd seen him without Spike, it seemed as if an essential part of him – a hand or a foot – was missing. I wondered whether I could get a new toy dog shipped from the States, how long it might take, and whether Billy would accept a substitute for Spike. But even if I could pull that off, it would be the least part of mending Billy. His elbows were already scabbing over, and eventually he would get over losing Spike, but . . . *bloody niggers*?

When Rashmi arrived with a suggestively raised eyebrow, I simply couldn't bear it. I told her Billy hadn't slept well and to let him nap, adding, 'I might be late coming back. I have errands in Simla.' Rashmi bobbed her head cheerfully, and I left.

I cycled down the hill past the Himachali houses, noticing that the graffiti was still there, but everything else appeared normal. I thought of Walker's remark: 'This country goes from doldrums to maelstrom in the blink of an eye.' I looked around for the boy who had taken Spike, but of course he wasn't there.

The children sat under the banyan tree, chattering in Hindi, but fell into a respectful silence when I arrived. I hurried through the day's lesson, letting sloppy pronunciation slide. I shortchanged them – they deserved better, but it seemed spectacularly unimportant that day. I wanted to get to the rectory at Christ Church to talk to Reverend Locke about Billy. I needed someone trained in the art of offering wisdom and sympathy.

Reverend Locke opened the door, but he did not display his gap-toothed smile and declare me splendid. He said, 'I heard about the row with your little boy yesterday. Is he all right?'

'Minor bruises, but . . . no, actually, he isn't.'

Reverend Locke showed me into his study, and we sat in the overstuffed chairs. I said, 'Yesterday's incident introduced Billy to bigotry, the exact opposite of what we wanted him to learn here. I don't know how to make him understand how poverty twists people. Not that it justifies stealing, but . . . well, you see, I'm getting muddled even talking to you.'

'I understand.' The good reverend sat with his hands composed in his lap; his sympathetic expression seemed practised and professional, a mask, and for the first time I wondered who he was.

I said, 'Do you have children?'

He nodded slowly. 'I had a daughter.'

'Had?'

'She died.'

'Oh. I'm sorry.'

'Yes. The war, you see.' He smiled wistfully. 'But we were talking about your son.'

In light of a dead daughter, a stolen toy seemed embarrassingly trivial. I said, 'I don't want him to learn to hate. He's terribly angry.'

'No doubt. But this won't be the last time he's angry. Perhaps this is an opportunity to teach him how to deal with anger.'

He was right, of course, but how could I teach Billy how to handle anger when I didn't know how myself? I said, 'How would you do that?'

He examined his hands and I had the feeling he was thinking of his lost daughter. He said, 'Forgiveness is a good place to start.'

'Forgiveness?' I thought of the little band of brats who had knocked Billy down in the dirt, his tear-stained face and scraped elbows, their laughter, Spike gone. I could understand them, their want and poverty, but there was also Billy, my Billy. It was too soon for forgiveness.

Reverend Locke smiled. 'I wish I could be more helpful, but that really is my best answer. People do dreadful things for all sorts of reasons – poverty, passion, power, ideology . . . it's a long list. Teach your son to forgive.' He stood as if it took a great effort. 'I'm awfully sorry, but I have an appointment.'

'Certainly.' I stood, nervously gathering my purse. 'You didn't know I was coming. Thank you for your time.'

He took my hand and tried to hold his smile. 'It wouldn't matter if I had more time, Mrs Mitchell. Forgiveness really is the only answer.' His face hung above me, long and bereaved, but he gestured at the bookshelves, saying, 'I'm terribly sorry to run out like this. Perhaps while you're here you'd care to have another peek at the church records?' He opened his hands as if apologizing for having nothing more to offer.

I thanked him, and he shambled out of the door looking diminished. I regretted having made him remember his daughter, but of course he had never forgotten her. He simply knew how to get on with his life in spite of his pain. I wished he could have told me how to do that.

I took down a faded volume and opened it to January 1858, the year of Adela's death. I turned the pages, scanning the banal details of parish business, and came to a page that appeared to have been torn out of another book. It had been folded and tucked into October 1858.

8 October 1857
The christening of Charles William.

The name seemed incomplete. In my experience, English children always had at least one middle name before their surname. But this child apparently had either no middle name or no last name. I went to the bookcase and flipped through the earlier volume until I found the place with a page missing in October 1857. I fitted the torn edge of the page to the torn edge in the earlier book, and the saw-tooth pattern matched perfectly. I went back to the later volume and saw that the torn page had been inserted alongside ordinary church business, including a death notice.

14 December 1858 – Adela Winfield laid to rest
after a long illness.

Someone had placed a christening record in with Adela's death notice, but Felicity was the one who was pregnant. A consumptive could have a healthy infant, and this must be her baby, but why would the christening notice be placed with Adela's death notice? Felicity would not have gone home and left Adela here with her baby. And if Felicity died, why was there no death notice for her, and where was her grave? If they both died, what happened to the baby?

I hailed a tonga and rode home, wondering what had become of them. I was still distracted when I arrived to find Rashmi waiting on the verandah, wringing her hands. Rashmi's unfailing good cheer had failed. When she saw me, her face twisted with anguish, and the red bindi on her forehead disappeared in a deep crease between pinched eyebrows. English forgotten, she babbled frantically in Hindi. I didn't understand, but the tears streaming down her face made me sick with dread, because everyone cries in the same language. Rashmi pulled me into the house and led me to Billy's bedroom. The bed was empty. The blue shutters and the window were wide open. Billy was gone.

Chapter Twenty-Seven

I DROPPED MY PURSE and flew out of the house. I hit the pavement running, first one way, then another, rushing wildly up and down the road. I shouted his name, 'Billy!' Then again, louder, 'Bii-lly!' I ran down the road. *No, no, no, no, no.* I called his name again, because I didn't know what else to do. 'Bii-lly!' I ran like a mad woman – *No, no, no, no, no.* My hat flew off and my hair bounced as I ran. I kept shouting, 'Bii-llyy!' My blouse pulled out of the waistband of my slacks, and sweat blossomed under my arms, in the small of my back and on my face. I sped past Morningside and saw Verna peek through her curtains, curious and alarmed. I screamed, 'BILLY!' She threw open the window, but I could see by her confusion that she knew nothing.

I raced down the hill, calling his name and scanning both sides of the road. When I came to the house with the red graffiti, I walked around it. Someone had tried to wash off the red paint and the wall was a disturbing mess – as if someone had tried to clean up after a firing squad. A sloe-eyed woman flipping chapattis on a hot rock paused to inspect me, tilting her head at my dishevelment, my air of frenzy, and then went back to her work. Men rumbled along on bull carts, mangy dogs lay in the sun, and women strolled along the road, swaying gracefully with water jugs on their heads. The calm that had so comforted me before now infuriated me. My son was missing. I wanted someone to *do* something.

I dashed into the crush of Himachali huts and ran between them, dodging cows and children and goats. A woman in an apple-green sari stopped me and said, 'Madam, in the road your little boy I am seeing.'

'Where?' My head whipped around.

'Not now, Madam. Towards Simla he is walking.'

It seemed unlikely that he could walk to Simla – almost ten kilometres – but could someone have taken him? That question sent my head and stomach into free fall, and I rushed out to the road to hail a tonga. I asked the driver to go slowly, and I called Billy's name over and over, trying to scan both sides of the road at once. With every passing kilometre, my panic deepened.

In Simla, I paid the tonga driver and headed for the Lakkar bazaar, Billy's favourite place. As usual, the streets were packed shoulder-to-shoulder with people, and I knew Billy's head would only reach hip level. I strained to see through the dense, shifting crowds, but everything looked impossibly normal, and it drove me crazy. The world was ending; how could everyone be so complacent?

Billy hadn't eaten breakfast that morning or dinner the night before. He'd be hungry and, oh God, he was probably still wearing pyjamas and a flimsy pair of moccasins. I imagined him picking his baby way through the bazaar, and when the pitiful children approached me with their hands out, I remembered the slavers.

It wouldn't take them long to spot a little boy with curly blond hair tramping around in teddy bear pyjamas, and I knew what slavers would do with a five-year-old white boy. I doubled over, hugging myself – *Oh God, Oh God, Oh God.*

People looked, but they didn't stop. They walked around me with eyes averted, the same way I averted my eyes from their lepers and ramshackle slums. Martin had told me what they thought of white women – morally suspect, and one wrong word to a white woman could get you arrested. When it came to white women, it was best to mind your own business. Saris and kurtas parted around me, and a rush of panic made me dizzy.

My breathing turned fast and shallow; my lungs refused to expand. I tried to take a deep breath, but a vice gripped my chest. *Oh God, Oh God, Oh God.* I felt lightheaded. I struggled to pull in one good breath, and the vice tightened. I raised my arms but it didn't help. Pinpricks of light flickered in my peripheral vision, and I felt my heartbeat stuttering like a flame in the wind. My vision began to blur, colours and sounds ran together, and I sucked at the air like a fish out of water. Gasping and crying, I stumbled to the telegraph office.

Martin didn't waste any time. Within minutes he had called the police and had half the office staff out on the streets. Martin and I went with Walker to the Simla kotwali to file an official report, and then all three of us tailed a policeman – a short, portly man in a black turban and khaki uniform – while he questioned people. He talked to tradesmen and customers and rickshaw wallahs and housewives, he stopped at temples and huts and shops and stalls. No one had seen Billy.

'How is that possible?' I pleaded. 'A blond five-year-old in pyjamas? How is it possible no one saw him?'

'It's a delicate matter, Evie.' Walker rubbed his beard.

'People would be afraid to pick him up, but no one would want to admit seeing him and not picking him up. Anyone who might have taken him might now be afraid of kidnapping charges.'

'No! No charges! We'll offer a reward . . . tell them.'

'Yes!' Martin said. 'No charges. A big reward.'

'Right.' Walker rubbed his beard.

Rewards were not the way things were done in India; the situation required money up front, baksheesh. Martin took out his wallet, but he didn't have much cash so we sped home and I raided the tea tin while Martin waited in the old Packard. We drove back to Simla and dispensed baksheesh freely, forcing rupees into people's hands. The police were the first with their hands out and that surprised me, but only me. We stopped people on the street and halted tongas and rickshaws, and Martin passed out rupees to everyone. He stuffed paper money into hands and pockets, but no one knew anything. We didn't need a photograph. A five-year-old blond boy in Western pyjamas was description enough.

I wanted the shops to close and the streets to empty. I thought it would be easier to spot a small child without the shifting masses of people. But streets in India are never really empty, and I felt a sudden rage at the crowding. I wanted them all to stand still, make way, go home, do *something*.

Martin and Walker huddled in conference with the policeman, and I shoved my way into the middle of them. 'You don't talk without me. This is my child.'

Martin took both my hands in his. 'Honey, there's a place they want to check, but I'm not sure you should go there.'

'If Billy might be there, I'm going.'

Martin put a hand on my shoulder. 'It's a slave market.'

My knees went weak, but I said, 'Let's go.'

We followed the policeman down slanted stone steps into

increasingly narrow lanes, twisting and turning, going up and down and up again, until I knew I could not have found my way out alone. In a filthy alley piled with rotting garbage and alive with vermin, the policeman stopped and said, 'In here.' He stood at the entrance to a lane so narrow that it disappeared into deep shadows even now, in the middle of the day.

Martin peered into the dark and said, 'Evie, are you sure? Walker can wait here with you.'

I said, 'I'm sure,' and stepped past him.

The little policeman looked at me with baleful eyes. 'So sorry,' he said, shaking his head. He looked helpless and I felt sorry for him. He did not want me there, but he did not know how to refuse an insistent memsahib. 'This is no good place for Madam.'

He was chivalrous, in his way, and uncomfortable dealing with a white woman. But the thought that Billy might be anywhere near this awful place seized me with a sense of urgency. I turned to Martin. 'Tell him to stop apologizing and go. Every minute counts.'

Martin nodded at him and the policeman sighed. He said, 'Please be walking carefully, yes?' He pointed down and I saw a narrow black canal of open sewage snaking down the middle of the lane. 'So sorry,' he said again, 'but Madam must be walking like so.' He placed his feet on either side of the foul water and began a slow, rocking waddle into the darkness.

I followed, trying not to step in the filth that flowed between my feet while the evil stench rose up in my face. I heard Martin and Walker sliding along behind me in the mud, and I had the sudden thought that, when we got home, I would have to throw away our shoes. Immediately I felt disgusted with myself for having such a trivial thought when

Billy was missing. I was chastising myself for pettiness when the policeman stopped abruptly in front of a sagging wooden door, and I almost slammed into him in the dark.

He said, 'No tourists in people market. You pretend you come to buy, OK?'

I felt sick, but Martin quickly said, 'Yeah, sure.'

The policeman rapped a series of coded taps, and I heard scraping and cursing as a wooden bolt was lifted on the other side. A woman shrouded in black opened the door, but only a few inches; she squinted at us suspiciously. A reek of garlic and boiling mustard oil seeped out of the partially open door.

The policeman spoke to her in whispers while she watched me with kohl-lined eyes. Then she made a contemptuous gesture, a sideways flick of the hand as if swatting at a pesky fly. She said, 'Neh.'

The policeman wheedled and cajoled, and finally Martin shouldered past him and thrust a wad of rupees at her. She counted the money, gave me a sharp look, then swung the door open. She led us along a narrow hallway stinking of garlic and laid with filthy rush matting, and then out to a secluded courtyard. The woman plodded ahead of us like a tired workhorse, and I wondered whether she was a slave.

Her house (if it was hers) had been built right up against a crevice in the mountainside, accessible only through the garlic-scented hallway. There was a cave entrance on the far side of the courtyard, where six young children sat on the ground, silent and unmoving. Daylight was blocked out by a canvas awning stretched overhead – no doubt intended to thwart prying eyes – and the effect was an eerie artificial dusk. Oil lamps shed a sickly yellow light, and men in djellabas and kurta pyjamas were clustered in one corner, chatting quietly. They looked up when we came into the courtyard, and there was a rush of whispers. I distinctly heard 'white woman' but I couldn't tell which was the greater offence, my colour or my sex. We hung back and after a minute they resumed their conversation.

One man walked over to the cave and bent down to inspect a little girl. He made the child stand up and turn slowly, parting her matted hair and scrutinizing her scalp with a look of distaste. He pulled down her lower eyelids, then looked in her mouth, probing with his little finger, and finally lifted her ragged tunic and took a long look at the thin naked body. The girl, no more than six years old, registered no emotion. She did as she was told and then sat back down. I started to tremble and Martin put his arm around my shoulders and held me tight.

The policeman talked with the slavers – they seemed to know him – but they were clearly annoyed with him for having brought us there. We pretended not to notice the scowls and gesticulating in our direction. After a while, the policeman came back shaking his head. 'Ten times a fair price I am offering. I'm sorry. They are not having him.'

We left the way we had come, single file, inching along the putrid alley. When we got back to the bazaar, I felt myself spinning. It was too much – the slavers, the stink, the heat, the sound of unseen drums. My breathing speeded up, my lungs constricted, and my heartbeat became erratic. I clutched at my chest and rasped, 'Martin, Martin, tell them to check the cars. The cars! Slavers have cars. They could be driving him away right now. Martin?'

Walker gave Martin a veiled look and I turned on him like a whip. 'What the hell?' My fingers retracted into a fist. I felt heat rising in my face and I could barely breathe, but I made my voice cold. 'My child is missing. Don't you *dare* patronize me.'

'I apologize, Evie.'

The police asked me to go home. I refused. The one in charge, a short thick man with kind eyes, said, 'People are not being restful these days, Madam. I am assuring you, we are most capable.'

Martin took off his glasses and rubbed his eyes. 'I think he's right.'

'No.' I crossed my arms over my chest. 'I can't go home and do nothing.'

Walker stepped up and took a small brown bottle out of one of his pockets. He said, 'If you insist on staying, take one of these.' He shook out a yellow pill.

'What is it?'

'It'll help.' Walker offered the pill along with his water flask. After a moment, I downed the pill with a few swigs from the flask, and within an hour, I woozily allowed Martin to take me home.

Martin laid me down on our white bed and said, 'It wasn't your fault.'

My speech came out drug-slurred and nasal. 'If we don't find him—'

'No.' Martin put a finger to my lips. 'We'll find him.'

'Billy,' I moaned. 'Oh, God.'

Martin wrapped his arms around me and held me fast beneath Rashmi's wilting mala, and I wept and wept and wept.

Chapter Twenty-Eight

VERNA ARRIVED WITH Lydia, and Martin left to rejoin the search. As soon as I saw the women, I wanted them to go away. Neither of them had children. They couldn't possibly understand. They stood in the doorway, saying, 'You poor dear.' I knew they were there to make sure I stayed home, but I was too drug-addled to argue with them.

I decided to run a bath – the only way I could think to escape them. While the bathroom filled with steam, I peeled off my clothes, which were wrinkled and limp with sweat that held the sour reek of fear. I left the clothes in a heap on the Mercurochrome-stained floor and stood naked beside the tub, watching it fill and caressing my stomach. The skin there felt a bit slack and I knew there were translucent stretch marks from pregnancy, spidery silver shadows meandering under the skin. I remembered the secret joy of feeling Billy move inside me, under my heart, warm and safe. Now he roamed God knew where, hungry and unclothed and alone, and it was my fault. How could I ever have left his side in this terrible place? Lydia was right. I shouldn't have brought him to India. I put one foot into the tub and a tingling burn seized me up to the ankle, but I resisted the impulse to pull back. I got in and let the scald take me. Penance. A monsoon of pain spread through my body, searing and biting, and it was a relief to feel something other than fear.

I sat there, hugging my knees, long after the water had cooled, and I listened to the women's muffled voices in the next room, hushed, the way people talk at a funeral. I wanted to march out there stark naked and say, 'You don't know *anything*.' I splashed water on my face and climbed out of the tub, and then opened the door a crack to listen. They weren't talking about Billy or me at all. They were talking about wires having been cut in Pathankot, and their circumspect tone made me angry. Who cared about cut wires now? I trudged into my bedroom with a towel wrapped around me, crawled into bed and drew the mosquito netting.

Once in a while I found myself weeping, but I couldn't remember having started. The sedative must have begun to wear off because I sat up, intending to get dressed, push past Verna and Lydia and go find my child. I stood up just as Verna came in with a cup of tea. She said, 'Sit down, dear,' and set the cup on the bedside table. I obeyed rather than argue. I wanted her to leave.

Verna wasn't smiling, and her lips looked wrinkled as a used handkerchief. Lipstick bled in rays around her mouth, and I realized that without the big smile Verna's whole face drooped and her neck puddled like melted wax. Maybe Verna wasn't childless. Maybe she had grown children, even grandchildren. Not that it mattered. She patted my hand and left.

I drank the tea quickly, thinking it would help counter Walker's sedative, and then I only remember feeling as if I were being pulled underwater and wondering what they had put in my tea. I was half asleep when Verna came back.

'A message has come, dear.' Verna put something on the side table and picked up the empty cup. I glanced over and saw a rolled note on long Indian paper – probably from Harry. I ignored it. Verna said, 'Would you like me to read it to you?' I started to say it wasn't important, and then it occurred to me that the note might be from a local who had seen Billy. I sat up and unrolled it. The writing blurred and swam and I had to blink to clear my vision.

Dear Evie,

I have secured a translation of the Urdu reference to Miss Winfield, and it is interesting. Please come to the temple at your convenience. I'll be here every afternoon from now on. The ashram is driving me mad.

Your friend,
Harry

I tossed the note on the table and lay back down. I said, 'It's nothing.' She nodded and left.

When Lydia came in, I rolled away with my back to her. She said something, but her voice seemed to come from far away and her words didn't string together the way they should. I let her stand me up stark naked and slip bra straps over my shoulders. When I didn't move, she gently fitted the cups over my breasts and fastened the hooks. Obedient as a child, I stepped into my panties and allowed her to pull them up. Then she draped my chenille robe over me, threaded my arms through the sleeves and tied the sash.

Verna had made tea and cucumber sandwiches, but in spite of the kettle steaming and the women sitting at the table, the kitchen seemed cold with no curry pot simmering on the stove. I said, 'What happened to Habib?'

'We sent him home, dear.'

'Oh.'

'Don't worry, we paid him.'

'Thanks.'

I stared at the sandwich they'd set before me while Lydia complimented the dessert Verna had served at their last dinner party. Verna explained the fine points of constructing a strawberry trifle, and after the trifle recipe had been beaten to death the women shared amazement at the outcome of a recent cricket match. I understood that they didn't really know me and didn't know what to say to me, but . . . *trifle and cricket?*

Martin came in around three in the morning and the memsahibs left.

I said, 'Does anyone know anything?'

'Not really.'

'What does that mean?'

'We haven't found him yet. But lots of people are on it. Lots. We'll find him. Simla is not Delhi. I only came home to see how you are.'

'I'm fine.'

'We'll find him.'

Martin went to the bathroom to splash cold water on his face, and I slumped on to the camelback sofa, dizzy and disoriented. After a while, I lay down, hating myself for being so sleepy, and absently pulled a loose thread out of the seam on a down pillow. I watched the thread unravel and the welting come loose, thinking things fall apart too easily. It seemed wrong; things should be sturdier than that. Half the welting hung limp and desultory, ready to fall off. I gave it a tug and the pillow ripped open, exposing feather guts, looking the way I felt.

Martin came out of the bathroom and leaned over the back of the sofa. He said, 'I'll bring him home.'

I twisted at the waist and threw my arms around his neck. Ah, the comforting familiarity of his touch. He said, 'I have to go.'

'Yes.' I let him go. 'Find him.'

After Martin left, I wandered into Billy's room and stared at the empty bed. The sequinned camels hung under the mosquito netting, and his wooden blocks lay in a heap under the window. I picked one up, turned it over in my hand and threw it against the wall as hard as I could. It didn't help, and I sank to my knees on the floor. I sobbed and hit the ground with a fist, crying out when a loose plank popped free with a sound like a gunshot. As I pulled out the plank, intending to set it properly back in place, I saw a small tin box tucked into the space under the floorboards.

I took it out, wiped off a crust of dirt and mould and lifted the lid. The box contained two rubber hot-water bottles, each with one end sliced off to make a sort of pocket. Inside, I found a hand-made book with a mauve suede cover, sewn neatly with silver thread. The stitches were small and regular, like tiny silver teeth clamped all around the edges, and on the bottom right corner of the cover I saw the initials A. W. It was Adela's journal.

Now? Now, when I didn't care any more? I almost laughed.

I fanned the pages, disinterested, and saw the place where several pages had been torn out – February to June 1857 – the pages I had found in the Bible. Listlessly, I opened the back cover and one heavily underlined word in the last entry caught my eye – _sorry_?

August 1857

Is there no end to this nightmare? I returned to find Lalita crying & Felicity gone. He left a thick, cream-coloured calling card on her bed with a scribbled note. 'I have taken her. I'm sorry.'

He's sorry?

He's sorry?

Where has he taken her? And why?

There were more entries, but I didn't care. I closed the journal and dropped it in the tin box. Then I lay down on Billy's bed, under the sequinned camels, and curled up like a drugged snail retreating into its shell.

Chapter Twenty-Nine

THE DOORBELL RANG and I woke to the sound of feral dogs barking and brawling. Verna and Lydia must be waiting patiently on my verandah, no doubt carrying more sedatives in their purses. Why couldn't they leave me alone? My hand had fallen asleep under my hip and pins and needles prickled up my arm, but I didn't move. The bell rang again, and then they began knocking, but I lay still. After they went away I would get dressed and go out, and I would stay out until I found him.

A fist pounded the door so hard the wall shook. God! What was wrong with those women? I'd have to go out there and send them away. I'd physically push them off the verandah if I had to. I marched to the door barefoot, and when I opened it, my hands flew to my mouth. James Walker stood on the verandah, holding my son in his arms.

Billy's pyjamas were streaked with mud, there was hay in his hair and his teeth were chattering. He said, 'Mom?' and he reached his short arms out to me. My throat swelled and my eyes smarted. I grabbed him, pulled him tight and breathed in his grubby, little-boy-in-summer smell. He nuzzled his face into my neck and kept it there as I carried him inside. My throat felt blocked and tears blinded me, but I've never been that happy before or since. I sat on the sofa with Billy on my lap and examined him: his face was dirty, he smelled like hay and dung, and his moccasins were gone. Other than that he appeared unharmed, but his teeth still chattered. 'Are you cold, Billy?'

'Nuh-uh. Are you mad at me?'

'No, Baby.'

'I wanted to find Spike.'

I hugged him. 'I know.'

'You and Dad were fighting about Spike.'

I winced. 'It's OK. It's all OK now.'

'I thought if I got Spike back you wouldn't fight any more.'

'Oh God.'

Walker put his hands in his pockets and looked away for a moment. He cleared his throat and said, 'The little fellow might be in a bit of shock, but he's not been harmed. Nothing a warm bath and a meal won't put right.'

'Does Martin know?'

'Oh, yes. Poor chap broke down, but we gave him a stiff whisky. Hell, we all had one. He's at the kotwali right now, filling out a final report.' He ruffled Billy's hair. 'Our little sahib got lucky. Edward found him on the road this morning. We made the mistake of thinking someone had taken him to Simla, but he was less than a kilometre away the whole time, right here in Masoorla.'

'Edward found him?' Billy clung to me and I rocked him.

'Worthington stayed out all night with a lantern, knocking on doors and roaming the countryside like some medieval ghost. Said the cops were useless and stayed at it by himself.'

'Edward did that?'

'I suppose he couldn't give up because of the boy they lost.'

'What?'

'Didn't you know? Lost their son in the Blitz. Lydia had a complete breakdown. Edward's been her salvation. He can be irritating as hell, but he coddles her like a wounded bird. That chap has a side you'd never suspect.'

'Edward?' I remembered him comforting Lydia at the telegraph office. Oh, but poor Lydia, gently placing my breasts into a bra, pulling up my panties. What heartbreaking memories had Billy's disappearance brought up for her?

Walker said, 'Damn lucky, really. We made such a public stink about him being missing, I'm afraid some rather unsavoury types were searching for him as diligently as we were.'

My stomach heaved. 'Unsavoury? You mean . . .'

'Well, he's here now, and that's what matters.'

'Mom?'

'Yes, BoBo?'

'Mr Worthington bought me a roti, and I said *kripya*.'

I covered his face with kisses.

When Rashmi arrived, she screamed, 'Beelee!' She flew to him and combed her fingers through his hair.

He said, 'Hi, Rashmi,' and he reached for her. Her eyes brimmed as she swept him up and held him out in front of her like a dangling doll. She asked, 'Coconut?' He nodded, and then the tears fell.

Billy had climbed through the window and walked down the tree-shaded road without the slightest twinge of fear. We had walked that way many times. He said, 'I remembered to keep to the side of the road, like we do with the wagon.'

'That was good, sweetie.'

'I saw some kids, but not the bad boy who took Spike.'
He looked at me sideways. 'My moccasins got real dirty.
I was worried you'd be mad.' He shrugged. 'Now they're
gone.'

'We can get new moccasins. Did anyone try to stop you?'

'A man in one of those flat round hats tried to talk to me.
But he looked mean, so I ran away. Then a lady in a green
sari shook her finger at me and said I should go home. But I
don't talk to strangers, so I stuck my tongue out at her.' He
demonstrated, and I laughed in spite of myself.

At the house with the red graffiti he went to the door. He
said, 'A lady was sitting on the ground, and I asked her if she
knew where Spike was.' He paused, then said shyly, 'I had to
ask somebody.'

'I know.'

'She didn't wanna talk to me anyway.'

After that he wandered off the road so Kamal wouldn't
stop him, and then he got lost.

'Where did you sleep last night?'

'In a cow shed. A nice goat kept me warm. But when I
woke up my moccasins were gone.'

'Oh, baby.'

He rubbed his eyes. 'Mom? I'm kinda hungry.'

Wanting to be alone with Billy, I sent Rashmi home. She
kissed him a dozen times, then a dozen more, and then
gathered up the garbage and left, smiling.

After feeding him a dish of yogurt and sliced banana, I
bathed my prodigal son slowly. I filled the tub with warm
water, and his smooth little body slid under my soapy hands.
I rinsed him as if I were washing rose petals. He'd been
returned to me whole – a gift, a miracle. I shampooed his
fine blond hair, tipped his head back under the tap and

watched the lather rinse out, leaving his head slick as a baby seal. He was still hungry, so I boiled an egg and spread strawberry jam thickly on a roti, grateful to feed him, grateful to watch him eat. Afterwards, I lay in his little bed, spooned around him, smelling the soap and jam on his skin, until he dozed.

But I had not eaten in twenty-four hours, and after he fell asleep I felt it – a deep, hollow ache in my belly. I pulled myself away from Billy, kissed him one last time, and headed for the kitchen.

After eating a boiled egg, I made a cup of tea and took it to the living room, but I stopped short, shocked at the sight of the plundered pillow. It lay on the sofa, gaping open and spilling feathers. They were soft and white and incredibly small, the tiny quill tips sticking like pins into the upholstery. The landlord must not be allowed to see the ruined pillow. The stained bathroom floor was bad enough, but that pillow was an antique, possibly valuable. I would have to buy a sewing kit from a box wallah and try to repair it, but I wasn't much good with a needle. If I couldn't do it I'd have to get a *durzi* to set up with his sewing machine on the verandah and do it right. How much would that cost?

After all the baksheesh we had paid, on top of my secret splurge on perfume, there wasn't enough to cover the rent. Thank God Martin didn't know. I decided to write an invitation to tea and give it to the post wallah who came by every day before tiffin. He could deliver it to the landlord and then, face to face, I could ask the man for a grace period. But I hoped he wouldn't charge a penalty or interest.

I had just given the note to the post wallah when I remembered the journal under the floorboards. I went to Billy's room with a butter knife, quietly prised up the loose board, and took the tin box back to the living room. I removed the little suede book from the hot-water bottle and it fell open at the spot where a ridge from the torn pages acted as a natural bookmark I turned to the beginning and began to read.

Chapter Thirty

July 1857

The Indian has not visited for several days & I am relieved. Felicity says he has gone to his silk plantation near Pragpur, & she seems at peace with it. Perhaps we've seen the back of him. Probably not, but I will not dwell on it now. There is enough to deal with here, her illness & the pregnancy, the skittish servants.

The new plank floor looks superb, & I have loosened one board in my room. I will leave some portion of my story in the space beneath this house, to be found by whomever Fate decrees.

We hear reports of more rebellious sepoys, bloodbaths in Haryana & Bihar.

July 1857

Once again the monsoon came late. For a week, one could see mango-wood fires along the road & farmers flicking water into the flames. Felicity says they call the rite 'havan' & they believe it will bring rain.

When, finally, it came, the first drops fell lightly, but in seconds it became a torrent & created a watery green twilight. It fell in sheets, making it difficult to breathe, but people came out to kneel in the mud & dance barefoot in the puddles, the same as last year.

It went on & on & eventually everyone simply sat & stared at the continuous downpour whilst lightning flashes illuminated brown faces huddled in the godowns.

It has rained thus for a week & if it goes on too long the farmers will again perform havan to make it stop.

British troops have formally been dispatched from Simla and other places to put down the rebel sepoys.

July 1857

Kanpur! The sepoys held 206 of our women & children hostage in the Bibghar for two weeks. It is said that after hearing reports of entire Indian villages being massacred by British troops, the rebels hired a handful of peasants & thugs to murder the women & children with knives & hatchets. They say the walls of the Bibghar are covered with bloody handprints, & the floors littered with body parts. The dead & dying were thrown down a well & when the well was full the rest were thrown into the Ganges.

I have not told Felicity, nor will I.

July 1857

I fear there has been an outrage near Masoorla. No one speaks of it, at least not to me. The servants' faces are blank, but there is a distinct odour in the air, the cloying stench of decay. Kanpur has provoked a ferocious thirst for revenge & villagers whisper about a British Army of Retribution sweeping the countryside, wreaking vengeance not only on insurgents but everyone in their path. They are calling it the Devil's Wind.

Here in Masoorla we have only farmers & servants & shopkeepers, but there are rumours that reprisals are unrestrained & indiscriminate. I find this hard to credit. Surely no British soldier would murder innocents.

And yet, the smell is most oppressive on hot afternoons, & the flies have become insufferable. It is impossible even to take tea on the verandah without one's cup being covered by a black writhing mass.

July 1857

I have discovered why Felicity was not despondent when her lover ceased his visits. He did not go to his silk plantation near Pragpur; he has been sneaking in at night. When the moon is high & I am deep in slumber, he comes in through her bedroom window. The punkah wallah has confessed to seeing him.

Felicity says she asked him to come to her this way because she cannot bear my look of disapproval. She points out that I cannot even force myself to say his name, which is true enough. I think of him always as 'the Indian', or 'that man' or 'her lover'. Still, I have worked hard to put away jealousy & I know that they are hopelessly drawn to each other. Well do I remember how it was with Katie. I have striven to accept him & did not realize that my reservations showed so clearly on my face.

But much of what Felicity sees in my countenance is worry & even fear. Indians & Britons have never been so violently opposed as they are at this moment. This liaison of hers is dangerous!

However, I cannot change their hearts, & so I apologized to her & asked that he come by day, through the front door. I will try to be cordial for her sake in spite of my misgivings.

Felicity says her lover – I should say Jonathan, his family is anglicized & his name is Jonathan – Jonathan has commenced coughing. We do not know whether he has a simple catarrh that will pass or whether he has contracted Felicity's consumption.

August 1857

When her first twinges came in the afternoon, I sent the post bearer to Simla for the doctor, hoping it might be early enough to find him sober. I walked through the house & into our new kitchen & stood there, seeing nothing, trembling. Then I collected myself

& went back to her. She smiled at me. 'By tomorrow we shall have a child.'

I pulled a chair up to the bed. 'The doctor will arrive soon,' I assured her.

'That old sot?' She grimaced. 'Send for a midwife from the village. Lalita will know who to bring.'

'A native midwife?'

'Why not?'

I looked at Lalita, who said, 'My sister is having a baby last year. Many, many hours a first baby is taking, memsahib. No baby before morning is coming.'

Felicity nodded. 'The pains are mild.'

Allowing about an hour for the post bearer to get to Simla & the same for the doctor to ride out, it seemed we had plenty of time. Even if he arrived drunk, there would be time for him to sober up. But doing nothing was nerve-racking.

Lalita stood near the door, a frightened child, holding her veil over her mouth. I told her to fill the washstand & I took fresh sheets from the almirah – I was sure at least that much would be needed.

When I sat by the bed again, Felicity grabbed my hand & squeezed hard as she moaned. It began to rain & Felicity laboured to a backdrop of water beating on the roof. By dusk, I knew the muddy roads would make the journey from Simla more arduous, especially for a half-drunk rider. When Lalita brought a lighted lamp, I told her to go out in the road to see if the doctor was coming. She came back shaking her head & biting her lip. She whispered, 'Memsahib, much rain is falling. I am getting village woman?'

Would anything have been different if I'd said yes? But I said, 'The doctor will arrive soon.'

I gave Felicity small sips of water between her pains, & listened to the rain pound the roof. Lightning flashed & thunder rolled, &

what did I know of childbearing? How could I know if it was pro-ceeding normally? Shortly before dawn, I went to the verandah & saw a swamp surrounding the house. I could not even tell where the road began & still the rain fell in sheets. Even a sober man would have difficulty riding in that.

Panicked, I shouted for Lalita to get the midwife. She flew off the verandah & ran down the hill, slipping & sliding in the mud. She fell once, got back up & ran, mud splashing up to her knees. As I went back in, an eerie chanting started in the godowns, the servants making puja for their memsahib & her baby.

I went back to Felicity, who said, 'It will be all right.' So kind of her to allow me the beautiful lie that we all need to hear at times like that.

Within the hour, a tiny boy was born into my hands & the mid-wife arrived, half-drowned, in time to cut the cord. Despite Felicity's consumption, he is plump & rosy. He has a fuzz of black hair & a lusty cry; I believe he might live.

I swaddled him & placed him gently in the crook of Felicity's arm, but she was too weak to hold him. The midwife handed him back to me & pushed me roughly aside. Felicity was bleeding copiously & although I believed this to be normal, the midwife shouted something at Lalita, who ran out at breakneck speed & returned with a stone mortar & pestle. The woman crushed a con-coction of leaves & berries, then stirred it in a glass of water. She coaxed it between Felicity's lips whilst I stood there, holding the squalling child, helpless.

I watched Felicity grow weaker & paler whilst the midwife massaged her belly to no avail. There was a great surging of blood & when I understood she was truly in danger it was like a thunderclap within me. But when I saw no more could be done, I lay down with her & a calm came over me.

August 1857

The child is sleeping & the servants are nowhere to be seen, but tablas & wailing can be heard in the godowns. I wonder whether her spirit has already departed this place she so loved, or has her soul entered a dragonfly in order to linger near her new son?

As her body cooled, I washed her & dressed her in the lavender sari of which she was so fond. I brushed her hair & drew the netting round the bed. Her skin looked like alabaster, & I waited senselessly for the rise & fall of breath. I don't know why. I must pull myself together & leave the baby with Lalita whilst I make her final arrangements in Simla. This climate demands she be buried within twenty-four hours.

I have sent Khalid out for a tonga.

August 1857

Is there no end to this nightmare? I returned to find Lalita crying & Felicity gone. He left a thick, cream-coloured calling card on her bed with a scribbled note. 'I have taken her. I'm sorry.'

He's sorry?

He's sorry?

Where has he taken her? And why?

Martin came home wrung out and relieved. He hadn't shaved in two days and his eyes were bloodshot, but for once he seemed alive and happy. He went straight into Billy's room, gathered him in his arms and held him tight. Billy woke up and said, 'Hi Dad.'

'Billy boy.' Martin ran his hands and eyes over our child's face and body, looking for damage.

'I'm OK.'

'You can't go out alone like that,' Martin said. 'There are bad people out there. You could get hurt.'

'I know. The bloody niggers are out there.'

Martin laid a finger over Billy's lips. 'I don't ever want to hear that from you again. That's a terrible thing to say. Those children were naughty, but they're very poor. They'd never seen anything as swell as Spike. They were wrong to take him but ... they have nothing, Billy. We should feel sorry for them.' Billy stuck out a stubborn bottom lip and Martin ruffled his hair. 'A little sorry? They didn't know how much you love Spike.'

Billy stared at his hands, sullen and unconvinced.

Martin said, 'You think about it, OK?' Billy nodded and Martin continued, 'As for calling people names because they're different, you should know there were plenty of Indian people out looking for you, hoping to find you safe.'

Billy said, 'I don't hate those boys 'cos they're different. I hate them 'cos they took Spike.'

'I know. It was wrong to take Spike. Sometimes people do things that are wrong, but hating them and calling names won't help. It will only make you act like them.'

'I can't help it.' Billy shrugged. 'And it made you and Mom fight again.'

'We weren't fighting about Spike.'

'Uh-huh. I heard you.'

Martin raked his hair. 'I'm sorry you heard that, but it's OK now.'

'I still want Spike back.'

'I know.' Martin hugged him and I could see that he wanted to say more, but how do you make a five-year-old understand that human nature is complicated and life is unfair? Billy had a right to be angry. And if Martin were to be completely honest, he would have to admit that he'd like to smack the brat who robbed our little boy. I was sure of it.

*

After I got Billy back to sleep, I checked the latch on his shutters. Silly. It was a simple latch meant only to keep out monkeys, but I had to do it. I resolved to check the import shop for a more sturdy lock and I left his bedroom door wide open so that I could hear him if he woke.

I found Martin sitting at the kitchen table with his head in his hands. He mumbled, 'Stupid.'

'What?'

He looked up and his angry eyes confused me. He said, 'I was stupid. Flashing money around, acting desperate.'

'We *were* desperate.' I slipped into the chair next to him.

'Every criminal in Simla was looking for him. They would have sold him to the highest bidder and had him in Peshawar by next week. I was fucking stupid.'

I said, 'We were scared.'

'I thought he'd be hurt. Because of me.'

I took his hands in mine. 'What do you mean?'

His face had that frenzied look he got after one of his nightmares. 'You have no idea what people are capable of, what could have happened.'

'Nothing happened. He's fine.' I pressed his hands.

'I thought he'd have to suffer because of me. Sins of the father and all that . . .'

'Sweetheart, it was war. You did what you had to.'

'You don't understand.' He shook his head slowly and emotion drained from his face. 'I did nothing.'

Something faltered in my chest – his suddenly stony eyes, his cold tone. I said, 'Are you talking about the concentration camp?'

He nodded. 'When I told Billy that hating people makes you act like them, I was speaking from experience.'

My hands closed over his. After all my pleading for him

to open up, I was suddenly frightened. 'Martin, maybe we should just—'

'No. You need to understand. I'm going to tell you.'

Chapter Thirty-One

'WE'D BEEN ON THE march for weeks, bivouacking in the Bavarian woods and occupying little towns. The last village we took was half-wrecked but it still had a couple of basic shops going; some towns weren't hit as badly as others because they didn't produce anything for the war effort. This one still had a sausage shop where they stuffed roadkill into the casing and a farmer who somehow coaxed potatoes and cabbages out of the scorched earth. There was a small bakery, too, with a cracked window. Funny what you remember. It was only open two days a week because Elsa couldn't get enough supplies to bake every day, but she did her best to feed the few locals that were left. Nice girl, Elsa. Seeing her in there, blonde and pretty, standing behind the counter, the smell of bread baking – it reminded me of you in Linz's.'

'I *knew* you remembered Linz's.'

'Yeah.' He shook an Abdullah out of my pack and I was surprised. I'd offered him my smokes before, but he said they were effeminate. I watched in paralysed silence as he lit up. It was one of those moments when you simply do not interrupt. He blew two streams of smoke from his nose and said, 'Elsa complained about not having enough flour, but she always managed to have a loaf of rye for me and my guys. I liked going there; the shelves were mostly bare, but the place was embedded with that smell of fresh-baked bread. It made me think about you, safe at home. The only sign of war in that bakery was me, and I couldn't see me, so it was nice.

'I always paid her. Oh, yeah. I said thanks and I paid.' He tapped the cigarette on the edge of the ashtray. 'We weren't like the Krauts in France, who took livestock and chickens, every damn thing they could find, and left farmers to starve. I paid her and she was grateful. Some of the guys said I was nuts to buy bread from a Kraut. They said she could have poisoned it. Well, she could have, but she didn't. They used to feed a slice to a dog before they ate it, but I knew it wouldn't be poisoned.

'Elsa had a kid, a boy about five or six. He was shy. He'd be there sometimes, peeking out from behind his mother's skirt. I'd smile at him, and he'd duck away. Kids in wartime. Jesus.' He tapped the cigarette again. 'I always left a piece of chocolate on the counter for the kid. Sometimes Elsa's mother was around, too, griping about her bad back; she looked about a thousand years old, hunched and wrinkled, and she wouldn't talk to me. But she was just scared. They were all scared.' He took another drag. 'Elsa could have been nasty about giving me the bread, but she wasn't. She said, "We're all just trying to survive."'

'Martin, I'm not understanding this.'

'One day I went in for the bread and she was gone. Well, it was war; people disappeared all the time. About a week later we moved out, and a few weeks after that we came to one of those fucking concentration camps. The first thing we saw was a string of open boxcars full of dead bodies. Most of them were naked and they were just skin and bones. Their legs were only a couple of inches around. It's crazy, but I remember wondering if Elsa and her kid could be in there. I'm thinking, maybe somebody ratted her out to the Gestapo about the bread. It was a strange thought to have, but if you'd seen . . .' He took a long drag and blew it out slowly. 'Nobody talked. We walked past those boxcars in silence, staring. We'd seen plenty of bad shit by then, but this . . . Well, we didn't talk, just moved on to the camp.

'There was a big gate, and this German came out – a big handsome specimen of the master race, over six feet tall, broad shoulders, blond, and he's wearing a Red Cross shield and waving a white flag. A Red Cross! I thought, you son of a bitch, where have you been? You sure as hell weren't taking care of the people in the boxcars. Guy next to me whispered, "Come on, you bastard, make one funny move, just one." He was holding his tommy-gun real tight.

'We went through the gate and all these . . . these people came at us from all directions, thousands of them, dirty, and starved, and sick as hell. A couple of them sat in a tree, waving. Some sat on the ground, too weak to move. Others swarmed the yard, laughing and crying, and I thought one of them looked a little like Uncle Herb.' Martin started to smile, but it turned into a grimace and he smashed his cigarette out. 'They tried to grab us, tried to kiss our hands and our feet. Skeletons, grabbing us.'

'Your nightmares.'

'Yeah.'

'Honey, maybe—'

'One of the Nazis came forward to surrender, expecting the usual protocol. He was wearing all his ridiculous decorations.'

Martin's voice had become clear and strong, his face tough as a boot. He scared me. I said, 'Honey—'

'The dumb son of a bitch barked "Heil Hitler" and our CO looked around at the mounds of rotting corpses, the starving prisoners, and he spat in the Nazi's face. He called him a *Schweinhund*.'

'Good.'

Martin winced. 'I know. We all felt that way. But then . . . a few guys took the Nazi away and a couple of minutes later I heard two shots. The guys came back and one said, "Fuck protocol." Somebody else said, "Damn straight." '

There was a flint of anger in Martin's eyes, and goose bumps rose on my arms. He said, 'This wasn't war. It wasn't about dropping bombs from a clean blue sky, or soldiers fighting to push the front line, and it sure as hell wasn't self-defence. Germany had surrendered; those guards were unarmed. But the place was a hell-hole of tortured people and rotting corpses and shoes – God, the shoes. Thousands of shoes piled up by the crematorium. A mountain of shoes. And the smell.' He scrubbed his nose with the back of his hand. 'I'll never be rid of that smell.' He pushed his glasses up and looked at me. 'That camp wasn't war; it was personal. It ran on hate, and we wanted revenge.'

He looked away and I was relieved. He said, 'There were a few Germans dumb or arrogant enough to shout insults. Can you imagine? Waving a white flag and shouting insults. One Kraut yelled, "The Geneva Convention requires you give us a trial." Willie yelled back, "Here's your trial, you bastard! You're guilty!" And he shot him in the face.'

'But he *was* guilty.'

'Are you sure?'

'He was there, wasn't he?'

'There were hundreds of Germans there. By '44 the Nazis were running out of men and they drafted women and kids and old men. You didn't say no; if the SS wanted you, the choice was to be a guard or an inmate.' He paused and took a breath.

'Things calmed down for a while, and the colonel got about fifty Germans lined up against a wall. He left this young private holding a machine gun on them, and when he walked away the damn kid started firing. The colonel yelled, "What the hell are you doing?" The kid started crying. He said, "They were trying to get away." Well, they weren't, but everybody was so disgusted nobody cared. The kid was blubbering, "They aren't soldiers; they're criminals. They don't get to say, 'I quit,' and get off free." The colonel didn't argue with him, and the medic refused to patch up the ones who weren't dead, just left them to bleed to death. You know, it still didn't bother me.'

'I understand.'

'Then it started. There was nothing organized about it, just a lot of shooting and screaming and running around, corpses everywhere. I remember this Nazi running towards me, waving a white flag, and one of our guys, a corporal, running after him, yelling, "Oh, no you don't, mother fucker," and he shot the Kraut in the back. The inmates killed some of them with shovels.'

'Did you . . . ?'

Martin shook his head. 'I didn't kill anybody that day.'

'Well, then? What could you do? And, Martin? I can understand the others. I really can.'

'I know. I did too, until I saw Elsa.'

'The girl from the bakery?'

'And here I thought she might have been in a boxcar. There were nineteen female guards at that place. I don't know how Elsa wound up as one of them, but I know she must not have had much choice, and I know she couldn't have been there very long. I don't know what happened to her boy or her mother, but she was there, getting pushed up against a coal bin by a kid with a gun. She recognized me. She yelled something and reached her hand out to me. I don't know what she yelled, maybe it was only a scream, but I did nothing. I was an officer; I could have taken her prisoner. One word: *Stop*. But I did nothing.'

'You were traumatized.'

'I was an officer and a human being. She reached out to me, and I watched that kid blow her brains out. That wasn't war; that was murder. And I just stood there. Part of me will always be standing there.'

'Oh God.'

'There was a court-martial after the war. Charges were filed against a handful of guys, but Patton dismissed them. No witnesses were questioned and no one was found guilty. They argued a lot about exactly how many unarmed Germans were killed that day. Fifty? One hundred? Five hundred? Damned if I know. It was chaos. But I know Elsa deserved a trial. I know it today and I knew it then.'

'Oh, Martin.' My hands fell into my lap. I wanted to say something, but I felt bludgeoned. He waited, but I couldn't speak.

He said, 'So now you know.'

I forced myself to make words. 'You couldn't have stopped it.'

'Don't you get it?' He smiled and it was grotesque. 'I didn't *want* to stop it. She was wearing that uniform. That *uniform*. There were skeletons in rags, and naked corpses in the boxcars, and the smell and the shoes, and then there were those Nazi uniforms. I'd been shooting at that damn uniform for two years. Elsa's face was out of place, but she was wearing that god-damn uniform, so I did nothing. And I have to pay.'

I said, 'That's crazy.' But then I understood Martin's weird combination of paranoia and recklessness. If life didn't make him pay, he'd make himself pay. I said, 'Martin? Honey?' But he wasn't there any more. His mind was staked to a horrific memory and he stared at the table as if it were taking place there. I touched his arm lightly. 'Honey?' He pulled his gaze from the table and said, 'I know we met in a German bakery. I just wish we hadn't. I don't like to think about German bakeries.' Then he got up quietly and went to bed. I sat there for a while, trying to find room inside myself for this. All of my sniping and stewing and secrets suddenly seemed meaningless.

I don't know how long I sat there, but suddenly I couldn't keep my eyes open. I wanted to rest my head on the table and sleep right there, but I didn't want Martin to sleep alone, not that night. I didn't want him to think he disgusted me the way he disgusted himself.

I dragged myself to the bedroom and, lo and behold, he was sleeping peacefully. His clothes hung off a chair like a dead thing, and mosquito netting diffused moonlight around him. His face was as smooth and placid as I'd ever seen it. He'd been living with his secret for more than two years, and he'd finally unburdened himself. After that night, Elsa belonged to both of us.

Chapter Thirty-Two

I WOKE UP EARLY, with my heart pounding and my stomach knotted and queasy. I dressed quickly and hurried to the kitchen to fix Martin a big breakfast. While Billy ate his roti and jam, I made coffee and toast and eggs sunny side up – firm whites, runny yolks, the way Martin liked them. I set the table, fumbling with the fork and knife, clattering the cup and saucer. My hands weren't working right. Billy watched me, and I tried to smile. I wanted Martin to walk in on a scene of domestic tranquillity, to feel that we were fine, he was fine, everything was fine. I wished I had a crisp white apron to wear. If I could make it look OK, maybe it would be. But when he walked into the kitchen with that tightness around his mouth, the obscene images came back, and an irrational rush of shame and pity (but for whom?) made me turn away. I sprinkled borax powder on a stain in the porcelain sink and scrubbed hard. I asked, 'Breakfast?'

He said, 'Sure.'

He kissed the top of Billy's head and sat down at the table, and I forced myself to sit with him. He dipped his toast in his yolk, asking, 'To what do I owe all this?'

I said, 'Now that it's all out, maybe we can put it behind

us and be a family again.' I should have looked at him, maybe touched him, but I shook an Abdullah out of the pack and lit it.

He stopped chewing. 'Oh, brother.' He put his fork down. 'I get it.'

'What?' I took a long pull on my cigarette and blew the smoke away from him.

'This is what I was afraid of. You don't know how to live with it.'

I tapped the cigarette that didn't yet have an ash to tap. 'Do you?'

'No, but one of us was enough. I shouldn't have told you.'

'No—'

'Oh, yeah. Bad mistake.'

'No. I—'

'I'm sorry, Evie. This isn't your burden, it's mine. You shouldn't have to . . . I'm really sorry . . .' His voice trailed off and he pushed away from the table and left the kitchen.

I listened to the front door click shut, knowing he was right. I didn't know how to live with it. Part of me wanted to comfort him, tell him he was forgiven, but another part of me wondered whether I could ever again look at him without seeing Elsa. I shovelled Martin's breakfast into the garbage and started scrubbing dishes until they squeaked.

I was battling dried egg yolk when a post bearer came to the front door. I wiped my hands and read the note from our landlord; he had received my invitation and would come by at eleven. I put the ripped pillow into the bedroom almirah, picked the feathers off the sofa cushion, and went back to the kitchen to finish the dishes.

When Rashmi came in and saw me labouring over a pile of dishes and pans, she slipped off her sandals and hurried to the sink, shaking her head. 'Arey Ram! What Madam is doing?'

'It's OK.' I buffed a coffee ring out of a cup. 'I'll do this. You sweep up.'

She moved closer and smiled impishly. 'Something good I am bringing for Madam.' She dug around in the cloth bag that served as her purse and pulled out a tarnished gold tube of lipstick. She opened it and rolled out a blazing-red lipstick, obviously used, and beamed at me. 'Sir will *love* it.'

I put down the dishcloth and said, 'Thank you, but I don't often wear lipstick.'

Her face dropped. 'But this is the trouble, neh? Madam has to try, isn't it?'

She was killing me. I said, 'Sure.'

'Gooood.' Her renewed smile threatened to crack her sweet face. 'Be putting it on now to keep me radiant.'

Anything to make her stop. I dabbed my lips with the waxy stuff, wondering who had used it last.

Rashmi grabbed her chest as if she were having a coronary. 'Sooo beauuutiful Madam is.' She sidled closer. 'Now only Madam is needing some jewellery. Why are white ladies never wearing enough jewellery? Verrry bad mistake.'

'I have earrings.'

'In the ears is good, but also the arms and nose and toes.' She pointed at her nose pin and her toe ring and jangled her bracelets. 'You can see?'

'Yes, very nice.' I dried my hands and edged towards the living room.

'And, excuse for saying, but Madam's hair is being too short.'

'I'll let it grow.' I headed for the verandah, licking the sticky wax off my lips. I called out, 'Make a pot of masala chai, OK? The landlord is coming.'

Rashmi launched herself into the living room and headed me off at the door. She made a couple of rough swipes at my lips with her thumb, saying, 'Not for him this is. For Sir only.'

'Of course.' I took the dishcloth from her and wiped my lips. 'Now will you please make tea?'

She retreated, mumbling in Hindi; I didn't understand the words, but the indignant tone came through loud and clear. In her world, men did not come alone to visit married ladies in the middle of the day.

I sat in the wicker rocker and checked my watch. I had dreaded this encounter when I wrote the invitation, but that morning I was glad for something to take my mind off Martin.

At exactly eleven, a black Mercedes pulled up and a chauffeur got out and opened the back door. Our landlord, Mr Singh, always wore well-tailored Western suits, and his turban always matched his tie. That day, he wore a grey silk suit and a slate-blue turban and tie. He mounted my front steps – his steps, actually – and strolled across the verandah with an air of ownership.

Our landlord had the manner of an English aristocrat and the reputation of a cagey businessman, the type Chicagoans called a shark. I did not expect him to throw us out on the street, but he could set whatever interest and penalties he liked, and we might come up short even after Martin's pay-cheque arrived.

I considered inviting him in and serving tea in the living room, but he might notice the missing pillow, and if he asked to use the bathroom, he'd see the orange stain on the tiled floor. None of that would put him in a generous mood. I felt like a Hun who had laid waste to his pristine dolls' house, and I reminded myself that at least it wasn't I who had gnawed those teeth marks in the wooden arm of the brocade chair.

He put out his hand and his white smile dazzled against

his caramel skin. I had the passing thought that he might use neem twigs to brush his teeth, but that was ridiculous; neem twigs were for peasants, and this wealthy man was as European as he was Indian. As I shook his hand, he made a small, efficient bow. 'Good morning, Mrs Mitchell.' His British English had no Indian lilt.

'Thank you for coming.' I gestured at the wicker chairs.

He took one of the faded chairs and sat as if his entire body was freshly starched; he flicked an invisible piece of lint off razor-creased trousers, and I called for the tea. In the history of the world, there has never been a negotiation in India without tea.

Rashmi brought it out, looking put upon and suspicious as she set the tray on the small table between the wicker chairs. After she had poured, she walked away, trying to catch my eye and shaking her head. The landlord picked up his cup and inhaled the fragrant steam. He took a sip and said, 'Very nice, Mrs Mitchell.' He put his cup down without a sound. 'Now, how can I be of service?'

Where to start? I said, 'Perhaps you heard that our little boy went missing.'

'I did. And I was relieved to hear that he is safe.'

'Yes, but, you see, we paid out quite a lot of money for . . . we paid people to help us find him.'

'You paid baksheesh, Mrs Mitchell. I know how things work.'

'Yes, well, I'm afraid, we can't pay the rent. I hoped we might come to an arrangement. Something that would be fair to everyone.'

His face clouded. 'It would be a fine thing if life was fair, wouldn't it?'

I sat forward. 'Mr Singh, surely you understand that we intend to pay. Haven't we always? I'm only asking that you waive any penalties and set a reasonable rate of interest. We live on a budget.'

He held up a manicured hand. 'Mrs Mitchell, you misunderstand. I would never charge you penalties or interest. It saddened me to hear about your little boy.'

'Oh.' I sat back. 'Well, that's generous of you.'

He raised his teacup. 'It's nothing, I assure you.'

'I don't know what to say.' Something felt stuck in my throat, but it would have been mortifying to cry in front of that polished man. I took a gulp of tea to wash down the obstruction. Still, my voice came out strained. 'I expected you to be angry. Lately, people are so angry.'

He nodded. 'It's an anxious time – bad decisions and worse behaviour. As the British depart, we should be trying to get along.'

'You don't favour Partition?'

He shook his head solemnly. 'I think it's quite unfortunate.' He brushed more non-existent lint off his trousers. 'My beloved grandfather was my first mentor, and he would have been sorely distressed by Partition. He, too, would never have penalized you for your misfortune. In memory of my grandfather, I will not trouble you for the rent until you find it convenient.'

'My goodness.' I wanted to tell Martin, and then remembered – I couldn't.

For a week, the ghost of Elsa made us walk around each other as if avoiding some contagion; it hung in the air like a bad smell that neither of us acknowledged. Martin left every morning before I woke, and came home to spend half an hour with Billy before he went to the Club for dinner. He said he couldn't take Habib's cooking any more, but we both knew he was having trouble looking at me. When he returned, always late, he fumbled off his clothes and collapsed into our white bed smelling of whisky. I pretended to sleep and kept my back to him. I wanted to turn and say, 'I still love you.' But the memory of that woman and her little boy kept me quiet. He was Martin, and he was good, and I did still love him, but I couldn't rid myself of the images of her he'd given me – standing in her bakery wrapping a loaf of rye bread and, later, reaching out to him, pleading.

One morning, after he left, I sat up in bed and said, 'No.'

If it was a mistake for Martin to let that moment ruin his life, then it was a mistake for me as well, and if I had to lose Martin, it wouldn't be without a fight. We couldn't simply talk – words couldn't get past his guilt – but I could *show* him I still loved him. I could make a grand gesture that would shock Martin out of his dark place.

That afternoon, I left Billy with Rashmi – who now never let him out of her sight – and I took a tonga to the Lakkar bazaar. I never took my camera with me any more – India simply could not be squeezed into my viewfinder – but I had begun keeping a journal. I made my way to the tent of the henna artist, and my heart banged against my ribs as I pushed aside the flap and entered the dim, perfumed interior. The henna artist, a woman in a sari the blush-colour of passion fruit, bowed and said, 'Namaste, memsahib.'

'Namaste.' Then I took a shaky breath and said, 'I'd like a henna tattoo.'

She looked me up and down, then asked, 'Hands or feet?'

'Here.' I laid my hands over my breasts and belly. The woman stared at me for a moment, and then she smiled. 'Of course, memsahib.'

I undressed down to my panties and lay on the white sheet she spread on the ground, and she laid another sheet over my body. She disappeared behind a beaded curtain to mix powders and paints while I lay, listening to the bustle of the bazaar outside the tent, thinking how strange it was to lie there, almost nude, with only a piece of canvas between me and thousands of people hurrying by, talking, laughing, buying, selling. This feeling was foreign to me, and the henna on my body would be even more foreign, but it felt right. Martin would not be able to ignore this. The lines from Rumi came back to me.

> *You can't quit drinking the earth's dark drink?*
> *But how can you not drink from this other fountain?*

The henna artist came out carrying a small black-bellied pot filled with thick red mush covered with a metallic sheen. I lay still, feeling the tickle of a fine-tipped brush adorning me with vines and flowers. She turned my body into a lush jungle that bloomed over my breasts, twined down to my navel and spread across my belly, a tale of the ties that bind and how difficult it can be to locate beginnings and ends.

After the henna artist finished, she told me to lie still for an hour while the paint dried. I lay on the ground, waiting, feeling my heartbeat in the hollow spot at the base of my neck. A certainty came to me then that we would be all right; I would do this for him, only him, to show him that I could forgive him, that he was, in fact, forgivable.

That night, I waited in bed for Martin to return from the Club. When he climbed in beside me, I reached for him and said, 'We have to stop this.' He went still, and I whispered, 'I forgive you. I still love you.'

He said, 'I can't forgive myself.'

'I'll help you.' I slipped my nightgown off my shoulders. 'Look at me.'

He made a hoarse, choking sound. 'Evie, what have you done?'

I laid my hands over my breasts and my stomach. 'This is us, Martin. Intertwined. Still. Always.'

'Jesus.' His voice was husky.

I said, 'Touch me.'

He placed his fingertip in the hollow at the base of my neck and let it rest there while he took in the design on my body. Then took his hand away and said, 'Cover yourself.'

'What?'

He pulled my nightgown up over my breasts and shoulders, gently pushing me away at the same time, and humiliation, sharp as a broken bone, forced a strangled cry out of me.

Martin said, 'I'm sorry. I can't.' He got out of our bed, knocking Rashmi's marigold mala off the bedpost in his haste, and in his hurry to pull on his pants and leave me there, he stepped on it.

Early the next morning I found him on the sofa, awake, staring at the ceiling. He said, 'I had a wonderful dream.'

His happiness made me instantly angry. I said, 'Good for you.' I turned away, but he grabbed the hem of my nightgown, and I stopped with my back to him.

'Evie, please.'

I peered over my shoulder; his face was wide open, like a child wanting answers. He said, 'I don't remember all of it, but there was light, so much light, and I was playing the piano, and I felt . . . this is corny, but . . . I felt bliss.'

'Bliss.' I remembered the crushed mala still lying on the bedroom floor, my scathing humiliation and the henna tattoo, fresh and vivid on my pale skin. I'd have to live with it for months. I said, 'I'm happy for you.' I yanked my nightgown away from him and went into the kitchen to make coffee.

Rashmi arrived with chits from the butcher and the import store, and she watched me stuff them into the empty tea tin. She said, 'Not for worrying, Madam. I am making puja to Lakshmi, goddess of rich.' She nodded slyly, as if she'd given me an insider tip, then called, 'Come, *beta*,' and went after Billy.

That day I felt an irresistible urge to clean the hell out of something. I took dirty clothes out of the hamper and filled the bathtub with hot water and washing powder. I knelt on the hard, cold tiles and bent over a washboard with my hair tied back in a kerchief like an antebellum mammy. The work was back-breaking and the bathroom steamed up, jungle hot. I scrubbed and sweated and scraped my knuckles on the washboard, wanting to wash everything away. *Thwack!* That one is for Martin rejecting me. *Slap!* That one is for Billy and Spike. *Whack!* That one is for every stinking war men have ever waged. I battered Martin's shirts, I clobbered his pants, I bashed my blouses, and I walloped Billy's pyjamas . . .

'Arey Ram!' Rashmi stood in the bathroom door, holding her cheeks.

'It's OK, Rashmi.' I wiped my cheek with a curled wrist.

'Nooo!' She rushed over and knelt next to me. 'Madam is bleeding!'

My knuckles were torn and abraded; bits of skin hung off here and there, and the soapy water on the washboard dribbled pink suds. The blue blouse bunched in my fist was splotched with red.

When Rashmi prised the blouse away from me, I felt bereft and grabbed another, but she stilled my hands and studied my face. She said, 'Billy is one hundred per cent A-OK.'

'I know.' I smiled weakly, and then Rashmi held me. She didn't understand, but it didn't matter. I sank into her embrace.

Later, with Band-Aids on my knuckles, Rashmi and I carried the basket of wet laundry out to the compound to lay it on bushes to dry in the sun. I liked handling the fresh clothes smelling of carbolic soap, and I shook out Billy's yellow shirt, watching it flap at the sky like a prayer flag. Billy sat on the steps and stared.

Rashmi and I both knew that Billy was not A-OK. Without Spike, he shuffled around the house, breaking my heart with each soft step. When I tried to engage him in play, he played. When I told him to eat, he ate. At bedtime, he submitted to his bath and went right to sleep. I built forts out of blocks and he watched patiently. I read Aesop's Fables and he listened politely. I pulled him around our compound in his Red Flyer and he lay down on the pillow and went to sleep. He was a little Gandhi, defeating me with passivity, and if the British Empire couldn't fight that, what chance did I have?

While Rashmi and I spread the laundry on woody mimosa bushes, I recalled a moment of healing magic from my own childhood, a kind thing Da had once done for me. I went into the house and rummaged through my bedroom almirah until I found the cardboard shoebox that held my black, open-toe pumps. I'd bought them for the high, sexy heel and the patent-leather bow at the toes, but on the dirt roads of Masoorla and the broken steps of Simla, they would have hobbled me like a Chinese woman with bound feet. I hadn't worn them once since we arrived. I emptied the shoebox and drew a rainbow on the lid with Billy's crayons.

I wedged the lid in the box at a steep angle, and tossed a handful of shiny copper pice at the end of the rainbow and, *voilà* – a leprechaun trap.

Da had made one for me after Mum died. He promised that some greedy leprechaun would slide down the rainbow, aiming for the gold, and not be able to climb out. Leprechauns are tiny, you see, as small as Billy's pinky finger. Da said after I caught my leprechaun, I could put the lid on the box and the little fellow would be pleased as punch to live inside with his pile of gold. I had checked my leprechaun trap every day for a month until I got bored, and then it disappeared. But it had gotten me one month closer to healing.

I showed Billy the leprechaun trap, and he said, 'A real leprechaun?'

'Well, there are no guarantees.' I knitted my brow. 'I'm not sure there are as many leprechauns in India as there are in Chicago, but we can try.'

He nodded like a sad little sage. 'OK.'

I nestled the leprechaun trap in a stand of wild tuberoses, saying, 'Any leprechaun worth his salt wouldn't be fooled by a rainbow inside the house.' I figured we'd catch a few bugs, maybe a lizard – anything to distract him – but the next day, Billy came in with the shoebox under his arm. 'Got one,' he said.

'What?'

'A leprechaun.'

'Really?' What the hell? 'Can I see?'

'Nuh-uh. He's shy.' He hurried to his room and closed the door.

I wasn't sure whether to be glad or concerned. In the end I decided an imaginary leprechaun wasn't any worse than a fake dog, but Billy's leprechaun was not a garden-variety imaginary friend. Billy carried the shoebox everywhere, lifting the corner of the lid and whispering into the box, smiling a sneaky smile, as if he and the leprechaun were hatching a sinister plot. Whenever I looked at him, he stopped abruptly, but as soon as I turned away, he'd begin whispering again.

I said, 'You know leprechauns are good guys, right?'

'Uh-huh.'

'A leprechaun wouldn't do anything naughty.'

'Uh-huh.'

But the sly, shifty whispering continued. At the kitchen table, Billy slipped food into the box, and I worried about it rotting. But if I removed the food scraps, would he think the leprechaun had eaten it?

Of course, he took the shoebox to bed with him, and one night, while he slept, it fell on the floor. Then next morning he screamed like a banshee, and I came running. He was sitting in bed, sobbing and twisting the sheet the way Martin did during his nightmares. When I put my arms around him he collapsed like a marionette on cut strings. I saw the shoebox, half under the bed, and picked it up, but I had to press it against his chest and hold it there to make him understand he hadn't lost his leprechaun. He could barely catch his breath. He hugged the box while his crying subsided into convulsive hiccups. I watched him, thinking I should never have tried to replace Spike. But by then, taking the shoebox away was unthinkable.

I took Billy out for short walks in the colonial district, pulling him and the shoebox in the red wagon, singing 'Old MacDonald', but he didn't join in. Once, I took him to the import shop in a tonga, and he plodded through the congested aisles, inhaling the ripe air and hugging the shoebox under his arm. I offered him candy and toys, even with an empty tea tin and the rent in arrears. I would have bought him anything, but he said, 'Nah. We're fine.'

As always, the import shop was a cramped obstacle course with burlap bags full of rice and onions on the floor, tin cans and glass bottles lining the walls, mops and Borax and Jeyes cleaning fluid stacked in the corner. I lingered at a table heaped with apples and jackfruit, and selected six dull red Himalayan apples, which I set on the counter with a jar of strawberry jam for Billy's roti. I asked, 'How are you, Manesh?'

The round little man rocked his head from side to side. 'I am keeping radiant, even with uncles and aunties sleeping on the verandah. In the morning, over bodies I am stepping.' He shrugged and smiled.

'Has your family come for some occasion?'

'Indeed yes.' Manesh laughed. 'The occasion of Partition.'

'Excuse me?'

He explained that violence in the cities had caused thousands of people to flee to the countryside. In addition to his own relatives, Manesh was also sheltering a Muslim family who didn't want to emigrate. He said, 'Old friends they are. In the cow shed they are sleeping.'

Some families had taken in as many as forty displaced relatives. They lived shoulder to shoulder in their tiny houses, scraping by, sharing everything, always finding an extra potato to add to the curry pot, an extra handful of rice. And they seemed good-natured about it, accepting everything with enviable equanimity.

Listening to Manesh, I wished I could join them. I wished I could leave my comfortable bungalow with its emotional baggage and wrap myself in a soft cotton sari – pale green or maybe lavender would be nice with my hair – and sit on the floor of Manesh's crowded house. Billy could play with other children, and I could chop onions and grind coriander with other women, listen to an infant being comforted and the cow lowing out back. I'd feel the solid earth under me, and wallow in the closeness of people who cared about each other. But I couldn't find a place for Martin in my fantasy. Even with his dark skin and kurtas and bidis, he didn't fit because I didn't want him there. India wasn't lonely; I was.

I bought Billy a shiny, blue-lacquered yo-yo and signed my chit, then I took him home to Rashmi, who was surprisingly versed in yo-yo tricks and eager to demonstrate. I told her I'd be gone for the rest of the afternoon, and Billy said, 'Where are you going, Mom?'

'To the Club, baby.' I was sick of being lonely. It was Tuesday, bridge day, and everyone I knew would be there.

Chapter Thirty-Three

THE CLUB REMINDED me of an old English country house where all the guests knew each other, a temple of clubbiness with rules about clothes, and social politics, and plenty of alcoholic lubricant to loosen those stiff upper lips. I walked across a wide verandah, through a small antechamber and into a comfortable room full of leather chairs and chintz sofas arranged in intimate groupings. Only two men sat talking quietly, spirals of smoke rising from their cigarettes. The empty room could have accommodated at least fifty people, but in the mid-afternoon lull it had a deserted, defeated ambiance, a reminder of the dying Raj.

I passed a room known as the Study – so named because of a long, high wall crammed with books and Victorian antiques – dominated by a well-lit snooker table in the centre. That afternoon, two men played with rolled-up sleeves. One fellow bent over the green felt and sighted a line down his cue. I heard the clack of balls, followed by one man's laughter and the other's groan. Murky oil paintings of dead viceroys, glassy-eyed animal heads and faded sepia photographs covered the walls.

The airy main room of the Club had a high, open-beamed

ceiling from which a dozen fans revolved slowly. Sunlight sneaked through the wrap-around verandah and filtered through French doors to strike the polished parquet floor, and I spotted Verna and Lydia at one of the square tables across the room, playing cards. Four women in floral dresses and pearls played bridge, tapping their Abdullahs in glass ashtrays, and sipping their gin with the emblematic listlessness of the bored memsahib. The charmed enclosure of the British Raj was safe, but it was also hermetic and limited, and after the first year a predictable ennui and longing for home needed to be rigorously countered with games and alcohol.

A long, polished oak bar with rattan barstools ran along the side of the room, and I flinched when a shrill voice shrieked, 'Dickie, you scoundrel!' A blowsy woman with a painted Bette Davis smirk was perched sideways on a barstool, with her legs prettily crossed and one hand on the arm of a young officer leaning over her. She held up a drink with fire-red nails and wiggled it at a bearer for a refill. Her scarlet halter-neck dress did not allow for a bra, and her shallow breasts bobbed under the flimsy fabric. She screamed again, and I thought her voice could have grated carrots.

This was the other sort of memsahib: the jaded lady who spent months in the hills without her husband, listening to the same stale jokes from the same people, hearing the same gossip – herself often the subject – reading the same out-of-date magazines, wondering what was happening on the London social scene, flirting and more, until she went back to Calcutta or Bombay or Delhi for the cool weather. Her laughter sounded like glass shattering.

I walked past the bar and approached the bridge table, catching snatches of subdued conversation about the Liverpool Cup. In my slacks and sandals and a fawn-coloured kameez, I didn't fit with the finger-curl crowd playing bridge, or with the hard-drinking, philandering memsahib at the bar. Still, if I had to be lonely, it wouldn't be because I didn't try. Verna saw me and waved me over. 'Evie, how nice to see you.'

I pulled up a chair and set my purse on the floor. 'Well, I'm not much for bridge, but I thought I'd say hello.' I ordered a gin and tonic, and Verna passed me a dish of piquant Bombay mix. I took a spiced peanut, and she said breezily, 'We're not very good either. We're just passing the time until we can go home.' The women laughed, and even that sounded lethargic.

I said, 'Is that all you have? Bridge?'

'Oh, no,' she said gaily. 'There's dancing and amateur theatricals, tennis, cricket . . .' She studied her cards.

Lydia laid down a card and said, 'There's plenty of gaiety, but no real culture.'

A woman I'd met once before, named Petal Armbruster, said, 'That's not entirely fair, Lydia. There's the Asiatic Society, though I admit they're mostly bluestockings.' She pulled a face, and the fourth woman laughed without looking up from her cards. For the life of me I couldn't think of her name; she, too, had been at Verna's welcome tea, but whatever her name was, it was not as memorable as Petal Armbruster. Petal went on, 'They read dreadful papers about monoliths and ancient dynasties.' She bulged her eyes in mock horror.

Verna laid a card down. 'Some ladies mess about with charities – there's Lady Blebbin's Hindu Widow Institute and the East Indian Self-Help Society – but they're a rather morose lot.'

'Yes,' said Petal. 'We prefer cheerier types.'

'Like me?' The woman in the scarlet halter-top had left the

bar and stood smoking near one of the French doors. I looked at her, and she came over, teetering on her ankle-strap high heels.

Verna took a sip of her drink and grimaced as though it was too bitter. She said, 'Evie Mitchell, this is Betty Carlisle.'

Betty said, 'I've met your husband.' She threw me a nasty little smile, and I imagined bookish, withdrawn Martin fending off this abrasive woman. She said, 'He doesn't dance. That must be dull for you.'

The table fell silent and everyone hunched over their cards. Betty waited a beat, took a long drag on her cigarette, and said, 'Always lovely to see you too.' Then she wobbled back to the bar.

'Look at that,' said Verna. 'The Treacle Tart is already boiled.'

'She comes over here to annoy us.' Lydia tapped her cards into a neat stack, then fanned them out again.

'She's not fooling anyone.' Verna slapped a card down. 'Betty Bed-and-Breakfast is about as old as the antiques in the Study.'

'The room with the snooker table?' I lit an Abdullah.

Lydia nodded. 'Hodge-podge of taxidermy and old junk is what I call it. The historical committee is always nattering about donating any old thing you come across.'

'Why not donate it?' Verna asked. 'No one wants it.'

'True enough.' Petal sipped her gin. 'No one knows who the frightful old sticks in the photographs are, and it's not as though anyone wants to read their boring rants.' She put her hand on my arm. 'Sorry, darling. I just remembered that your husband is an historian. I suppose he'd like all that old stuff.'

I punished her with a cold smile as the bearer set down my drink. 'Martin is documenting Partition and the end of the Raj.'

The bearer smiled a little too broadly, and silence descended on the bridge table. The joy these ladies felt at going home was tempered by a sense of defeat, and none of them seemed entirely sure whether to celebrate or grieve. Petal cleared her throat. 'Well, with this new date for withdrawal I'm sure he'll have plenty to document.'

The fourth woman at the table said, 'I don't know what Mountbatten is thinking.'

'Nor shall we ever know,' said Verna. 'It's the Viceroy's divine right not to care a parrot's eyelash for anybody.'

Benny Goodman's clarinet spiralled out of a gramophone, startling everyone, as Betty came back to the table with a fresh drink and a cigarette drooping between languid fingers. She said, 'I had the bearer put on some music. This place is dull as a tomb – as usual.'

Verna tutted. 'It's a bit loud, isn't it? We're still playing bridge here.'

'Oh, honestly!' Betty stabbed her cigarette into the glass ashtray. 'I'm sick of bridge. I'm sick of all of it.' She glared at Verna. 'You are, too. You just won't admit it.' She turned, almost losing her balance, and wove out to the verandah with her drink. The young officer at the bar slipped off his barstool and went out after her.

Verna watched her go and mumbled, 'That outfit looks . . .' She rolled her eyes. Verna turned back to the table with a smug smile. 'I've heard she has the manager at the Cecil ring a bell early in the morning to warn her to get back to her own bed.' She sat back, happily disgusted.

I had replaced the memory of horsey teeth and hard-bitten Ts with the image of a kind, older woman who brought me drugged tea, mercy tea. And Lydia had been gentle and solicitous, and I had hoped it might have been an overture to real friendship, but . . . Verna held up her empty glass and called out, 'Bearer, gin and tonic. Look lively.'

I tamped out my cigarette and pushed back my chair. 'I wanted to thank you, Verna and Lydia, both of you, for your kindness when . . .' I thought of Billy sleeping in a cowshed and couldn't say it. 'When I needed it.'

Lydia made a dismissive gesture. 'We're all stuck here together. If we don't help each other, who will?'

'You were both exceptionally kind.' I picked up my purse. 'But I was rude. I was upset.'

'Of course you were,' said Verna. 'Having your child out *there*, among *them*.'

I said, 'Do you have children, Verna?'

The smile appeared in all its glory. 'Two boys, grown and flown, in England.'

'Do they ever visit?'

'Here? With all that's going on?'

'Well, not now. But ever?'

Verna stretched her neck to get closer as if she thought I was hard of hearing. 'They're in *England*. They're not Company men. I visit *them*, not the other way round.' She leaned back in her chair and unleashed the smile. 'Anyway, soon I shall see them whenever I please.'

'That will be nice for you.' I wondered whether Verna had some mild form of split-personality disorder. One moment she was kind, and the next she was a malicious gossip who abused the servants. I thought of Reverend Locke saying, 'People . . .' and the way his hand had circled around nothing.

Verna looked past me and her face lit up. She said, 'Darling!' I turned to see a tall, grey-haired man in a military jacket and Sam Brown belt walking towards us.

'Sorry to interrupt,' he said, giving Verna a peck on the cheek. 'Just popped in for an early peg.'

'Evie.' Verna beamed, newly animated. 'I don't think you know my husband, Henry.'

His eyes were affable and his smile genuine, and he wore colonel's pips on his shoulder. 'A pleasure,' he said, and I had the impression that he meant it.

Verna asked, 'Will you join us, darling?'

'Not today, love.' He patted her hand, and they gazed at each other like newlyweds. 'I don't want to disturb you. I'll have my peg with the boys at the snooker table, but I couldn't resist an opportunity to kiss my lady's cheek.'

They exchanged an intimate look and I wondered, how? How could they sustain such unwearied affection after decades of marriage? Verna wasn't a particularly nice woman, she certainly wasn't beautiful, and his job kept her far away from her beloved home and children, but there they were – lovebirds. This unexpected display of lasting love made me feel even more alone than I had when I'd walked in, hoping for companionship. 'Well,' I said, 'I should be going. I only have one servant at home and I have a lot to do.'

Verna's lips shrank over her enormous teeth and she said, 'Would that be your ayah, the little fat woman?'

'Her name is Rashmi.'

Verna's lip curled and the other woman studied their cards. 'The fact is, my dear, she's been selling your garbage.'

'What? Who would buy my garbage?'

'Oh, you are so innocent.' She looked at her husband. 'Isn't she innocent?'

Henry smiled warmly. 'This place is not easy to understand.'

'The point is,' Verna continued, 'she's been selling it instead of disposing of it the way she ought.'

I felt blood rush to my face. I *hated* that. I said, 'Actually,

Verna, I don't care what Rashmi does with my garbage. I expect she needs the money.'

Her face closed up. 'I suppose that's one way to look at it.'

I stood abruptly. 'I came to say thank you. Lovely to meet you, Henry.'

Martin's pay came through the next day and that evening, while he ate dinner at the Club, I filled envelopes for the butcher, the import shop and the landlord. Since the landlord had been so gracious, I thought it would be a nice gesture to deliver the rent to his home in person, rather than sending it with a post bearer. The following morning I asked Rashmi if she knew where he lived and she laughed. 'So high, high that family is standing, everyone is knowing. Tell the tonga driver, "big man Singh".' She smirked. 'Driver is knowing.'

A tonga took me up a hidden driveway, snaking through tropical foliage to a scrolled wrought-iron gate flanked by elephant topiaries with raised trunks. Space is the most precious commodity in India, and Mr Singh lived in a two-storey house surrounded by deep lawns and massive old trees. I asked the driver to wait at the gate, then I walked up a brick lane shaded by pomelo trees with glossy leaves, and jacarandas, dripping clusters of lilac-coloured blossoms. Coming upon a grand villa, I saw the chauffeur polishing the black Mercedes under a side portico.

I walked up marble stairs to a verandah many times larger than mine. It was strewn with teak armchairs upholstered in nubby red silk, and when I lifted the heavy brass knocker on the door it dropped like a gong. A turbanned bearer in a wine-red tunic and gold sash pulled the door open, revealing a cavernous foyer with a curved staircase. He looked more like a pasha than a servant as he ushered me in, with practised panache, to a spacious room decorated in the Indo-European style.

I sat on a low divan piled with embroidered pillows and surveyed the room: walls upholstered in watered silk, a carved wooden screen with an antique patina, and tall windows open to persimmon trees. A royal-blue Persian rug covered most of the inlaid marble floor, and two throne-like chairs with lion-paw arms faced the divan. In front of me, on a low table, a rangoli of lotus flowers, white with achingly pink tips, floated in a shallow crystal bowl. I bent over one of the great creamy lilies with a tiny phial of perfume at the end of each stamen, and I touched a petal, tracing the cool waxen surface. A deep voice said, 'Beautiful, aren't they?'

He stood in the doorway, poised as always, wearing a white linen suit, and I wondered how some people managed to look fresh even with wrinkles in their clothes. He wore a jade-green turban that day, with a matching tie. I said, 'They certainly are.'

Crossing the room with an easy gait, he said, 'The lotus represents purity of mind and body.' He sat opposite me in one of the carved chairs and rested his weight comfortably on an elbow. 'I'm not religious, but the beauty of the lotus does seem to embody something spiritual, don't you think?'

I feared that touching the lotus might have been a faux pas; Mr Singh seemed nonchalant enough, but of course he would. I took the envelope out of my purse and passed it to him over the rangoli. 'I can't thank you enough for your patience about this.'

'Glad to help.' Mr Singh laid the envelope on a side table as if it had nothing to do with him. 'A small gesture of gratitude for my life in this peaceful place.' He nodded at the butler and a tea tray materialized almost instantly.

While the butler poured, the wind riffled the persimmon trees and a dragonfly flitted in through the open window; it hovered for a moment, then disappeared. I said, 'It *is* peaceful, isn't it?' In the tonga on the way over, I'd seen men dawdling at tea stalls and women swaying easily along the road with brass vessels on their heads. In spite of the violence in the cities and the increase in the local population, Masoorla remained bucolic. I said, 'Even though the people here have taken in so many refugees, it's still peaceful.'

Mr Singh gave me a patient smile. 'The refugees are the ones who do *not* want trouble. That's why they come.'

But I felt sure he would know why that mob had burned the car and beaten the driver. I said, 'Of course, there was an incident on Cart Road.'

'The Muslim chap.' He nodded. 'A mudarris who had the unfortunate habit of taking Hindu boys to his madrasa. Proselytizing, you see, never a good idea here. He'd been warned, but he didn't stop, and when one of the boys actually converted it was like setting a match to dry tinder.' Mr Singh gave a helpless shrug.

'Is he . . . ?'

'Dead? Oh, very.'

'But there haven't been any others . . .' His face stopped me.

He said, 'In the bustees – the slums where Hindus and Muslims are pressed side by side – there have been incidents and there will be more. Calcutta and the Punjab will be particularly violent. You live among Europeans, and this area—' he gestured around him, 'is all Hindu and Sikh. The violence hasn't touched us and probably won't. Still,' he stared at the rangoli, 'one feels helpless, doesn't one?'

'Isn't Lahore in the Punjab?'

'Yes, and the trouble has already begun there.'

I thought of Martin, with his dark skin – now brown as a chestnut – kurta pyjamas and bidis, making him indistinguishable from the refugees, boarding a train to Lahore. I took a nervous sip of tea.

My tonga driver had dozed off. His chin rested on his chest and a thin red line trickled from one corner of his mouth; even the horse looked heavy-eyed and languorous, swishing at flies with a lazy tail. I listened to the buzz and snuffle of the driver's snores and shaded my eyes to survey the road lined with slow-moving people and squeaky ox carts. Mr Singh had said this area was all Hindus and Sikhs, meaning safe, and I decided that if the colonial district and this neighbourhood were the only places I could venture freely, I wouldn't waste the opportunity. I would walk a while before hailing a tonga to the Buddhist temple. I paid the driver, slipped on my sunglasses, and set out.

Chapter Thirty-Four

AT THE EDGE OF Mr Singh's estate, the pavement ended and a dusty road wound past a sun-washed Hindu temple. A bundle of rags with two thin brown legs sticking out of them huddled on the steps. While I fished around my purse for a few coins, I heard the eerie resonance of a conch being blown inside the temple, summoning the gods. Then came the clash of finger cymbals and low chanting. Mr Singh had said he was not religious, but he seemed to have a spiritual side, and I wondered if he ever hungered for the comfort of ritual.

I placed a coin in the beggar's hand and saw, through the open temple door, a statue of Hanuman, the monkey god with his wise simian face, smiling faintly. The god's neck had been draped with marigold garlands, and people bowed before him in earnest obeisance. Some touched their foreheads to the floor and one man lay prostrate, holding incense in his outstretched hands. Aromatic smoke swaddled the air inside, and a woman knelt to receive a tikka from a spider-thin pandit. It struck me then that I had never seen a Hindu temple without people in it, no matter what time of day. Whatever the act of prayer might or might not accomplish, it clearly satisfied a profound human need.

I walked on, keeping to the quiet residential streets, enjoying the sight of women hanging strange but beautiful laundry on trees and a man in a doorway brushing his teeth with a neem twig.

Then I saw the corpse.

She lay on the ground under the thatched roof of an open-sided funerary hut. A few people dressed in white sat on their heels beside a mound of fresh flowers, and a man with a freshly shaved head moved the body so that her head faced away from me. Martin had told me that Hindus positioned their dead facing south, the direction of death, before they prayed over the body. I stayed back, not wanting to intrude, but I stood spellbound. Death breeds a queer fascination.

The dead woman was shrouded in yellow, and the chief mourner knelt beside her, trickling sanctified water over her face. He cupped his hands and carefully dribbled water on her forehead and cheeks. Then he took the corner of his sleeve and tenderly dabbed at one of her ears, where water must have pooled. I thought he must have loved her. Perhaps he was her son. He dipped two fingertips into a small pot to apply sandalwood paste to her forehead, and then other family members helped to lift her on to a bamboo stretcher. They covered her body with roses, jasmine and marigolds until she was virtually buried in flowers but for her face.

The mourners lifted the bier on to their shoulders, and one man took up a drum and beat a slow, funereal rhythm as they began their solemn procession to the cremation grounds. When they carried her past me, I was startled to see that she was disturbingly young. The chief mourner was probably not her son but her husband, and, naturally, I imagined Martin preparing my body that way – or I his.

I watched them go and something seized inside my chest. I said, 'We die.'

It hit me like a train. This ordinary knowledge suddenly had emotional reality, and I stood there, trying to whittle things down to what really mattered – Billy and Martin. That was it.

As I struggled with the reality of death, something big and heavy hit me in the back of the head and almost knocked me over. I didn't understand what had happened until I looked around and saw a monkey sitting on the ground, a few steps away, holding my sunglasses. I'd almost forgotten I'd been wearing them. He sat there, tawny and wizened and smug, dangling my glasses from one bony finger, like a taunt. The petty thief must have been sitting on a rooftop or in a tree, waiting. I stared at him, Hanuman incarnate, and in that moment, without my sunglasses, I saw the utter futility of guilt and regret. We just didn't have that kind of time.

I didn't care about the sunglasses. I hurried to the Buddhist temple with an urgency I didn't understand. I found Harry kneeling at the feet of the Buddha, tidying scattered offerings, throwing dry brown apple slices and wilted flowers into a paper sack while he sang, 'We're off to see the wizard . . .' His voice was flat but completely un-selfconscious. '. . . the Wonderful Wizard of Oz.' Such a funny little man.

'Hello, Harry.'

He turned with his mouth open as his song halted. 'Evie. How nice to see you.'

'I hope I'm not disturbing you.'

'Not at all.' His compact features loosened in a gentle smile. 'What can I do for you?'

I wanted to ask him why we have to die, and what we should be doing in the meantime. Instead I said, 'I came about the Urdu translation.'

'Oh, right. That was interesting.' He put down the paper sack and dusted his hands. 'It recounted an incident of suttee in 1858.'

'Suttee?'

'The practice of widows being burned alive on their husbands' funeral pyres.'

I shuddered. 'I thought that had been outlawed.'

'Yes, it was, in 1848, I think. But . . . well, it goes on to this day.'

Goosebumps rippled up my arms. I tried to block the image, but in spite of myself I vizualized Martin's corpse blackening and shrivelling on a high pyre. I knew, without a doubt, that I would never join him in the flames, and I was absolutely sure he wouldn't want me to. I said, 'Why would a woman do that?'

Harry hesitated. 'Tradition and a sense of destiny. Widows who sacrifice themselves to honour their husband's memory are considered courageous martyrs.' He reflected a moment. 'Women from every caste commit suttee, although, strictly speaking, one does not commit suttee, but rather enters into it, as into a state of grace. Of course, the motives are not always so high-minded. Sometimes, if the widow is facing a life of beggary, and, well . . . Gandhiji says poverty is the worst form of violence.'

I wondered whether the widow climbed on to the pyre quietly or whether she recklessly threw herself into the flames. Might she be forced or drugged? Would she be overcome by smoke, or would she scream when the flames touched her? I didn't want to think about it. I said, 'What has this to do with Adela Winfield?'

'Apparently, Miss Winfield witnessed the suttee.'

'Why? Whose cremation was it?'

'The record only tells of Miss Winfield being present. That

was the strange thing. Indian women are not even allowed to stand near the pyre. So an Englishwoman witnessing suttee would have been extraordinary.'

'I can't fathom it. Deliberately burning to death?'

'There are things worse than death.'

I became aware of the Buddha watching us. 'Because you reincarnate?'

'No.' He shook his head decisively. 'The point of re-incarnation is to evolve far enough so that you no longer need to reincarnate.'

'You aspire to oblivion?'

'I would say it's more like peace.' He hesitated. 'Oh, but I'm being a bore.' His squashed little face broke into smile. 'Can I do anything else for you?'

Was he dismissing me? I shook my head. 'You've been very kind.'

'Then I must say goodbye. I've wasted enough of every-one's time at the ashram trying to be something I'm not. I leave next week to join Gandhi in Calcutta. It's time for me to get on with it.'

My heart sank. 'Isn't Calcutta dangerous?'

'Life is dangerous.' He inclined his head as if indulging a child. 'But what kind of world can we make if we seek only personal safety?'

Chapter Thirty-Five

AFTER I PUT BILLY and his shoebox to bed, Martin came home from the Club, and I stood on the verandah, watching him manoeuvre the Packard in the old stable. Rain began to fall as he walked across the compound in the twilight. He came up the steps, shaking his head like a wet dog, and when he pushed his glasses up on his nose, I regretted having cut him off when he had tried to talk about his dream. I met him at the top step and kissed his cheek; he flinched, and looked confused.

Inside, he changed into dry clothes and put an Ethel Waters record on the turntable, 'Stormy Weather'. The chorus – a slow lament about lost love and endless rain – hit me like a slap in the face.

He stretched out on the sofa, but when I lay at the opposite end and playfully tangled my legs with his he got up and sat in the wingback chair. The house held on to the day's humid heat, and we listened to the rain pound the house while Ethel pined for her man. Watery sheets of grey and green closed in on all sides, trapping Martin and me in a hot, sticky centre. The song finished as the rain let up, and a woman's haunting voice reached us from someone else's godowns. I much preferred her sacred raga to Ethel's sorrow, and I said, 'I like this place.'

'Yeah,' he said. 'It gets under the skin.'

'Tell me about your dream,' I said. 'The good one.'

He got up and put on another record – Duke Ellington's 'Things Ain't What They Used To Be'. He said, 'I was playing the piano, and I felt . . . the way I used to feel, before Elsa.'

'It means you can still feel joy.'

He tipped his head to one side. 'Well, I can dream about it.'

'No, you felt it. If you forgive yourself, it will come back.'

He gave me a withering look. 'Have you been reading Robert Collier? Rah, rah, you can do it, and all that jazz?'

'Don't mock me.'

He heard the edge in my voice and we fell silent until the record ended. The needle began to scratch and I said, 'I can't stand this.'

He said, 'I'll change the record.'

'I'm not talking about the record.'

But he got up and went to the phonograph anyway. He said, 'I told you about the war. Isn't that what you wanted?' He lifted the needle, replaced it carefully in its cradle, and then picked up the album sleeve.

I said, 'I want you to stop punishing yourself.'

'You're imagining things.' He slid the record into its sleeve and examined the cover, the Duke suave and cool at his piano.

I sat up on the sofa and stared at him. 'You want to punish yourself, but you're punishing us. You have to stop being angry.'

'You make it sound simple.'

'Maybe it *is* simple.'

'No, it isn't.'

'But—'

'OK. Enough.' He put the album down. 'I think I know where Spike is.'

'What?' I knew he was dodging the conversation, but suddenly I didn't care. 'Spike?'

'I always ask the families I interview if they heard about the incident. One of them knows the boy who did it.'

'Where is Spike?'

He lit a bidi and sat down. 'The family's name is Matar. But they live in a very dangerous area.'

'No kidding.' Sarcasm made my voice flat.

'It's treacherous. It's a bustee where Hindus and Muslims are packed together in the worst conditions. You don't want to go there.'

'You mean *you* don't want me to go there.' All the old combativeness was right there, near the surface, ready to rush out, *whoosh*, just like that. But I remembered the corpse . . . *we don't have the time.* Martin pushed his glasses up on his nose, and that simple, familiar gesture cut through my anger and touched me.

He said, 'That's right. I'll handle it.' He raised a palm to hold off my objection, and I felt an opportunity for us to do something together slipping away.

I said, 'Let me go with you. Please. This is important. I won't talk; I'll do whatever you say, but let me do this with you.'

Martin took a long drag on his bidi and exhaled like a gasket letting off steam. 'The father's a drunk, and the mother runs a small black-market operation. She scavenges bidis and yarn, whatever she can get, and sells them door-to-door like a box wallah. Sometimes she gets a deal on shawls or something special from up north, but she never gets ahead because her husband spends the money on arrack as fast as she makes it. They're basically destitute and they live among people just as badly off who don't get along. You can't march in demanding things.'

'It doesn't have to be like that. We'll be nice. They're poor? We'll pay them.' I reached for him, but he moved back in his chair. I said, 'None of it has to be like this.' I thought of the dead woman buried in flowers and the quote from Rumi about choosing darkness or light. I thought about Felicity and Adela choosing to live on their own terms, choosing joy. I said, 'We can choose, Martin.'

'Choose what?'

'We can choose how we will meet each day, just that day, and those choices, those days, they add up and they *are our lives*. But some day we're going to die. We don't have the time to be . . . like *this*.' I reached for him again and this time he let me touch his face. I wanted to tell him about the corpse, Mr Singh, the monkey . . . I wanted to tell him about Felicity and Adela, long dead and everything but their stories gone with them. But it was too much. I wanted to kiss him, but I feared he might push me away. I said, 'If we keep this up, we'll lose each other.'

He laid his hand over mine. 'If I lost you I wouldn't want to live any more.'

I met his dark eyes and saw my Martin – a *good* man. 'We can't go on like this.' I slid off the sofa to kneel before him, and relief washed through me when he stroked my hair with his fine, long-fingered hands. I said, 'I can forgive you because you're a good man. That's why it's killing you, because you're *good*.' I moved closer to him and he sat very still. I said, 'Don't shut me out, Martin. Let's start over by doing this together.'

Martin rolled the back of his hand down my cheek, the way he used to, and after a moment he said, 'OK.'

*

The next day was hot and close with heavy monsoon clouds bearing down to hold in the heat. Rashmi spread a sheet under the sandalwood tree and Billy and I sat in the shade to drink limeade. I wrote in my journal while the brain-fever bird made his annoying racket in the thickest part of the tree, where no one could see or shoot him. A pye-dog slunk by the low compound wall, whining for food, and I warned Billy not to touch it. In the hills, where people raised sheep or yak, dogs might be trained as herders, but in Masoorla and Simla dogs were simply disease-ridden nuisances.

Billy sat in the shade with me, whispering to his shoebox, and I thought about Martin, arranging the rescue mission for Spike, finding out exactly where the Matar family lived and how much we should pay them. We would bring fresh fruit for the family and toys for the little boy. I imagined both of us giving Spike back to Billy, and him getting rid of the sinister shoebox. I closed my eyes and leaned against the tree; drowsing in the heat, listening to the hum of insects, it seemed everything would be all right.

When an itinerant sweet wallah came up the road calling, 'Toffee! Toffee!' Billy jumped up, and Rashmi flew out of the house, bangles jangling. The sweet wallah trotted into our compound with a cloth-covered tray on his head. In one hand he carried a stand for the tray and in the other a pair of scales made of wicker and twine, with river rocks for weights. He was a small man with large brown eyes and a thin white beard, and he reminded me of a goat.

He set up his sweet stand in our compound and Billy and Rashmi deliberated over coconut toffees cut in diamond shapes, hard red candies that stick to the teeth, and fat twists of barley sugar. They made their selection, and I paid the sweet wallah while they carried their treats to the sandal-wood tree and sat down, sucking on sugary fingers.

As the sweet wallah trotted away with his paraphernalia, a barefoot mango man, bent and hobbling under his load, made his slow way up the road. I shaded my eyes to watch him and saw, far in the distance, another bearer, shimmering in heat waves and dust, with a long wooden ladder on his head. So much had happened since I ordered it, I had almost forgotten about the ladder. I watched him come, remembering Adela, and Felicity, her lover and their baby. I glanced at the sandalwood tree and my heart leaped like Indian drums.

Chapter Thirty-Six

RASHMI HELD THE ladder while I climbed, and Billy, chewing a piece of barley sugar, watched. Three rungs from the top I was able to reach the hollow, but I hesitated. There could be a rabid squirrel or a monkey in there. I stepped up another rung to scout the inside, the ladder wobbled, and Rashmi screamed, 'Arey Ram!' I steadied myself on the trunk and looked inside the hollow.

The edges had grown smooth with time, and the inside was filled with snarled webs, rotted birds' nests and dead leaves. Gingerly, I reached in, grabbed a handful of damp debris and dropped it without looking down. From below I heard, 'Arey Ram!' and Billy laughed. I pushed leaves around until my hand hit something hard, which I teased forward with my fingertips. It was a clay urn, and I nudged it out and balanced it on the edge of the hollow to inspect it. It was covered with dirt and mould, and the lid had been sealed with paraffin. I held the urn against my chest as I descended, very slowly, with one hand on the ladder.

At the bottom, Billy said, 'Is that buried treasure?'

'Sort of, Cutlet.' I whisked dirt off the top and examined it. The sealing wax was old and dry, and I thought the lid would come off with a few careful taps. I picked up a rock and rapped the edge lightly, first on one side and then the other. The third try did it, and the seal broke with a muffled crack. I lifted the cover, and three heads, red, blond and black, bent over it.

It was an ordinary tin box, rusting at the seams and covered in a skein of cobwebs. When I lifted it out, one side fell off, and a rubber hot-water bottle dropped to the ground. We sat under the tree to examine it. Once again, an end had been sliced off to make a rubber pocket for a book – another of Adela's hand-bound journals.

Billy said, 'Aw, nuts. It's only an old book.'

Rashmi, who didn't read English, looked disappointed. 'Come, *beta*,' she said, giving Billy a kiss. 'Let Mama read.'

August 1857

A message on embossed writing paper has arrived. He has had her body cremated according to the custom of his race. Jonathan, indeed. It takes more than an anglicized name to make a civilized man. I cannot bear to picture it – my fair friend consumed by flames on a Hindoo pyre. I understand that he was important to her, but she was not his property to dispose of. It is done, & cannot be undone, but I will never allow him into this house again.

The infant cries & cries as if he understands the heinous act committed on his mother. He is an unpleasant child, loud & malcontent. His hair is dark, & his skin already turns from pink to brown. He screams as if he knows he will never fit anywhere in this world. But he is hers, & I will care for him.

August 1857

I am delirious with lack of sleep but afraid to call a wet nurse. I have heard too many stories of those who feed their own children whilst they allow the memsahib's baby to starve. I give him goat's milk whenever he demands it, but often nothing will quiet him. He is capable of screaming for hours, & nothing pacifies him.

I barely know night from day with this infant's incessant howling. When I ask Lalita to do something with him she runs off, crying, herself only a child & traumatized by her memsahib's death.

So constant are the infant's demands I cannot even grieve. Sometimes I imagine smothering him with a pillow, or throwing him against a wall. My thoughts frighten me.

September 1857

Thank God. At last I have found a soporific for the tiny beast. I remembered Felicity's supply of Mother Bailey's Quieting Syrup & poured a tablespoonful in a bowl of goat's milk, then soaked a cloth in it. He sucked greedily & his eyelids drooped in a matter of minutes. I believe opium is one of the ingredients & I must take care with the dosage, but the silence brings a relief so profound I could weep. I slumber with the insensible bundle on my breast & must admit that asleep he looks almost angelic.

Felicity once told me that if she had a son, she would name him Charles. She considered it a noble name, & so I have named him Charles, in accordance with her wishes, & William for her father. I believe she would approve, although I am not at all sure this ill-tempered infant deserves a noble name.

Jonathan wishes to see him. I suppose he has a right, but I simply cannot face this man who brought about her death & then robbed me of her body. Not yet.

September 1857

The Mutiny has been put down. A message came from Simla saying it is safe to travel. I am free to go to Calcutta or even back to England, but why? There is nothing for me in those places, & certainly not with this brown child. I sit under the sandalwood tree *with him in my arms, & his eyes try to follow the marigold I dangle before his face.*

Now that I have contrived a method to make him sleep, the world begins to right itself. In slumber he curls up with his knees against his chest, looking utterly defenceless, & something in me stirs. I have no words for it, something as great & ineffable as the Himalayas, but far more intimate.

I have decided he is too small a being to support the weight of a name like Charles, & so I call him Charlie. His grip on my finger is surprisingly firm. He is a healthy boy & Felicity would be pleased to know he did not contract her illness. Consumption is airborne & her death might actually have spared him. I sit beneath the tree, watching his chubby legs pump & his hands grasp at nothing, & I wonder how we will manage when he needs more than goat's milk & Mother Bailey's.

Felicity's annuity will cease when news of her death reaches Calcutta. I do not know when it will happen, only that it must. I have no means of my own, & have not communicated with my parents since I refused to go to Calcutta for the season. My instinct is to pray, but to which god, & for what?

September 1857

Jonathan has asked again to see his child, but I am not ready to face him. I know I must forgive. I must stop being angry. Harbouring anger is like taking poison & hoping it will kill the person who has made you angry. I must put these poisonous feelings to rest, but I need time.

I have summoned the fortitude to go through Felicity's things & will donate her clothing to the mission. I will keep her ivory & jet brooch to remember her by. Sometimes she wore it to fasten the folds of her sari & we laughed at the incongruity. I called her the Hindoo memsahib, & I can still see her face shining with mirth as she pinned it.

I have found messages from Jonathan in the form of poetry in her almirah – loose notes on all sorts of paper. His notes are written on his embossed stationery, & early drafts of those she wrote for him cover pages torn from her sketchpads. They were all folded & tucked in with her intimate things.

September 1857

Jonathan has sent money, a generous amount, & though I find it uncomfortable to accept, I am at a disadvantage, expecting Felicity's income to cease at any time. I am compelled to accept his charity, but something in me shrinks from it.

He has asked again to see his child & even as I struggle with his request I hear Felicity's gentle admonition from beyond the grave – do not judge.

Charlie can focus on the marigolds now, & he grabs for them with wiggling fingers. I am taken by his perfectly articulated fingernails, & by the delicate whorls & crevices of his small, faultless ears.

Today, I think he smiled at me.

October 1857

I have had him christened Charles William. I wrapped him in a soft cashmere shawl of green paisley & took him to Christ Church in a tonga. I had sent a message ahead, & the minister met me at the font. It was a quick unceremonious affair with no one in attendance but Lalita & me: a sprinkle of sanctified water, a few words spoken in a monotone, & a name inscribed in the church record.

I could not think what surname to give him. Chadwick would imply that his father is unknown, but I could not bring myself to hang an Indian name on him. I feel he belongs to Felicity & me. Perhaps this was wrong of me, but he is simply Charles William. To me he is Charlie.

Money continues to arrive regularly, along with repeated requests to see Charlie, & I feel myself softening. It would be a relief, actually. I would enjoy showing Charlie off, his twinkling eyes & impish smile. Lalita carries him about, singing quietly, & Hakim cooks him sweet rice porridge & makes a great fuss over his plump cheeks.

I am certain that Charlie smiles at me, & most charmingly at that. He is a handsome child.

November 1857

Jonathan sent a long & earnest letter. He begged to see his son in the most moving & respectful language, & I am at a crossroads. I must put aside judgement & anger, knowing that this letting go is the price for an untroubled heart. I have decided to invite him to tea, & it is easy to imagine Felicity's wonderful sudden smile at my decision.

However, Jonathan did indeed contract Felicity's consumption. Now I must find a way to bring Charlie & his father together whilst protecting Charlie from infection. It is reasonable to assume that as the child of two people with consumption he will not have my immunity. I must give this dilemma a good think, for I have resolved to let Jonathan visit.

Diwali, the triumph of light over darkness, has come again & Charlie stared in wide-eyed wonder as we lit the lamps. Whilst Charlie & Lalita watched the fireworks, I wrote Jonathan a gracious invitation to tea with the stipulation that he cover his mouth & nose & not touch his child.

November 1857

I do not understand how such a tiny creature can keep me so busy. When he is asleep, I confer with Hakim about his diet, & with Lalita regarding his clothes & nappies. I instruct the dhobi (repeatedly!) to use only the mild soap I provide, & remind the sweeper to remain alert for scorpions & snakes. I personally make sure the legs of his bed always sit in dishes of water to prevent insects from climbing up, & I caution the servants to boil not only the drinking water but also Charlie's bath water lest some enter his mouth. Then I walk to the godowns to ensure the goat's milk is fresh & the ponies are fed. All this must be done whilst he sleeps, because I want to be with Charlie when he is awake. I have neglected my journal & feel the tiny rascal has usurped my life.

But there is no doubt that Charlie smiles at me – he smiles a good deal now – & sometimes I fancy I see something of Felicity in his suckling face, but surely that is only my imagination. He has his father's complexion, black Indian hair, & dark, dark eyes.

I feel a profound satisfaction when he quietens in my arms. I believe he must think I am his mother. Do babies think? In any case, I suppose in some sense I am.

He is a beautiful boy, & I begin to understand why poets sing of motherly love.

November 1857

Jonathan came yesterday. We sat on the verandah & when Lalita brought Charlie out he unwound the end of his turban & covered the lower half of his face. I held Charlie up, an arm's length away, & he surprised me by saying, 'He looks like her.' I stared at Charlie's cocoa skin & silky black hair, & then I saw it, the thing that made me fancy I saw something of Felicity in him. There is irrepressible joy in Charlie's eyes.

December 1857

Christmas approaches & I think of England: roast goose & carol singers in the snow, wassail & a kissing ball with mistletoe. I sing 'Hark the Herald Angels' to Charlie & he stares up at me with such purity of expression that my voice falters.

Last night, with Charlie asleep, a fire crackling in the grate &

the house as silent as snow, I gazed out at a full moon & a fierce loneliness seized me & brought me to my knees. In that moment, I wished Jonathan were with me, simply to share memories of Felicity & delight in Charlie's perfection. Tears stung my eyes as I took out my writing paper & hurriedly wrote Jonathan another invitation to tea.

December 1857

I took a hacksaw & cut pine boughs from a tree behind the house. I have fashioned a rather crude kissing ball, nothing so elegant as those Martha made, but it will suffice. I raised my hands to my face to smell the resin on my fingers, & I began to weep. I cried for a good while, then I washed my face & decorated my kissing ball with cloves & woody cones plucked from the blue pines. It hangs now in the drawing room, & I have crocheted a gift for Charlie – a yellow jumper.

On Christmas morning, I entertained Charlie with a poem from my own childhood, & I smiled at the last two lines because they sounded like Charlie & me:

> *He was chubby and plump – a right jolly elf –*
> *And I laughed when I saw him, in spite of myself.*

Charlie didn't understand a word, but the sing-song rhythm made him lie still in my arms & stare up at me. I held him under the kissing ball & when I pecked his tender cheek, he grabbed my hair to pull my face to his. It was the finest Christmas gift I have ever received.

That night he slumbered in my arms & there was no sound except the house settling in its corners, a sound to exaggerate silence, & it was enough.

January 1858

Felicity's annuity has ceased & I am now entirely dependent on Jonathan.

He has accepted my second invitation & will come tomorrow, but his handwriting is shaky & I wonder how quickly he is deteriorating. Of course, I have Charlie, but he has no one. Can grief hasten one's demise?

January 1858

I met Jonathan on the verandah with Charlie in my arms, but my smile faded when I saw him struggle up the steps. He is gaunt & grey & already leans on a walking stick. Still, his face broke into a smile & his eyes filled at the sight of his son. I could not put Charlie into his arms, but his eyes devoured the small, perfect face, the dimpled arms & curled fingers. He fairly collapsed into a chair as I set Charlie in a basket & Khalid served the tea.

I have invited him to come whenever he wishes & as often as he likes.

February 1858

This morning I received an envelope from Jonathan; it contained money & regrets that he would not be visiting again. There can be only one reason: he is too ill. But so soon!

March 1858

The news has come at last. His mother wrote a brief message to inform me that her son, Jonathan Singh, has died. The woman writes in a beautiful hand, & her English is flawless. She included the customary amount of rupees & I realized, with a start, that she is Charlie's grandmother.

I wrote her a thank-you note. Then I took a chance on her good-will & asked whether her son might have kept some of Felicity's *ashes, as they sometimes do. If so, I asked if I might be allowed to take possession of them.*

I do not understand my longing, but having Felicity's remains near by would give me comfort.

March 1858

Oh God! To think I had regarded those people as civilized! I attended Jonathan Singh's cremation, intending to beg his mother for Felicity's ashes, if she had them. I persuaded myself that in that moment of watching her son reduced to ash she would appreciate my need.

I stood apart, with the other women, wishing not to disrupt the ritual in any way. But before I could discover which of the white-shrouded women to approach, Jonathan's widow emerged from the crowd in a red wedding sari & climbed upon his pyre. She lay on the corpse as though in a trance & they covered her with wood. A rich family can afford enough wood to burn even two bodies quite thoroughly.

I watched, horrified, as this wealthy family piled many layers of wood on top of the living woman, & then put fire to four sides of the pyre. She did not move or make a sound as two men held the ends of long bamboo poles to keep her pinned under the wood. The flames rose up around her & I thought she must have fallen unconscious, overcome by smoke, but then she screamed. It was a raw, piercing, animal sound & one of her arms shot out from under the wood. But she was too weighted down to escape, & those closest to the pyre appeared ready to keep her in place. The bodies blackened & shrivelled, melting & fusing together. Did the fire cause her muscles to twist & contract, or did she writhe & struggle that long?

It is an ancient practice called suttee, an abomination, & I recoil at the memory. The Crown has outlawed it, but there is no way to stop isolated cases. It is not as if we are in the habit of monitoring these barbaric rites. I stood transfixed by the roar of flames whilst the charred air scratched my throat. The smell of burning flesh was acrid & unnerving. A cry escaped my throat when, near the end, the chief mourner, with his hair shorn, broke the blackened skulls to release the souls. Did they do that to Felicity?

My mind has exploded & I cannot hold a thought. Now, at the beginning of the hot weather, even as the punkahs go up, my teeth chatter, my body shivers & I cannot get warm. Charlie cries & cries & I cannot comfort him.

April 1858

I cannot rid myself of the images; I dream of suttee & wake with my heart pounding. It sickens me to take that family's money now, & I do not want to raise Charlie in this heathen land.

I must put away my pride & write to Mother.

April 1858

I've confessed! Felicity, Jonathan, Charlie, the suttee – everything. I've asked forgiveness for my headstrong behaviour in the humblest words I know. I've begged in the most contrite tone to be allowed to return to Rose Hall with Charlie. And I have made the ultimate compromise: I have offered to marry any man of my mother's choosing & sworn never to utter a word of complaint.

I hired a photographer to make a portrait of Charlie to send with my letter. I dressed him in his hand-embroidered christening gown & topped it with the yellow jumper I crocheted. He smiled for the camera, & who could resist that face? I had a copy made to keep for myself. Sometimes I gaze on it after he has gone to sleep for the night & my hand wanders over his smile, his twinkling eyes & his dimpled hands. I kiss the picture, but only on the edges so as not to damage it.

I estimate three to four months for my letter to reach England

and the same again for an answer although Mother might respond immediately by telegram. Perhaps I should allow an interval for her to consider my plea. She will be getting what she has always wanted – an obedient, properly married daughter – but she will need to convince herself that she is being magnanimous. I have a bit of money put aside, & by September I should have enough for the passage to England.

Felicity & Jonathan are dead, & now Charlie is my son. I will make him an English gentleman & tell him, again and again, how brave & good his parents were. I will never let anyone hurt him.

May 1858

He has both front teeth now, they dazzle against his smooth cocoa skin. He eats enough for three babies. I think he does, but of course I have nothing for comparison. Hakim even cooks in the new kitchen, preparing the soft lamb meatballs & tamarind chutney that Charlie loves, whilst my son plays at his feet.

Charlie's appetite astounds me. I have to ration his portion of rice pudding when Hakim makes it with saffron & sultanas; I swear the child would eat the entire pot if I let him.

He crawls fast, & laughs gleefully when I come after him. Today he pulled himself upright on a chair, & soon he will be walking. Imagine the amazement on Mother's face when I stroll off the ship with this beautiful child!

June 1858

Last week I felt unaccountably lethargic. Perhaps the hot weather is sapping my strength. The grass tatties are up & watered & the punkah waves day & night, but I feel drained. Perhaps I should hire another ayah, but I don't even have the energy to conduct interviews. Playing with Charlie has become especially fatiguing, Yesterday, I was unduly short with him for being petulant. But the poor child has prickly heat, & I must make a greater effort.

I had one particularly hard day when I found myself imagining nightmarish scenarios – myself falling desperately ill, dying, & leaving Charlie with no one. God forbid. But the next day I felt much better. Who knows what ephemeral afflictions are borne on these Asiatic winds. Moods & maladies will come & go, but I must not be impatient with darling Charlie, & I must not let morbid visions carry me away.

Charlie has stopped his play in the marigolds to listen to the bamboo wind chime on the verandah. He's such an attentive child! I'm sure his intelligence is well above average. I know all mothers think that, but with Charlie there is no doubt.

July 1858

I am in a whirl. The voyage will require much preparation. I have been diligent about budgeting & already have almost enough for our passage, but there are other considerations. The amount of clothing needed to keep Charlie clean & dry will require three trunks. Then there are his glass nursery bottles & his playthings. Should I bring my own rice & sugar in case rations run short aboard ship? Perhaps I should consider keeping a goat in the hold to ensure fresh milk. But then I would need a goatherd & provisions for the goat, & what does one do with an Indian goatherd in Yorkshire? I would have to pay to send him back.

Will I be able to find Katie? Should I even try?

I must send to Simla for more Mother Bailey's syrup, oh, & I'll need plenty of soap & Jamaican ginger-root for seasickness. Should I take Lalita? Would she agree to come? I know I must be forgetting something . . .

No matter. When we get to England all problems will be resolved & all hardships forgotten.

August 1858

I must make arrangements to close up the house. The landlord is a Scotsman & will expect everything to be left in good order. Easier said than done. Charlie, in his teething agonies, gnawed the teak arm of that lovely brocade chair. He also left an appalling stain on the dhurrie rug when he had an upset stomach. The brick wall in the kitchen has darkened from cooking smoke, but I believe that is to be expected & not for me to refurbish, especially since we built the kitchen at our own expense. I wonder how much notice I am required to give before departure. I cannot give the landlord a date until I hear from Mother.

Oh, to see the moors again. I will bundle Charlie in a warm jumper & take him walking in the woods. I cannot wait to see his face when he witnesses his first proper Christmas, the house decked out with holly & a long table lit with candles & heaped with roast goose & sugar plums. We will make snow angels & eat roast beef & Yorkshire pudding, & I will give him a gaily painted nutcracker. I wonder how long he will he believe in Santa Claus?

September 1858

The house is in good order, but there is simply nothing to be done about the teeth marks in that chair arm. Perhaps no one will notice. Lalita & Khalid have begun packing my things & I am organizing Charlie's. He goes through so many pieces of clothing in a day that I am having more made so that we have enough whilst en route downriver. The durzi sits on the verandah with his caged mynah, sewing tiny shirts & hemming nappies. All day long we hear the whine & clatter of the new machine, of which he is inordinately proud.

I wonder which of Charlie's toys will keep him best occupied in the dhoolie? That will be a trying six days!

I have put off writing to Mrs Singh about our departure for fear she might object to my taking her grandson away. In quiet moments I know my fear is baseless. The woman has never even asked to see him, & I am glad. If ever she saw how wonderful, how beautiful he is, she might want to keep him, & what a snarl that could be.

I have no idea what the laws are in this country regarding children, if there are any, but he looks Indian & I am not his natural mother. Still, she has not met him, & that is for the best. I will give Charlie a good life in Yorkshire. I will shore up his spirit to withstand any prejudice he might encounter. A proper education will compensate for much, & I will see that he gets it. Will he like cricket? His temperament is agreeable & he will surely have many friends.

As for Mrs Singh, I will wait until the last minute before I write to her. I do not think she will be sorry to see me go, but I hope to be packed up & on my way by the time she gets the news.

September 1858

All we really have are our stories, & before I leave I will wrap this journal against the weather & put it in the sandalwood tree. This is my story, or at least some part of it, & I trust to fate that the right person will discover it. If such a thing should come to pass, I hope that whoever reads my words will benefit from them in some way, as the stories of Fanny Parks & Honoria Lawrence set Felicity & me on our rightful paths.

Chapter Thirty-Seven

1947

I PUT ASIDE THE QUESTION of how Adela's journal might benefit me. And I put aside the question of how she could be
buried in Masoorla if she went back to England. And I put
aside the question of how, if she didn't go back to England,
she could have raised a half-caste child alone in India, and
what might have happened to him. I put it all aside to devote
myself to the quest for Spike.

Martin had confirmed that the boy carried Spike around
with him daily, and that the family did indeed live in one of
the worst bustees around Simla. We would go there at
dinnertime, when they would most likely be at home, but it
would not do for us to pull up in a car, looking too rich, or
by coolie rickshaw, looking too colonial. A tonga wouldn't
fit through the narrow lanes of the bustee, so we settled on a
bicycle rickshaw. I would even wear a skirt and cover my hair
with a scarf. We would lay down a full day's pay in cash – the
equivalent of a month's wages for a labourer – and say a
respectful thank-you as well as namastes and salaams, whatever they wanted. If we saw the boy we would try to smile at
the little thief as we gave him the yo-yo and candy and kites
we had bought him at the Lakkar bazaar.

We did not tell Billy about it, but the expedition to retrieve Spike had been talked about at the Club, and Lydia had offered to sit with Billy. At first, we resisted the idea of leaving him with Lydia, but we owed Edward a huge debt for staying out all night to find him, and after learning that they'd lost a child in the war we felt terrible for both of them. Martin said, 'I don't think even Lydia can turn him into an imperialist in an hour. And if he's bored, he'll forget about it when we give him Spike.'

Lydia and Edward were waiting in their suite at the Hotel Cecil. I hadn't seen Edward since the day Spike had been taken, and we'd never really had a conversation since that uncomfortable meeting in the bazaar when I'd mentioned Amritsar. After Edward found Billy, Martin had sent over a bottle of Scotch, but I owed him my personal thanks as well as an apology. When we walked into the room, Edward put out his hand. I took it and said, 'How can I thank you? And after I—'

'Nonsense.' His silly tongue flashed and disappeared. 'Relieved to find the little fellow.'

Martin shook Edward's hand, a firm, honest shake, during which some sort of manly comprehension seemed to pass between them.

Lydia's lips and cheeks were flushed, and somehow she seemed younger than I remembered. She gave us a distracted greeting and beamed at Billy. On the tea table, she had set out a pitcher of limeade, a platter of ginger biscuits and a few children's books. The room had a small bookshelf stocked mostly with out-of-date magazines and an ancient set of *Encyclopaedia Britannica*. Lydia had combed the shelves, pulling out anything she thought Billy might like.

Martin squatted and said, 'Mom and I are going out for a while, Buddy. You're going to stay here with Mrs Worthington.'

Billy glanced at Lydia. 'OK, I guess.'

'Do you like limeade, young man?' Lydia smiled like a girl.

He looked at the frosty pitcher. '*Nimbu pani?* I sure do!'

'I suspected as much.' She waved us away. 'Push off, then,' she said. 'We're going to have a grand time.'

Our rickshaw jolted us into the destitute area of dilapidated shacks on the outskirts of Simla. I had often passed the place, but I had never ventured into the throng of tumble-down sheds and sagging shelters made of rags and paper and rusted tin. A haze of smoke from dung fires hung low over the bustee, and the air smelled like burning sewage. Women sat on their heels to stir their rice pots, and unemployed men sat in disgruntled clusters and stared as we passed, eyeing the basket of apples and toys on my lap. Others smoked or slept; no work, no money, no hope; why not smoke or sleep?

A grimy, half-naked toddler sat in the dirt, crying and slapping her knees, and the rickshaw went around her. Now and then the rickshaw wallah called, 'Matar?' and someone pointed the way. We passed a woman veiled in black, sitting on her haunches, grilling kebabs over a dung fire. The rick-shaw wallah shouted something at her, and she looked over, long-faced and bitter, and shook a charred kebab at him. The rickshaw wallah glanced over his shoulder at Martin and me and smiled grimly with paan-stained lips. 'They eat cows,' he said. Then he leaned sideways and spat a stream of red saliva.

We halted in front of a collection of frayed and filthy rags thrown over bamboo sticks with a dung fire smouldering at the front. Martin and I got out and stared at the home of the family named Matar. It looked like the tattered remains of a tent after a bad storm. The front gaped open to the elements, and I wondered what the family did for warmth in the winter. We stepped past the dung fire and Martin put his palms together, saying, 'ram ram,' the country version of namaste. The woman sitting on the ground inside narrowed her eyes at us, furtive and suspicious. A yellowing bruise covered her cheek. Her face was rough and bleak, and her neck was stringy as beef jerky. She'd been slicing an apple into a clay bowl, and at the sight of us she moved it behind her, as if we might try to take it.

A spindly man in a stained dhoti tottered out of the gloom. His right arm dangled crooked and useless at his side, and his eyes swam, unfocused. He said something, but his speech was so slurred Martin couldn't understand him. The rickshaw wallah said, 'He asks what you are wanting.'

I had imagined walking into a spare little hut and seeing Spike lying on a rough wooden shelf or even on a charpoy, but these people had nothing. A battered tin pot and a covered basket sat next to a jumble of blankets in a corner. That was all. The place smelled of dung and arrack and smoke, and I set our basket of bribes on the ground.

Martin spoke to the man in his heavily accented Hindi, and when he got no response he called to our driver. 'Tell him we want to buy the American doll. The toy dog.'

The rickshaw wallah relayed the information, and the drunken man looked befuddled; red saliva dribbled from his bottom lip, and the woman laughed. She got up heavily and walked over to the jumble of blankets. Only then did I see the little boy who had harassed Billy. He sat in a dark corner with his head down, thin arms around bony knees. I remembered sitting like that in the bathtub, scared to death when Billy was missing.

The woman cuffed the boy's head, but he made no sound. She kicked his ribs hard enough to make him rub his side, and that's when I caught a glimpse of red plaid and blue denim in the boy's lap. The woman reached down and wrestled it away from him, then gave him one more kick for good measure, but the boy only put his head down on his knees, and his shoulders heaved. The woman gloated in listless approval as she threw Spike at Martin's feet. The cowboy hat and boots were gone and the toy was filthy. One eye was missing and one leg torn off; I imagined the boy having to fight the other children to keep it for himself. The woman put out her hand and said, 'Rupee.'

'We can't give it back to Billy like that.' I picked up what was left of Spike and glanced at the boy in the corner. He was small and pitiful, still crying, but one hand had crept into the basket next to him. His skinny arm moved as if he were playing with something inside.

His mother followed my gaze and when she saw his hand in the basket she marched over and kicked it away from him. The boy covered his head and turned his face to the wall. But the lid had been thrown off, and the basket rocked back and forth. I heard scrabbling, and a tawny head with a black nose peeked over the side. The puppy had floppy ears and liquid brown eyes, both too big for his small face. I grabbed Martin's arm, and he said, 'Yeah, I see it.' He said something to the woman, and she squawked, 'Neh, neh,' and waved her arms. She chattered angrily while she pushed the puppy down in the basket and replaced the lid.

Martin said, 'Usually she gets blankets and shawls from up north, but now and then she gets a Kashmiri sheepdog. That's a big deal for her. She sells them to traders going to Delhi. They're good pets, trainable and immune to the mange. But only the rich keep dogs for pets and there's no market in Masoorla.'

'Can we—'

'She says she already has a buyer.'

'Offer her more.'

He spoke to her again and they went back and forth; I recognized the ritualistic haggling I'd so often seen in the bazaar. Finally Martin said, 'She can see we really want it. She'll sell, but it's going to cost plenty.'

'Can we cover it?'

Martin bit his lip. 'Maybe. How much have we got?'

I gathered the rupees I had taken from the tea tin for Spike and added everything else I had in my purse, while Martin emptied his pockets. He counted the money out on the woman's leathery palm, and then she counted it again. The money disappeared under her dirty kameez, and she gestured with her chin at the basket. Martin walked over and picked the basket up, but she grabbed it away and pulled the puppy out by the scruff of the neck, his hind legs scrambling for a foothold. The basket wasn't part of the deal.

Martin handed me the puppy and the soft little thing curled against my chest like a contented baby. I said, 'Oh, he's perfect.'

A long gut-wrenching sob came from the corner. I picked up what was left of Spike and offered it to the boy. He looked surprised, but only for an instant. He snatched it and hugged it to himself, staring at me, frightened that this might be some cruel joke.

We climbed into the rickshaw and the little dog coiled in my lap and slept. Martin scratched behind the puppy's ear and said, 'This little guy was probably headed for the life of Riley, napping on satin pillows and eating figs in Delhi.'

'Well, he's going to have to settle for a dhurrie rug and a bone in Masoorla.'

As we mounted the stairs at the Hotel Cecil, I held the puppy behind my back – he was no more than a handful –

and we found Lydia and Billy in the suite playing hide-and-seek, the pitcher of limeade empty and the ginger biscuits gone. Lydia's finger waves were mussed and frizzy, and her eyes sparkled. She prowled around the room peeking under tables and behind curtains saying, 'Is he here? No? Is he here?' A giggle came from behind the sofa, but she ignored it and lifted a pillow off a chair. 'Is he here?' When she finally moved the sofa to expose him, they both squealed.

Martin said, 'I'll be damned.'

'Mom!' Billy ran to us. 'Dad!'

'Have a good time, BoBo?'

'Mrs Worthington makes the best *nimbu pani*. And she read me the best book about Big Boy Puffington.'

Lydia gave him a heartbreaking smile. 'Big Boy Puffington is strong and brave, like you, my boy.'

They grinned at each other.

'Gosh. That's swell.' I cast around for the shoebox and saw it abandoned in a corner. I said, 'Billy? Look what we found.' I brought the puppy out from behind my back.

Billy stared. 'Who's that?'

'He doesn't have a name.' I held him out to Billy. 'You'll have to give him one.'

Billy took the puppy carefully and whispered, 'Wow.' The little dog planted his paws on Billy's chest and shyly, tentatively licked his chin. When Billy kissed the wet black nose, the puppy's stumpy tail wagged urgently. 'Hey, he likes me! I'm gonna call him Pal.'

'My boy had a dog.' Lydia sidled up and petted the puppy. 'We had such fun training him.'

I looked at Martin and he nodded; we could still talk without words when we needed to. I said, 'Lydia, I wonder if you would be kind enough to help Billy train his puppy. I'm sure you know more about it than we do.'

Billy and Lydia grinned like two children who had been given permission to ride a flying carpet to a forbidden kingdom. Their joy was so naked it was embarrassing. She said, 'I'd like that.'

Billy pointed to a couple of books on the table. 'Mrs Worthington said I could take those home.'

'Why, thank you, Lydia.'

I gathered up the books while she petted Billy's hair. 'Such a lovely boy,' she said. 'Do bring him round again.'

One of the books was contemporary, a picture book about Big Boy Puffington, but the other looked old. I opened it and checked the copyright, 'Why Lydia, this is a first edition of *Uncle Remus*.'

'Is it? They have so few books here, and even fewer for children. Well, there really aren't any children here, are there? Do take it for him. Take one for yourself, if you like. They won't be missed.'

'Thank you.' I went to the little bookshelf and ran my hand over the soft leather of the old *Encyclopaedia Britannica*. I said, 'They don't bind books like this any more.'

'Too costly,' Lydia said absently. She couldn't take her eyes off Billy.

Martin said, 'We should be getting home. But thanks again, Lydia.'

'Pity.' Lydia petted Billy's hair.

Martin picked Billy up and said, 'Want your leprechaun?'

'Nah.' Billy held Pal next to his cheek and the puppy twisted to lick his face. 'Pal might eat him. Will you keep my leprechaun, Mrs Worthington?'

Lydia's eyes and mouth softened and I saw the woman she might have been before she'd been crippled by grief. She said, 'I'd love to.'

It had been a day of good surprises. I took in the staid,

comfortable suite and felt no irritation with the English décor or with Lydia or even Edward. I ran a hand over the row of leather spines one more time and a title stamped in gold leaf caught my eye – *The Collected Poems of a Lady and a Gentleman, 1857*. Having been so immersed in 1857, I automatically slid the book out and riffled through the pages. Near the front, I saw a poem formatted like a letter. It was addressed 'My Dearest', and signed 'Felicity'.

Lydia repeated, 'Please feel free to borrow any books you like.'

I closed the book and said, 'Thank you, Lydia. I'll take this one.'

Chapter Thirty-Eight

THE NEXT DAY, RASHMI arrived in an uncharacteristically sour mood. 'Those crazy lorry drivers are always playing the horn. So noisy, like Delhi Masoorla is sounding.'

'Have you ever been in Delhi?'

'No. Filthy place.'

'Then how do you know how it sounds?'

'I know. Full of Muslims who eat cows.'

'There are Muslims in Masoorla.'

'And all day they are playing the horn.'

'I'm pretty sure there are Hindu lorry drivers too.'

'Hindus are not playing the horn.'

'Um . . .'

'Nooooo.'

'OK.'

She wobbled her head, slightly mollified, and the mischievous smile appeared. 'A verrry special mala I'm bringing your good self.'

'Oh, wonderful.'

Rashmi dug into her cloth bag and whipped out a fat orange garland – three strands of marigolds woven together. 'Triple first class, this mala.'

'Very nice. Thank you, Rashmi.'

'This excellent mala I am hanging on the bed.'

'OK.'

'Guaranteed money back hundred per cent.'

'Great.'

Her smile vanished. 'I'm telling you for truly, Madam. If this mala not be working, I'm veerrry sad for you.'

'Don't worry.' This was clearly our last chance, and I considered mussing up the bed as if orangutans had been tussling in it, even leaving a damp spot in the middle, anything to silence her.

Rashmi wagged her head solemnly. '*Big* puja for this mala I'm making.'

I took the book of poetry out to the verandah and opened it, immediately disappointed by page after page of that flowery, Victorian nonsense that had irritated me in college. 'Dewy-eyed doggerel,' I mumbled. A young Victorian girl was in love. So what? Anyone can be starry-eyed for a while, but how do you manage the long haul after life throws you a few fancy curves? I thought of Verna and Henry and felt more confused.

I flipped through, thinking the poems were uninspired and mawkish to boot, then dropped the book on my lap and put my feet up on the railing. Billy was in the kitchen, singing with Rashmi; his childish voice melded with her alto, and a unique version of 'A Bushel And A Peck' sailed out to the verandah. I smiled at the thought of the leprechaun trap, forgotten in Lydia's suite. It wasn't only the puppy; Billy and Lydia were good for each other. Now there was a curve I hadn't seen coming.

I drummed my fingers on the book and shifted in the creaky wicker rocker. Billy and Rashmi launched into a boisterous rendition of a Hindi folksong, and I heard Rashmi's ankle bracelets clashing; no doubt she was twirling around the kitchen with Billy in her arms. I opened the book again and flipped through a few more pages to the poem with a salutation and a signature, as if it had been sent as a letter.

My Dearest,

Moonlight bathes
your Face in light,
my dusky Lover,
Life's Delight.
Beneath the Moon
we both are bright.
No Colour taints
our Love at Night.

Yours,
Felicity

Felicity's poetry was sentimental, and why not? She was young and in love. Of course she wouldn't have put her name on the cover. It was considered unbecoming for a lady to write, and downright embarrassing for her to publish. Activities like that carried the stigma of being a bluestocking. Typically, Victorian women who published did so anonymously, but Felicity wasn't typical, and I was a little surprised that she would adhere to that convention. Then I realized she hadn't. She had died. Someone else had published this collection.

The River shines in Sunlight like
a Chain of Gold
thrown carelessly across the land.
Beauty quite ineffable
& yet
Nothing
to the Sunlight in
my Lady's fine-spun Hair

My Lady? Why would Felicity write a love poem to a woman? Then I remembered the title: *The Collected Poems of a Lady and a Gentleman*. I read another:

I love a Riddle, so I ask
What Miracle would have us bind
the unseen Future to the Past?
What ancient Mystery
will save
our Hearts to beat beyond the Grave?

And the next:

The only Mystery known to me,
both young & old as Spring,
is one for which I have long prayed,
the Gift most sought by Kings.

Felicity and her lover had written those poems as messages to each other. I recalled Adela complaining that '. . . *messages come & go and she does not show them to me*.' Adela said Felicity's lover had lived in England and spoke the Queen's English, which made him as much a Victorian as she. Felicity told him that she was pregnant with a Victorian riddle, and he answered in kind. In spite of the scandal, they were happy about the pregnancy. But how did all of it come to be bound together in a book? I turned back to the first page and read from the beginning.

> *You are a Gentleman*
> *& so*
> *when first our Fingers touched by Chance*
> *you pulled away from me*
> *as if your Flesh by Flames was licked.*
> *But why must we do Penance, Sir?*
> *I see no Blame in Love.*

He had responded:

> *I am not free*
> *in terms that Men respect.*
> *There is a Contract to constrain*
> *my acts*
> *though not my Heart.*
> *Your Friendship is a humbling thing*
> *which I accept in Gratitude,*
> *& care not whether Men absolve Agape.*
> *Yet I confess*
> *My Lady C*
> *you take my Breath away*
> *& make me ponder Eros.*
> *Can it be?*

For Victorians, the mention of Eros would have been risqué even in England. But in India, with issues of race and class, the Sepoy Rebellion raging, and him being married, it would have been insanely dangerous. Yet the book appeared to be a full account of their secret romance. How bold they were!

> *Beloved Sir,*
> *When I saw your changeling Face*
> *– in our winged Garden –*
> *the Moon was round & bountiful*
> *yet not as full as my full Heart,*
> *quickened*
> *by your Touch.*

The last poem was his:

> *My Lady lost,*
> *I sink*
> *I drown.*
> *My Body*
> *and*
> *my Spirit*
> *both*
> *descend*
> *into*
> *the black*
> *Abyss.*
> *I would despair*
> *but for one thing –*
> *Our Child*
> *lives!*
> *And thus*
> *shall we*
> *cheat*
> *Death.*

But did they cheat death? Did their child live? I turned the
book over and examined the fine binding, the good leather.
Professionally done, but who did it? These dead women kept
goading me into finding the rest of their story, and the first
place I thought to explore was that mighty wall of books in
the clubroom known as the Study.

That night, we took Billy to Lydia at the Cecil, and I went
to the Club with Martin.

Chapter Thirty-Nine

WE SPOTTED WALKER at the bar, swigging Indian beer and talking politics to a military man with grey hair sprouting out of his ears. As we came up behind him we heard Walker say, 'I wouldn't be surprised if there are a million dead before it's over.'

Martin clapped him on the back and Walker turned. 'There's my drinking chum,' he said. 'And with his lovely wife for a change.'

The military man seemed relieved to excuse himself, and I wondered how long Walker had had him cornered. We sat on the rattan barstools and ordered drinks. Walker said, 'I was just telling old Cromley that more than twelve million people might be displaced. Think of it. Miles of homeless families trudging along dusty roads, dragging everything they own – Muslims going one way, Hindus the other. Someone throws an insult, or a stone, and then God help us.'

'It's the agitators.' Martin lit my Adbullah, and then his bidi. 'I don't think it would be half so bad if extremists didn't keep stirring them up.'

Walker nodded. 'They start an argument between neighbours and let them chew on their rancour overnight. The next day a cow is killed. The day after that, the cow killer comes home to find his daughter's been raped. A day or two goes by and the rapist's daughter is found with her throat cut. Within a week the whole city is burning, and old tribal hatreds are fanning the flames.'

Martin, the scholar, put his elbows on the bar and made a tent with his fingertips. 'Confucius said, "Before you embark on a journey of revenge, dig two graves."' He gave me a knowing look as the bearer set down our drinks.

I took a quick sip of gin and stubbed out my Abdullah. 'I'm going to poke around the books in the Study.'

'Not much current there, I'm afraid,' said Walker. 'Bound volumes of *Punch* and *Tatler*, a few novels by Rider Haggard and all the year-old newspapers you want.'

'I like old books.' I remembered the journal in the sandal-wood tree and said, 'After all, all we really have are our stories.'

Martin caught me with a sharp look, and I thought I'd said something wrong. He stared at me as if I'd said something profound or profoundly stupid, then he turned back to his whisky. I said, 'You two can figure out how to achieve world peace.' I slipped off the rattan chair. 'I'll be back.'

Standing in the open double doors to the Study, I inhaled cigar smoke and old leather. The walls were solidly covered by oil paintings, animal heads with staring glass eyes, and faded photos in battered frames. Shabby books, dusty vases, faded needlework, antique jewellery and odds and ends of every description filled the bookshelves. The room reeked of Victoriana, and I stepped across the threshold like a spelunker entering a cave looking for buried treasure.

The room was larger and more ornate than it appeared from the lobby, stuffed with game tables, leather chairs and hassocks, with the snooker table in the centre. Everything was braided and tasselled and bordered, and a heavy blue-velvet curtain with deep folds covered a tall window. I turned my back to the men at the snooker table and perused the collection of old bric-a-brac on the bookshelves. A sign had been posted on the one of the shelves: PLEASE DO NOT HANDLE THE ARTEFACTS. I let my eyes roam over the hoary bits and pieces, idly thinking that the brown tea cosy looked drab next to a pillowcase embroidered in raspberry and mango and gas-jet blue. I recalled Adela's mention of embroidering pillow covers and ran a fingertip over a fuschia lotus petal, wondering whether it had been created on my verandah.

An ivory and jet brooch carved with a woman's profile lay on a sachet pillow that still gave off a weak whiff of lavender. I studied the miniature profile, the strong nose and chin, hard angles chiselled in cold stone, and I thought of the sketch of the woman riding astride in a split skirt. Another shelf held a row of silver-framed sepia photographs, people in formal poses, looking dour and uncomfortable. Petal's voice came back. '. . . *no one knows who the frightful old sticks are . . .*' I picked up a photo in an ornate silver frame, a baby wearing a sweater over a long white dress with fine embroidery around the collar and hem. But it wasn't a bald, blue-eyed English baby. This baby looked Indian, with black hair, dark eyes and a dazzling, impish smile. I whispered, 'Charlie?'

In a glass-fronted shadowbox, a display of gold and green silk moths achieved immortality, mounted on black velvet – fabulous for ever – and the box had been positioned on top of a book to give it height, a sculptural statement. I angled my head to read the title on the book's spine – *The Collected Poems of a Lady and a Gentleman 1857*. That volume, like the one I had at home, looked pristine, as if it had never been opened. Petal again, *'. . . it's not as though anyone wants to read their boring rants . . .'*

On a low shelf, a pile of crocheted doilies and anti-macassars, yellow with age and sadly flaccid, fanned around a small hand-bound book with a mauve suede cover and tiny silver stitches around the edge. I had to fold my hands behind my back to keep from grabbing it.

PLEASE DO NOT HANDLE THE ARTEFACTS.

I glanced out to the lobby. An Indian bearer stood at the open door, watching me, but when I met his eyes he quickly looked away. The men playing snooker had moved around the table and had their backs to me. I opened my purse and nabbed the mauve journal with one quick swipe. I snapped my purse shut and moved the doilies and antimacassars to cover the blank space, then I strolled back to the bar.

Walker was saying, 'God forbid Gandhi kicks the bucket on one of his fasts. Each side will start blaming the other. All they have to do to stop a train is to park a cow on the track; then they can board it at their leisure and chop "the enemy" to bits. And they will.' He pinned Martin with his eyes and said, 'I'm telling you, my man, this is not a good time to go to Lahore.' He gestured at Martin's clothes and his noxious bidi. 'At least, not looking like that.'

Back at the Cecil, we found Billy spooned around Pal, sleeping with his head on Lydia's lap. She stroked his hair, and her eyes were red-rimmed and glassy. I wriggled the puppy out of Billy's embrace, and Martin slid his arms under Billy's knees and shoulders. Lydia reluctantly handed him over, gently, like something precious and fragile. She gave us a detailed account of everything he had done, how many ginger biscuits he had eaten, the cocoa he had drunk, the stories they had read, the adorable things he had said. She handed me a bottle of calamine lotion, saying, 'This will help the mosquito bite on his left leg.' I had calamine lotion at home, but I took the bottle and thanked her.

She continued to fondle Billy's hair as he dozed on Martin's shoulder, and absently asked, 'You had a nice evening?'

'We did.'

'I'm glad. Bring him back again. Any time.'

As Martin and I moved towards the door, I said, 'That's kind of you, Lydia.' I wanted to say, *I'm terribly sorry about your boy*, but I said, 'Thanks again.'

Lydia followed us to the door. 'When do you think you might have an evening out again?'

Martin and I exchanged a coded look. He said, 'Soon. I'll call you.'

'Please do.' She followed us out of the room, and watched us start down the stairs. 'You know, you could leave him overnight if you like.'

'Not tonight, Lydia.'

'Another time then.'

'Yes. Goodnight.'

'Remember,' she called. 'Any time.'

After we had tucked Billy into bed with Pal, Martin said, 'Did you see that smile on his face?'

I shuffled record sleeves and said, 'You're still going to Lahore tomorrow?'

'Please don't start. I'm tired.' He took off his glasses and squeezed the bridge of his nose. 'It's my job.'

I put the records down. 'You are not a soldier or a journalist. It is not your job to put your life in danger. What about Billy and me?'

He put his glasses back on. 'Don't get hysterical.'

'Why can't you go somewhere else? Why can't you wear Western clothes? Why can't you smoke Lucky Strikes or Camels? You want to hurt yourself, but you don't care that you're hurting us too.'

'Of course I care!' Martin massaged his forehead. 'Jesus, Evie, I love you and Billy.'

I dropped on to the sofa and lay my head against the high back. 'Then why?'

He stared at me a moment, and I thought I saw something happen behind his eyes. But he only mumbled, 'You're getting worked up over nothing.' He rubbed the back of his neck. 'It's late. We'll talk in the morning.'

He was right. It was later than he knew. 'Fine,' I said. 'Go to bed. I'm going to read a while.'

He stood there for a moment, with his arms limp at his sides, but when the silence became oppressive he slouched away, and I heard the bedroom door close. I kicked off my shoes and pulled my feet up on the sofa, then I opened my purse and pulled out the journal I'd stolen from the Club.

Chapter Forty

September 1858

Mother's letter arrived yesterday. She says she is delighted to hear I have come to my senses about marriage & she has just the chap for me: a fifty-year-old bachelor accountant. She enclosed a photograph of a pig-eyed fat man with no hair. My heart sank when I saw him &, knowing he has never been married, I presume his personality must be as unpleasant as his appearance. His income is modest, but this match will get me out of her house & save her the embarrassment of a spinster daughter about whom there may have been odious rumours. Still, I hugged Charlie & said, 'We're going home!'

Then I read, 'But surely you understand that you cannot bring a whore's half-breed bastard into this house.' I read it three times & questioned whether I might have forgotten to include Charlie's photograph with my letter. But I did not forget. She closed by saying, 'There must be orphanages in that godforsaken place.'

I shall not see my parents or England again.

October 1858

Charlie has taken his first steps. He grows more spirited daily, but I am unnaturally fatigued. I sink back on my pillow after chota hazri, & must drag myself through the day. I nap when Charlie naps & still, at night, I fall into my bed & sleep overtakes me almost before my head meets the pillow. But sleep does not refresh me. Every morning, I wake achy & exhausted.

The station doctor came, almost sober this time, & poked & prodded. He says I suffer from an abscess of the liver. 'Filthy business, but not contagious.' Then he remembered to say, 'Awfully sorry.'

'But what's to be done?' I asked.

'Well, we will bleed you, of course, & then we will see.' He mucked about in his black bag, eventually producing a brass lancet & a bowl to catch the blood. 'Let's have your arm, then,' he said, coming at me with his knife. I remember a sharp pain in my forearm & bright red blood pooling in the white enamel bowl. The next thing I remember is waking to the smell of rose-water. He was gone & Lalita was bathing my arm. She said, 'Let me bring a healer, memsahib. This bleeding business is no good.'

I smiled & I told the dear girl to go ahead & bring her witch-doctor.

October 1858

The witch-doctor turned out to be Lalita's mother, Anasuya. She is a pretty woman who has a gold pin embedded in one nostril & a melodious voice that I find calming. After spooning a truly vile orange liquid into my mouth, she brought Charlie to me. I was too weak to hold him long, & she comforted him when I gave him back & he cried. She & Lalita now sleep on the verandah & together they care for both Charlie & me.

My skin has developed a jaundiced hue, my urine has turned brown, & I itch. The itch is an unrelenting torment that cannot be scratched away. This bizarre affliction does not respond to any of the medicines I brought with me. Anasuya bathes me in cold nilgiri tea for the itch. It helps, but not for long. I must endure.

October 1858

Fever waxes & wanes, & I have developed an ache on my right side. Anasuya continues to nurse me with bitter tisanes & strange herbal concoctions, but they have not helped.

All day she & Lalita run between Charlie & me, God bless them. But worry weakens my spirit as surely as this disease wastes my body: what will happen to him if I die? Will Anasuya take him? She could not even feed her own daughter, putting her into service as soon as possible.

And Charlie is a half-caste. What will become of him?

October 1858

I can no longer rise from my bed. It is an effort to hold my pen. I lie here thinking of all the sordid backstreets in India overrun by starving urchins, ragged & begging, sleeping in gutters, eating from garbage heaps. Felicity said a four-year-old girl is worth two horses in Peshawar. I suppose they would take him at the orphanage, but I have never seen a child there over the age of nine or ten. What becomes of them?

Anasuya brings Charlie to me twice a day, & after she takes him away I weep.

The rest was blank. I closed it and sat still in the moonlit room, feeling the pinch of grief. They died so young. And what about the baby?

Although Singh was a common name in India, wealth was rare. The odds of another wealthy family by that name living in Masoorla were slim, and the possibility that my landlord was connected to Felicity's lover, Jonathan Singh, made my sleuthing heart beat faster.

Martin planned to leave for Lahore the next day on the three o'clock train. I couldn't stop him, but I could take my mind off it by paying Mr Singh another visit.

Chapter Forty-One

M R SINGH OPENED the front door himself. He wore an exquisitely tailored ecru suit of heavy silk and a claret-coloured tie with a matching turban. He shook my hand, saying, 'Always a pleasure, Mrs Mitchell.'

As I walked through the lofty foyer, I noted a delicate spicy scent coming from a jasmine rangoli in a shallow Meissen bowl. It occurred to me that my little bungalow must look like servants' quarters to Mr Singh. I said, 'Thank you for seeing me.'

'Do come in.' He waved me into the same room in which we'd spoken last time, and once again I sat on the low divan piled with an array of down pillows covered in ice-cream-coloured silks. Mr Singh gave a subtle nod to the butler and said, 'Tea, Daksha.' He sat back and crossed his legs in the European manner, saying, 'I hope there's no problem with the bungalow.'

'Oh, no. The bungalow is fine.'

Mr Singh looked at me expectantly. I said, 'There's a loose brick in the wall of the kitchen.'

'I'll have it repaired immediately.'

'No. I mean . . . that's not why I'm here.'

He cocked his head and waited.

'It's this.' I opened my purse. 'I found these hidden behind the loose brick.' I pulled out the packet of old letters and laid them on the table between us.

Mr Singh glanced at the letters but did not reach for them. He seemed slightly amused and said, 'How peculiar.'

I said, 'They're the letters of a woman named Felicity Chadwick. She—'

'I know who Felicity Chadwick was.' The amusement in his face vanished like sun behind a sudden cloud.

'You do?'

Mr Singh uncrossed his legs and sat forward, elbows on knees, fingers laced. 'Why have you come here?'

Daksha walked in with the tea tray and conversation halted while he poured a cup and offered it to me. I said, 'Thank you,' and as he poured the second cup I had the sensation of walking a tightrope. If Mr Singh's ancestor had been Felicity's lover, it would have been a scandal for his family and might still be a touchy subject. After Daksha left the room I said, 'May I ask how you know about her?'

'My great-grandfather knew her.'

The tension in the room was suddenly tangible. 'May I ask his name?'

'Jonathan Singh.'

I nodded. 'Your great-grandfather and Miss Chadwick—'

'They were lovers.' Mr Singh set his teacup on the low table between us. 'But I have a feeling you already knew that.' He said, 'What exactly do you want to know?'

'Forgive me, Mr Singh. I know this is personal, but I've found Felicity's papers as well as the journals of her companion. Their story has affected me. The bold joie de vivre with which they approached life has led me to consider taking a very serious and painful step in my own life. My marriage . . . I might even . . .' I set my teacup down next to his. 'This has become important to me.'

'I see.' He took a monogrammed leather cigarette case from his breast pocket. 'You know,' he said, opening the case, 'Jonathan was married.'

'Yes. And his widow committed suttee.'

He nodded curtly. 'It was a shameful episode, and my parents refused to discuss it.' He offered me a cigarette, and I noticed they were English Ovals. I declined, and he lit his with a silver Ronson table lighter.

I said, 'Your parents were ashamed of the affair, or the suttee?'

'The affair, of course.' He exhaled a thin stream of smoke, and I heard the susurration of silk on silk as he re-crossed his legs. 'Suttee is considered honourable, the act of a chaste and loyal wife. But an affair with a white woman . . . well, excuse me, but that was repugnant. Grandfather was the only one who would even acknowledge that Jonathan knew her.'

'What did your grandfather tell you?'

Mr Singh sat in his carved throne, his face blank and unreadable. 'I was a child, Mrs Mitchell. I heard whispers and I sensed secrets, as children do. Grandfather told me his father had once befriended an Englishwoman. I sometimes had the feeling that he wanted to say more, but he never did. Well, I was quite young. It wasn't until I was older, after Grandfather died, that I understood what he meant by "befriended", and why my parents wouldn't speak of it.'

'So your grandfather never mentioned Felicity and Jonathan's child?'

'Child?' He smiled. 'There was no child.'

'Oh, but there *was*.'

Mr Singh's cigarette paused in mid air. 'I'm sure you're mistaken.'

But the expression on his face was far from sure; he knew his grandfather had kept something back. I said, 'Felicity died in childbirth, and her friend, Adela, took care of the child, a boy, for more than a year before she herself died.'

'If this is true, that child would have been Grandfather's half-brother, and my great-uncle.' Mr Singh uncrossed his legs and sat forward again. 'But a half-caste orphan . . . well, he might have been put into an orphanage, but if not . . .' He shook his head.

I said, 'I know children are sold into slavery.'

Mr Singh took a long pull on his cigarette and exhaled slowly. 'Some children are mutilated to make them more sympathetic beggars.'

'Dear God.' I took out my Abdullahs and tapped one out nervously. He leaned across the table and lit my cigarette with the Ronson, and I thought of Charlie, eating rice pudding, crawling around the cook's legs, playing in the marigolds. Then I imagined him among the roving street urchins, perhaps blinded or maimed, finishing each day with a handful of rice or a beating. I said, 'But the child wasn't a secret. Jonathan's mother knew about him.'

Mr Singh shrugged helplessly. 'Grandfather and I were close, but he never mentioned a child.'

'But Jonathan's mother knew. She might have made some provision for the child. After all, he was her grandson.'

Mr Singh spread his hands as if asking for mercy. 'Mrs Mitchell, you're talking about my great-great-grandmother. She died with her secrets a very long time ago.'

I couldn't let Charlie go. I said, 'Jonathan's mother helped Adela. She sent money to support herself and the child.'

'I beg your pardon?'

'I've read Adela's diaries and I know she wrote to

Jonathan's mother. They might have made arrangements for him in the event of Adela's death.' I smoked, waiting for his curiosity to overcome his reluctance to re-open the family scandal.

He pursed his lips, and I couldn't tell whether he was pensive or annoyed. He said, 'I don't see how we could verify that.'

'Those Victorians kept *everything*.' I tapped the letters on the table. 'The letters between Adela and Jonathan's mother might still be here.'

'Here?'

'Didn't Jonathan's mother live in this house?'

Mr Singh made a disinterested gesture at the room. 'We have several family homes – Delhi, Jaipur, London. But . . .' He drummed his cigarette on a heavy crystal ashtray. 'If she wrote from Masoorla, I suppose she would have lived in the old wing of this house. It has no electricity and no one lives there now.'

'Mr Singh, perhaps you sensed that your grandfather had more to say because he did want to tell you about his half-brother. If you had been older, or if he had lived longer . . . If he were here today, would he tell you?'

Mr Singh's disinterest cracked. 'My grandfather was an honest man. He would have wanted me to know the truth.'

'Then shouldn't we try to find out?'

His smoky eyes softened. 'Interesting, isn't it? How a family secret can linger like a ghost even after everyone who knew it is gone?'

'Our secrets are part of our stories. It's our stories that linger.'

'Well, if an abandoned child is part of my family's story, I think Grandfather would want me to know.' He crushed out his cigarette in the crystal ashtray.

'Grandfather's suite is in the old wing. It has been closed up since his death.'

'Could we . . . ?'

'Yes.' He stood brusquely. 'Let's have a look.'

We walked across the yawning entry hall and up the curved staircase. The mahogany railing slid under my hand, butter smooth from generations of servants with polishing rags. I followed him down a long corridor laid with a richly patterned rug, coppers and greens worn to a soft lustre, and walked past a series of deep doorways. I wondered how many rooms the house had – a dozen? Two dozen?

We turned a corner and entered an older corridor, wider but creaky and a bit musty, and stopped in front of an intricately carved door. Mr Singh opened it and motioned me into a room that was large but airless, having been closed up through many monsoons. He said, 'The servants dust in here, but otherwise it hasn't been disturbed since Grandfather died.'

Heavy silk drapes covered a bay window and when he opened them, dust motes swirled in sunlight. Nestled in the bay, two grey silk armchairs flanked a small octagonal table of inlaid marble. A massive four-poster bed surrounded by tired mosquito netting dominated the room, and bookshelves flanked a cold fireplace. Mr Singh said, 'My grandfather died in this room.'

I wasn't sure what to say to that. I nodded my sympathy and moved towards the shelves. My eyes travelled up to a domed ceiling painted a deep indigo with a dull matt finish and inset haphazardly with bits of mirror. At the top of the dome, a translucent disc of white alabaster glowed faintly. It appeared to be an attempt to simulate the night sky with a full moon in the centre; a whimsical and rather childlike notion for a bedroom, I thought.

A rattan trunk squatted at the foot of the bed, and in a shadowy alcove, I spotted a writing desk – ebony carved with mythic creatures, and a rococo Chippendale chair. Mr Singh walked to the chair and ran his hand over top. He said, 'I spent a great deal of my childhood in this room. This old chair –' he gave it a solid pat, 'Grandfather often sat here and read to me while I sat at his feet.'

I went to the rattan trunk. 'May I?'

'By all means.'

I lifted the lid, imagining bundles of ribbon-tied letters, a bonanza of secrets, and my heart sank at the sight of blankets and bed linen. I said, 'Can we search the bookshelves?'

We examined every shelf. We took out books and fanned the pages. We peered into a ginger jar, tipped over a porcelain vase and opened a carved wooden jewellery box. The gold hinge gave a faint creak, but the box was empty except for a powdery grey residue that reminded me of moth dust. After searching every book on every shelf I said, 'That's strange.'

'Well, I didn't really think we'd find anything.'

'I mean it's strange that there's no copy of Felicity and Jonathan's poetry here. Someone had their poems printed and bound. I found one volume in the Hotel Cecil, and another at the Club.'

He shook his head. 'I've never seen such a book.'

'The desk?' I pointed at the alcove, and he nodded.

We opened tiny drawers and found old-fashioned fountain pens with ink dried on the nibs, yellowing invitations to teas and dinners, a few loose coins, blank sheets of writing paper, and the book of poetry – this one well used. But no letters.

Mr Singh slid his hands into his pockets and shrugged his perfectly square shoulders. 'Well, we tried.'

'I'm sorry to have to put you through this. Thank you for showing me this room.'

'Charming, isn't it? Did you notice the ceiling?'

We both looked up and I searched for a convincing compliment about the rather clumsy facsimile of moon and stars. Before I could think of something, Mr Singh said, 'Of course!' He looked oddly satisfied, as if the last piece of a jigsaw had fallen into place. He said, 'Grandfather had this ceiling put in; he used it to teach me the constellations – the *Rasis* – and I spent much of my early childhood staring at it. It was only after his death I noticed that flaw.' He pointed to a thin white line between the deep-blue crown moulding and the domed ceiling. It looked as though the painter had missed a long, slim streak. Mr Singh said, 'I first saw that flaw after Grandfather's death and thought I hadn't noticed it as a child because I was busy studying the stars. But maybe it wasn't there when I was a child.'

I was shocked when he took his shoes off to climb up on the bed and then step up on to the higher bedside table. I understood when he reached up to tease a piece of paper from behind the moulding. He unfolded it and said, 'Grandfather, you devil!' He pulled out another and another until the thin white line, which was not a painting flaw at all, had disappeared.

There were seven letters in all, the first dated September 1858, and, without a word, Mr Singh and I took them to the octagonal table in the bay window and pushed the grey silk chairs together.

Chapter Forty-Two

September 1858

Dear Mrs Singh,
I am deeply indebted for your support these past months, but
now I must ask even more. I am afflicted by a malevolence of
the humours & fear I will not live much longer. The child,
your grandson, will have no home once I am gone. Might I
impose upon you one last time? Could you find it in your
heart to make arrangements for him? Perhaps you know of a
family who would take him in & be kind to him?
                                        Respectfully,
                                        Adela Winfield

I said, 'I knew it!'
Mr Singh unfolded the next note.

September 1858

Dear Miss Winfield,
Before he passed away, my son asked me to provide for his
child. It is not for me to judge Jonathan or Miss Chadwick. I

am sorry to hear of your illness, but yes, Miss Winfield, I will make arrangements for the child.

Also, I would like you to know that I did not withhold your friend's remains due to any grievance on my part. My son committed her ashes to the holy Ganges. After his death, I did the same with his remains & with those of his wife, Makali. All three are mingled for ever in the sacred water.

In kindness,
Charumati Singh

September 1858

Dear Mrs Singh,
I was horrified by your daughter-in-law's suttee. I will not pretend otherwise, nor will I pretend to understand such a custom. But I agree that it is not for us to judge.

Anasuya, the child's ayah, will bring him to you after my death. I cannot bear to part with him sooner. Dare I ask that your kindness extend to her as well? Perhaps you could arrange for her to go with him, wherever he is placed. He is very fond of her, & he will already have lost two mothers.

Anasuya will return your letters, when the time comes, should you wish to keep them for your grandson.

Respectfully,
Adela Winfield

October 1858

Dear Miss Winfield,
You may rest your mind in the matter of the child's ayah. They will not be separated.

You must not judge Makali too harshly. She could not

conceive a child & she became bitter, feeling she had failed in a woman's most important duty. Having no children, Makali had nothing to live for after Jonathan died. According to custom she could not remarry, she must shave her head, wear white for the rest of her life, & eat only bland foods. But all that was nothing compared to her melancholic nature and her disappointment in life. She was a good woman & she saw suttee as an honourable choice. She believed martyrdom would finally give her life meaning. I tried to dissuade her.

I hope you will not hold her memory in contempt.

In kindness,
Charumati Singh

Mr Singh put the letter down, his handsome face puzzled. He said, 'But my great-grandmother did have a child. She had Grandfather. Oh, my God. Do you suppose . . . ?' He picked up the next letter.

October 1858

Dear Mrs Singh,
I hold no one in contempt. I wish only to die in peace.

I am sending you the poetry your son wrote for Felicity in the hope that perhaps the child might know his parents by these poems. I beg you to see that he learns English so that he might read them. If nothing else, these poems will assure him that his parents cared deeply for each other, & that they did not regret his birth.

Respectfully,
Adela Winfield

October 1858

Dear Miss Winfield
Thank you for these poems, in which my son lives for me
again.
I have found Felicity's papers amongst my son's effects &
will have all of them printed & bound for posterity.
As for the child, his surname will be Singh. He will learn
English, & he will know that his mother was Felicity
Chadwick.

> *In kindness,*
> *Charumati Singh*

October 1858

Dear Mrs Singh,
I have one last request. I have named him Charles William,
names I believe his mother would approve of, & I ask that
you allow him to keep those names. However, I call him
Charlie, & that is the name to which he responds.

> *Respectfully,*
> *Adela Winfield*

Mr Singh gave a strange little cry. 'Charlie? You didn't say
the child's name was Charlie. Charles William Singh? That
was Grandfather!' He sat back in his chair, as if pushed. 'We
used to joke about Charlie being an undignified name for a
grown man, but he preferred it to Charles.'

'That means . . .' I let him finish the thought.

Mr Singh laid a hand flat on his impeccably tailored
chest. 'Felicity Chadwick was my great-grandmother.'

We stared at each other, wondering at the unexpected
ways people are connected and how we touch each other

through space and time. It could almost make a person believe in . . . something. I said, 'I wonder why your grandfather didn't tell you.'

'I'm sure my parents told him not to. They always referred to Makali as my great-grandmother.' He glanced up at the domed ceiling. 'But this explains Grandfather's obsession with this ceiling and the time he spent making me study it. If you knew the hours we spent here . . . but they were happy times for us. He left those letters where only I would find them.' He stood up, saying, 'I want to show you something.'

He pulled the heavy drapes closed over the bay window, and the room fell into darkness. Then he went to the bedside table, took a box of matches out of the drawer and lit the oil lamp, which he carried purposefully to the middle of the room. He said, 'Look up.'

I looked up and gasped. The domed ceiling had burst to life. The indigo background had disappeared and a thousand tiny mirrors reflected the lamplight, glittering and twinkling with the movement of the flame. I saw Ursa Major and Orion and in the centre the disk of alabaster moonstone glimmered. It seemed that the roof had peeled away to display the cosmos, because it was too fantastic to be the work of human hands.

Mr Singh's voice came from nowhere. 'We Sikhs worship one God, whose name is Truth. Grandfather used to say, "Gaze at the night sky and see the truth." He had always meant for me to discover the truth.'

I don't know how long we stayed like that – lost in space. It might have been a minute or it might have been ten before he blew out the flame. As he pulled open the drapes he said, 'It's a recreation of a ceiling in the palace at Jaipur.'

'It's breathtaking. Thank you.' The spectacle had reminded

me of the ridiculously romantic night years ago when Martin
and I had stood under the stars by the moondial in Pulaski
Park. That cosmos had been real, but our infatuation had
not stood up to reality. This cosmos of paint and mirrors was
an illusion, but there was a more enduring reality under that
ceiling than there had been in our moonlit park. All my
sleuthing had brought me back to the beginning, but a new
beginning. Our marriage could not be sustained by a fairy-
tale of young love; it had to be durable enough to survive
life's realities, or it must end before it dragged us into
bitterness.

Mr Singh smoothed his tie into the V of his jacket. We had
shared an intimate moment, and I saw he felt it as well. He
stared out of the bay window, possibly to avoid my eyes, and
I said, 'Are you married, Mr Singh?'

His colouring warmed and intensified, and then he said,
'Yes, Mrs Mitchell. I hope you don't think—'

'Not at all. That was too personal. Forgive me.'

He shrugged and his blush subsided. 'Today we've shared
more than facts. I've been happily married for many years.'

'Was your marriage arranged?'

'Of course. In a Sikh wedding ceremony we pray that we
may always live as friends. I have been fortunate. My wife
and I have become good friends.'

'I see.' How Indian to face reality head on and acknowledge the challenge right from the start. 'So, in India,
marriages are simply friendships?'

He smiled. 'Only the good ones.'

Riding home, I tried to recapture the sense of awe I'd felt in
the darkened bedroom, but it had already begun to fade.
That is the nature of emotion. And then I knew how it must
be: Martin and I had to forge a friendship that could survive

the past and create a future worth living. Like Harry, it was time for me to get on with it. I would not join Martin in his suicidal hell, and I would not raise Billy in one.

The word 'divorce' formed in my mind in bold black letters, an apocalyptic announcement of disaster. I loved Martin and I would always love him, but I would not let my life be a monument to his guilt. Like Felicity and Adela, I would choose joy, and Martin could join me, or not.

I checked my watch; the train for Lahore did not leave for another hour. I called out to the tonga driver and he pulled up on the reins. I said, 'Take me to the train station.'

Chapter Forty-Three

MARTIN WASN'T THERE, so I waited. The train chugged in on screaming brakes, and the shifting tide of humanity, enduring and ephemeral, flooded the platform. Young men with hennaed hair hawked paan and tea; a man dressed in nothing but a handkerchief held by a thread around his waist stood with gold bracelets all the way up his outstretched arms, and a patient Indian cow with beautiful eyes meandered through the crowd.

Snacks and tea were bought and sold in a grand rush, displaced Hindus disembarked, and displaced Muslims climbed aboard, heaving trunks through windows and shouting at family members to hurry. Eventually the train huffed out of the station in an angry hiss of steam, and the hawkers sat on their heels to wait for the next one. In spite of his tan and bidis and kurta pyjamas, I would have recognized Martin, even from behind. He simply wasn't there, and I wasn't sure whether to be worried or hopeful. I hailed a rickshaw to take me to the telegraph office, but when I got there Walker said, 'He took the train to Lahore.'

'No, he didn't.'

'Well, he's not here.'

I went home, because I didn't know where else to go, and found him sitting in the wicker rocker on the verandah, watching Billy play tug-o-war with Pal. The puppy growled with youthful ferocity, small pointy teeth clamped on to the twig Billy jiggled, while Rashmi lay curled in a corner, napping. As I came up the steps, Billy said, 'Mom! Dad's waiting for you.'

'Oh?' I kissed the top of Billy's head, and Rashmi sat up and yawned.

I stood there, uncertain, and Martin smiled at me. He pushed his glasses up on his nose, and my heart broke. I steeled myself for what I had to say – it would be the first time he heard the word 'divorce' from me – and it took me another second to notice that he was wearing Western clothes. I said, 'You're not going to Lahore?'

'No.'

'But your thesis . . . ?'

'I can write my thesis without Lahore. Hell, I can talk to the people coming and going at the train station right here.' He held his hand out, and I took it. He said, 'I did go to the station, and I'm glad I did. Watching those refugees, I finally *got* it. They were all families sticking together through a civil war, and there I was sitting alone like a stupid martyr ready to sacrifice my family to my guilt. What a jerk.' He squeezed my hand and his eyes shone.

Rashmi saw us, our faces, and understood. She lumbered to her feet, saying, 'Come, *beta*,' and she took Billy out to the compound with Pal scrambling behind.

Martin surprised me by pulling me on to his lap and wrapping his arms around me. He said, 'Remember that night we went to the Club? You said something that stuck with me. You said, "All we really have are our stories." '

I had been quoting Adela, but he didn't know about

Adela, so I just nodded, surprised that he had remembered my offhand remark.

He said, 'I couldn't stop thinking about that. I thought, yeah, that's why I'm doing this, why I'm an historian. I'm going to tell the story of India at a turning point, and my story will be useful. It might even be important. But something kept bugging me.' He paused, searching for words. 'Today I went to the bazaar for cigarettes, and while I was walking around the sun got to me.'

I opened my mouth, a sarcastic quip on the tip of my tongue, but he headed me off. 'OK, I admit it. Sometimes I feel like my brain is frying. But I hate those colonial topis. So I bought a shawl and wrapped it around my head.'

'Oh, for heaven's sake!'

His arms tightened around me so that I couldn't get up off his lap. He said, 'I know. I stopped to light a bidi and saw my reflection in a shop window. I didn't recognize myself. I blended into the crowd and I knew then that you were right; I was looking for trouble.'

'Well, thank God for that.'

'But I went to the train station anyway. I was early and I sat there, with my head wrapped, smoking a bidi, trying not to think about anything, just watching the families coming and going. No matter how anxious they were, they had one thing in common – they were sticking together. If somebody got hurt or killed along the way, they'd know it. They'd be there to mourn together and comfort each other.

'And I was sitting there all by myself, dressed like a goddamn fool. I thought about someone having to tell you that I'd been killed in Lahore, how you might not even recover my body, what you'd tell Billy, and I was revolted by my own selfishness. Then I knew why your remark had been bugging me. The history of India isn't my story. *I* am my story. *We* are my story. I unwrapped my head – it felt like taking a bandage off a head wound – and I came home.' He shrugged. 'Do you think we can start over?'

His eyes pulled me in – their earnestness – but the frantic edge was gone. *That* was my Martin, saving us with his courage and honesty. What hubris to think that all I had to do was forgive him, offer myself, and he would be healed. It had to come from *him*, of course it did. And then I acknowledged my own part in the last two years – dismissing his fears, keeping secrets, sniping, nursing grudges. I said, 'I never stopped loving you.'

I felt his body relax against mine. The tension went out of his arms, and he said, 'No more blame, I promise. It's self-indulgent.' He drew me close and said, 'It's not that the past doesn't matter, it's that the future matters more, and the present matters most of all.'

I remembered the henna tattoo, still fresh on my body, and felt ashamed of my skin-deep attempt at reconciliation. We had been playing our parts clumsily, but now, finally, we had come to a moment of shared grace.

Martin said, 'I promise you our story won't end with that war. There's enough misery in the world. I won't perpetuate it any more.'

I touched my forehead to his and whispered, 'Martin.'

'Evie, you're trembling.'

'I almost gave up. You don't know how close I came to giving up.'

He winced. 'I wish—'

'No.' I laid a finger over his lips. 'Just this.' I searched his face. 'But you'll have to let it go every day. Every day, Martin.'

He smiled gently. 'I know.'

The invisible barrier between us dissolved and I sagged against him. Billy whooped as a flashy parrot shot out of the hibiscus bush, and I thought, anyone can be happy when you're young and in love under a full moon, but *this* . . . *this* was solid. We held each other, our broken selves, with no moonlight or music, only the punishing Indian sun, pesky monkeys chattering, Rashmi scolding Pal, and our little boy rolling in the dirt.

'There's something I want to do.' Martin reached down and fished under his chair, pulling out the clay pot I'd taken from the sandalwood tree. I remembered putting it away in the old stable and asked, 'What are you doing with that?'

Martin said, 'I found it when I parked the car; funny I never noticed it before.' He ran his hand over the cool, round surface. 'It's a Hindu funerary urn.'

'For ashes?'

'No. After a body has been cremated, the chief mourner walks away from the pyre and throws a clay urn over his shoulder. It shatters and he doesn't look back; it's the final letting go.'

Martin nudged me off his lap and went to the verandah steps with the urn. He faced me and threw the pot backward, over his shoulder, and we heard it break on the steps. My eyes stung, and I went to him, and he folded me into his arms.

Billy and Rashmi chased Pal around the sandalwood tree, while Martin and I sat on the verandah, and I told him my secrets. I started with the loose brick in the wall and finished with Charlie Singh's star-studded bedroom. Martin asked to see Felicity and Adela's papers, and we read them together, our heads bent over the old journals, now and then reading a sentence aloud. Martin said, 'They lived for joy.'

I said, 'Isn't that beautiful?'

He nodded, and then we both smiled. I said, 'I'm going to donate Felicity and Adela's papers to the Historical Society, but I've been keeping my own journal and I've decided to leave it in the sandalwood tree. Do you think that's corny?'

He smiled that open, hopeful smile I so loved and said, 'Corny as hell. But I like it.'

Rashmi left, and Habib arrived, and the sky burst into flames as the water wallah came up the road, calling, *'Pani! Pani!'* We put our child to bed together, his skin smelling of sandalwood soap and his breath of parsley, and we settled Pal on a quilt on the floor, knowing he would find his way on to the bed before morning. We ate dinner together, and then we went back to the verandah. There was so much to say, like old friends catching up after a long absence.

We talked while the monkeys quietened, and the moon rose to backlight the blue monsoon clouds. The thump of tablas reached us from the godowns, a muezzin called the faithful to prayer, and still we talked. When it rained, we stopped to listen; Martin lit two Abdullahs, and we smoked while the eaves dripped and the rain settled to a steady drone. We grew sleepy, but we kept on talking.

The rain stopped and the swift Himalayan dawn flashed over the sandalwood tree and caught us by surprise. The sun ignited one icy peak after another, and the sky brightened. It was a new day, excellent and fair, and when Martin took my hand, I wondered why I might ever want for more when moments like that, when they come, are all my heart can hold.

Author's Note

Epiphany in Old Delhi

India!

I had yearned to see it for as long as I could remember. But, intimidated by the profound otherness of the place, it took many years of travel in Europe, Southeast Asia, and even Africa – seasoning, if you will – before I worked up the nerve to visit in 2001. I remember standing in a street near Mumbai harbour, feeling swamped by the intense sun, the smell of diesel and dung fires, the ceaseless swirl of colour and movement, and the masses of people and traffic and animals . . . I thought, yes, I had been right to be intimidated. The place was a perpetual-motion kaleidoscope, dizzying, dirty and beautiful in a way I couldn't understand. I'm a writer, but it would take enormous hubris to try and capture that ancient, layered, paradox-ridden subcontinent in a novel. It took several more years for me to calm down enough take a stab at writing a novel set in India.

After two years spent researching and writing a first draft of *The Sandalwood Tree*, I went to India again in March 2009 to check facts and remind myself of Indian sights (marigolds heaped before stone idols and opulence alongside poverty), smells (curry and smoke), sounds (small drums and winding flutes and the swell of a billion voices), colours (all I'd ever seen and some I'd never imagined) and tastes (complex and hot).

When my husband and I landed in New Delhi, we plunged into the smoke and noise and crowds, gobsmacked by heat and a vibrant human mosaic. Porters – mostly children and old men – vied to carry our bags, and taxi drivers called out and motioned urgently for us to get into their cars, quick, quick, as if someone were chasing us. Chaos reigned, and when we finally arrived at our hotel, I remember feeling vaguely ashamed of how happy I was to sit down in a quiet, posh, air-conditioned lobby with an efficient staff at my beck and call. I looked forward to a nice cool shower followed by room service. And everyone had a British, not Indian, accent. What a relief!

The female staff wore saris, but they were all the same cobalt blue with a rich gold border – a sumptuous uniform to amuse the tourists. One of those lovely girls served me Earl Grey tea while my husband checked us in, and I thought she looked like Miss Universe. I really enjoyed sitting in that clean marble lobby where everyone spoke in hushed voices, and it worried me. If I could be overwhelmed by a ride from the airport, so glad to sip milky tea in a hotel with all the comforts of home, how would I survive a month in a car, swerving around rickshaws and bullock carts and beggars? Eating . . . what? Sleeping . . . where? Even though I'd already spent two years working on *The Sandalwood Tree*, I wondered whether I, an American, could really get close enough to that enigmatic place to write a believable novel.

The next morning we woke jet-lagged but excited, and we wasted no time getting out, hoping to lose ourselves in Old Delhi. We hired a car and driver (we're adventurous, not crazy) and headed for the bazaar. Our driver twisted through

the choked improbable trans-species traffic, idled behind
rusted buses and alongside men and women carrying
platters or jars or bundles on their heads. We dodged bullock
carts, suicidal dogs and a camel, and squeaked around three-
wheeled tuk-tuks spitting noxious fumes and stuffed with
people sitting on each other's laps or hanging perilously off
the sides. We stopped for the occasional bony cow who, of
course, always has the right of way.

In Old Delhi, where the streets are too narrow and congested for cars, we climbed into a bicycle rickshaw and
bumped along alleys packed shoulder to shoulder with
shoppers dressed in a rainbow of turbans and skullcaps, veils
and saris and a multitude of fantastic costumes I couldn't
name. The lanes were packed full of tiny shops open to the
street and spilling over with colour and sparkle. There is so
much glitter in an Indian bazaar I got the feeling that if I
dropped a leg of lamb it would come up with gems stuck all
over it like some meaty sceptre. It was dirty and the air
smelled of smoke and the women, in their brilliant saris,
looked like tropical birds fluttering through a veil of dust. I
held on tight while the rickshaw bucked and rumbled down
Silk Street, Paper Street, Bird Street, Tassel Street, Shoe Street,
Barber Street, Samosa Street . . . you get the idea. I was the
very picture of a wide-eyed, rubbernecking tourist, but I
couldn't take it all in. It was just too much, and I wondered
again whether I had made a colossal mistake and wasted two
years.

Maybe some of my disorientation was jet lag, but I
became increasingly aware of what a huge and baffling thing
I had chosen to write about. How could one month possibly
be enough to scratch the surface of such a rich, ancient, con-
voluted culture? But there I was, sitting in a rickshaw, and it
was too late to turn back.

Instead, we turned down an unexpectedly quiet and deserted lane and I assumed we would now be murdered for our credit cards and passports. (Surprising myself, I became curiously philosophical. Oh, well, it had been an interesting life and I probably couldn't pull off a book about India anyway.) But the sweating rickshaw wallah dismounted his bike and gestured graciously for us to enter an unmarked shop. We walked into a small room lined with shelves of luxurious Kashmiri needlework – pashminas, tablecloths, pillowcases, bedspreads . . . a breathtaking abundance.

The merchant wore kurta pyjamas and had orange hennaed hair, and he stood behind the counter with his perfectly beautiful eight-year-old son who had big, dark, liquid eyes. The man spread out his wares and I selected a one-of-a-kind-god-that's-fabulous pashmina. I'm not going to wear it; I'm going to frame it. It's *that* gorgeous. The little boy watched the transaction solemnly, learning the family business. After the merchant showed me how a drop of water would not penetrate the fine wool, the boy carefully tipped the single drop of water back into the cup; his father smiled and said, 'Water is precious.' I will never forget watching that drop of water slide back into the cup, the child's gravity and his father's approval.

The orange-haired merchant served chai and kindly asked us to visit him at home in Kashmir. He invited us to be his guests in his houseboat in Srinagar; he seemed sincere, and I was intrigued. I've always wanted to see Srinagar – the elaborate houseboats furnished with crystal chandeliers and velvet settees, the ghost of George Harrison playing a sitar. Outside I'd see faded palaces reflected in the water, and in the background the mighty Himalayas, rising enormous and powerful, a white mirage hard against the blue sky. Tempting.

I thanked the merchant but suggested that it might not be the best time for an American to go to Kashmir, which is still hotly disputed between India and Pakistan and shares a border with Afghanistan. He shrugged, as if I was being overly cautious. For him, a Kashmiri, ongoing war was a way of life. He said, 'Come any time. You only have to know someone.'

Putting Srinagar on hold, he took me on a tour of his Delhi house, of which the shop was only one ground-floor room. The building was an old Moghul mansion that had been sectioned off into apartments, and his family lived in two floors of rooms that opened on to a cracked cement courtyard. He was justifiably proud of his home in a city where millions live under a tarp thrown across a couple of shaky bamboo poles. He grinned and pointed proudly to a dusty houseplant, listing in a corner, and said, 'See? Greenery everywhere!'

He introduced me to his scrawny, smiling, barefoot mother, who appeared to be doing nothing but sitting on her rope bed (a charpoy, I later learned). She didn't speak English but was obviously proud to be the widow of a freedom fighter in the Indian War of Independence. She pointed up to a formal black and white photo of a stiff, unsmiling man in a Nehru-style cap. I was forced to crane my neck to look up to that man, whose photo hung only about a foot from the high ceiling, the placement symbolic of his stature in the family and in India

The friendly merchant let me take pictures of everything and everyone – the shop, the charpoy, his mother – and we talked about Indian history. I asked him what he thought of Partition and he said it was the worst thing that had ever happened to India. He said, 'When you create a border based on ideology, you create something to fight over.

When you live side by side, you create a reason to get along.'

I looked at him, his orange hair and kurta pyjamas, his shy son and proud, if withered, mother, and I had the sudden thought that maybe India wasn't really so different, after all. It runs on human reasoning, human love and hate, human greed and generosity, human war and peace. And that's when I knew I could write my book. As any novel worth its salt should be, *The Sandalwood Tree* is not about a place, it's about being human – in India.

Acknowledgements

This book owes its existence to a multitude of good people around the world.

In India: I would like to thank Ramesh Kumar, who navigated some of the world's most hair-raising roads while graciously answering all my questions and generally keeping me alive. In Delhi: thank you to DK of Mysteries of India, who made last-minute travel arrangements, even when my requests were unreasonable. In Dharamsala: thank you to Colonel Naresh Chand, who kindly granted a rare interview and shared memories of India under the British Raj and his experiences in the Indian army. In Varanasi: thank you to Narottam Kumar, who explained Hindu beliefs and funerary rites while sitting in a rocking boat on the Ganges. In Amritsar: thank you to Mandeep Singh, who ushered me through the Golden Temple and offered insights into Sikh customs. In Agra: thank you to Muddassar Khan for a delicious lunch and a fascinating conversation about arranged marriages. In Shimla: thank you to Manish Patwal, who generously volunteered family anecdotes, and also to Apoorv Chanan for a personal guided tour of the colonial Peterhof Hotel.

In New York: thank you to Emily Bestler, whose brilliant editing once again created a much better book, and my meticulous copy editor Isolde Sauer. Thanks also to my peerless agent, Dorian Karchmar, who is always in my corner. In London: thank you to Sarah Adams for pointing me in the right direction, and Kate Samano for a superb copy edit that went above and beyond the call of duty. In Santa Barbara: thank you to Ginny Crane for furnishing details of her life as an American memsahib in India in the 1960s.

In New Mexico: thank you to my daughter, Tess Light, for helping me through the final notes and enabling me to deliver this book from a hospital bed, and to my son, Michael Lavezzi, who made sure it got to New York on time.

I extend heartfelt thanks to fellow writers in San Diego, San Francisco and Denver, who patiently read and re-read this manuscript, and gave me the benefit of their skill and wisdom. They are: Seré Halverson, Peggy Lang, Eleanor Bluestein, Chelo Ludden, Laurie Richards, Walter Carlin, Susanne Delzio, Al Christman, Judy Grear, James Jones and Felice Valen.

I also owe a debt to the intrepid Victorian expats Fanny Parks, Honoria Lawrence, Sara Jeanette Duncan, Julia Curtis and Mrs Meer Hassan Ali, whose diaries and journals painted a vivid picture of an Englishwoman's life in nineteenth-century India. Thank you to Margaret MacMillan, whose book *Women of the Raj* was a valuable resource. Thank you also to William Dalrymple, whose books *The Last Mughal* and *White Mughals* provided a rich historical context for my characters.

To my husband, Frank, thank you for allowing me to retreat into my own head for months at a time. And thank you, Dad, for making dinner when I was writing ten hours a day.